SMILE, YOU'RE DEAD

Robert C. Novarro

authorHOUSE®

AuthorHouse™
1663 Liberty Drive
Bloomington, IN 47403
www.authorhouse.com
Phone: 1 (800) 839-8640

Published by AuthorHouse 03/02/2018

ISBN: 978-1-5462-3197-4 (sc)
ISBN: 978-1-5462-3195-0 (hc)
ISBN: 978-1-5462-3196-7 (e)

Library of Congress Control Number: 2018902858

Print information available on the last page.

Any people depicted in stock imagery provided by Getty Images are models, and such images are being used for illustrative purposes only. Certain stock imagery © *Getty Images.*

This book is printed on acid-free paper.

Because of the dynamic nature of the Internet, any web addresses or links contained in this book may have changed since publication and may no longer be valid. The views expressed in this work are solely those of the author and do not necessarily reflect the views of the publisher, and the publisher hereby disclaims any responsibility for them.

DEDICATION

To all my fans past, present and future, I hope
you find enjoyment in this book.

"In a time of universal deceit – telling the truth is a revolutionary act."

Unknown

CHAPTER

1

H ANK WELDON'S HEAD flopped hard onto the bar with a thud. He was sitting in a place called The Dive, his fourth scotch and rye still clasped tightly in his hand. The noisy customers' voices began to slowly fade from his ears. The Dive was a fitting name for the dump where he usually got drunk a few times a week. Losers in life were the preferred clientele.

All at once, the room seemed to shake violently. Earthquake? But no one was screaming. "Get up!" a peeved voice barked out. "This ain't no flop house!" Hank's head rose with some trepidation as his stomach churned like a stormy sea. The private detective was able to finally focus on the large, bald, tattooed bartender whose name was Ivan.

"What's going on?" Weldon managed to slur.

"This is no place for you to crash for the night! Drink up and get out!"

"This is no way to treat a regular paying customer!" Hank retorted incensed by the barkeep's nasty attitude.

"Get out or I'll throw you out!" With a few swallows, Weldon finished his drink and slammed the glass on the counter.

"I'll go, but only because I want to!" Weldon rose from the bar stool and staggered his way out the door.

The garish lights of Brighton Beach, Brooklyn hurt his eyes as he stepped out onto the street in the hot humidity of a mid-August evening. Hank groaned, covering his eyes with his hands as he leaned against the stucco wall of the building. *I'm too drunk to drive home. I wonder if I can hail a taxi.*

He was just about to lose his footing, slip down the wall, and sprawl on the sidewalk when what seemed like his guardian angel took his arm and lifted him back on his feet. Hank tried to focus on the magnificent winged creature before him, but as his eyes reached a sense of clarity, he acknowledged that this was no heavenly guardian. "Wake up!" A voice echoed in his inebriated cranium. When Weldon didn't respond, a giant, hairy paw struck him hard across the face.

"Cut it out!" screamed the detective as he swung wildly at the blurred figure. An open hand struck him across the face again, even harder. It seemed to do the trick, because Weldon's bloodshot eyes began to clear of their alcohol-induced fog.

"For Christ's sake Kaz, what the hell is wrong with you?" It was Kazimir Titov, an enforcer for a local Russian mob that had infiltrated and laid down roots in this part of New York City. He had occasionally cooperated with Hank as a lookout on jobs involving cheating spouses. "I'm taking you home to sleep it off. You are no use to me in this condition," he sneered out loud.

He threw him over his shoulder like a limp rag doll, walked him to his car and dumped him in the back seat. The enforcer drove to Weldon's small, one- room apartment building, climbed the three flights, and unceremoniously dumped him onto his unmade bed. Hank never woke up. Instead, he drifted off into a deeper sleep.

Kazimir Titov was one of the few Russian-Americans in Greshnev's band of brutish bullies. Most of the rest were Russian immigrants. His mother and father had met through a family arrangement and were married in the small town of Kasimov on the banks of the Volga River.

His father, Nikolai Titov, was a bull of a man with broad shoulders, and large hands, which were very useful at his occupation as a blacksmith. His new wife Natalia, was a demure, raven-haired young girl with a sweet personality, who adored her husband. For many years, they had tried to have a child with no success. Natalia could be found at their local Russian Orthodox church lighting candles so that they could be blessed with a baby.

Their lives together were uneventful until the invasion of Nazi Germany shattered the small town's serenity. With the entire town, the family marched northwest in the hopes of getting around the invading enemy, but the trek was so arduous that many of their friends and neighbors died along the way. It was with the grace of God that they eventually found themselves over the border of the Soviet Union and into Finland.

With the money they had saved, they were able to buy their passage on a Finnish ship on its way to New York City. On the open sea, there was always the threat of a German U-Boat sinking them, and although there were many scares, the ship arrived safely in port.

Nicholai had sent a telegram to his aunt and uncle who had immigrated to Brooklyn years before, telling them that they were coming to the United States. They were on the dock to welcome them as refugees. Taken into their home, his uncle got him a job at a clothing factory where he swept the workshop floors of debris.

Within a few months of their arrival to America, Natalia became pregnant. The couple was overjoyed by the news. Nine months later, the infant boy was stillborn, breaking the hearts of his parents. They gave up on the idea of having a family as they were convinced that a black cloud hung over their heads. It came as a complete shock nine years later that Natalia was once more expecting a child. She prayed that this time they could have their dream fulfilled. Little Kazimir was born on a hot Summer's day to his elated and adoring parents. They poured all their love onto the young child.

Kaz grew up resembling his father. His brute strength led bullies to cower when he appeared on the scene. Although his parents tried to guide him down a law-abiding path, Kaz grew up in the streets, playing stickball and basketball with the neighborhood punks. It was there that he met Maxim Greshnev and a close bond was formed between them.

As he grew into adulthood, Maxim taught him how to steal from street peddlers, and how to lift a wallet from a man's back pocket without the victim realizing it. Eventually, the two were sent to Juvenile Court where they were sentenced to a work camp in Westchester County. If the two boys had been tight before, their internment forged an even stronger alliance. Kaz became Maxim's bodyguard at the camp and not one of the other internees wanted to tangle with him.

Once they were released, Maxim took the skills he had learned on the mean streets of Brighton Beach and formed a gang that extorted money from local merchants for protection. In a short time, Greshnev's enterprise grew by leaps and bounds and Kazimir Titov took the ride with him.

His body guard could be affable and pleasant at times, but everyone knew not to cross him. The good-natured Kaz could turn into a beast who lusted for blood. Max found this characteristic in his bodyguard very useful when dealing with unwilling debtors. As soon as Kaz walked into their establishments, the owners were only too willing to pay what was owed.

As time went by, and Maxim's fortune grew, he branched into other illegal undertakings, including a brothel named the Russian Doll House. With the greatest of satisfaction, Maxim Greshnev watched as his new enterprise took off. An added benefit to this business was the local politicians and city officials who visited the "cat house" and eventually wound up in the mob boss's back pocket. As Maxim's fortunes rose, Kaz was right by his friend's side.

He was born Henry David Weldon on June 6, 1959 to the proud parents, Phyllis and Steven Weldon. As far back as he could remember, little Henry grew up in a household more resembling a battlefield than a nurturing home.

His father, a door-to-door vacuum cleaner salesman, spent more time complaining about his aches and pains than actually pounding the pavement looking for new customers. As a result, his mother began to take in wash from her neighbors and continually harped at her husband about their teetering pecuniary situation. "Get out of the house and go to work before you lose this job!" Phyllis kept bombarding him with her resentful, furious words.

"Shut up!" was his father's usual quick return. "You're going to drive me to drink one day!" And as if to prove his prediction, he eventually took to hitting the bottle. With their constant bickering, it was obvious to everyone that Henry would be their only child. Hank, as his father called him, became a problem in school. Disruptive in class and combative with his fellow schoolmates by the time he was in the 4th grade, he could usually be found after school in the playground battering some poor boy who was the object of his frustration.

Bloody and bruised, he would be separated from his opponent by a teacher, and escorted to the principal's office. "You again?" ponderous principal, Mrs. Miller, would ask, her chubby, accusatory index finger pointing at him in a stabbing motion. "What do you have to say for yourself this time?" Hank remained obstinately uncommunicative. "You have nothing to say? Then I guess I'll just have to get your mother back here again." As he waited outside her office, his mother was contacted. She would always arrive with a scowl on her face. After the meeting, his mother would drag him to his feet and out the school door. "When is this going to stop?" she would yell at him as they walked to the bus stop.

"The other kids don't like me," Hank would defend himself.

"How can they like you when you're always picking fights with them?"

Hank would answer with an adolescent shrug and the words that always infuriated his mother, "I don't know."

"I know one thing," she replied with severity as they boarded the bus and she dropped her money in the fare machine. "You're going to wind up in reform school if this kind of behavior doesn't stop right now!" They took two seats near the driver. As he stared out the window, Phyllis continued. "Don't I have enough trouble with your father! Do you have to be a problem too? You took me away from the wash I was doing! It's the only way I can keep a roof over our heads and food in our stomachs! It's not likely your lazy lout of a father will ever do anything to help us, and now you have become another source of worriment to me!"

Hank sullenly remained silent. "Say something!" she demanded of her son. "What's your problem?"

"You and daddy are my problem." Like a flash, her hand was raised and slapped him across the cheek.

"How dare you speak to me with such disrespect!" The other riders could not help but see what was going on between mother and son, and embarrassingly looked in other directions. Although his cheek burned from the clout, it wasn't the reason for his face turning red. It was because of his mortification of being physically rebuked by his mother in front of a bus full of strangers.

When they got home, his father was in his familiar position, drunk and asleep on the couch, a half-finished bottle of scotch by his side. "Go to your room," his mother screamed at him. *With pleasure! I'd do anything to get the two of you out of my sight!*

These circumstances continued as he went through his school years, getting into trouble and barely passing his classes. Finally, he was of the age to graduate from high school. "The Army or the Police Academy," his mother snidely suggested to the 18-year-old. "With your temperament, you wouldn't be suited to any other profession." Hank couldn't have disagreed with her even if he had wanted to.

It was the Police Academy that he eventually chose, and where he met another cadet named Archibald Malone. Archie, as the other cadets called him, had arrived at the academy with circumstances that were quite close to those of Weldon's dysfunctional family, and their similar backgrounds proved to create a tight bond between them. They both graduated and were lucky enough to be assigned to the same police precinct. This cemented their friendship even more.

An even closer connection was forged as they patrolled the streets of Brooklyn. After work, they would patronize a little bar a couple of blocks away, named O'Halloran's. It was there that he met a lovely barmaid named Clare Gallagher. Weldon was attracted to her fair face, strawberry blonde hair, and her quick Irish wit. He was smitten right away. She was drawn to him because of his ruggedly dark, handsome features, and his personable demeanor.

The two courted for over a year, and then to Hank's own amazement, he popped the question to her. Clare's answer was an immediate, "Yes". They were married in a small ceremony at a Roman Catholic Church named St. Aidan of Lindisfarne. She had invited her parents, but Hank did not bother to let his parents know that he was to be married.

They could not afford a honeymoon, and spent their time in the apartment of her parent's home doing what newlyweds normally do. Almost a year later, Clare told her husband that she was pregnant. Hank was elated by the news. *Now I can prove myself to be a better husband and father than my father!* Everything had proved to be as perfect and wonderful as he could have ever hoped for.

####

A dark haze came across Weldon's whisky soaked brain as he lay in his bed, remembering. He recalled that Clare had been almost 7 months pregnant that 94-degree Sunday morning in August before he went on duty. "Be careful," she warned him, as she did every time he was going to work. "I will," he'd replied as he touched her swollen womb before he left their Sayville apartment. Hank left that day with the idea that once he got home, they would enjoy dinner and relax for the rest of the evening, but that was not how things would wind up.

It was a few hours later, while on patrol with his buddy Archie in Bensonhurst that a patrol car with its siren whining, came to a halt while they were walking their beat. "Get in!" the officer behind the wheel yelled to them.

"What's going on?" Patrolman Malone inquired.

"There's been an accident!"

"What do you mean?" Hank demanded.

"Get in and I'll explain it." Both men got in as the car moved down the street, its siren once again wailing.

"Well, what's happening?" Malone repeated.

"There's been a fire."

"And?" queried Weldon.

"It's your wife." These words conjured up anxiety in both men's minds.

"Clare?"

"Yes."

"Is she hurt?" he yelled, his heart suddenly beating like it would burst from his chest.

"I don't know, but I'm taking you home."

The patrol car sped along, its siren moving all the cars out of their way. Anxiety gripped Hank's thoughts as Archie tried to keep him calm.

"She'll be alright, you'll see," he tried to placate his friend, but he could not help think black thoughts about what they would find. Before they had pulled up to the residence, Hank gasped at the covered body on the sidewalk. He jumped from the car before it came to a complete stop. He noticed that his landlords were standing on the sidewalk, the wife crying uncontrollably.

"Who is this?" he demanded of the fire chief who was standing next to the body. The chief lifted the sheet. Archie had to hold him back as Hank recognized his wife's sooty face. "What happened?"

"There was a grease fire in the downstairs kitchen that got out of hand. Your wife was trapped and died of smoke inhalation."

"And the baby?" The fire chief shook his head.

He lost interest in everything as his self-hatred grew ever stronger. It became his constant companion, haunting his every waking and sleeping moment, consuming him in the flames of regret and guilt that he had not been there to save them.

Weldon even lost interest in his job, and spent many hours trying to drown his sorrows at the bottom of a bottle of liquor. Each night, Archie had to get him and bring him back to their shared apartment. As time went by, Weldon sunk deeper into alcoholism as a coping mechanism.

His friend and colleague registered him into an alcoholic rehab center, which Hank loudly protested against. But Archie knew that this was the only reasonable choice left for him to recover from his culpability and chronic drinking. Months later, he was out, claiming that he was a changed man. But nothing had changed for him. He had refused to discuss anything about his deep-seeded hatred of his childhood, or the incident that had taken his wife and child. He kept his emotions tightly bottled up, afraid that if he released them, he could never come back as a whole person.

The inner conflict brought him down to the depths of depression. He felt ostracized from his former friends because of his continued drunkenness. No matter what small pleasure he was enjoying for a moment, the vision of his dead wife dispelled it from his mind and replaced it with horrible visions he could not completely eradicate.

After being kicked out of the police force for his drunken behavior, he tried to live an abstinent life, but the same self-recriminations and dark thoughts began to crop up in his mind. Before long, Hank found himself back at The Dive, indulging in alcoholic stupors that helped him to forget.

The last straw for Archie Malone was when he had asked his friend and former partner to be the best man at his wedding. Hank Weldon had agreed. On the day of Archie's marriage, Hank never showed up at the church. After the ceremony and reception, the groom went back to their apartment, gathered up Hank's belongings, and went straight to The Dive, where he knew he would find him. He was not surprised to find Hank perched on the same customary stool at the bar.

Laying his one piece of luggage at his feet, Malone spun Weldon around. "It's over!" he proclaimed to the drunkard.

"What's over?" Hank slurred his words.

"I've packed up your things and brought them here to you!"

"What for? Am I going somewhere?"

"Yeah, your leaving my apartment! I was going to let you live there now that I'm moving out, but I'm not going to waste any more time and money on you! You're just a hopeless drunkard."

"So, what are you saying? Are you telling me that you're not going to help me anymore?"

"That's it exactly! You're completely hopeless and I can't have you in my life now that I'm married!"

"That's right," Hank barked. "Just rub it in! You're married while my family lays in a grave!

Archie countered. "Stop feeling sorry for yourself! Only you have the power to pull yourself out of this funk you've been in for years!"

"That's easy for you to say. You're not responsible for the death of my wife and child. I am!"

"Excuses, always excuses for the reason that you can't stop drinking. You're no better than the alcoholic father you've ranted against over the years, and you're on your own as far as I'm concerned! I've tried to help you in every way I could think of, but you've thwarted me at every turn! Whenever you needed me, I was always there for you. All I asked from you was to be my best man and stand next to me in church. But you couldn't do that one thing for me, could you?

"I never asked for your help!" Weldon snapped back. "I never wanted it!" Hank took a drunken swing at his friend, but he was way off mark.

Archie looked with disgust at the red-eyed alcoholic who stared back at him.

"Go on, go! I don't need you! I don't need anybody!" he yelled back, his arms gesticulating wildly. "And if I never see you again, that will be just fine!"

Archie turned and walked out, never looking back.

Nothing has changed, Weldon thought as he drank to try and forget Archie's grilling. Nothing has changed at all! "Give me another bottle," Weldon directed his command toward Ivan, the bartender. "I'm not fully drunk yet!"

###

When he turned over in his bed, the morning light hit Hank directly in the face, waking him with a terrible throbbing in his head. *Stinking hangover!* Slowly, he raised himself to a sitting position trying not to further upset his churning gut. His face felt as if it had been put through a meat grinder. He was astonished when he looked down to find he was still in yesterday's clothing. Hank tried to remember what had happened to him after he left the bar, but no amount of concentration helped to retrieve the memory.

Staggering to the bathroom, he leaned against the cold porcelain sink and stared at his visage in the mirror. He had expected to see the red swollen eyes, scruffy whiskers, and the tussled hair, but there were red marks emblazoned across both cheeks. "What the…" Suddenly his bedroom door swung open and Kaz stood in the doorway, his bulk effectively blocking the light that would have shown through.

"So, you're finally up?"

"What are you doing in my apartment so early in the morning?"

"It's after eleven. Most people have been up and working for hours."

Thrusting his hand through his disheveled hair and walking back to his bed, Weldon replied, "I'm not most people."

"Yeah, I know."

"Say, how did you get into my apartment anyway?"

"I used your key when I took you home last night."

So, that's how I got home.

"I don't suppose you know how I got these red marks on my face, do you?"

"Yeah, I gave them to you."

Enraged, Weldon made a staggering attempt to get to his bed. Titov walked over and pushed him down on it. "Sit down, tough guy before you fall down on it!"

"Just who do you think you are, roughing me up?"

"A client." The words caught Weldon by surprise.

"What are you babbling about?"

"I found you yesterday in The Dive, but you were in no condition to talk. That's why I took you home and waited and let you finally sleep it off."

"You stayed here all night? And you want to hire me?"

"That's right!"

"Well then, let's get to it! What's on your mind?"

Titov removed a photograph from his pocket and thrust it into Weldon's hand. Hank stared at the blonde woman in the picture. He recognized her right away. It was a local prostitute who worked in a bordello called the Russian Dolls. Her name was Albina Lukashenko but her "Johns" simply called her Albina." Weldon knew that since he had "visited her" many times.

Hank decided to play dumb. "Who is she?"

"Her name is Albina Lukashenko and she's my fiancée."

Shit! I slept with this guy's intended. I'm glad I kept my mouth shut! "Congratulations! So, what do you want from me?"

"She's been missing for a couple of days."

"And…"

"And I want you to find her!" Acting as nonchalant as he could under the circumstances, he replied, "Maybe she's visiting her mother."

"Her mother is dead."

"Maybe she is staying with a girlfriend and forgot to tell you."

"I know where she goes and who she sees."

Hank wondered if Kaz already knew about his occasional assignations with his fiancée. Titov gave no indication that he knew of their trysts.

"You want me to find her?" he inquired as he stood up. *Maybe she ran away from you…you big gorilla!*

"Have you gone to the cops?"

"No police!" he was emphatic. "You're going to do this job for me!" He had made his mind up and wanted only Weldon.

I guess going to the cops for any reason would make Kaz a marked man in the eyes of the mob!

"Okay, okay…I'll do it."

"Here's a couple of hundred dollars to get things started." He pulled a wad of rolled up cash from his pocket, removed the rubber band, peeled off a couple of bills before he rolled it up again and returned it to his suit jacket.

"Have you ever stopped to think that maybe she just doesn't want to be found? Besides, I think that I'm the wrong man for this job."

Kaz roughly lifted him off the bed, his eyes blazing like two active volcanoes. "You find her or else!" Weldon didn't want to know what the "or else" was.

"Okay, there's no need for the tough act! I'll look for her!" Titov pushed him back on the bed like a sack of potatoes. "And remember, no cops!"

"Yeah, I got it!"

"Good, I'll call you tomorrow to see what you've found out." Not waiting for a reply, he stormed out of the apartment.

That guy has a short fuse and I hate playing with dynamite.

Weldon shuffled over to the bathroom sink. Once more he saw his horrific appearance in the mirror and he knew he looked ready to be picked by the "Grim Reaper." His head was still aching as he threw cold water on his face and combed out the bird's nest on his head. He needed a shave, but he just wasn't in the mood for it. He looked at his rumpled clothing and changed into something a little less tousled. I need some coffee in a hurry!

The afternoon sun now blazed directly over head as he walked to the neighborhood diner a few blocks away.

Finally, he had a case of a suspected missing person. The woman was one whom he had slept with many times, and whose fiancée was a bone crushing head breaker who had broken Weldon's arm once. Just my damn luck!

He turned and opened the door of the Tick Tock Diner, and walked over to his usual booth in the back. The familiar waitress named Lil walked toward him. "Hey, Hank", she said in a voice that reflected their comfortable familiarity with each other. "What's shakin'?"

"Morning, Lil."

"It's afternoon, sweetie."

"Yeah, well whatever. Give me a cup of hot coffee."

"Looks like you've had a rough night, honey!"

"My life story. Bring over the coffee and keep it coming until I tell you otherwise."

"You got it, Hank."

Weldon took his first sip of the high-octane brew. *I've got to get my head screwed on straight before I go out there looking for Albina.*

CHAPTER

2

F IVE CUPS OF coffee and two trips to the bathroom later, Hank floated out the door and took the downtown bus. Before long he was standing in front of the Russian Doll House. He had made his way there many other times but never during daylight hours. He was confronted at the door by a huge hulking humanoid. "What do you want?" he demanded in a thick Slavic accent.

"I'm here to see Fat Zoya."

The incredible bulk blocked his way. "You got appointment?' Serge demanded.

"Tell her I'm here about one of her girls who may be missing."

"You wait." Walking a few doors down the hallway, he stopped at an open door and said, "Weldon is here to talk about Albina."

Weldon did not hear what the madam said, but in a moment Serge turned and waved him forward. He found Fat Zoya (although no one called her that to her face) balanced on a chair in a corset and slip. Her bulging breasts appeared big enough to crush a man's head like a walnut in a nutcracker if he were ever foolish enough to find himself in that predicament.

"It's you," remarked the madam as she slipped a cigarette from between her nicotine-stained teeth. "You're usually a night owl. What brings you here at this time of day?" she knowingly winked.

"No, I'm not here for that. I'm on a case."

"You," she laughed heartily, her flabby body shaking violently. "You've got a real case?"

"Yeah," he answered with annoyance at her skepticism. "I'm looking for a missing girl."

"And what does this have to do with me?"

"She is one of your girls, Albina Lukashenko."

"Albina missing? Well you don't need to worry. There are plenty more dolls here. She was your favorite, no? You visited her quite often as I recall."

Ignoring her, he continued. "Has she been around the last couple of days?" Zoya's emotions turned on a dime, and she became hostile. "That bitch has been gone for the last three days! I'm like a mother to my girls and that is how that bitch repays me!"

"Did she have any friends here? Someone who I can talk to."

"Sure, she made friends. The girls are happy here."

"Who would know her best?" Zoya thought for a moment before she answered, "Karina, I suppose. They were always huddled together whispering about something."

"Good, and what room would she be in?"

"Just a second," Zoya looked straight into his eyes. "You need to pay for her time just as any other John does!"

"I'm not here to have my whistle waxed. I just want to ask her a few questions."

"Makes no difference. No money, no visit!" She held her hand out. With a sigh, Hank dropped 60 green backs in her hand. She folded up the bills and stuffed them into her already overstretched bra.

"Room 12. Remember, you've only got 30 minutes here or I'll have to send Serge to show you the way out. As you probably could tell, he doesn't have a very gentle way about him."

"I noticed." Before Hank got out the door she added, "And if you ever do find that little trouble making drama queen, tell her she better get her ass back here if she knows what's good for her!"

Weldon made his way down the hallway past the doors with numbers surrounded by fake roses in the shape of a heart. *Cheesy!* He walked up to number 12 and knocked. A curvaceous, raven-haired beauty opened the door in a silky dressing gown and fuzzy pink slippers.

"Come in," she cooed taking him by the hand and leading him inside, closing the door behind him. She dropped the robe revealing her flesh to him. "Come," she enticed, as she went to the bed. "I've wanted you for a long time."

Hank cleared his throat. "I'm not here for that."

Taking her robe from the floor, she replaced it on her body. "Hey, it's your 30 minutes. I'll do whatever you want."

"I have some questions about your friend Albina Ludashenko."

"Albina? Now I recognize you. You are one of her steady customers. You're Hank, right?"

"Yeah well…Do you know where she is?"

"What Albina does and where she goes is her business. It has nothing to do with me."

"Zoya tells me that the two of you are friends?"

"I guess we are something like that."

"Then you must have an idea where she's gone."

Karina looked at him without making a sound. Finally, she declared, "I might, but my memory is kinda fuzzy, you know what I mean?" With a sigh of exasperation, he took a $20 from his wallet and placed it in her hand.

"Does that bring you any clarity?" he smirked.

"It's doing wonders for my memory."

"Alright then, give!"

"She told me a couple of days ago that she had met a man."

"So what, the place is full of men!"

"There was this one guy in particular."

"Got a name?'

"That she wouldn't tell me, but he was taking her away from this life and marrying her."

"I want my $20 dollars' worth of information!" he exclaimed with frustration. "So, you're telling me that they eloped?"

Karina shrugged. "I suppose so."

"And she never said where they were going?"

"Never said a word. I suppose she didn't want Kaz to find out."

"Weren't they engaged?"

"I think that's what he wanted, whether Albina agreed to it or not."

So, she was trying to get away from that big gorilla after all!

"Are you sure about this?"

"I'm sure! I'm no liar!"

Hank checked his watch. He had spoken to her for only a little more than ten minutes. *After all, I did pay for 30 minutes.*

"Take off your robe.

"I knew you couldn't resist me."

As he dropped his pants, Hank stated, "Shut up and get into bed."

Five minutes later, he walked out of the room and down the corridor.

As he passed Zoya's office, she called out, "So, did you get anything out of Karina?"

"Enough to tell you that Albina probably isn't coming back.

"Good riddance to bad rubbish!"

That evening, Hank was awakened by a constant pounding on his door. He hadn't had a drink, so he knew it wasn't part of a hangover. He looked through the peephole and opened the door. Kazimir brushed passed him as if he were on fire.

"No greeting, no how are you doing, Hank?"

"I'm not here to play games, so tell me what I want to know!"

"Let me begin by advising you not to lose your temper."

"What's wrong? What did you find out?"

"It seems that Albina has run off with another man."

Kaz stood as still as a statue trying to comprehend what he had just been told.

"Impossible!" he at last blurted out as if he had been holding his breath. "You are wrong!"

"Listen, Kaz...I got it from a reliable source."

"Who told you this lie about my Albina?"

"I know it's tough to accept but your girl has eloped."

Kaz grabbed hold of Hank and shook him like he was doll. "It's a lie!" he kept screaming.

"Stop shaking me!"

Kaz threw him across the room and Hank landed on the floor with a thud.

"I'm telling you to cut this rough stuff out or you can get yourself someone else to find your girlfriend! Understood?"

"Yeah!" he barked. "But it is a lie I tell you. Albina loves me. She would never leave me for another man."

"I'm afraid you've been suckered!"

"Who told you this monstrous lie? Who was it?"

"A reliable source."

"What reliable source? Did this person ask you not to give me their name?"

"Well…no."

"Then what is the problem? Give me the name!"

"It was Karina."

"That slut, she has never spoken the truth about anything since the day she was born."

"Now Kaz, don't do anything foolish."

"I'll beat the information out of her! If she is telling the truth, I'll beat the name of the man who took my fiancée away from me or I'll kill her trying!"

Kaz made a turn for the door. Weldon hesitantly put his hand on his shoulder to stop him. The big Russian turned with an icy stare that would have stopped anyone in their tracks.

"You can't beat her. You'll be arrested and thrown into jail. That won't help you find your fiancée." *I can't believe that I'm giving advice to this big lug after he threw me across my flat.*

"Then what am I supposed to do?"

"I'll go visit Karina again. If she knows anything, I'll get it out of her."

Kaz shrugged. "Okay but I tell you once more that it is a lie. My Albina would never have left me for another man.

All women leave, you big dope!

"I'll see Karina the first thing tomorrow morning."

"Good."

"Go home and take it easy." Without another word, Kaz left more meekly than he had arrived. Hank was thankful for the peace and quiet.

CHAPTER

3

A GOOD NIGHT'S sleep and no hangover allowed Hank to drive back to the Russian Doll House. His 1967 Volkswagen Beetle, held together with tape, spit, and a prayer, chugged its way downtown. Pulling into a parking spot near the building, he got out and did not bother locking the car. *Nobody's going to steal this piece of shit!* He was met inside by the same 300-pound ape who had stopped him the day before.

"You're back?" Serge inquired as he rose from his chair. Weldon thought he heard the armchair groan in relief.

"Yeah," Weldon proclaimed as he tried to push passed him.

"Not so fast," the brooding behemoth sneered, as he laid his paw on Hank's chest. "What you here for?"

"You know damn well what I'm here for," he retorted adding a little wink at the end of his sentence.

"You here to see Karina?"

"That's right!" Weldon took the $60 from his wallet and tried to hand it to the body guard

"You pick someone else. Karina not here!"

"Don't give me that, I'm here for Karina, now get out of my way!" he said raising his voice in anger.

"You leave now!" Roughly, the guard laid his hand on his shoulder, and without much thought, Weldon unleashed a powerful karate chop to his throat. The big man grabbed his neck as his face turned red, and like an ancient redwood tree that had just been chopped, he crashed backwards into the chair which fell apart from the force of the fall.

I'd better get to Karina's door before this guy fully recovers! But before he got too far, Fat Zoya, who had heard the commotion, waddled out to the hallway.

"What the hell's going on out here?" When she saw her protection on the floor, she screamed at Hank. "What do you want?"

"I'm here to talk to Karina," he announced once again, pushing passed her.

"She's no longer employed here." Not believing a word out of her mouth, he opened the door to room 12. A buxom redhead was lounging in a lacy nightgown.

"Where's Karina?" Hank yelled. The woman simply shrugged.

From down the hall he heard Zoya yell. "I'm calling Greshnev!"

Maxim Greshnev, the boss of the Russian mob! I better get out now!

Wherever there was graft, bribery, head bashing, or a dead body found in Brighton Beach, you could be sure Maxim Greshnev was involved.

Not wanting to run into his revenge-seeking nemesis, Weldon left through the room's window.

He was headed to his car when he noticed a commotion on the beach. Making his way over to the barricaded crowd where a police investigation was in progress, Hank noticed an old friend, Detective Archie Malone. He shouted to get his attention. "Archie, over here," he waved trying to catch the detective's eye. Malone looked up to see who had called his name. Treading through the sand, he finally stopped in front of Hank.

"What are you doing here?" he asked, not too pleasantly.

"Aren't you going to say hello?" Weldon held out his arm for a friendly handshake. Malone did not reciprocate.

"I'm on a case, so make it quick! What do you want?"

Archie's still not anxious to see me after I was thrown off the force all those years ago, I guess.

"What's going on?"

"A dead female washed up on the beach last night."

"Who is she?"

"No identification, she's nude."

I wonder if it's Albina?

"I might know who she is." With great skepticism, Malone held up the yellow tape so Weldon could pass underneath. They both plodded back to the scene of the crime. Immediately, Hank realized that this was not Albina. The black hair of the victim was that of Karina. Her body was bruised all over. He sucked in air with surprise.

"You know her?' Malone inquired.

"Yeah, her name is Karina. She worked at the Russian Doll House.

The dead woman's skin was pale and lifeless, unlike the woman he had encountered the day before. Her body and hair were entangled with green seaweed. Around her pretty neck was a knotted rope. Before she was dumped, a heavy weight had been attached to the ligature, but those who had disposed of her, thinking she would never be found, didn't know the rope would break. The frayed end laid near her feet.

Malone smirked, "Did some business with her in the past?"

"Yeah, you could say that." *What have I gotten myself into?*

"I need you to come in for questioning. Can I trust you to come in this afternoon or do I have to have a couple of these patrolmen haul your ass in now?

"Geez Archie, we're still friends, aren't we?"

Through Malone's demeanor it became obvious that their friendship had died long ago.

"Well, what will it be?" Archie queried out of sorts.

"I'll be there this afternoon."

"Good, now get out of here!"

Hank made his way back to his car. He sat for a while on the torn, discolored upholstery. He wished he had a glass of any kind of liquor in his hand right now, but he realized that he better have his wits about him. *Did Kaz follow through on the threat he made last night?* He could still hear the mob enforcer's words playing over and over in his head. I'll kill her…I'll kill her!"

Hank began to go over a possible list of suspects in Karina's death. At the top of it was Kazimir Titov. The motive was there as was his accessibility into the bordello. He was primary, but it could have been anybody in the Russian mob. Perhaps her conversation with me yesterday signed her death warrant. The idea that he might have had a hand in her death, even indirectly, made him sick to his stomach.

As he parked outside his apartment building, he was too much in thought to notice the black limousine parked a few spaces away. It stood out like a sore thumb in that rundown part of town.

Weldon climbed to his second-floor apartment and took out his key.

As he went to insert it into the lock, he noticed that it had been broken. He reached for his weapon in the back of his waistband. Turning to move quickly away, the door flew open and Kaz grabbed him by the shirt collar dragging him inside.

"What's the idea?" Weldon inquired testily. As Kaz let him go, Hank realized that they weren't the only two in the room. Sitting in his ratty armchair was Maxim Greshnev. The mob boss's diminutive size, 5 feet 6 inches, reminded him of Napoleon. Standing by his side was another strapping young Slav who looked as if he could crush bowling balls between his hands.

"So, to what do I owe this pleasure?" greeted Hank.

"Put down your gun," Kaz demanded. Weldon laid it on the table. "Sit down," responded Maxim as if he owned the joint. Weldon saw no reason not to make himself comfortable in his own apartment. Max smiled in a way that almost had Hank involuntarily emptying his bladder.

"So, why have you come to visit me?"

"I've been hearing your name, and out of curiosity wanted to meet you."

"I've heard about you too." He didn't bother to mention in what context he had heard Greshnev's name.

The boss's lips turned upward into a threatening grin exposing a gold tooth in the front of his mouth. "I've heard you were at one of my places of business the last couple of days. Is this true?"

"You've heard correctly."

"And that you attacked one of my employees by chopping him in his throat."

"Guilty as charged."

"And that you created a commotion when you were told to leave."

"I guess I did."

"That wasn't very smart!"

"Well, I've never been accused of having brains. While I've got you here, perhaps you can answer a question for me. Do you know who killed Karina last night and tried to dispose of her body in the ocean?"

"You are being a very foolish man! Tell me, why did you want to see Karina?" Hank looked back into Kaz's eyes. They were emotionless as he stood with his arms folded across his chest.

"She's a great lay and I came back for another go-round."

"You're lying to me! That's your second strike!"

"How about we stop playing games and you tell me why you're really here." Maxim's eyes narrowed into evil slits. "You have a smart mouth and you need to be taught a lesson. Boys..." he added turning to Kaz and his other henchman. Both moved toward him threateningly.

"Now, there's no need for the rough stuff." He held out his hand in a defensive manner. Kaz yanked him out of the chair and spun him until he had both Hank's arms locked behind his back.

"Hey!" Weldon yelped in pain. Before he could get another word out, the other goon's fist came crashing into his nose. Immediately blood spurted onto the floor. That did not stop the young hoodlum. He alternated giving out punishment from the solar plexus to the face. Weldon was soon doubled over in pain. Kaz let go of his arms and Weldon fell to the floor.

"Get smart and stay out of my affairs or you could be the next body washing up on the shore!"

Maxim and the young bully left, but Kaz stayed behind to remind him of one fact before he walked out. "Remember, no police."

Hank wanted to explain that he was ordered to see them this afternoon, but after the beating he took, he felt no more loyalty to the big Russian.

Stemming the bleeding as best he could, Hank glanced in the mirror at his reflection. It wasn't pretty. His chest felt as if a wrecking ball had hit it multiple times. God, I'm a mess!

Although he badly wanted a drink, he refrained from going to The Dive. I've got to be sober when I'm questioned this afternoon.

Weldon knew he would now be under surveillance on the orders of Greshnev, and that his visit to the police would get back to the mob boss. He wished that Kaz would hire some other private dick to find his missing fiancée, but he knew that there was no way out of this.

Changing out of his bloody clothes, he went downstairs and started his car. As soon as he pulled away from the curb, he noticed a black Lincoln Continental do the same thing. He watched as the car shadowed every turn he made. Once he arrived at his old precinct and parked, the Lincoln did the same, a few yards away. He nonchalantly looked over at the car as he made his way into the station. No one had gotten out and he could not see who was behind the wheel due to the tinted windshield.

Inside, a million feelings flooded back to him. Almost everything is different. He noticed that most of the faces were younger and new. "What can I do for you?" the young woman behind the desk inquired.

"I'm here to see Detective Malone."

"Have a seat on the bench and I'll see if he's available. Your name?"

"Henry Weldon." A few familiar faces turned around to look, but they turned quickly back once they recognized him. Hank hadn't expected anything different.

Weldon sat down on the bench reserved for visitors. For him, it felt strange sitting there.

After almost ten minutes, Archie appeared. "I'm ready for you," the detective reposted icily. Malone glanced at his eyes to detect if he was on a bender. That's when he noticed Weldon's appearance. "What happened to your face?"

"I had a mean run in with my apartment door." Hank followed him to Interrogation Room 3. Both men took a seat at the table.

"There's still a few recognizable faces around," he mentioned, trying to break the ice between them.

Malone wasn't having it. "No one's your friend here anymore, Weldon. Those days are gone."

They sat on opposite sides of the table. The detective got down to brass tacks. "I hope you're ready to answer my questions fully and honestly?"

"I'll do the best I can."

"What do you know about the woman found dead on the beach this morning?"

"I know her name's Karina and that's about it."

"You knew she was a prostitute, didn't you?"

"Yeah."

"And you told me you had been with her the night before."

"Correct."

"And this morning you were visiting her again?"

"You could say that."

"Do you know how she wound up dead?"

"That I couldn't say."

"How are you involved with the Russian mob?"

"I'm not and never have been."

"And yet, I've seen you around with a hood named Kazimir Titov. Isn't that, right?

"We have some business dealings together. I can assure you that it's all very innocent."

"Innocent," he laughed rising from the table. Now there's an adjective I've never associated with Titov!"

"Listen, sometimes he goes on surveillance and takes pictures of cheating spouses when I'm not available. He makes a little extra money on the side."

"You mean when you're too drunk to do the job yourself."

"I haven't had a drink in two days!"

"Yeah, I've heard that song and dance before."

"It's the truth!"

"The truth is that you're holding back information from me!" he yelled getting into Hank's face.

"If this is your feeble attempt at intimidation, I invented that game when I was on the police force!"

"There's more to your association with Titov. For some reason, you're now running with the wrong crowd."

"I have no association with Maxim and his followers."

"That's a lie!" Archie threw down his evidence. They were photos taken of Grehnev and his two body guards.

"They entered your building this morning. Is that how you got roughed up?"

"I told you already, it was a door."

"Yeah, a door. Were you a part of Karina's demise?"

"Now you're calling me a murderer?"

"I've learned early in life that when you lie down with dogs, you shouldn't be surprised if you have fleas!"

Weldon wanted so badly to tell the detective how Kaz had hired him to find his missing fiancée, and how he threatened to kill Karina, but he couldn't because Kaz's voice rang in his head, *Don't tell the police!*

"If you had any evidence that I killed Karina, you'd already have me in cuffs and would be reading me my rights. But you have nothing! This is just a fishing expedition, isn't it?"

"Wise guy! One day you're going to trip yourself up!" Hank stood up, pushing back the chair.

"I'm leaving!' Malone did nothing to stop him.

I'm being squeezed from both ends, the Russian mob and the cops! How do I let myself get into these situations?" I've had it! When Kaz comes over tonight, I'm going to tell him that I'm off the case. No more Mister Nice Guy! I'm through with the whole sordid situation!

Feeling better with this promise, Weldon walked through the detective room to the front door. Screw all of you! He walked to the car and observed the black vehicle still parked in the same spot. When he pulled away, so did the Lincoln Continental. *And screw you too!*

CHAPTER

4

WHEN HANK CAME home, a green-eyed redheaded female was camped outside in the hallway. She stood up immediately. "Hank Weldon?"

"Yes," he responded, recognizing her from the Russian Doll House.

"I need your help."

Not another one!

"Come in." Unlocking the lock that had been replaced, they both walked in. She asked, "Could you draw the shades?" Weldon looked at her with a confused expression, but did as she bid.

"Who are you?"

"My name is Renata Dubov."

"I've seen you at…"

"The Russian Doll House? Yes, I've seen you there too."

"Why have you come to see me?"

"I'm scared. A lot of the girls there are also afraid."

"Is this about Karina?"

"And about Albina, since she left so mysteriously. The women feel as if they're being targeted one by one." Weldon doubted that Greshnev would be picking off his money makers one at a time.

"Sit down," invited Hank as he saw that the girl was under great duress. Renata sat in the armchair.

"Maxim doesn't like his women to go outside his establishment."

"I know. Even though the girls all agree about being threatened, I was the only one who was willing to try and sneak out to see you."

"I see."

"I can't go back! I've already missed a couple of scheduled customers. They realize I'm missing now and will beat me!"

"You can't stay here! There's barely room for me." The pretty redhead broke down into a cascade of tears. Suddenly, Weldon could feel an emotion that he thought was long dead, well up inside him - compassion.

"Please, I have nowhere else to go!"

"Alright, you can stay. Would you like a cup of tea?"

"Yes, please."

He chose the least chipped cup in his cupboard and placed the bag and hot water into it. He set it before Renata.

"Thank you," she smiled dunking the bag a few times before she took a few sips.

"I'm sorry but I don't have much more to offer you."

"This is fine."

Although Hank had visited several girls in the bordello, he had never questioned them before about their backgrounds. "Where are you from originally?"

"I grew up outside of Minsk, went to school where I learned to speak English, took secretarial courses, and when I graduated I worked as a receptionist at a local doctor's office."

My God, she wasn't always a prostitute?

"How did you get involved in this current line of work?"

"I was approached by a man who said I could earn a much bigger salary doing the same job in America."

"So, you did it?"

"It seemed like a dream come true. I just couldn't pass up the opportunity. I had to pay them for my passage, but when I got here, I found that it had been all a lie. I was held against my will and had to do awful things." One more tear escaped from her eye.

"And are all the other girls in the same circumstances?"

"For the most part."

"What about Albina and Karina?"

"Karina's story seems similar, but I don't know about Albina's."

"I'm sorry," was all he could think to say.

"I won't be a problem for you. I can sleep on the floor. My cooking and housekeeping are very good." Weldon could not see how he could gracefully get around it. He now had inherited a houseguest.

"Alright, we can do this for a while."

"Thank you so much! I will cook for you my specialty, Beef Stroganov."

"Sounds like an expensive dish. Do you have anything else you can cook that won't cost me a lot of money?"

"I can cook borsht." Renata gave him a list of ingredients and he left for the supermarket, spending most of what was left of the money Kaz had given him.

When Weldon returned, Renata got busy in the kitchen. While the meal was cooking, she tidied up the small apartment. Soon the wafting aroma of homemade food was filling the living space.

Watching Renata work reminded him of Clare, and he wanted a drink so badly, but he refrained from giving in to the urge. Soon his head rested on his chest as he fell asleep in the arm chair.

"Mr. Weldon," he heard a voice calling him and felt a hand shake his shoulder gently. "Wake up, it's time to eat." Hank opened his eyes to see the food on the small card table. Soon they were both sitting down sipping their soup.

"This is delicious!"

"I'm glad you're enjoying it!" The two of them slurped away in perfect harmony.

"That's the best meal I've had in a long time!"

"Were you ever married?" inquired Renata as she tried to learn something about her protector.

Weldon's face became suddenly sullen. "I was married but I don't want to talk about it, understand?"

"Of course." The girl brought the empty dishes to the sink and began to wash them. They were interrupted by a banging on his door. Renata's eyes stared at Weldon with terror.

"Get in the closet and don't say a word because your life depends upon it." Without making a sound, she entered the closet and closed the door. Hank went to the door and found Kaz on the other side. The big man stomped in.

"It smells like borsht in here."

"Take out from a Russian deli," he lied.

"What the hell were you doing at the police station today?" Kaz's eyes became slits of ferocity.

"I don't like being tailed!"

"Answer me!" he screamed his temper reaching a boiling point.

"The cops would have brought me in if I hadn't gone myself. Besides, it was about a whole different matter."

"And what was that?"

"They wanted to question me about Karina."

"Is that it, nothing else?"

"I gave you my word that I wouldn't go to the police. I've kept my promise."

The big Russian pulled the plug on his anger. "And you better keep it or I'll…" Interrupting him, Weldon stated, "Do you want to know what I've found out about your fiancée or not?"

"What have you found out about Albina?"

"It seems that someone in the mob may be responsible for both Albina leaving as well as Karina's murder."

Kaz stopped to absorb this information. "You mean to tell me that someone I work with has taken her?"

"Someone you work with or work for."

"Are you suggesting that Maxim had a hand in Albina's disappearance?"

"It's a distinct possibility."

"I don't believe it."

"Have you made any enemies?"

"Enemies? Don't make me laugh! Every day I make enemies!"

"What about people you've hurt trying to collect what they owed your boss?"

"Those weasels? They don't have the balls to stab me in the back."

Don't be so sure of that! "I don't know what else I can tell you."

"You can tell me where my Albina is and who abducted her. That's why I paid you!"

"Speaking of pay, if you want me to continue, I'll need more money." Hank hoped his demand for money would end his obligation.

Kaz dropped a couple of hundred dollars onto the table." "I want results," he growled. "I want results soon!" He left, not bothering to close the door.

Weldon walked over to the closet and let a frightened Renata out.

"I suppose you heard our conversation?"

"Yes," she answered with a terrified voice.

"He's gone. You have nothing to worry about."

"Kaz scares me and the other girls."

"More than Greshnev's other henchmen?"

"He has a black heart! I wouldn't be surprised to find out that he had a hand in Karina's death!"

Days quickly flew by and became weeks, and Renata became an important part of his life. He began to develop a fondness for her. He could not bear for her to sleep on the hard floor, so he gave up his bed. His back was sore each morning, but that was compensated by Renata cooking breakfast. Hank didn't know how long he could keep her hidden, but for now it just seemed like the right thing to do. When he was at home, he was comforted by her presence as she cleaned his apartment or stood by the stove, concocting something delicious. If Weldon had to leave because of a case, he warned her, "Don't open the door to anybody unless it's me, and don't make a sound!"

"I understand," she would tell him, no matter how many times he repeated himself.

Once she had even convinced him to go to a steam room to relieve the stress he was under with Kaz's nightly visits. At first, he refused, but with her constant coaxing, he finally relented. The old bath house had been converted into a modern spa. Women were not allowed, since everyone knew that this was sometimes a mob hangout. The man behind the desk eyed him suspiciously. "What can I do for you?"

"I'm here for a steam."

Looking him over, the man continued. "I've never seen you around here before."

"Yeah, so…it's my first time. Am I breaking some law?" Hank suggested sarcastically.

Shrugging, the employee pointed to a sign behind him that read "$20 for one hour." Placing the bill on the counter, he was given a key for locker 27.

"Place your clothing in the locker. You will find fresh towels and flip-flops. Make sure you lock it and keep the key around your wrist. Then follow the red arrows to the steam room."

Hank arrived at the locker room and started to disrobe. He hadn't undressed in front of other people other than his wife, and the prostitutes he had seen. Hank was feeling a bit flabby compared to the well-built men who surrounded him, and he wrapped the towel around his waist quickly.

Self-consciously, he moved swiftly through the locker room, his flop-flops slapping against his heels, until he reached the steam room. Small groups of men sat around speaking Russian. They glared at him as if he were some sort of alien. Weldon came to an uninhabited corner where he could hide. Sitting on the tiled bench, he put his back against the wall, closed his eyes, and let the steam work its magic.

He didn't know how long he slept when he was awakened by the sound of voices. He took a quick look to see who had invaded his space. He realized that it was Maxim Greshnev, Kaz Titov and another guy he did not recognize were sitting around the corner. They all had prison tattoos with various symbols, but one significantly stood out. Weldon recognized the rose tattoo on Kaz's chest indicating he was a member of the Russian Mafia. On Maxim's shoulder was a star, revealing he was a man of status and discipline. Another on his knees meant that he kneeled before no man. On his chest was the Madonna and Baby Jesus revealing that the man would never betray his friends to the police. The third man had a tattoo of a knife sticking out of a neck, that denoted that he was an assassin for hire. He listened carefully as the three of them spoke. "He is a loose cannon," Kaz spoke to his employer.

"He cannot be trusted any longer," the other man added.

"Yet he has given us vital information over the years as to what the police are up to," replied Maxim. "He has been an essential link to police activities."

"He has been warned off the Karina Davidenko investigation many times, but continues to pursue it!"

Could it be Archie Malone they were referring to? No, it couldn't be!

"If Malone opens his mouth, we are all in for it! He has to go!"

My God, it is Archie! How long has he been on the Russian's payroll? All this time he's ostracized me when he's been a dirty cop!

"Don't be so quick to slit his throat! Kaz, go to him. Tell him again to lose this murder in the cold case files, and warn him that if he opens his mouth we will make sure that his body is never found!" With a grunt of approval, the men talked about betting debts that had to be collected. Hank sat nervously hidden trying not to get a bullet in his forehead.

Once they got up to leave and their voices faded in the distance, Weldon felt safe enough to reveal himself. *Shit! What am I going to do with this information?* He stood in the steam room internally debating the pros and cons. *Should I tell Archie that I know about what he's been involved in and warn him that his life could be in danger? Or should I leave that piece of crap to discover it on his own?*

Remembering how Archie had treated him the last time they'd been together, he really felt like letting him swing in the wind. Hank thought back on the pleasant memories of them as rookies at the academy, how he had been his best man when he married Clare, how he had been there when she had died, and how he tried to help him with his alcoholism. But when he proved to be unreliable and sometimes violent while he was drinking, Archie washed his hands of him. Malone's last words were, "If you're not going to help yourself, no one will be able to help you!"

"Go on, get out!" he had retorted. "I don't need anybody's help!" That was the last time he had seen Malone until they had met on the beach with Karina's body.

Assuming the mafia boss and his henchmen had already dressed and left the building, Hank cautiously returned to the locker room. Skipping the shower room, he furtively glanced around, but he did not catch sight of them. Hurriedly, he unlocked his locker and got dressed and returned the key to the front desk.

He had come to a decision. I'm going to warn Archie for old time's sake! He played it vigilantly because even though he had not caught sight of a car, he knew he might still be tailed by Kaz. Weldon would have to contact Malone using his house phone.

Hank spent a restless night going over how he was going to approach Malone with the information. The next morning, he waited for Renata to get into the shower before he picked up the phone. He didn't want her to know anything that might endanger her life. The phone rang a few times before being picked up. "Twenty-Third Precinct, Detective Cunningham, how can I help you?"

"I want to speak to Detective Malone."

"He's busy on a case, but you can speak to me."

"No I can't!" he said emphatically. "Get him on the phone. Tell him it's a friend calling about a life and death situation!"

"Hey, Harry!" Weldon heard the cop on the other side of the line shout. "Where's Archie?" Hank didn't hear the answer, but Cunningham responded, "Well, go tell him he's got a phone call".

A minute or two passed before he heard Archie's voice ask, "Who is it?"

"He won't give his name but says he's a friend with a life or death situation." Ripping the phone out of Cunningham's hand, he yelled

"Who the hell is this?"

"Listen to me and shut up!"

"Weldon, is that you? What part of "I don't want to be bothered with you" don't you understand?"

"I said shut up! Your life is in danger! I overheard a conversation in the Russian Bath House today."

"Is eavesdropping one of your private detective techniques?"

"It was a conversation between Maxim Greshnev and two of his men, and your name was mentioned." There was silence on the other side of the line. He had finally gotten Archie's attention.

"I don't know what you're talking about."

"How long have you been on their payroll?"

"Come over and say that to my face and I'll knock you down!"

"They said that you're a "loose cannon" and that if you didn't back off from Karina's murder, your life would be forfeited." Again there was silence. "Did you hear me?"

"Yeah."

"I'm warning you for the sake of the friendship we once had. What you do with the information is now your business."

More silence. At last in a low and humble voice, Archie replied,

"Thanks." The phone went dead.

CHAPTER

5

W ARM SUMMER DAYS began to fade, and the morning air became chilly. Like the weather, Hank's investigation of Albina's disappearance had also become cold. Wherever he turned, it became evident that the tips he received were useless. The only evidence seemed to indicate that Albina and Karina had been victims of an inside job at the Russian Doll House, but convincing Kaz of this had become a lost cause. The prospects of finding the man who had run away with her were as bleak as the outlook for the upcoming winter.

For Hank, the presence of Renata in his studio apartment made everything around him cheerier, but then he realized it was his own attitude that was different. Watching her clean and cook brought back pleasant memories of the years he had been married. In fact, he had put on some weight, all in his stomach, due to the Russian woman's talents as a cook. It remained very idyllic between the private detective and the prostitute. It was all quite platonic, since sex was not part of the equation.

Life could have gone on this way, until one morning when there was a loud pounding on his door. "Who is it?" he demanded. The voice of Kaz was clearly heard from the other side.

"Unlock this door or I'll knock it off its hinges!"

What is he doing here at this time of the day?

Renata had been standing by the stove making stroganoff. "Go to the closet!" he whispered to the horrified woman. She made a dash to her familiar hiding place and closed the door. The pounding on the door continued.

"Open up, now!" Titov's words were not an empty threat. Hank had to have his front door fixed when Kaz had been impatient once before, and he was not going to let that happen again. Weldon unlocked and opened the door.

Immediately, Kaz remarked about the aroma in the room. "Stroganoff?" he inquired and made his way to the stove. He grabbed a spoon and sampled the dish. "Excellent stroganoff. Who made it?"

"A neighbor woman sends me food every once in a while."

"A whole pot? She is very generous to you."

"Why are you here, Kaz?"

"I want to look around."

"Look for what?" Kaz did not answer but pulled his gun out. "What's this all about?" Hank looked over to the kitchen chair where he had hung his holstered pistol. *He'll gun me down if I try to go for it.*

Kaz opened the bathroom door and peered inside. Once he was satisfied, he closed the door. He moved to the closet and took hold of the handle. A scream came from the interior.

"Now what do we have here?" Titov opened the closet door and pulled out Renata by her wrist. "Well, look who you've been hiding all this time."

"Don't Kaz, please!" yelled Hank.

"Where's my Albina? He retorted with a voice full of anger. For months, I have come to you, paid your expenses and all you've come up with is that someone in the mob is at fault!"

"Please!" Renata begged him. Don't take me back!"

"Be reasonable," Weldon tried to appease him. "You know what they'll do to her if you take her back!" Renata burst into tears.

"Every time I came here, I wondered about the smell of food. The deli… a neighbor, all lies!"

"Just forget that you found her here. Leave as you came and no one will be the wiser."

"If Maxim ever found out I knew where Renata was and never took her back, he would have my head. I like my head just where it is!" He dragged the girl to the door as she vainly tried to fight him. Kaz kept his gun trained on the detective. "Don't even think about going for your gun!"

"Don't do it, Kaz!"

"Now you stay exactly where you are." Renata looked back to Hank, her eyes pleading for him to save her. Weldon was helpless to make a move toward her. When they were gone, Hank was desolated.

###

When he tried to start up his Volkswagen, it at first wouldn't turn over. *Damn it! Not now!* After the third try, the engine roared into action. Weldon followed Kaz's car at a safe distance, keeping it well in sight. He knew that if he were ever going to get Renata back, he would have to confront Kaz somewhere along the line. The difficulty was the Russian's use of her as a shield. *God, I could use a drink to steady my nerves!*

Hank shadowed the black Chrysler sedan, already knowing where it was heading. He kept his eye on the car even though there was heavy traffic. Once they arrived at the Russian Doll House, Hank grabbed his pistol. Renata must be so scared thinking that I abandoned her. I must get her out of this! Weldon screamed, "Titov, let her go!"

"Hank!" Renata shrieked when she heard his voice but Kaz did not heed his warning. Aiming his gun at the detective, he dragged the crying woman into the building. Weldon had held out hope that Titov would come to his senses and release her, but now he was in his sanctuary, a place he knew like the back of his hand. Running to the door, the private detective opened it expecting Serge to be waiting for him, but the entrance and hallway were clear. Cautiously, he made his way forward. Zoya came out of her office holding a rifle. "Put that rifle down and get out of my fucking way!" he warned her.

"You're not welcome here anymore! Turn around and leave now!"

"I'm not leaving without Renata! Where is she?"

"You will never see her again!"

"That's where you're wrong." His argument with Zoya had only been a distraction. As they went back and forth, Serge crept up behind him, and hit Weldon in the back of his head with a pistol. Everything went charcoal black and his mind felt like it was swimming against a strong current.

He didn't know how long he had been out, when a sudden pain brought him back to consciousness. The back of his head pounded like the hangovers he used to have after his alcoholic binges, but he then remembered the wallop he received. *Son of a bitch!*

He emitted a low moan and then with a start, Weldon realized that he wasn't the only one in his car. Next to him sat poker-faced Kaz, still training his gun on him. "Did you do this?' he confronted his tormentor.

"No, but you're lucky that's the only thing that happened to you!"

"Who hit me?"

"It makes no difference. I needed to get your attention. You haven't been listening to me."

"I want Renata back!"

"Forget her, at least for the time being."

"What does that mean?"

"I want my Albina returned to me."

"I've tried to explain to you many times…"

"Again, you haven't been listening to what I've told you. It is nobody in the organization that has taken her! I want you to stop repeating that to me! Go out and do the job I paid you to do!"

"Listen, Kaz…"

"No, you listen! I have a bit of insurance to force you to find my Albina!"

"You mean, Renata?"

"That's right! You'll never see your precious girlfriend again until you bring Albina back to me!"

Weldon hesitated before he declared the next question. "But what if she is already dead?"

"Then you've seen Renata alive for the last time." The look of shock was evident on the private detective's face.

"Go home Hank and get started. Renata's life depends upon your success."

Kaz got out, slammed the door, and strolled slowly back to the building.

Now what? Hank's head was full of multiple possibilities, each of which seemed to lead to a dead end. A feeling of utter hopelessness soon overwhelmed him.

The next morning, with a battered and painful hand that he had iced almost the entire evening, Hank Weldon started off for the post-war Building of Public Records. Bounding up the marble steps, he entered the vaulted anteroom and headed straight for the information desk. A young man with pock-marked skin looked up from his desk. "And what can I do for you?"

"I'm wondering where I can find a list of paroled rapists living in and around Brighton Beach?" One of the man's eyebrows raised in surprise.

Clearing his voice, he answered, "You can easily get that from your local police precinct."

"I know that, but I'm here now," Hank answered sarcastically.

The man stared at him for a moment and then replied, "Third floor. Elevators are to the right."

Hank made his way to the elevator bank and pushed the "Up" button. As he waited, he glanced around to see that the building wasn't busy at all.

The elevator arrived and a woman pushing a cart of files stepped out. Hank took her place in the elevator cage. He rose to the third floor. When the doors opened, they revealed numerous reading tables and green shaded lamps at each of the seated areas. Weldon walked to the front desk. A young woman, her disheveled dirty blonde hair put up haphazardly with hairpins, got off the phone and looked up.

"Yes," she said with an exasperated attitude.

"I'm searching for the file of rapists living in this area."

Her nose crinkled with distastefulness. "And what would you want with that?" she answered with disdain.

"None of your business! As a civil employee, your job is to provide a service to the people who come here for help. Do your job!"

The woman pointed, "Section Eight. The file cabinets are alphabetized."

Hank searched the room until he located the file cabinet he was looking for. He fingered through the file folders until his eye fell upon the one entitled "Rapists". Weldon went to the nearest table and opened the manila envelope and laid the documents out on the table. He read through the names, addresses, and whether each was deceased or interred in prison. Hank peered up and found a pad of paper and a chained pen. He wrote down the addresses of those currently living in the area. Weldon compiled a list of 17 names, ripped the page from the pad and folded it, putting into his pant pocket.

After going through about a dozen names of those who lived in the neighborhood, Weldon came upon an Alexander Kurkov living along Coney Island Avenue.

He drove to the dilapidated semi-attached house, and parked the car. He found the gate was rusty and off one hinge. Weldon pushed past it and climbed up the steps that had several loose bricks. The doorbell hung loose from the building exposing its wires. *No use in trying to ring that.*

Instead, he knocked on the door. There was no response. Shading his eyes and looking through the window, he saw somebody moving around inside. This time he pounded on the door. "I know there's somebody in there, so open up before I kick this weak-ass door down." A minute passed before the door opened at a crack. "Get the hell off my property or I'll call the cops!' A husky voice came from behind the front door.

"Go ahead, call the cops! I'm sure they would be interested in hearing what you've been up to lately!" Weldon had no idea what Kurkov was up to, but the ruse worked. The door opened wide. Immediately, Hank noticed a line of sweat appear on Kurkov's upper lip and forehead. "Feeling warm?"

"Who are you? Why are you here?" the 50-something man with the unshaven face demanded. Pushing past him, Hank entered the living room. The room looked like it had never seen a dust rag or carpet cleaner. Scattered around in various piles were old yellowing newspapers.

"Who I am isn't important. I've been canvassing the neighborhood looking up former rapists like you. I have some questions for you, the first of which is are you Alexander Kurkov?"

"Who are you to come barging in here and asking me anything! I'm calling the cops right now!"

"I work for the cops!"

"Where's your badge?"

"Tell you what, I left it at the precinct but I can drive you over to show it to you! I'm sure Detective Malone would like to see you again."

At the mention of Archie's name, the man in the food-stained plaid shirt and khaki pants blanched and cast his eyes to the floor. *I wonder what that's all about.* Hank pressed on. "So, what do you do for a living?"

"I'm disabled."

"Really, in what way?"

"In a way that nobody can see." Mentally disabled?

"According to my records, it says that you were convicted of raping five women, is that correct?"

"I did my time for those crimes and was released three years ago. I haven't done it again."

"I see. Do you get out much?"

"What are you, my social secretary?"

"I'm wondering whether you have visited the Russian Doll House over the past few months?"

"I don't even know the place."

"I wonder if any of the girls would recognize you."

"Okay, I've been there a couple of times but that's nobody's business!"

"Well, if you'd rather answer these questions for Detective Malone, I'll drive you there right now." Once again Alexander turned white and bit down on his lip.

"That won't be necessary."

"Have you ever slept with one of the girls whose name is Albina?"

"Listen, I don't ask for their names and I don't give them mine!"

From his jacket pocket, Hank withdrew the picture of the woman he was talking about. "She looks like this." Weldon watched Alexander's face for some sign of guilt.

"No, I don't remember being with her."

"The other girls tell a different story. They say you were one of her steady customers," he lied.

"They're flat out wrong!" Walking around the slovenly room and looking through various doorways, Weldon inquired, "Do you live here alone?"

"Yeah, why? Are you looking for a housemate?"

"If I were, it wouldn't be you! When's the last time you saw Albina?"

"I already told you that I've never seen her before."

"A couple of days, a couple of weeks, a couple of months ago?"

"Are you hard of hearing! I don't know her!"

"You know Mr. Kurkov, I feel you're holding back with me. I think you have been with Albina, but for the life of me, I don't know why you refuse to admit it."

"I've given you enough of my time today. Please leave my house."

"Okay, but I have the feeling we'll be seeing each other again real soon."

As Weldon got to the first step outdoors, the door was slammed shut.

With the rest of his list of names he had to still visit, he doubted that anyone else would give him the creepy feeling that he had gotten when talking to Kurkov. *With a little more pressure, I believe I can break Kurkov down until I extract the truth from him.*

CHAPTER

6

WELDON LEFT THE house, and as soon as he did, a black unmarked police car pulled up and the passenger window came down. Surveillance still on! "Weldon," the man in the passenger seat called out his name.

"Yeah?" Hank asked with curiosity.

"Detective Malone wants to see you right away!"

"What for?"

"You'll find that out when you get there!"

"Fine," he replied resigning himself to the fact that there was no way he was going to wriggle out of this. "I'll follow you in my car."

"Get in the back seat!" the officer commanded. "If you're worried that someone will steal the Beetle, don't. Even from a distance, anyone could tell it's a piece of shit!"

As soon as Hank got into the back seat, the car sped off. The tension in the car was thick enough to cut with a knife. They came to a halt in front of the precinct building. The cop in the passenger side came out and opened the door. Walking through the precinct door, the cop asked the receptionist, "What interrogation rooms are free?"

"Three and five," the answer came back.

"Tell Malone that Weldon will be in five." He opened the door saying, "Take a load off! Detective Malone will be here in a while."

Hank wanted to ask how long a while, but the door was closed without another word. *I hope Malone doesn't keep me here forever. I still have the last names on my list to get into.*

He looked out the wired window and onto the busy city below. He cursed the day that Kaz Titov had ever come to him to locate Albina. *I could be at The Dive throwing back a few beers right now.* He revisited in his mind the day Clare and the baby had died and realized he would have been close to retirement and his child would have been sixteen. Things could have turned out so differently for me. "It's too late for that!" Hank turned when he felt another presence in the room. "Talking to yourself?" Archie asked. "That's usually the first sign of mental incapacity!" Malone closed the door.

"I'm still sharp enough to remember the topic of our last conversation on the phone."

"Shut up!" Malone seethed, his hissing was like a coiled snake ready to strike. "Now sit down!" Hank took a seat at the table.

"So, what is so important that you had to see me right away?" Malone looked down at his former friend's left hand.

"How did you hurt your hand?"

"Skiing accident at San Moritz!"

Ignoring his sarcastic answer, the detective took a seat opposite Weldon and proclaimed, "Well, you've been a busy beaver today."

"I suppose that mean's something to you but it's a mystery to me."

"You've been observed riding around Brighton Beach and dropping in on certain people."

"Your bloodhounds never miss a trick!"

"I'm interested in your visit with just one of those people..."

"No, don't tell me. Let me guess... Alexander Kurkov. Am I right?"

"What were you doing there?"

"I had some questions for him."

"What questions?"

"It was a private matter."

"Really?"

"I noticed while I was talking to him that he had a very strange reaction each time I mentioned your name."

"I don't know what you're talking about."

"He acted all nervous and sweaty, and couldn't look me in the eyes... Oh wait a minute, now I get it!"

"What do you get?"

"He's your informant, your stoolie. Is he feeding you information about the Russian Mafia?"

Archie did not address the accusation. "You need to stay away from him if you know what's good for you!"

"For my own good? I think that you don't want your decoy uncovered because he's your pipeline inside the mob. Isn't that it?"

Malone slammed his hand down hard on the table as he stood up. "Drop it!"

"You mean like I dropped the idea that you were on Maxim Greshnev's payroll?"

"Keep your mouth shut or I'll shut it for you!"

"Well," Weldon began as he stood up. "I guess I'll be going now, although being with you was like a little slice of heaven."

"Weldon, watch your step before you trip yourself up," he advised.

"I'm not the one who's going to fall hard if the truth comes out! The game you're playing can only lead to one conclusion, a bullet to the back of your brain. Watch your step!" As Hank left, his mind started turning. *That will give him something to think about for a while instead of me.*

Weldon went home to his lonely apartment and got on the phone. He dialed Kaz's number. He was greeted brusquely with, "Have you located Albina yet?"

Ignoring his query, he retorted, "Do you know a character named Alexander Kurkov?"

"Yeah, that pervert comes to the Doll House to have sex every once and a while, but mostly to play poker with Greshnev and people who owed me favors. Why do you ask?"

"He may have a connection to Albina's disappearance."

"I'll kill him!" the bodyguard's voice responded overflowing with lividness. "And I told you already that I don't think anyone in the organization is involved."

"Listen to me very carefully. All the girls are watched like a hawk. How could Albina get out without someone looking the other way?"

For the first time since he had suggested a conspiracy, Titov fell silent. At last he answered, "Sokoloff!"

"Who's that?"

"Serge is the girls' bodyguard. The one you hit in the throat and the one who returned the favor. Wait till I get a hold a hold of him!"

"Don't do anything rash! I'll get the information I need out of Kurkov and don't tip your hand too early to Sokoloff!" I can't let Kaz know he's a police informant, because if something happens to Kurkov, Malone will know that I spilled the beans to a member of the mob.

"I want to see Renata."

"Yeah, and I want to see Albina!"

"Give me a break! Let me see Renata so I can explain what's been going on."

"Why should I? You've brought me a theory as to why my fiancée is gone. There's no concrete evidence that it is right!"

"Please, I know she must be scared."

"Alright, meet me in the Russian Doll House bar at three this afternoon. I'll try to arrange a short meeting between the two of you."

"Thanks, Kaz!" The phone was hung up.

###

The hands on his wristwatch seemed to drag, moving as if it were suddenly in slow motion. Weldon tried to eat, read, get some sleep, but his mind was working overtime and he could concentrate on nothing else but seeing Renata again. He wore out the wood on his apartment floor as he paced across the room, stopping a few times, only for a minute, as he glanced outside to the streets below. He noticed the sky becoming gray and overcast. He wanted to be optimistic, but the sky was reflecting his mood. It's going to rain soon.

At 2:45 p.m., Hank got into the car. It was drizzling as he turned on the ignition and the windshield wipers. He started on the ten-minute drive toward his rendezvous. The parking lot was crowded, and Weldon had to find a spot on the street. Inside the bar, he noticed that the booths were crowded with men looking for a cheap thrill, while the girls milled around the customers. Hank looked around but could not find Kaz. After a minute, the back door with the words "Employees Only" opened and Kaz stepped out. "Right on time," remarked Kaz casually as he approached Weldon.

"Where is she?"

"You're not very observant for a private dick." Weldon looked at him with a puzzled expression. "She's up there," he announced pointing to the stage just beyond the bar. Three beautiful girls were writhing on poles to the delight of the patrons. One of them was Renata. Hank knew that the girls who gave the owners trouble, talked back, or didn't follow the rules were taken out of the bordello and made to dance in high heels and skimpy underwear as the men stuffed dollar bills in their waistbands or bras. Weldon turned angrily to Kaz. "What is she doing up there?"

"Trouble maker!" he answered with a cruel smile. "Her set is over in about ten minutes."

"Then I can see her?"

"Sure, I'll send her back to one of the private lap dance rooms. He held his palm out.

"What does that mean?"

"Fifty dollars for ten minutes."

"I just want to see her and have a talk."

"You're not seeing anybody until Ulysses S. Grant crosses my palm!"

Taking out a fifty, he placed in his hand.

"Candy!" he yelled at one of the scantily dressed waitresses. "Take this gentleman to room One."

"This way, sir," she replied walking him back through a red velvet curtain and into a private room. "She'll be right with you."

Hank sat down on a red velvet couch in the dimly lit room. On the walls were framed photographs of the strippers wearing nothing but alluring smiles. Weldon looked toward the door in anticipation of Renata's arrival. At last, she stepped in. It had been a few weeks since he had seen her, and he noticed a distinct physical difference. Her face was slightly swollen with heavy makeup covering facial bruises. Hank proclaimed, "What have they done to your face?"

"I'm here to give you a lap dance and nothing else." Pushing him back on the couch, she took off her bra and sat on his lap. She began to seductively move around on him.

"Renata, it's me…Hank!"

"No names," she casually said as she worked him. He looked into her eyes that seemed as vacuous to him as her voice. Weldon noticed the puncture marks on her arm revealing that she was probably being drugged to make her more cooperative.

"I'm going to get you out of here." As soon as he said it, she got up and sat on him with her back to his face.

"Didn't you hear me?"

"Do you like it like this, lover?" she answered her voice breathy and seductive. Hank felt nothing but empty inside. Once more, in a low voice, he called out her name.

"Renata."

The dancer got up from his lap and put on her bra. Facing him, she announced,

"What's the matter, lover? Are you having trouble getting it up today? No matter, you can always come and see me again." Without another word, she left the room.

Hank Weldon stood up, his mind disturbed by the vacant Renata that he had witnessed. Before he could get out the door, Kaz stopped him. "So, did you have a nice conversation?"

"What did you do to her?"

"I don't know what you're talking about."

"Who's beaten her?"

"There are rules that must be obeyed and if they are not, there are severe consequences."

"If you or Sokoloff touched her…" Kaz just shrugged the comment away. "Have you drugged her? Her personality has changed!"

"Now you're talking crazy!"

"If she has received any permanent damage at your hands or anybody else's…" Kaz grabbed him by the lapels and got in his face. "Blame yourself for anything that has happened to her! I've been a patient man with you and still my Albina has not been returned to me! I will not wait forever!" Pushing Hank away gruffly, he left the private detective behind.

Hank left the building, the rain coming down with the force of Niagara Falls. Running to the car, he got in and slammed the door. I could catch my death of cold if I just sit here waiting to get dry. He knew just what to do. Driving through the puddled avenues, he made his way to an old familiar haunt, The Dive. As soon as he arrived, he ran to the door and went in. The same bar flies occupied their familiar seats at the tables or bar.

"I haven't seen you in here for a while," Ivan the bartender commented.

"Yeah, I know." It's been almost five months since I've had a proper drink.

"What will it be?" the bartender queried wiping his hands on the white towel that was hanging from his waistband.

"A double whisky…neat!"

"Comin' right up." Ivan walked to the bottle on the glass shelf on the back wall of the bar. Taking a tumbler, he poured a double and placed in front of Hank. He gulped the liquid down in a couple of swallows.

Ivan began to walk away to return the whisky when Hank got his attention. "Pour me another and leave the bottle here."

"It's all yours!" the bartender said placing the bottle on the bar.

"This is just for medicinal purposes," he explained to Ivan. "I feel a nasty cold coming on and I'm trying not to get sick."

"Yeah, I know. All the others that are here have come in every day for their dose of medicine too!" he snickered as he walked away.

"Jackass," Weldon proclaimed under his breath, and so he sat there until he was blind drunk in the hope that he could forget. Unfortunately, the events of the last few months kept rewinding and playing over and over in his mind.

CHAPTER

7

"UGH!" HANK LOWLY moaned as he tried to open his eyes. The fact that he hadn't had a drink for months made this hangover much worse. He sensed that he was in a bed. *Is this my own bed or someone else's?* Once again, he attempted to open his eyes, and this time he was successful. The room seemed to spin around.

"Finally, you're awake!" a voice said from somewhere near.

"Who's there?"

"It's Archie. Fell off the wagon again, did you?"

"Where am I?" Weldon wondered out loud as the room began to slow down.

"You're home."

Slowly sitting up, Hank queried, "How did I get here?"

"I got a call from Ivan at The Dive. He told me that you weren't fit to drive yourself home."

Putting his hands on his head to stop the throbbing, he said, "Is Ivan your paid informant?"

At first Malone didn't answer, but Hank could hear him going over to the refrigerator and opening it up. Suddenly, he felt the freezing touch of an ice bag on top of his forehead. "Or maybe," Hank continued, "he's a part of the mob that you're now involved with."

"Shut up! I'm not talking to you about that."

"Tell me, have you spoken to your wife and children about your arrangement with these animals?"

"I don't ever want you to mention it or talk to me about my family again, understand?"

"Touchy subject, is it? By the way, since when did you care enough to see that I got home safely?"

"Can't you just shut up? You're starting to annoy me!" He stared into Hank's eyes. They were void of any emotion.

Malone decided to go on the offensive. "When are you going to get your life together? Do you think Clare would be happy about the way you're living now?"

"My life literally went up in smoke and flames 15 years ago."

"When are you going to stop using that as a crutch? Do you think that you're the only one who ever had someone you love die?"

"You don't know!"

"I know that Clare's looking down on you right now and is not happy about what she's seeing."

"What's the real reason you took me home and decided to sit with me? Did you do this in exchange for keeping my mouth shut about your lapse of judgment with the Russians? "Why did you go to them in the first place?"

"I'm afraid it's a long and boring story and one that you're not fit to listen to at the moment.

"Will you tell me someday?"

"I'm afraid I have to go. I told my wife I'd be working late and it's almost dawn."

"Well, thanks."

"Lie back down and get some more sleep so you can feel better later in the day. And stay off the sauce for God sake!"

"Don't worry! I won't be doing that again." As Weldon laydown, the ice pack still balanced on his head, he felt himself drift back into slumber.

He didn't know how long he had been out before he heard a constant pounding on his door. "Go away, I'm not well!" The door was flung open and Albina's fiancée looked over to him as he lay there as still as death. Kazimir threw something light on his chest.

"Sit up!" he screamed "and look at what I've brought you!"

"Didn't you hear what I said? He remarked never opening his eyes. "I'll look at it tomorrow." Before he knew it, Titov dragged him out of his bed and onto his feet.

"Look at this!" he yelled waving something in his face.

"What?" Weldon sighed as he took what looked to be a photograph out of his hand. He tried to focus his eyes on the image. It was a picture of a blonde woman. As his vision cleared, he realized in horror that it was a snapshot of Albina and she was dead.

"What happened?" he asked not being able to tear his eyes away from the photo.

"What happened is that she is dead!"

"How did this happen?"

While Kaz raved on, pacing from one end of his room to another, Hank examined the image more closely. The crime scene seemed staged. Albina was placed in a chair, her legs crossed and a lit cigarette between her thumb and index finger in her left hand. Her head was rolled over on her left shoulder and her red lipstick had been purposely smeared across her face. The pearls around her neck were knotted and Weldon noted the black and blue dotted image that indicated that they had been pressed in her neck. She was strangled with her own necklace! *Who could have done this? She looks as if someone had taken her picture just as Albina had fallen asleep.*

He tore his eyes away to see that across the image, a sentence had been written in red ink. It read, "Smile, you're dead!"

Was it a coincidence that Weldon always used a similar phrase, "Smile, you're caught" when he would snap the picture of someone who was caught with his pants down? *Is someone trying to pin this murder rap on me?*

"You were supposed to find her!" he heard Titov's deranged voice scream. "I paid you to find her before something like this happened!"

"You haven't told me everything about Albina's disappearance, have you? What have you been holding back from me?"

"You accuse me of Albina's death?" Hank was no longer sure that Kaz hadn't been involved. Someone was muddying the water, preventing Hank from seeing the clear picture, and that maybe it was Kaz himself.

"Did you have something to do with her death? Perhaps you had a lover's quarrel and it got out of hand. Whatever it was, I can't help but feel that you're holding something back from me in this case."

"You bastard!" yelled Kaz as he swung his fist connecting with Weldon's jaw. Hank fell backwards onto the bed. It was then that he felt his holstered gun. He withdrew it quickly and pointed it at the out-of-control mobster.

"Don't put your hands on me again, Titov or it will be the last thing you ever do!"

"She's dead now and you did nothing to find her!"

"You can blame yourself for this tragedy. You gave me nothing to work with and placed obstacles in my way."

"You're talking crazy! What obstacles?"

"Not telling the police!"

"I hate cops! I didn't want them involved."

"Again, I feel as if you're holding back!"

"Crazy, crazy, crazy…" he repeated, using his finger to make circles at his head to emphasize his point.

"And then there was your refusal to accept my theory that a member of your mob had some kind of implication with her disappearance."

"Nobody I work with would dare to cross me like that. You were wrong then and you're wrong now!"

"I can tell that you're still not willing to tell me what you know. I did the best that I could. Until you're willing to tell me the truth, I quit working for you!"

Kaz's eyes seethed with a hatred that scared him. "Watch your back, Weldon," he hissed walking toward the door leaving the photo behind.

"Is that a threat?"

Stopping at the door, he said, "Just watch your back, buddy!" he opened the door and left the room.

That afternoon, Hank was sober enough to know that he might be on his own in solving this murder. *It's a damn shame!* Albina and Karina are dead. The murders were linked. Renata was beaten and drugged. Somehow, these three cases were tied together. *I'm the one who will have to discover the connection and unwind it.* "No point in keeping my promise to not get the police involved!" he said out loud.

He drove to the police station, and walked quickly past the receptionist who kept repeating, "Can I help you…Can I…" until he reached Archie Malone's desk. He had his head buried in paperwork.

"Archie." Malone looked up, his reading glasses perched precipitously on the end of his nose. "You clean up well."

"We need to talk."

"Talk about what? I'm trying to get my reports done so I can get home on time for a change."

"This is important. Can we speak somewhere privately?" Malone gave him a skeptical look, as if seeing him would be a waste of his precious time. At last, he relented. "Come with me." Weldon followed him out the door and towards a police car. Archie got into the driver's side while his former partner and friend joined him in the passenger seat.

"This has to be kept completely confidential.'

"Even more confidential than what is admitted to a priest in a confession booth. Now, what's so important that you had to drag me away from my work?"

Weldon took out the photo from his jacket pocket and handed it to Malone. The detective stared at it without saying a word.

"Well?"

"Well what?"

"Don't you recognize her?"

"Yeah, it's a photo of Albina Ludashenko." His voice sounded far away. "She's dead!"

"Any moron could see that!" He handed the photograph back without saying another word. "What's happened to you?"

"I don't know."

"When we started in the police department together, you were a compassionate guy. What's changed you?"

"What changed me?" he questioned. Eighteen years of seeing the bodies of innocent victims hardened my heart. I thank God that it did, or I could have easily had a mental breakdown by now."

"But Albina is dead!" reiterated Weldon.

"She was a prostitute who gave herself to anyone who could afford her. In this city, prostitutes die all the time and their killers sometimes get away with it. It's a sad fact of life, Hank and you've got to get passed it."

"I knew she was missing because Kaz was her fiancée and came to me to find her."

"Well, I can see how well that worked for him."

"Kaz didn't want the police involved in the search."

"Titov can be very persuasive."

"Now that she's dead, I've come to the police to help me find her killer."

"Hank, I'm going to give you the best advice you've ever received."

"What's that?"

"Let it go!"

"What are you talking about? Two girls have been murdered and you want me to let it go?"

"For your own health, forget about it!"

"I'm thinking that Kaz or someone in the mob did this."

"Kaz?" Archie queried with disbelief. He's just a teddy bear when it comes to the girls at the Russian Doll House. He'd never hurt them much less kill them."

"Their murderer has to be brought to justice!"

Malone simply shrugged his shoulders. "Nobody can say that I didn't warn you. What you do now is your own business, but the police department will not be helping you. If there's nothing else, I'm going back to my paperwork. "Archie got out and left a stunned Weldon behind.

For the first time since Kaz hired him, he felt truly alone and vulnerable. Titov's words came back to haunt him. *"Just watch your back, buddy!"*

CHAPTER

8

*G*OD, HOW THE *hell did I get myself in the middle of this damn mess! If I had a dollar for every time I've asked myself the same thing, I'd be able to move out of this cheap dump and buy myself a new car.*

One thing had rung true to Hank when he had spoken to Malone. Clare would not be happy with his current circumstances. *Maybe I should do what Archie advised and just forget about the whole thing.* But he knew that if he would ever have a chance of redeeming himself, this was his best opportunity. In saving Renata, he would be saving himself.

Sitting in his chair by his studio window with a cup of coffee, Weldon began making a mental list of possible suspects in the double murder. *At the top of my list is Maxim Greshnev, mob boss and all-around Great White Shark. Perhaps, he had found out about Albina's leaving and took violent measures to stop her. And maybe Karina saw the murder, and once Albina was disposed of, he knocked off Karina so she wouldn't talk. I'd hate it if it were true, but Archie must be part of this list. Possibly, he's warned me off because he murdered them both.*

Then there's Zoya's trained gorilla, that bastard Serge. What if he caught her trying to get away from the Russian Doll House? Maybe he stopped her a little too roughly and killed her? What if Karina had witnessed the murder? She was as good as dead too.

Now I get to Alexander Kurkov, the police informant and rapist. What if he were the man who promised Albina to take her away to a new life, and instead led her into months of sexual abuse until she met a horrible death? This would come as no surprise to me.

And finally, there was Kazimir Titov, Albina's so-called fiancée. I know firsthand of his unbridled temper and the damage he could do. Renata had said that all the girls were terrified of him. If he had found out Albina was leaving him for another man, there would be no one to stop his vengeance. Of course, there could be a remote chance that someone outside of this group was guilty, but as time went on, that theory began to rapidly fade in the background.

Checking through his list of suspects, Weldon decided to revisit Kurkov. But this time, he had to somehow avoid the police surveillance at his home. Out of all of them, Hank believed he would be the easiest nut to crack and he could squeeze more information out of him. *It's best if I go there under the cover of night.*

He noticed the sun beginning to make its swan dive into the horizon. In a few hours when darkness cloaked the earth, he would be able to call upon the first of his suspects.

He parked his vehicle several blocks away, and traveled quietly through neighboring backyards to reach his destination. A dog would bark occasionally, and he would have to crouch down to avoid being spotted. One incessant barker was stopped when his owner opened up the window and screamed, "Shut the hell up! I'm trying to watch television!" The dog cowered and lay down, chained to a pole.

He trained the beam of his flashlight on the most disgusting domicile on the block. The weeds were so out of control they partially covered the patio, and he could have used a machete to hack his way to the back door.

As Hank approached the house, he noticed there were no lights on. He hoped that a building in this much disrepair would not have a working lock. He nearly fell on the broken wooden steps to the back door. Someone could break their ass in this dump! The screen door was tilted off its upper hinge, making an easy access to the back door. He discovered that it was unlocked. He's certainly not worried that anything will be taken from this house except lice.

He flashed his light inside and entered the kitchen. The sink was piled high with dirty dishes, and the counters were covered with open boxes and cans of food. Roachville! The table had papers strewn about, except for a small place that was cleared at a single chair where the suspect probably sat to eat his meals. This place hasn't experienced a good scrubbing in decades! Cautiously he moved into the living room where he had last confronted Alexander. Thinking that he should check the bedrooms to see if Kurkov had turned in for the night gave him a reasonable excuse to check out the rest of the house for whatever he could find in the way of evidence. Hank soon discovered that the ex-con was not at home, and that he could not uncover any evidence with all the crap that lay around. *I'm going to sit and wait until this bastard shows up.*

Sweeping the pile of newspapers from a nearby armchair with his hand, he sat down and made himself as comfortable as possible for the duration. Checking his watch with the flashlight, he saw it was 11:17 p.m. He sat back and waited.

Weldon didn't know how long he had drifted into sleep before he was awoken by the sound of a car door slamming and a voice calling out, "Thanks guys. I'll see you tomorrow night." He heard footsteps come up the walk and stumble up the steps. The front door was at last pushed open and the shadow of a man passed through, closing the door behind him. A loud yawn was admitted as the ex-con went to turn on the lamp by the armchair. He was startled by the man who had been sitting there in the dark. Alexander backed away in fear until he recognized the face. "What the hell are you doing here? You scared the crap out of me!"

"Welcome home, Al!" Looking as his watch to discover it was a 2:45 in the morning. "Had yourself a late night, didn't you?"

"Get out now while you still have the time or I'll call the cops who are just down the street!"

"You're not going to do that!"

"And why not?"

"Because if you do, or mention to Malone that I was here like you did the last time, there won't be enough of you left to sweep into an evidence bag!" Hank could see the man's enlarged Adam's Apple as he swallowed.

"What do you want from me now?"

"I came to explain to you that we are now going to have a working relationship."

"What is that supposed to mean?"

"Instead of being Malone's bitch, you're going to become mine!"

"I…I don't know…"

"Oh, you're going to report to Malone as you always do, but from now on, you're going to feed me the same information."

"I'm not going to do that!" he said defiantly as he rediscovered his balls.

"Oh, you're going to do it alright if you want to live. One less rapist in this world would mean I'm doing humanity a favor." Hank pulled the gun out of its holster, and resting his arm on the chair, aimed at his opponent. The sudden flush of testosterone the former prisoner had experienced quickly evaporated under the constant glare of the man with the gun.

"Alright," he meekly replied.

"Good! Now I can get down to the second reason I'm here."

"What's that?"

"To ask you more questions."

"I told you everything I know."

"We'll see about that. Where were you tonight?"

"At the Russian Doll House. What do you care?"

"Gambling, drinking, whoring, or all of the above?"

"I got into a poker game."

"The last time I was here I asked if you knew Albina Lukashenko."

"My answer is the same. I don't know her." Hank took out the photograph and handed it to Kurkov.

"That's her. You might notice that she's dead." Alexander shrugged indifferently.

"So what!"

"She was a living, breathing human being until someone snuffed out her life. Is this your handiwork?"

"I did my time. I see my parole officer. I don't do that anymore."

"Prove it!"

"How?"

"You see the words scribbled across the picture?"

"Yes."

"Write it out on a piece of paper."

Through the debris, Kurkov managed to find a working pen and a clean piece of paper. Gazing at the words, he shakily wrote it out and handed it to Weldon. Hank could tell, even in the shaky handwriting, that Alexander hadn't written the sentence, but that didn't mean that he was off the hook.

"Which one of the girls did you have sexual relations with tonight?"

"I wasn't with the women. I played some poker, had a few drinks and left."

"If this relationship between us is to work, then you need to be completely honest with me."

"I'm telling you the truth. I didn't see any of the girls tonight."

With his thumb, Weldon pulled back the hammer of his pistol. "Come again?"

"Okay, I was with Renata." Hank could taste the bile rising to his throat. He wanted to lay his hands on the slime ball and beat him to within an inch of his life.

"Do you like to play rough with her?" Alexander swallowed hard before he answered.

"A little."

No wonder Renata had a bruised face. Weldon wanted to put a bullet between his eyes, but he fought off the urge, knowing that he could use Kurkov for the information he would be gathering.

"You are never to be with her again, understand?" he asserted, trying to control his temper.

The rapist saw his rage and didn't ask why. "Okay."

"What do you have to do with the death of Karina Davidenko?"

"Nothing! I never killed that girl!"

"You had better be telling me the truth," he remarked in a threatening voice, "or I'll kill you now and bury your body in that trash heap you laughingly call a backyard. With all the shit back there, the police wouldn't find your body for a while."

"I'm not lying to you."

"And you better never lie to me if you want to keep living. Remember, not a word to Malone or the cops outside about our new arrangement."

"I won't say a word." How will I contact you?"

"I'll be visiting you from time to time just as I did this evening."

Kurkov remained silent.

"Well, it's getting late and I'm sure you're ready for bed," he said to him as if he were speaking to a child. He returned his gun to his holster. He yanked the photograph out of the stunned man's hand and returned it to his jacket pocket. "Start making your way upstairs to bed."

Hesitantly, Alexander made his way from step to step. With a flick of a switch, the room was once more plunged into darkness.

Hank left by the back door and carefully crept through backyards until he was at his Volkswagen. He drove back thinking about who he would question next. *I've started questioning at the bottom of the food chain, but I think I'll change it up and go to the top of the food chain, Maxim Greshnev.*

CHAPTER

9

E VERY TUESDAY, LIKE clockwork, Maxim Greshnev was chauffeured around town to check on his numerous enterprises. Besides dropping by to see that things were being done the way he wanted them, he went over the books, questioning his managers about every dime that was taken in. God forbid the books didn't add up, the unlucky person would be fitted for a cement overcoat and dropped into the nearest body of water or vacant lot and someone else was put in his place.

Greshnev was a natural-born killer, a trait that had taken him to the top of the underworld's feeding chain. But all this was masked behind designer clothing as he was considered a natty dresser. Maxim's look was topped off by a diamond ring that could have knocked an eye out. Anyone who was fooled by this masquerade of a gentleman was reminded, if they were foolish enough to cross him, that he would kill at the drop of a hat.

Outside the Russian Doll House, Hank waited patiently in his jalopy with a paper cup of coffee in his hand. As he sipped, he watched the seagulls soar in a blue sky and heard the early morning traffic, as people made their way to their jobs. Weldon hoped that he had impressed Alexander enough that he wouldn't go running to Malone, but only time would tell if he had browbeat the pervert enough to keep him under his thumb.

He noticed a black limousine approaching. It entered the bordello parking lot and one of Maxim's henchmen got out to open the back door. The mob boss got out impeccably dressed as usual. He moved toward the door, which was opened by the same lackey. Hank could just picture the bowing and scrapping going on by the flunkies who managed his business. Bracing himself for his encounter, Hank finished off his coffee and exited his car. He opened the door and came face to face with Serge. With a big grin on his face, he announced, "We are closed for now. How is your head?" Serge snickered.

"I'm not here to see one of the girls."

"Then what do you want?"

"I've come to speak to your boss."

"Zoya is busy right now so you can go away."

"I'm not here to see Zoya. I want to speak to Mr. Greshnev."

Out of his mouth came a loud belly laugh. Hank watched him with a straight face.

"You want to see Mr. Greshnev? You're funny! No one sees the boss unless he calls for them."

"Tell him it's Hank Weldon. I'm sure he'll see me."

Shaking his head back and forth in disbelief, the guard answered, "Go away!' and he flicked his hand as if he were chasing away a bothersome fly.

Pulling out his gun, Weldon replied, "I've got my appointment right here!" The burly Russian was startled by this turn of events. His eyes turned into narrow slits.

"You're making a big mistake."

"Take me to him before you make a terrible mistake."

With eyes full of hate, the man turned and walked down the hallway. Reaching a door, he knocked gently.

Zoya came to the door and opened it. "I told you I was not to be disturbed." The Russian moved to the side exposing Weldon holding a pistol. Fat Zoya's face fell. "And I told you that you were not welcome here anymore."

"Move out of my way!" Greshnev's henchman Boris, who stood next to his boss, already had his gun out as Maxim looked up at Hank.

"Put away your gun," ordered Maxim to his bodyguard. He did as he was told. *Either this guy is really ballsy or stupid.* "Come in and sit down. There's no need for any gun play here." Weldon replaced his pistol and took a seat at a chair against the wall, making sure he could see everybody easily. He noticed that Kaz who usually accompanied the boss was nowhere to be seen. "And you are?"

"Hank Weldon. I've come to talk to you."

"Barging in on me like this must mean your mission is very important."

"It is to me."

"Go ahead, I'm listening," he replied, folding his arms across his chest as he sat back on his chair.

Hank got up and placed the photograph on the desk. Greshnev looked for a minute before he raised his head up. "This is what you came here to speak to me about?" Weldon returned the snapshot to his pocket.

"Her name was Albina Lukashenko."

Greshnev looked placidly at him. "Why would I be interested in that fact?"

"She worked for you."

"Many women work for me. I do not memorize their faces or names."

"The rumor is that she left with a man who promised to take her away from the life she was living."

"What do I care about that!"

"She was engaged to one of your men."

"And who would that be?" *Kaz has been keeping secrets.* "I still don't see what any of this has to do with me."

"Did you have her murdered because she had tried to escape this place? And did you have Karina Davidenko killed because she saw something she shouldn't have seen?"

Greshnev smiled from ear to ear like the proverbial cat that swallowed the canary. "What do you see when you look at me?" Hank had no idea what kind of answer he expected.

A cheap hood in expensive clothes? "I'm not sure what you're asking me."

"I was born outside the city of Odessa, Russia and when I was about five, my parents emigrated to the United States."

I hope he doesn't relate his whole life story.

"I played hooky from school until my parents gave up trying to send me. Instead, I got my education on the streets of New York City, where I learned how to hustle and survive, and I did whatever I had to. Finally, I worked my way to the top, a self-made man."

More likely, you murdered your way to the top!

Now, I'm the man who runs this town! I am a realization that the American Dream can come true!" he announced with great bravado. "I have the police department in my back pocket."

So, Archie's not the only cop Greshnev has on his payroll.

"I run this town from top to bottom. Even the mayor doesn't take a crap until he gets my approval."

"In other words, you know exactly what goes down in this city."

"That's right, but I do not involve myself in the petty lives of prostitutes."

"By the way, where is Kaz?"

"I believe I've given you enough of my time this morning. You may leave."

Something's up with that. He avoided my question.

Immediately, his henchman moved forward. "No need for any rough stuff," he told his underling. "I'm sure Mr. Weldon can find his own way out."

There's no way of knowing whether Grehnev told me the truth about the women's deaths, or was just handing me a line of bullshit.

Weldon opened the door only to bump into the great ape again. "Leaving so soon?" Serge grinned. "Let me show you out."

"Say, what is your name anyway?"

The man looked at him suspiciously but threw caution to the wind. "Serge Sokoloff, you want to make something of it?" he challenged in a raised voice that indicated he was spoiling for a fight.

"Not at all. Tell me something, how did Albina manage to get past you the night she got away?"

"Keep your nose out of my affairs!"

"Were you getting busy at the time with one of the lovely ladies here?"

"I don't need to go to any of these cheap sluts!

Probably, he takes care of business by himself.

"Or maybe Kaz paid you off to look the other way."

"Nobody gave me anything."

"Then I guess you were pretty pissed off when you discovered she was missing. How did Greshnev react when he found out?"

As they approached the front door, Serge said, "You ask too many questions. That will land you in a body bag." He added, "Don't forget. You are not welcome here! The next time you are foolish enough to show up will be your last time!"

Weldon was left crestfallen. He had hoped to encounter Renata while he was there, but although he saw some of the girls, she was not among them. While he stood outside, he stopped to think. *More and more this is looking like an inside job.* Checking his watch for the time, he decided to stop at his next suspect's place of work, the local police precinct.

###

At the precinct, Hank was told that Archie was on vacation. Hank got in his car and wondered if he had taken the family away. There's only one way to find out. Hank drove, remembering exactly where Archie and his family lived. Turning onto Blake Court, he stopped in front of the house. *Things have certainly changed since the last time I was here.* No longer was it a split-level brick dwelling. The house had been redesigned to look like a mini-mansion. Instead of the Dodge Dart that Malone formally drove, a beautiful white Cadillac Escalade and a black Mercedes-Benz sedan were now parked in the driveway. For a moment, Weldon hesitated, wondering whether another family had moved in and made these changes. He pushed the doorbell. A familiar face greeted him, Archie's wife Eileen. "Hank!" she said with great delight. "How have you been?"

"I've been well," he lied with a straight face. "And you?"

"Just great! Come on in!" *They had to have dropped a lot of dough in this place to have it look the way it does now.* Hank entered the house and took it all in. "Come into the kitchen and have a cup of coffee with me." Weldon sat at the table while Eileen continued to chatter. "How long has it been since we saw each other?"

"Almost 15 years."

"How have you been doing?"

"I've gotten over it." *But not completely.* Eileen poured two cups of coffee and brought them to the table before she sat down.

"Tell me, did you re-marry?" She must have noticed that he was not wearing a wedding ring but women just love gossip.

"No, I just never found another woman I wanted to spend my life with."

"Are you seeing someone?"

"Not really."

"Because I have a friend a few years younger than you. *Not another blind date!* She's very pretty with a bubbly personality. Her name is Sheila."

"How are the boys?" he asked, trying to get her off the subject.

"They're doing fine. Craig is a sophomore at Brown University and Jake is a senior in high school. It's been a long time since you've seen them."

"Yes, it has." *Enough of the socializing. I've got to get down to the reason I've come here.* "Is Archie home?"

"Yes, he's up in his den. He'll be thrilled to see you after so much time." *Obviously, he hasn't mentioned seeing me. I'll play along with the charade.*

Eileen went upstairs and after a few minutes came back down. "Go on up, Hank! He can't wait to see you! It's the first door on your left." As Hank climbed the stairs, Eileen called out, "Let's get together for dinner real soon."

"Sure." Archie will never agree to that.

Hank knocked on the door. "Come in," a voice answered. He opened the door to what would be a techie's Wonderland. Archie sat at his desk surrounded by the latest computer gadgetry. Hank emitted a low whistle.

"This is quite a set-up you have."

"Close the door!" he demanded irritably. As soon as Weldon had done what he was told, Malone went on the attack. "You have a nerve coming to my home!"

"Well, Eileen was happy to see me."

"She doesn't know about what a mess you've turned your life into."

"Tell me Archie, have you told her how you've come to afford all of this, or does she believe this all comes from a police detective's salary."

"You leave Eileen out of this!"

"I wish I could, but Eileen and the boys are going to be affected when you are finally taken down."

Laughing, Archie responded, "I'm too smart to be taken down by anybody, especially a drunk like you! You see all of this?" he inquired spreading his arms wide open. "I even have a summer house at Lake Saranac. You could have had my life too if you hadn't become a hopeless alcoholic!"

"I don't want your life! Not the way you've earned it!"

"Don't be so naïve! This is how business is conducted now. You've been out of the police department too long! It's the only way things work today."

"You've sold your soul to the devil! What kind of favors did you do for Greshnev?

"I've warned you over and over again not to bring that up!"

"Perhaps knocking off Albina Lukashenko got you the Escalade and maybe murdering Karina Davidenko helped you buy the house at Lake Saranac!" Archie sprang from his seat. "I'm not a killer for hire!"

"As far as I can see, Greshnev says jump and you say how high!"

"You're not going to back away from these cases, are you?"

"No, I'm going to keep digging through the dirt until the person or persons who committed these murders have been brought to justice!"

"Then I can't be blamed for what will happen to you!"

"On the contrary, my blood will stain your hands just as the blood of the two girls already does!"

"Get out!" Malone pointed at the door. "Get out and don't come back to my home with your ridiculous accusations!"

"That's right. Keep your family in the dark about all your nefarious activities! I won't have to tell them what you're up to. Sooner or later, like all crooks, you'll go down, and where will that leave them?"

Malone's hands balled up into fists as he screamed, "Get out of here before I forget you were once a friend and I kill you!"

"Have a nice life, Archie," were Hank's departing words. As he came down, Eileen was waiting at the bottom of the stairs, a concerned look etched on her face. "What went on up there?"

"Just a little disagreement, Eileen. There's nothing to worry about. You take care of yourself."

"You too," she answered in bewilderment.

As Weldon walked to his car, he thought about what Malone had told him. *Perhaps he had told me the truth about not murdering the two girls. What better way to ensure Archie's loyalty then to have him mixed up in murder? Malone can never turn him in because Archie would be ratted out to Greshnev. And yet, Archie has Kurkov infiltrating Greshnev's gang to feed him information. If he's playing both sides against each other, he's involved in a dangerous game. How can I really trust his word when Greshnev has him by the throat? I wish I knew the answer.*

Archie rushed out of his home and grabbed Hank by the arm before he could get back in his car. "I'm going to tell you this even though it might jeopardize my life."

"What is it?"

"I'm undercover, jackass! If you don't keep it to yourself, I'm a dead man!"

CHAPTER

10

WHERE WAS KAZIMIR Titov? Weldon's last suspect had not been seen in days, not since he had warned Hank to "Watch your back!" His usual place was glued to Maxim's side. He had been replaced by a mobster named Boris. And yet, Greshnev had seemingly not been disturbed by his absence. Has Kaz done something to tick off his boss? Hank remembered how Greshnev had asked him about Albinas's fiancée and when he told him, Maxim appeared to be unruffled by the news.

Maybe, I unwittingly confirmed his suspicions. If that's the case, has Maxim already done away with his right-hand man? Perhaps, Kaz's warning was not about what he would do, but what the mob would do to me if they suspected that I knew who killed the two women!

Weldon was ensconced outside the cat house, watching as Greshnev arrived the following Tuesday. As he had the week before, the boss exited his limousine followed by another hood. Kaz was nowhere to be seen. Every night he made a trip to The Dive in hopes of catching him there, but Ivan only confirmed his worst fears. "No, he hasn't been here in days."

It maddened Weldon that he didn't have a home address for the Russian pit bull. At least, I could break in and perhaps find a clue as to where he was. *How do I get the address? Perhaps Kaz confided something to Ivan*, he thought as he swilled down vodka.

Following his nightly routine, he approached the bar. The night was chilly and was the harbinger that autumn was rapidly turning into winter. The crowd at the bar was like they were every night, loud and inebriated. Weldon bellied up to the bar and called Ivan over. Placing his big, hairy paws on the counter, Ivan asked, "What can I do you for?"

"I haven't come in for a drink." Ivan shrugged his shoulders and began to walk away. "But I would like something else." Ivan walked back, his face screwed up.

"Listen, I run a clean place here. I don't sell any kind of drugs!" Hank doubted if that was true.

"I'm looking for information."

"What information?" he queried distrustfully.

"Has Kaz been in tonight?"

"Look, for the hundredth time, I haven't seen him in days!"

"Do you know anything about him?"

"I should! He's my cousin."

What a stroke of good luck.

"Then you know where he lives?"

"I've been having trouble with my teeth, lately. I need dental work, but it's very expensive, and I can't afford it! You know what I'm getting at?" Hank knew exactly what was needed. Slipping a $20 onto the bar, Ivan grabbed it like a drowning man reaching for a life line.

"So, what about the address?" Ivan ripped a sheet of paper from a pad and scribbled out the address. He folded the paper and handed it to Weldon.

Driving to the block with a dead-end sign, Hank got out of his car and looked around. The street seemed deserted as a full moon shone down brightly. *If I get caught by the police breaking and entering, I'll be in some deep shit.*

Looking at the address, because all these brownstones looked alike, he found the one he was searching for and climbed up the stairs to the front door. He used a credit card between the lock and the door frame until he heard the "click." Weldon opened the door and entered. There was some conversation going on in the apartments as he made his climb to the second floor. Finding 2B, he tried the doorknob. This one was not locked.

Funny that Kaz should leave his own apartment door unlocked.

The door swung open and Hank felt around for the wall switch which he turned on. "What the hell!" The room was cluttered with turned over furniture and objects that lay broken on the floor. *There had to be a scuffle in here! I wonder who got the upper hand?* He couldn't conceive of just one man getting the best of Kaz. It would have to be at least two. Questions, questions, and more questions but never any answers!

Weldon quickly searched the two-room apartment, and was about to give up when from the bottom of the underwear draw, he withdrew two airline tickets. They were for Aruba, but the plane had taken off two days ago. *These had probably been purchased by Kaz for Albina and himself for a honeymoon. It made sense!* Hank realized if Kaz wanted to leave town he had the perfect opportunity to use one of the tickets. *Perhaps he drove out of town and is in hiding. Or he could be dead lying in an unmarked grave, or like Karina awash in the Atlantic Ocean as fish food. I wonder if I'll ever really learn the truth.* Being careful not to be seen, Hank got into his car and drove away, determined to check with the hospitals tomorrow morning in the hopes of finding Titov.

By a quarter to ten the next morning, Hank had showered, throwing down a piece of buttered toast and a cup of coffee, dressed and was out the door. The overcast skies reflected the private detective's gloomy mood. As the days went by, Hank believed that the Russian would never be seen again. Every place he went, the receptionists' answers were all the same. "Has any unknown person checked into the hospital?"

"Can you be more specific?"

"He's a male of Russian descent, late 20's early 30's, around 6'3", weighing about 310 to 320 pounds whose name is Kazimir Titov," he inquired at each hospital. The answer was always the same. "No such person with that description has been admitted here recently, sorry."

The following idea was gruesome, but Weldon felt obligated to check funeral homes. Each time he was turned away without success. *What the hell! How does a person as imposing as Kaz just fall off the face of the earth without someone knowing what happened to him?* Weldon thought his best bet was to return to Ivan to see what he knew about his cousin's disappearance.

The next evening, he strolled through the door of The Dive, got to the bar and knocked on the counter. Ivan, who was having a conversation with another customer as he dried a glass, glanced in Hank's direction. It was

Alexander Kurkov who caught his eye. Hank got up and occupied the bar stool next to the ex-con. "What do you want now?" Kurkov asked defiantly.

"Information."

"About?"

"About Kaz Titov's whereabouts."

"I'm not in the mood to answer questions right now."

"Well get in the mood and be quick about it!"

"Are you crazy? Do you know who owns this joint?"

"Maxim Greshnev, am I right?"

"That's right and if he knew you were here threatening me for information, he'd kill you!"

"Well, I'm not going to tell him. How about you?" Alexander shook his head slowly back and forth.

"So, where is he?"

"I already told you that I didn't know."

"I find that hard to believe. What are you keeping from me?"

"Listen, Weldon. I try to keep my nose clean around here before I catch a little disease known as a bullet to the brain. I suggest you take my advice and drop the whole thing."

"You're staring at a man who wouldn't think twice about passing on that disease to you."

"Greshnev's men would kill me!"

"Not if they don't know. Besides, I'll kill you right where you are if you don't!"

"In front of all these witnesses?" Weldon looked around at the few customers in different stages of inebriation.

"These drunks will never get the story straight, and the cops will believe you were killed during a simple robbery at the bar."

Alexander hesitated for a moment and swallowed hard before he drew close to Hank and whispered, "The last I heard, they had him.

"Who has him?"

"Greshnev's men of course!"

"Where are they holding him?"

"I'm not sure, but the talk is Greshnev owns a warehouse in the old Brooklyn Navy Yard."

"And you haven't gone to the police with your suspicions?

"First of all, any trouble that Kaz is in, he must have brought on himself. Besides that, who in the police department could I trust? Greshnev controls them."

Maybe, he's right about that. Weldon nodded and put his pistol back.

He knew that tomorrow's destination would be somewhere near the Brooklyn Navy Yard.

Driving back and forth the next day, Weldon realized that one dilapidated warehouse looked like another. *God, it's like looking for a needle in a haystack!* He let out a deep sigh, not knowing how he was going to find the right place if he didn't devote days to personally searching each one. The task seemed daunting.

From the corner of his eye, Hank caught the image of someone moving in his side view mirror. A man was passing through the gate and onto the street. A black limousine turned the corner and picked him up before speeding away. Weldon recognized the vehicle. It was the one Greshnev was driven around in. Leaning over to lay his head on the passenger seat, the limo passed him by and continued on. It's a good thing that this beat-up car doesn't look out of place in this neighborhood. Getting out, he walked casually, but ever alert to his surroundings.

Going through the same gate he'd seen the Russian boss use, he entered a complex of three warehouses. He headed straight for the middle one, in the hope that it was being used by the mob. His guess had paid off. After plowing through the weeds, he stopped at a broken window and peered in. Two men wearing rubber aprons and gloves were mopping a red-spattered floor. Hanging down from an iron track was a large hook suspended from a metal link chain. The sight of this made Weldon involuntarily shutter. One of the men that he recognized was Maxim's new bodyguard Boris, the one who seemed to have replaced Kaz.

As he stared, Boris started hosing off the floor and then turned the hose onto a nearby table. He began to wash different-sized saws that were stained red. The scene was grisly and gruesome. Weldon was ready to go, when he observed the two men begin to load big black bags onto a dolly. Hank wondered if the bags contained the body parts of Kazimir Titov. He was bound and determined to find out.

As they piled up the bags, Weldon made his way to his car and waited patiently. In time, a van pulled around the building and into the street. Hank followed at a safe distance so as not to be detected. *By dumping the body in the daylight hours, these killers are thumbing their noses at all the law-abiding citizens in this city!* Pulling into a garbage dump, the gatekeeper waived them on. Hank parked and observed where the two bags were thrown.

Tonight, I'll come back. He waited for the sun to go down before he retraced his steps.

###

The search lights were on, but that wasn't going to intimidate him. Weldon had to know what was in the bags. He made it over the wire fence and dropped onto his feet. *Ouch! I'm not as spry as I used to be when I was 20-years old.* He tried to remember exactly where the bags were dumped. In the dark, he had trouble getting his bearings. The malodorous air of rotting garbage permeated everything in the area.

He took out his flashlight and pointed up. Moving the beam back and forth, he could not locate the bags. He moved further down the road. After a few yards, he trained his light up in the middle of the pile. He strained his eyes until he caught sight of a black bag that looked like the one he was searching for.

Making his way up and occasionally losing his footing, the stench became even more unbearable. At last, he reached his destination. Cutting the cord that kept the bag closed, he slowly opened it with hesitation. He saw shredded paper. *Damn it! I'll never find the bags like this!* In frustration, he tossed that one aside. When he looked down, another black bag was visible. *Probably, just the same shit that was in the other bag!*

He did not climb down, which was his first inclination. Instead, he cut the cord and looked in. The odor was putrid, and Hank shone the light in. Weldon knew what he expected to see if this plastic bag held body parts, but when he looked in, he felt as if he were going to puke. He willed himself to keep his stomach contents down. It was not Kaz. The polished nails of a hand attached to a dismembered arm lay in front of his eyes. Below that was a foot, and below that seemed to be something yellow. Shifting the bags contents, a blonde-haired head appeared. Looking closely, he recognized the features of what looked like Albina Lukashenko. He quickly closed the bag and made the sign of the cross. He wasn't religious, but it was the only thing he could think to do. *Your death will be avenged, or I'll die trying!*

Weldon was almost light-headed as he started his way down the pile. *These guys are totally arrogant to have left this out in the open. I'm sure a barge will soon carry the bags beyond the 12-mile limit before the evidence is unloaded into the Atlantic.* He staggered back to the street, climbed over the fence and got into the car. He opened the windows to try and get some fresh air, but all that he could smell was the scent of death. He drove home, his stomach doing somersaults. At one moment on the way, he stopped the car, opened the door and vomited on the road, but he still felt sick to his stomach.

When he finally reached home, he climbed the stairs and took every stitch of clothing off, because the odor seemed to cling to everything he was wearing. He jumped into a hot shower and let the stream of water work on the kinks in his neck and back muscles. He scrubbed and scoured every inch of his body. The last thing he did was shampoo his hair and rinsed himself until he was squeaky clean and then made himself a pot of coffee.

He tried to drive the night's images from his brain. He was not successful. In bed, he tossed and turned for hours. *Well, now there's no doubt about it. Albina had been kidnapped and killed by someone in the mob. If only Kaz had listened to what I was trying to tell him! But, where is he? Had he met the same fate as his fiancée?* Obviously, he got very little sleep that night.

CHAPTER

11

THE MORNING OF a new day usually promises the hope of a new beginning. Hank Weldon held no such hope. Instead, it all felt so desperate. His avenues to bringing the killers to justice were blocked. There was no way he could go to the police, because he did not know who was on the take and who wasn't. It was all spinning out of control and he felt like he was being sucked into the vortex. Albina and Karina's killings needed to be resolved. Kaz must be found. And then there was Renata. He had let her down and he had to save her from the life she was caught up in before it was too late.

Can I go to the Police Commissioner or the Mayor? How far reaching were Greshnev's tentacles into the hierarchy of city government? If I do go to one of them for help, would I be signing my own death warrant? Nothing he could think of would have him arrive at a happy ending.

It was at that moment that Hank arrived at a singular conclusion, the Federal Bureau of Investigation. The idea sounded preposterous even to him. After all, would they even believe a broken down ex-cop? Still, who else could he turn to? Screwing up his nerve, he called Information and asked for the number of the FBI branch in New York City. He waited as the phone rang. A female picked up saying, "Federal Bureau of Investigation, how can I help you?"

"Hi, I'd like to talk to one of your agents."

"What's this in reference to?"

"There's a situation in my town I fear may have cost three people their lives."

"What's your name, sir?"

"Henry Weldon."

"Please hold for a minute while I connect you." The phone rang a few times before it was picked up.

Weldon heard a man's voice as it commanded, "Tell him that I don't care how long it takes, the surveillance continues until we have something on him! Agent Baker here, who is this?" He brusquely inquired.

"My name is Henry Weldon. I want to report two murders and a missing person."

"You need to contact your local police department." he answered with disinterest.

"I can't. Some of them are on the take from a man named Maxim Greshnev."

The name caught the agent's immediate attention. "What town are you calling from?"

"I live in Brighton Beach, Brooklyn."

"Who are you?"

"I'm an ex-cop and now a private detective."

"And how are you involved in all this?" Weldon related the circumstances by which he was now a part.

"I see." For a short time, there was silence before Agent Cassidy Baker spoke up. "I need to clear my calendar for the next couple of days. Will you be available for me to visit in two days?"

"I'll be here."

"Good, let me have your address and telephone number."

After giving the agent the information, Weldon hung up and sat back in his chair. For the first time since he had become embroiled in this mess, he felt a sense of relief. *Finally, I won't have to deal with all of this by myself!*

The next day was dark and dreary. A steady rain began to fall by mid-morning and persisted off and on the whole day. Hank tried to occupy his time as best he could. He walked over to the Tick Tock Diner and ordered a toasted bagel with cream cheese and a hot cup of coffee. Purchasing the morning paper, he ate and read undisturbed. He paid the check, slipped the newspaper under his arm and walked back home.

He had noticed that in the last few days, he was no longer being followed. *I guess no one believes that I'm a threat any longer.* They'd realize very soon that he was still a force to be reckoned with. Hank stared at television shows, but saw nothing but the images that reran in his brain. Afternoon slowly melted into evening, and the rain still pelted on the windows. The streets seemed deserted as everyone sought shelter and warmth within their own homes.

Sleep came fitfully, and he spent more time watching the clock than in the arms of sweet slumber. By dawn, the rain had slackened, but the sky remained gray. He waited impatiently for the promised visitor. At one in the afternoon, there was a knock on his door. Hank stood face to face with two men in blue suits. The taller and older of the two had a square jaw with salt and pepper hair, and a look of hardened determination in his eyes. By his side stood the shorter, younger man with slicked-back black hair and the appearance of coldness on his unsmiling face. Both men took out their F.B. I. identifications and showed them to Hank. "Come in," he said to the two government agents.

"I'm Agent Cassidy Baker, but you can call me Cass, and this is my associate, Agent Parrish Wilson. I presume you are Henry Weldon?"

"I am. Please have a seat." The three men sat around the kitchen table.

"Mr. Weldon, we are here to get some information about the situation you explained to me on the phone," stated Baker. Agent Wilson removed a small recorder from his suit pocket.

"This conversation will be recorded," he said.

"I understand," Weldon reposted.

"What do you do for a living?"

"I'm a private detective."

"So, you've worked on the police force?"

"Yeah," Hank muttered.

Cass picked up on it right away. "How long were you on the force?"

"Almost five years."

"And you left because…"

"I was let go because of an on-going alcohol dependency."

"I see," Parrish answered with no emotion.

"And what is your current status with it now?"

"I've been off the sauce for months." Both men simply stared at him. "I give you my word!"

"You know," Cass began. "This is not going to work if you're still addicted. We've been waiting to get something on Greshnev for a long time, but so far, he has outsmarted us. We don't want any foul ups to occur!"

"I tell you, I'm clean!"

"Okay, what's your history with the Russian mob here in Brighton Beach?"

"I don't really have a history with them."

Baker looked doubtfully back at him. "If we are going to understand the situation here, you'll have to be totally honest with us. Is that understood?"

Hank answered, "My history is limited. I have visited a bordello they run called, the Russian Doll House and have frequented their bar known as The Dive, but that's all of it."

"Have you had any contact with Maxim Greshnev?" queried Parrish.

"Yes. I confronted him a few days ago about the killings of two prostitutes who worked for him, Albina Lukashenko and Karina Davidenko."

"And what was his reaction?" added Cassidy.

"He denied even knowing them much less murdering them."

"What do you know about either of these women?" continued Cassidy.

Weldon took out the dog-eared photo that Titov had left with him. "This is Albina Lukashenko."

Both men studied the photograph. Parrish spoke up first. "How did you come into possession of this picture?"

"Her fiancée, a man named Kazimir Titov, hired me to find her when she went missing."

"And where can we find him?" Parrish continued.

"That's a good question. He's been missing for over a week."

"Who is he?" Baker inquired.

"He was one of Greshnev's bodyguards, but when I went to see Kaz, he was nowhere around. If you knew Greshnev, you would know that Kaz was like his shadow. His disappearance leads me to believe that he was knocked off by Maxim!"

"What's your relationship with Titov?"

"I've hired him for side jobs, taking pictures of unfaithful husbands and wives that could be used in divorce court hearings."

Parrish Wilson looked at the photo again. "Without evidence or an eye witness to the crime, this case will go nowhere fast."

"I found evidence in a black bag in the city garbage dump that was disposed of by Greshnev's boys. I discovered the arm, foot, and head of Albina. That's when I called you."

Baker entered the questioning again, addressing Wilson. "Get someone on it. What about the other woman who was killed? Did you get a photograph of her dead body?"

"I didn't need one. Her body washed up on the beach the day after I spoke to her."

Both men raised their eyebrows.

"Yes, I also paid for sex with her the day before."

"Quite a coincidence," noted Cass. "And what did she tell you?"

"She said that Albina told her that she was running away with a man who was going to take her away from the business, marry her and give her a new life. I think that man was Titov. I now believe his hiring me to find her was a ruse to throw Greshnev off their scent. Obviously, it didn't work. Once Karina knew what was going on, and Maxim found out, she was marked for death."

"Not to be brutally blunt," Parrish replied, "but why haven't they killed you yet?"

"I have to believe that they don't really see me as a threat."

Baker came directly to the point. "And why is that?"

Weldon took a moment before he answered. "Probably because they see me as a disgraced ex-cop who is an utterly hopeless alcoholic."

"And are you?"

"A disgraced cop, yes. A hopeless drunk, no."

"You realize that to prosecute, we'll have to send somebody in with a wire," Baker said matter-of-factly. Hank knew what the next question would be. "Would you be willing to do that?"

"I would, but I've been told a couple of times that I was not welcome back to their establishments."

"Well, you're going to have to change their minds, aren't you?" Parrish vocalized mockingly.

"I guess so."

"We'll be in touch." The agents stood up to leave.

"I only ask for one thing," Hank remarked.

"The bureau doesn't provide financial remuneration in exchange for people's help on cases."

"That's not what I want."

"Name it and we'll present it to the Bureau Chief if we think it's appropriate."

"There's a girl working at the Greshnev's brothel, named Renata Dubov. She tried to escape and ran to me for help. Before long however, she was found here and brought back against her will."

"You want us to get her out of there?" Cassidy questioned.

"That's right."

"But how do you know that she's not already dead?"

Weldon remembered when he last saw her and how she reminded him of a mechanical zombie. "I saw her there just a few days ago. I want both of us placed into the Witness Protection Program and relocated anyplace else. Our lives would be over if we stayed here!"

The two agents looked at each other before they turned back to him. Cassidy Baker answered. "I believe we can convince the Bureau Chief that your lives would be in danger."

"Thank you."

"When will all this begin?"

"Sit tight and wait for one of us to contact you. Just a word of advice. When you do infiltrate the gang, do not have any contact with this Renata woman. If Greshnev smells anything out of the ordinary, you'll both most likely be eliminated without a second thought!"

"I understand."

Parrish turned off the recorder and replaced it in his suit pocket. "Fly under the radar and stay home as much as possible. We'll contact you in a few days."

After both men left, Weldon stopped to contemplate. It won't be long now before they'll all pay!

Hank looked out his window to realize that the sun had at last made a re-appearance.

###

Hank was damned if he were going to sit tight and leave all the control in the hands of government boys. Too often they would screw things up. It was up to him to keep them on the straight and narrow for Renata's sake.

Weldon had purposely not revealed the deal he had with Kurkov. It was the ace that he meant to keep up his sleeve to reveal when he chose to do so.

The next day the sun once more came out from behind gray clouds, but with it came a cold November wind that chilled to the bone. Hank walked briskly to the diner where he had his usual and read the paper. He watched pedestrians scurrying hurriedly from place to place trying to stay as warm as possible. The bitter cold reminded him of the cold bodies of both Karina and Albina and the most likely death of Kaz. They had not died peacefully in their sleep, but violently, floating in the sea, or stuffed in a plastic bag that was most probably dumped into the ocean. *The poor fools who live in this city know nothing of the menace and the deep-rooted corruption that encompasses all of them! Ignorance may be bliss, but reality is a harsh teacher!*

Hank broke out of his inner thoughts to ask the waitress to refill his cup. Drinking it down to brace himself for the walk back to his apartment, he left a tip on the table, paid his bill, and started out. He made his way along the cold, concrete sidewalk. Alone in his empty apartment, he felt as cold as a cadaver, no one to love and no one to love him. Weldon threw his coat on the chair in anger. *Why am I condemned to spend my life in isolation, away from human warmth and affection?* The fault lay deep inside his psyche. He knew he was an emotionally broken man who had pushed others away over the years while he wallowed in the sorrow of a lost wife and child. He had only come alive again when Renata had shared his life for those few weeks. *Could there be another life for me with this Russian girl?*

There was the sticking point, because in all the time they spent together, she had never shown him that she wanted an attachment to him. *Am I making too much of all of this? Have I fallen in love?* It had been such a long time since he had felt that emotion that he wasn't sure if it was just infatuation.

A purpose! He needed a purpose in life, and that purpose was to save Renata, whether she was in love with him or not. It was then that Hank resolved he would pay a visit to his informant, Alexander Kurkov. A night visit was best if he were to avoid the crooked cops that kept the lowlife under surveillance for his protection.

The time went by as slowly as the sand in an hourglass until it became nine in the evening. He left by the front door to walk to his car. The cold was even more biting that night. There was the distinct feeling of snow in the air. *The first snow of a long, dreary winter is upon us.* The car reluctantly started, and Hank turned on the heater. Making his way through traffic, he parked where he had before, a few blocks from where the cops were. Making his way through alleyways and backyards, he came to the shack that Kurkov called home. He shone his flashlight inside and made his way to the familiar living room armchair. It seemed just as cold inside as it had outside.

The hours slipped by, until he could hear his pigeon's voice saying goodnight to his official police escort. The front door opened and slammed shut. Immediately, Hank turned on the lamp. Kurkov emitted a yelp of shock. "I'll never get used to you sitting in the dark waiting for me!"

"Get used to it!" Weldon shot back. "We'll have a lot of clandestine meetings just like this one!"

"I know what you want."

"You should after the last time. Just coming back from a poker game with Greshnev and some of his cronies?"

"Yeah."

"Was Kaz around?"

"He hasn't been around at all. It is as if he has fallen off the face of the earth."

"And no one speaks about him or where he might be?"

"They're all tight lipped on the subject. I'm sure Greshnev has forbidden them on pain of death to mention his name. He wasn't at the abandoned Navy Yard?"

"No."

"I see. So, you've learned nothing new?"

"Not there."

"What do you mean?"

"I believe that I might be able to get something out of his cousin Ivan, the bartender at The Dive. With a few drinks in him, he might open up to me."

"Is that all of it?"

"Everything that I know at this moment."

"Keep pumping Ivan for information and keep your mouth shut." It's better to keep him in the dark about this information! Remember what I've said about telling Malone about our arrangement."

"I haven't forgotten."

"It's best that you keep it in mind or you will breathe your last breath on this earth!"

Moving out the back door, he saw the first snowflakes were now falling and sticking to the ground. He walked through the frozen winter land making sure that he wasn't seen.

As he drove back, he was hit with the idea that Kurkov was trusted enough in Greshnev's inner sanctum that he should be wired by the government boys to go undercover. Maxim would never trust me enough to reveal his part in the murders, but Kurkov…he's already been accepted by the Russian mob. *Besides, I'm sure Mr. Kurkov wouldn't mind putting himself in the line of fire instead of me.*

He felt a flush of exhilaration at how good things were going. *Kaz may not be dead, but probably being held against his will. It will only be a matter of time when Greshnev tires of playing cat and mouse with him, then he too will be killed. Why was Maxim so angry about Kaz and Albina's engagement? I can't figure it out. He certainly went into a homicidal rage once he learned of it. Was jealousy the variable in this puzzle? But why jealousy? Had there been some connection between the dead girl and the mob boss that was more than an employee and employer relationship?* It was a new and fascinating theory that would need to be further investigated.

CHAPTER

12

A FEW MINUTES after ten the next night, a whole entourage of people appeared at Weldon's door, headed by Agents Baker and Wilson. "Who are all these people?" Hank demanded as they started to pour in.

Parrish Wilson spoke up. "They are technicians who are going to plant recorders in your phone and apartment."

"There's no need for that. They've never visited me here or called me."

"Makes no difference," Cass chimed in. "In case they do, we'll be prepared."

As the technicians went about their business, the agents sat down with Hank at his kitchen table. "We are going to plant a wire on you now," Cass instructed as he called for one of the technicians.

"We want you to go into the Russian Doll House and strike up a conversation with any of the girls or other employees." Parrish related.

"I've been thinking about this, and in my opinion that will never happen." Seeing the surprise on their faces, he continued. "There's a man in town who has access to those establishments and even plays cards with Greshnev."

"Who is this guy?" questioned Baker.

"His name is Alexander Kurkov, a rapist and ex-con. He is under the protection of the corrupt police department." Weldon purposely did not mention Archie Malone's name.

"Why does he have their protection?" added Cass.

"He's undercover."

"But I thought certain members of the police department are cooperating with the mob?" pointed out Parrish.

"I guess one rat doesn't trust another."

"We can depend on this guy?" queried Wilson.

"He knows better than to cross me!"

"When can we meet him?" Cass wanted to know.

"There's no time like the present. However, you won't need all these techs at his house. Just bring one who will put on the wire."

"Why is that?"

"His place is barely one step above a carton box on the street."

Cass turned to his partner and said, "You stay here and make sure everything gets done." Parrish nodded and went where the techs were working.

"Jerry," called out Cass. "Yeah," a young man with thinning hair and glasses answered.

"You're coming with us. Make sure you've got what you need to wire someone up." Giving Cass the okay sign, Weldon explained the special precautions that would be needed to reach Kurkov's house.

A couple of inches of snow had fallen as Hank went to Agent Cass's car, a dark blue Lincoln Continental while Jerry followed in a truck. Weldon directed him to their destination. Instructing Baker to park blocks away, the two men followed Hank as he led them into dark alleys and backyards. The snow beneath their feet crunched, but no one noticed their movements. All three walked through the back door as Weldon turned on his flashlight. The junk and garbage assaulted their eyes and nostrils.

"What a pig sty," commented Jerry.

"How do people live like this?" Cass uttered. Weldon didn't bother to answer. Hank sat down in his usual chair and suggested,

"Just shove his shit off the chairs and sit down. We'll have to wait for a while until he gets home."

They waited impatiently for over an hour before headlights appeared and a car door was slammed shut.

"Goodnight!" a voice from outside could be heard. The door opened as Kurkov yawned loudly. And then the light was turned on. "What the hell!" Kurkov yelled as three faces were there to greet him this time.

"Hey Kurkov! Did you have a good night at the table? "Weldon inquired.

"What do you care!" he sputtered annoyed with the intrusion on his privacy. What do you want now? You were just here yesterday!"

"Today I brought some friends. Why don't you sit down and join us?"

"Who are these jackasses?"

"Mr. Kurkov," Cass Baker began. "We are from the FBI."

"So, you've brought in the big guns, huh!"

"And we'd like to ask you a couple of questions."

"It's late and I'm not in the mood!"

"Sit down!" Weldon responded gruffly "and shut your mouth until you are spoken to!" Kurkov's bravado quickly crumbled, and he did what he was told. Wilson spoke up.

"Mr. Weldon has told us that you have carte blanche when it comes to gaining access to Greshnev's establishments. Is that true?"

"I suppose so."

"This is no time for modesty," Hank said his words dripping with sarcasm.

"You have received police protection in exchange for information about the mob?"

"That's right."

"But you also work for Mr. Weldon?"

"Yeah," he answered with disgust.

"Good. Mr. Weldon has indicated to us that you would agree to wearing a wire when you visit any one of Greshnev's businesses."

"Have you lost your mind?" Kurkov directed his words to Hank. "If they catch me with a wire, I'm as good as dead!"

"They've never checked you for a wire before, and they're not going to check you now. Besides, if you don't do it, I'll expose you to Greshnev as a police informant! I don't even want to think about what he'd do to you!" threatened Weldon.

Cass looked over to Jerry and declared, "Get him wired up!"

"Now?" Kurkov yelled. "I'm dead on my feet!"

"You'll be dead on your back at the coroner's office if you don't shut up!" Without another word of protest, Alex took off his coat and lifted his shirt so that Jerry could wire his body.

"You're going back in, but this time your destination is The Dive, Hank instructed him. Kurkov nodded his head.

"Why there?" Cass queried.

"I told you about the bartender there, a man named Ivan. He could prove to be a fountain of information about the mob."

"Okay then, The Dive it is."

"I don't feel good about this." Kurkov revealed.

"Just make some easy conversation. Once he has had a little too much to drink, which you'll offer to buy one for him, he'll open up like the legs of a whore The rest will be a piece of cake." advised Weldon.

"Okay, check the connection," Cass advised Jerry.

"Everything is working."

"Now, call your chauffeurs back," Weldon instructed his pigeon. Giving them a grimace, Kurkov made his way to the door. "And make it convincing!" Hank turned off the light as Alex went to the sidewalk and waved the car up. He stopped to talk for a minute before he got back in the car which then drove away. Hank and the agents left the house immediately. They led him to a truck with a sign painted on the side reading, Sullivan's Heating and Cooling Co.

"We're getting into this?" Weldon inquired.

"To keep our cover," Baker responded.

As soon as Cass and Hank got into the back of the truck, Hank saw all the audio equipment. Jerry got in the driver's seat and took off after the black car.

Jerry parked close to the bar to pick up the signal, and yet remain inconspicuous to Kurkov's chaperones. Jerry went to the back of the truck and turned on the recorder. The three men sat in the dark until they heard Kurkov's voice say,

"Get me a vodka Ivan and pour one for yourself."

"Right away," a clear voice came back to them.

The conversation remained mundane for a while: the weather, football, women, but as the drinks were consumed, Ivan began to get very chatty. And then the topic was broached.

"So, have you heard from your cousin?"

"That jerk! He's gone crazy!" *Ivan can say that now that his cousin Kaz is not around to punch him in the face!*

"What do you mean?"

"He got himself into a real mess."

"How's that?"

"He knew Albina was Greshnev's girl, yet he went after her."

"Albina was Maxim's girl? She was just a cheap whore. Why would Greshnev want her?"

"The heart wants what the heart wants. Who's to say why these things happen."

"Hey bartender, what about some service down here!" another patron called out.

"I'll be right back," Ivan informed Kurkov.

"Are you getting all of this, Jerry?" inquired the federal agent.

"Every syllable." It wasn't too long before Ivan returned.

"So, what were we talking about?" he questioned Alex.

"You were telling me about how Maxim loved Albina."

"Oh yeah, Greshnev was pissed when he discovered that Kaz was trying to take her from the Russian Doll House.

It was Kaz that took her away? He had been used like a red herring throwing Hank under the bus by keeping him in the dark. Kaz knew all the time where Albina was being hidden.

"Do you know what happened to Albina?

"Rumor is that she's already dead."

"And what happened to Karina?"

"She was stupid! It's said that she confronted Greshnev about Albina's disappearance. A day later…" Ivan made a slashing movement across his neck with his index finger.

"My God…Do you think Maxim has Kaz under wraps?"

"I'd bet my life on it! Greshnev is probably getting his kicks torturing him. All I know is that I wouldn't want to be in his place right now."

"I know what you mean. Do you know where they have him?"

"That, my friend is the million-dollar question! Greshnev owns property all over this city!"

"Well listen, Ivan. I'm going to go home."

"Take care, Alex. I need to close up. I'll see you around."

When Kurkov arrived home, Jerry took off the wire.

"Can I go to bed now?" Kurkov asked in a surly manner.

"For now, yeah," answered Hank.

"In a few days, we'll try tapping the bartender again. Perhaps, he'll have more information," added Cass.

"I'll have to do this again?"

"You'll do it as many times as you're told," the agent dictated.

"Get upstairs!" commanded Weldon. Kurkov trudged up the steps.

Gathering the equipment, the three men went out the back door. If it were possible, the cold felt even more intensely biting than when they arrived. Their breaths were exhaled in short puffy vapors as they made their way back to the van and sedan. Baker turned on the ignition and the heater before he pulled out.

"It's looking more and more as if Greshnev was involved in Albina's killing," Hank theorized.

"Yes, but we still need a witness, because all of this is just hearsay."

"If we could find Titov, he might be convinced to loosen his tongue."

"But where do we start looking for him?" Weldon searched his mind for the answer, but it did not come.

A coordinated effort between the FBI and New York City police was formed, and based on the information about Greshnev's properties compiled by informants, a sweep was to take place in the early morning hours two days later. Some of those who held grudges against Maxim were only too happy to cooperate to bring the mobster down. Most of these had been cheated, squeezed out, or forced to "donate" their properties to the ruthless Russian tyrant.

Weldon had convinced a reluctant Agent Baker to allow him to accompany him on one of these raids. Parrish had warned him to stay under the radar and speak to no one about the sunrise search that was about to take place. Hank had agreed, but his mind was uneasy.

He tried to sleep the night before and tried to concentrate on something other than the next day, but Archie Malone remained in his head. He knew that he couldn't just walk into the precinct and confront him, since many ears might hear them. Weldon waited outside in his car until Malone was through with his shift. He saw a cop stop him at the top of the outside stairs and knew this was his moment. Archie was about to enter his forest green Range Rover when Weldon approached him.

Startled by Hank's sudden appearance, he said, "You again?"

"I need to speak to you."

"We're through. I don't want to hear anything else you have to tell me!" As he tried to close the driver's side door, Weldon grabbed the handle to prevent it. "Get your hand off my car!"

"Listen to me, you idiot. I've come to warn you!" Malone looked intently into his eyes and decided that this guy was serious.

"Get in!"

Hank began. "I haven't told a soul about your involvement with Greshnev."

"That again! I'm telling you for the last time that I'm not associated with the Russian mob. Now get out!"

"I don't care how often you deny it, I know the truth!"

"You don't know anything!

"I know one thing for sure. Tomorrow morning the FBI and the New York Police Department are making a sweep of Greshnev's real estate holdings. You need to make sure that you're not around any of them when they are."

Malone sat silent after this declaration and then his face turned red. "What have you done?"

"I could no longer turn a blind eye to these murders!" Hank's eyes reflected the fact that this was a fait accompli.

Once Archie settled down, he asked, "You're sure about all of this?"

"Dead sure!"

"What are they looking for?"

"I've told you too much already. For you and your family's sake, stay away tomorrow!" Hank opened the door to exit but Archie stopped him.

"Why are you sticking your neck out for me?"

"I owe you. I've never forgotten that, even after you wanted nothing more to do with me. But now my debt is paid. I don't owe you anything anymore." Again, Malone remained mute. "The only thing that I'm asking of you is to keep this information under your hat. If by chance, Greshnev is prepared for the raid, I'll have no choice but to tell them that I let you in on this information. What happens then will be on your head!" Weldon did not wait to hear his reply but exited the car.

My conscious is clear and I did what I had to, despite the government's warning for me to remain silent. I pray that Malone heeds my warning and keeps what I told him to himself. There's nothing else to do.

The private eye pulled out into the evening rush hour traffic, and decided to go to his favorite diner to get a hot cup of joe and read the morning paper.

###

Dawn came and Hank Weldon was already at Agents Baker and Wilson's side, waiting to enter a row house off Coney Island Avenue. It brought Hank back to his old days on the police force and like then, he could feel his adrenaline coursing through his circulatory system. It felt terrific! At the appointed time, Baker gave the word, and the rush toward this building was happening here, as well as in eight other places around the city. "Open up! FBI.!" Everything remained silent inside.

Waving his arm, Parrish called up the battering ram, and the door was knocked off its hinges. Women screamed, and men cursed in Russian. The inhabitants had all been caught by surprise.

Thank God! Archie has not warned Greshnev!

With guns pointing into the interior, law enforcement officers scrambled inside. It was a bordello and the people in it were caught in different stages of undress. "Get down on your knees! Put your hands on your heads!" The group that had broken down the back door was now also in the central hallway. While a few remained behind to cuff those that had been inside, the majority swept through the rest of the building looking for Kaz Titov.

After a few minutes of hearing the word "clear" being shouted from around the building, Parrish's walky-talky suddenly went off. "Yeah, okay," he answered in sharp, staccato syllables before he turned it off. "They've found him at the warehouse!" Leaving the others behind to haul the prisoners down to the precinct, the two agents and the ex-cop took off for the docks.

They came to a screeching halt and got out. Hank could count three dead bodies of Greshnev's gang. They found the rest of the gang kneeling and cuffed inside. "Where's Titov?" Cass demanded of one of the cops.

"Through the back door!" an officer replied. They entered in time to see Kaz being lifted out of a trap door in the floor. Hank was shocked by what he saw. Kaz's face was swollen so that his eyes were forced shut. It was red and purple with dried caked blood. His clothes had been ripped, and cigarette burns tattooed his chest, arms, and legs.

"Kaz" Weldon called out as they lifted him onto a stretcher. Titov made no response.

"How is he?" inquired Parrish Wilson.

"Incoherent," an officer replied. "But he keeps repeating "bean". Hank knew what he was trying to say. He was sure that he was trying to say Albina's name.

"Get him to the hospital," Cass directed the officers. An ambulance was called to the scene. The three men climbed down to the room below the warehouse. Forensics was already taking pictures and bagging evidence. The room was stifling, and one single bulb hung from the ceiling. It gave an eerie glow to the tiny space that had acted as Kaz's cell.

The walls and floor were spattered with dried red blood. The combined odor of sweat and blood permeated the air. Weldon had seen sickening crime scenes before, but this made him audibly gag.

"If you're going to vomit, go upstairs!" commanded Cass. "I don't want this evidence compromised!"

"I'm fine!" Weldon answered gruffly.

They returned upstairs to find that Kaz was already on his way to Coney Island Hospital. "Let's see how he's doing," suggested Parrish, and the three men were soon on their way. At the Emergency Room, they were greeted by the cacophonous noise of crying babies, children running around, and people speaking in all languages. Going over to the admissions window, Agent Baker brushed by several people who were complaining loudly about these men who had gotten to the head of the line.

"Hey mister," a woman with a Spanish accent yelled at Cass. "There's a line here. Get to the back!" Cass quieted them down immediately as he flashed his government identification.

"How can I help you?" the woman sitting behind the plexiglass window inquired.

"You should have recently received a patient by the name of Kazimir Titov, is that correct?" The woman scanned her computer screen and said, "Yes, he's on the eighth floor, room 812."

They walked to the lobby and got on the elevator. Once the doors reopened, they strode to Titov's room and looked through the window. The door of the private room was closed because a doctor was examining him. The patient was already hooked up to an intravenous drip in his arm, had an oxygen tube inserted into his nostrils, and his head was bandaged.

The doctor came out after conversing with the nurse. "Doctor, my name is Agent Baker," he remarked flashing his credentials once more. "This is Agent Wilson and Mr. Weldon."

"How do you do," the doctor replied. "I'm Doctor Greco."

"What's going on with your new patient," Cass pointed to the door.

"It looks like he may have a pretty severe concussion, but we'll learn more about that when he has an M.R.I. tomorrow, as well as other tests, to tell us how badly he's hurt."

"Is there anything else he's dealing with?"

"There are contusions in several places on his body, but it doesn't appear that any bones have been broken."

"Has he said anything?" queried Parrish.

"He keeps mumbling about a "bean" of some sort but I attributed it to delusions from his concussion."

Cass asked, "Can we go in and speak to him?"

"He's in no condition to talk for at least several days. Besides, he's just now going under sedation."

Turning to Parrish, Cass directed, "I want a cop placed outside this door 24/7 in shifts. No one's to go in unless their I.D.'s are checked, understand?"

"I know what he's probably trying to say," Hank revealed to Cass.

"What are you talking about?"

"I think that instead of meaning "bean" Kaz is calling out the name of Albina, his dead fiancée."

"You might be right, but we'll have to wait until he can speak to us about what happened to him."

CHAPTER

13

W HEN HANK STOPPED at the hospital room the next afternoon, he was greeted by a young cop who announced, "Let me see some identification!" Showing him his driver's license, the cop checked the name with a list of names on a clip board. "Go ahead," he said returning the license.

Weldon moved to the side of the bed where Kaz laid unmoving. God, they really did a number on him! He was aghast at what he saw as he scanned the patients face. It looked like raw meat. There were contusions everywhere and a broken nose. Not that Kaz had to worry about losing his good looks, he didn't have any. He saw tubes coming out of all areas of his blankets.

Hank got close to his ear and whispered, "Kaz, can you hear me? It's Hank." Titov didn't move a muscle. "If you can hear me, try to move your index finger." His finger remained still.

He took the chart that was hanging at the foot of the bed. One-hundred and one temperature and his blood pressure is high. Doctor Greco walked in with a nurse.

"Doctor, do you have the results of the M.R.I.?"

"Are you a family member?" The only family that Weldon knew was Ivan, and he didn't think the bartender wanted to get involved.

"His parents are dead and he has no wife or children, but I am his cousin," he fabricated.

"I guess that will have to do. The M.R.I. indicates some swelling of the brain and bleeding in the cranium."

"Can anything be done to reverse this?"

"We'll have to operate. Nurse, get me the forms."

"Will this operation affect his memory in any manner?"

"I won't be able to tell you that until the effects of the operation and anesthesia have worn off. Without the operation, he will die. Being his only living relative, you'll have to sign the permission form."

"Of course." *If anyone finds out what I've done, I'll be charged with fraud and who the hell knows what else!* "That's done!" he turned over the pen and form to the nurse. "How soon can his operation be scheduled?"

"We can get him into the operating room today. His case is a top priority!" Turning to the nurse, he instructed, "Get a couple of orderlies in here to prep him."

"Right away, doctor."

"You'll have to leave now, but you can wait for me in the visitor's lounge."

"That's fine." Hank sat down in the lounge occupied by a couple of other people and called Cass.

"FBI, Agent Baker speaking."

"It's Weldon. Kaz is on his way to the operating room."

"I know all about the operation he needs, but because I wasn't family, I could not give them permission. How were you able to get it done?"

"I lied and said I was his cousin."

"If he should die, we will lose his testimony against Greshnev."

"There's something else we need to worry about. The operation might affect his memory."

"You're kidding!"

"I wish I were. Either way, we will lose the testimony to convict Greshnev. All we can do now is sit and wait."

"I suppose so. Let me know what the doctor says after he operates."

"I will." Hank sat down to wait through the hours, a copy of last February's Town and Country magazine open on his lap which went unread. *This is going to be a long day.*

Time appeared to be purposely dragging its feet, seemingly just to piss off Hank. He had thumbed through all the available publications and now paced the floor trying to will the hands of the clock to move faster. Every time a door opened, he looked up with anticipation, but each time he was disappointed that it wasn't Doctor Greco.

In time, as the afternoon passed, one by one, those that had been waiting left, and he found himself alone. This did nothing but raise his anxiety level.

At last, when the clock had just passed 5:30 p.m, the doctor appeared looking exhausted, his operating gown soaked in sweat.

"How is he, Doc?" Hank was almost reluctant to hear the answer.

"He's pulled through, but it was quite an ordeal."

"How do you mean?"

"He needed three transfusions and his heart stopped during the procedure."

"My God, what are his chances of recovery?"

"That's something only time will tell. The next 24 hours will tell us if he has a chance of recuperation."

"Well, was the operation a success or not?"

"I was able to finally stop the bleeding, but he's in a fragile state."

"Can I see him?"

"He's recovering in ICU, and under heavy sedation. You can't see him now. He'll probably remain that way for the next couple of days."

"Thank you, doctor."

"You're welcome." When the physician had left the room, Weldon got on the phone with Baker. "He's in recovery."

"Did the doctor give you any idea when he'll be able to give us his statement?"

"He's not even sure that he's going to pull through."

"What are his chances?"

"He said that by tomorrow, they'll be able to tell much more."

"Where are they keeping him?"

"He's in I.C.U."

"I've decided to assign two cops outside that door as an extra precaution before Greshnev's goons get a hold of him again and finish the job!"

"When are you going to get Renata out and put her somewhere safe?"

"We can't get her out now. Without any evidence or testimony, a judge will never issue a warrant for us to enter the bordello."

"This waiting is making me very tense!"

"Keep your shirt on and don't do anything foolish that would put her life at risk."

"It's taking too long! Her life is in danger!"

"Once we get Titov's testimony, she'll be out of there."

"But what if he dies or never regains his memory?"

"Don't be such a pessimist, okay!"

"Yeah."

It didn't take long before repercussions from the raids and arrests were felt on the street. In one day, anyone that held a grudge against Greshnev vanished off the street or were dragged out of their homes. Maxim was determined to find the source of his betrayal and dispose of the person.

Weldon found out how serious it was the next day during his evening rendezvous with Kurkov. "He's gone crazy!" the ex-con explained.

"In what way?"

"All his business has come to a grinding halt. The bordello is closed and so is his bar."

"Why?"

"He is manic about just one thing. Who ratted on him."

"Geez, I never thought there would come a day when making money wasn't his first priority!"

"I'm scared!" Kurkov revealed and his terrified eyes were as big as saucers. "If he ever finds out that I've been pumping Ivan for information and that I was wearing a wire, there won't be enough of me left to put in a thimble!"

"If you walk around town with that defeatist expression on your face, he's sure to get wind of it, so do yourself a favor and lay low."

"Tell that FBI buddy of yours that I want protection and I want it right now!"

"Until Kaz comes across with his testimony, the agency can do nothing for us. We're all on the hot seat!"

"Not you, I'll bet. Now that you're in bed with the Feds."

"I'm not in bed with anybody!"

"You're going to convince them to put me immediately into witness protection or I'll…"

"You'll do what?"

Alex hesitated before he blurted out, "I'll go straight to Detective Malone and tell him everything you had me do, and how you are trying to stab him in the back!"

Hank was in no mood for verbal banter. He swiftly balled his hand into a fist and cold-cocked Kurkov in the nose. The man fell to the floor, his nose bleeding.

"Why did you do that?" he whined.

"That was just a taste of what you'll have coming to you if I find that you've told Malone about our little arrangement!"

"I think you broke my nose!"

"I'll break a lot more than your nose if you betray me!"

"What am I going to tell Malone when he sees my nose like this?"

"Tell him you were drunk and fell down the stairs. That's not stretching the truth too far." Hank turned on his heels and went out the back door, the same way he always came in.

What Kurkov said told him that he really had something to worry about. He wondered how much danger Renata was in. The feeling made him queasy with anxiety. Maxim Greshnev was not the kind of man to forget a slight. He certainly wasn't going to forget this attempt to incarcerate him. He was on the warpath, and that meant there was to be blood spilled; a whole lot of blood.

Wake up quickly Kaz and tell Baker all you know or we're all doomed to an early grave!

CHAPTER

14

TWENTY-FOUR HOURS LATER, Kaz was still breathing, which gave hope to Cass Baker that perhaps he could soon question the victim. In time, the patient was transferred to a private room, but his guards remained diligent outside his room. Baker had purposely not let the newspapers know about Titov's information saying, "The fewer people who know, the more chance Kaz has to stay alive!"

By the fourth day of his recovery, Doctor Greco granted visitation to Baker, Wilson, and Weldon for a short time. The sun streamed through the window blinds onto his bed sheets, making them look an even brighter white. Except for the room's basic accommodations, it was void of any flowers or get-well cards from family or friends. Titov was now marked as a pariah. No one would have anything to do with him now that he had crossed Greshnev.

The three men walked into the room and stood by Titov's bed. His nose had been straightened and was now bandaged. The former bodyguard's face was shaved clean, with only the slightly bloody bandages wrapped around it. There were far fewer tubes running out of his body, but the intravenous drip continued doing its job. Some of his bruises were already tinged with yellow, meaning that the healing process was under way.

Cass approached Titov, whose eyes had not opened since their arrival. "Mr. Titov…" Kaz made no response. Cass again called out his name, but nothing happened.

Hank slipped his hand into the patient's and spoke. "Kaz, it's me Hank Weldon. Can you open your eyes?" His eyes remained closed.

"You're going to have to speak to us sooner or later," Parrish Wilson threatened. "I'd rather not get a court order to make you tell us what we want to know, but if I must, I will!" Cass put his hand on Parrish's arm to restrain him from using intimidation at this point.

Suddenly Hank felt Kaz slightly squeeze his hand.

"He can hear us!" Weldon triumphantly announced. "Kaz, who did this to you?" They watched as Titov pursed his lips as if he were trying to speak. After a few agonizing seconds, in a low cracked voice, he whispered, "Bean."

"Listen, Kaz. Albina is dead!" he reminded the gangster. "Your boss took care of that just as he was going to take care of you. Somehow, he found out that it was you who was taking Albina away, and he wasn't going to let that happen. You don't want him to get away with this, do you?" Weldon thought it would be wise to hold back the fact of how his fiancée was dismembered and dropped in a garbage dump. Kaz did not respond to anything that was said.

"You can't let this guy get away with what he's done," added Parrish. "He must stand trial for his crimes!"

Cass now spoke up, "Mr. Titov, unless you can give us a statement that will tie all of this to Greshnev, he's going to get away with what he's done to you. You don't want that to happen, do you?" Once more, Kaz clutched Hank's hand and his lips began to move. The three men waited impatiently for his response.

"Bean." The trio looked at each other with frustration. It was at that moment that Doctor Greco walked in.

"Doctor, he doesn't seem any better than the day he was admitted," stated Parrish impatiently. "What's going on?"

Greco waved them into the hallway where he began to explain. "Mr. Titov received significant head trauma during his ordeal."

With an inquisitive look, Cass demanded, "What are you saying?"

"He may never recover beyond this point."

"You mean a human vegetable," blurted out Wilson. Greco frowned at the terminology. "If that's the case, he will have to be institutionalized."

"Of all the damned luck!" Cass cursed out loud.

"Gentlemen, that is not to say that he will remain this way, but only that it is a possibility. It is too soon to tell."

"When?" pressured Parrish.

"When what?"

"When will you know?"

"There's no specific timetable for all of this. Each patient recovers at a different pace."

"This is not what I wanted to hear," Cass replied gritting his teeth.

"If I were you, I'd check up on him every couple of days. There's nothing more that can be done." The doctor walked away, leaving them in the corridor.

"Now what?" bemoaned Parrish.

"It isn't totally hopeless yet," countered Hank. "He still may show enough improvement to give us his testimony."

"If we were at the racetrack," Cass began, "I wouldn't lay any money on it. It would be a sucker's bet."

"Have you got any other ideas?" quizzed Weldon.

"The only other chance we have is to get a confession rom that flesh-peddling murderer Greshnev."

"We have a snowball's chance in hell of that ever happening," sneered Parrish.

"That's where our stoolie Kurkov comes in."

"Have you gotten anything pertinent on tape over the last few days?" Weldon wanted to know.

"Yeah," sneered Parrish. "If you're interested in talk about women, money, and gambling there's plenty about that!"

"You mean you're going to try and have Maxim take responsibility for all of this while Kurkov is wearing a wire?"

"That's it."

"Are you saying that Kurkov will have to bring these incidents up during their poker game?"

"There's no other way."

"Kurkov will balk. He demanded that I ask you for witness protection the last time I spoke to him."

"I'll only agree to that if he can get Greshnev to admit to his guilt."

"At best that's a million to one shot."

"It's the only card we have to play now that Titov is the way he is."

"Given time, Kaz may still get better enough to testify."

"I'm not putting all of my eggs in that broken basket after what the doctor intimated."

Weldon continued to hold out hope for Titov's recovery, but he had to admit that Baker was right. A contingency plan had to be put in place.

"When do we break the good news to Kurkov?" inquired Parrish.

"There's no time like the present and no sense in putting it off."

Hank began to think. *I don't know if this plan with Kurkov is going to work. He's too much of a loose cannon, even if the Witness Protection Program is dangled in front of him like a carrot on a stick!*

"Are you all fucking crazy?" Kurkov screamed at the top of his lungs. "I'm as good as dead if I did what you wanted!"

"You don't ask him directly," Parrish Wilson stated. "Just mention their names and see how he reacts.

"Yeah," Hank concurred. "If he just twitches, pursue the same line of questioning."

"Get out!" yelled Kurkov pointing toward his door. "Get out now or I'll set the two cops outside on you!"

Cass Baker strode up to the raging man and put his hand on the snitch's shoulder. "What if the cops were to find out that you've been working behind their backs? How long do you think your guard dogs would remain outside to protect you?"

"You bastards!" Kurkov brushed the hand away from his shoulder.

"Are you going to do it?" inquired Cass.

The ex-con paced inside the room like a trapped animal. "Do I have a choice?"

"No choice," Parrish answered back.

"Tomorrow night we'll arrive to get you hooked up."

"What happens if he goes after me or gets one of his boys to do his dirty work?"

"We'll be in before anything can happen to you."

"It only takes a second to shoot a bullet."

"He wouldn't dare do that with all those witnesses around."

"I'm not sure."

"If you refuse, you'll have no one to protect you. Greshnev could get to you any time he wanted."

Seeing no way out of this dire predicament, Kurkov dropped into his chair and nodded his capitulation.

"Good!" Cass said in a soothing voice. "We will be here tomorrow night before your game. Make sure that you are here too." Once again, he nodded. His stare seemed distant and far away. *He now realizes the hopelessness of his situation.*

"We're going now, but we'll be back tomorrow night," related Cass. The former inmate sat motionless in his chair. The three men departed.

Hank wished with all his heart that he had the same access to the Russian Doll House as Kurkov had. *If I could only get Renata and tell her that a plan is being put into motion that will free her.* Still, it was probably better that she did not know. The knowledge of it might put her in immediate peril. *I wouldn't blame her one bit if she has lost faith in me. She probably hates me at this point.*

It was no use dwelling on his morbid thoughts. It always put him in a sour mood. He hoped the plan would work, but it was a long shot. If only Kaz would recover soon and tell his story, this whole mess could be cleaned up.

He went to visit Kaz every day, but there was no seeming change. After a time, the patient was sent to rehabilitation. Soon, he was able to walk with some help. His demeanor become brighter and a smile appeared on his healing face, but he still could only respond to any question put forth to him with the same one-word response, "Bean."

The wire was reconnected onto Kurkov's chest as the human pigeon stood motionless. "Okay, you can put your shirt back on," the technician instructed. As Cass coached him on how to broach the topic with the mob boss, the former jailbird remained strangely silent.

"Are you listening?" demanded Weldon

"Of course, I'm listening!" he bellowed back. "I've heard it so many times I could probably do it in my sleep!" *He looks as if he's already in a dream world.*

"I'm ready."

After his police dogs picked him up, the four men exited the house and got into the truck. Parking where they could pick up the signal, they waited impatiently. As expected, Kurkov was passed through the Russian

Doll House without being frisked. "He's through," related Jerry. There was a lot of background noise as everybody gathered in the poker room, but the crowd grew quiet once Maxim made his entrance. There were the usual platitudes of greeting before the sounds of chairs scrapping the floor were heard. One of Greshnev's boys went around filling tumblers with all kinds of libation while cigars were lit, and the smoke wafted over their heads.

The first game began and after a while, the winning hand was shown by one of the guests. There was some laughter but more cursing as the next man shuffled the cards. The next game was won by Greshnev.

Impatiently, Baker asked the tech, "Anything yet?"

"It's still early. Give him some time to ease into it." Parrish checked the time on his watch. "These games usually last until the wee hours of the morning. Kurkov will get to it when it feels right to him." The hours ticked by and the only thing that Alexander mentioned revolved around the game.

"What's going on with Kaz?" Alexander finally uttered as the cards were dealt for the next game. The table suddenly went silent.

"What did you say?" asked Greshnev.

"I was just wondering about Kaz. He hasn't been around lately."

Jerry told the others, "He's just asked about Kaz." The three men gathered around the tech with great anticipation.

The room was quiet and the tension was so thick that it could have been cut with a knife. Finally, Greshnev responded, "I've heard that he's laid up in the hospital because he had a terrible accident!" With that, he began to laugh. It was a cue for the others at the table to laugh along with him.

"What's happening?" Cass inquired.

"They're all laughing because Greshnev said he heard that Kaz had a terrible accident."

"Damn it! How the hell did he find out he's in the hospital?"

"The fact that he's laughing could only mean that the bastard has someone on the inside in the hospital staff telling him that Kaz is no longer a threat because of his condition."

"Son of a bitch! What's going on now?"

"They're still laughing...wait a minute. Greshnev is asking him something."

"Why are you so curious, Kurkov?"

"No reason." Jerry could detect the nervousness in his voice.

"Still, I wonder what's with the questioning?" All of a sudden, a tumultuous commotion was heard. There were yelling voices everywhere making it hard to distinguish Kurkov's voice.

"Who's talking?" demanded Parrish.

"Something is going down. Kurkov might be in danger…wait a minute!"

Jerry heard Greshnev say, "Put down the gun, Kurkov. We're all friends here!"

"Kurkov has a gun!" the technician related.

"How the hell did he get a gun?" Cass yelled.

"Don't be foolish!" Greshnev expressed with anxiety. Suddenly, a gun shot was heard.

"He shot Greshnev!" barked Jerry in disbelief.

"We've got to get in there" Hank croaked.

"No, contact the local police. We don't want to blow our cover." Parrish made the call. The cops assigned to Kurkov darted from the car with their guns drawn.

"What's going on now?" Weldon asked.

"I hear Greshnev's voice but there are too many other people talking at one time. The cops are inside."

"Who shot him?" Jerry heard one cop ask.

"He shot himself," responded Greshnev.

Jerry lifted the earphones from his ears and looked up with bewilderment in his eyes.

"Well," uttered Parrish.

"Kurkov shot himself."

"What?"

"We put him under too much pressure," Hank explained. "Is he dead?"

"They're not saying." The four men didn't have long to wait as a squad of patrol cars showed up followed by the coroner's van.

CHAPTER

15

W ELDON'S DOOR SOUNDED as if it were going to be beaten
down. "Who is it?" Hank infuriatingly shouted.

"Open up! Open up now!" Weldon went to the door and unlocked it.
The private dick was surprised by the face on the other side. "Don't you
know how to knock like a normal person?" he inquired of Archie Malone.

"Get inside before I knock your block off!" the detective threatened
forcefully. Archie slammed the door behind him.

"What's put you into such a foul mood this morning?"

"Don't play me for a fool, Weldon!"

"I have no idea what you're getting at, Archie!" Hank played dumb.

"No idea?" Detective Malone replied putting his hands on his former
friend's jacket lapels before he threw him back onto his unmade bed.

"Jesus! What's your problem?" wailed Weldon.

"You're my problem!" reposted a stressed Malone as Weldon attempted
to get up. Archie pushed him back down again viciously. "Stay where you
are before I sock you in the jaw!"

"If you've got something on your mind then get to it!"

"Kurkov is dead!"

"Really?" Weldon continued to play the game and hoped his voice
sounded somewhat incredulous.

"Yeah! A self-inflicted bullet to his cranium!"

"What happened?" Hank watched as a rising anger continued to show
on his former partner's face.

"You know damned well what happened!"

"I don't understand what you're talking about."

"You know what happened because you had a front row seat to his
suicide!" Hank realized that the game was over.

"I bet you can't guess what the coroner found on Kurkov's body." Hank remained silent. "You had a wire on Kurkov, didn't you?"

"Yes."

"I know you don't own that kind of equipment and that it didn't come from the police department, so where did it come from?"

"It belongs to the FBI."

There was the look of blood in the detective's eyes. "You got government men involved?"

"Well, I wasn't getting any cooperation from you, so I went above your head. I didn't believe I had any other choice."

"You idiot!" he screamed back at the top of his lungs. "Two years of undercover work has been compromised by your actions. I could kill you right now!"

"Undercover? Kurkov was working undercover for you? Weldon replied feigning ignorance.

"That's what I said, jackass!" Malone began to pace back and forth trying to get control of his emotions.

"You weren't on the take from Greshnev and the Russian mob?"

"I've been pretending that I was in his back pocket to get murder raps issued to him. Now you've gone and spoiled everything!"

"Gee, Archie! If you had only taken me into your confidence, I never would have brought in federal agents."

"I should trust you with that information? You're a pathetic alcoholic. I couldn't have confidence in you keeping your yap shut when you were in one of your drunken stupors! So, forgive me for not sharing with you!"

Penitently, Hank replied, "I'm really sorry. I wish I hadn't blown his cover."

"Too little, too late! What are the names of the government agents that were involved with you?"

"Cassidy Baker and Parrish Wilson."

"Contact them!"

"Now?"

"Yeah, right now!"

Weldon didn't see any diplomatic way out of the ultimatum and did what he was ordered. At last, the receiver on the other side was picked up. A voice answered,

"Baker here."

"Cass, it's Hank Weldon."

"Have you heard anything else about Kurkov?"

"No. The reason I'm calling you is because Detective Malone is here and wants to talk to you."

"You told him everything?"

"It's all out in the open."

"What the hell is wrong with you?"

"Give me the phone," Archie demanded, pulling the receiver from his hand. "Baker this is Detective Archibald Malone of the New York City Police Department. If you have any chance in hell of getting Greshnev convicted of murder, we are going to have to pool our resources and information." Malone wasn't giving the federal agent a chance to say a word. "Get over to Weldon's apartment now! I'll be waiting for you!" He slammed the phone down in its cradle.

Hank got up from the bed. "He's coming over?"

"Yeah, now sit down and shut up! This whole thing has given me a pounding headache!"

The two men didn't have to wait long before the sound of knocking was heard at the door. Baker and Wilson walked in, surveying Malone as if he were on the top ten Wanted List.

"Malone?" Cass queried as he drew closer.

"Detective Malone," Archie shot back to the agent.

"Well, we're here just as you demanded," was Parrish's dour hard-faced response. "What do you want?"

"What I want is Alexander Kurkov back! "Can you do that?" he asked acerbically.

"You know I can't! Why have you asked us here?" demanded Cass.

"I didn't want federal agents involved in this to screw it up, but now it's too late for that, thanks to Weldon!" He shot Hank a furious look. "Now we are going to have to cooperate with each other if we're going to convict Greshnev!"

"Are you trying to tell me that you're not involved with the Russian mob?"

"Kurkov and I were both infiltrating Maxim Greshnev's illegal operation until you blew Alexander's cover!"

"Who knew that he was going to blow his brains out in front of Grehnev?"

"Yeah, and who knew he would have been found with a wire on him!"

"That was unfortunate," added Parrish.

"Unfortunate? It was a disaster! Maxim is going to think that the police had planted the wire. He may never take me back into his confidence."

"What can be done now?" piped up Hank.

"What do you think? We have to find a new person on the inside to take Kurkov's place," Archie retorted.

"But who?" countered Baker. Malone's stare was turned toward Weldon.

"You can't mean me?"

"There's no one else," Archie barked back. "Your face is familiar to Greshnev and his minions."

"I'm not even welcome in the cat house!"

Parrish spoke up. "You'll have to find a way of ingratiating yourself to him."

"Besides, Greshnev may be looking for another person to fill Kurkov's place at the poker table, but don't approach him right away. Give it some time."

"I don't think…" Weldon didn't finish his sentence after looking at the three men. He knew from their facial expressions that his protestations would fall on deaf ears. Baker and Wilson had crossed the line to join Malone. He was now a minority of one.

Pulling Malone to the side, Hank said, "I'll do this under one condition."

"And what's that?"

"I want you to locate a girl named Renata Dubov."

The police detective shook his head in exasperation. "Don't tell me you've gotten involved with one of Greshnev's whores, have you?"

"That's my business. If you find her, I want you to remove her from Greshnev's grasp."

"I'll do my best."

Weldon realized that getting into the brothel was going to be difficult, but he knew that one way or another, he would have to talk himself back into the whore house.

When he got to the front door and rang the bell, a familiar face greeted him. Serge Sokoloff smirked and asked, "Are you stupid? You've been told you're no longer welcome here!"

"I need to speak with Fat Zoya."

"Well, Zoya doesn't want to talk to you!"

"Ask her again! I've done some thinking about my behavior. Tell her I've changed!"

After eyeballing Hank up and down for a moment, he ordered, "Wait here!"

Sokoloff walked off until he got to his boss's office. Weldon waited, worrying that he might be given the same response.

I've got to swear that I won't see or speak to Renata, and I better make it convincing!

Serge came out of the office and waved him forward. "Go in!" he commanded. Zoya sat behind her desk, a cigarette perched precariously from her lips and a tumbler of scotch over ice near her hand. A pile of her salt and pepper hair was stacked on top of her head and her fleshy body was bursting out of an imported pink silk robe.

"Well, what are you doing back here?" she queried with a thick Russian accent. "I've already told you to stay away!"

"I had to tell you something."

"Well say it and stop wasting my time!"

"I no longer want to be with Renata."

"Really," Zoya replied with skepticism. "Why should I believe you won't try to contact her behind my back."

"Because I give you my word!"

"Ha, your word? Do you think that I'm a fool?"

"Look Zoya, I promise on my dead mother's grave that I'm trustworthy!"

Zoya looked at him intently, not saying a word. She took a puff of her cigarette and a gulp of her scotch before she was ready to speak.

"Fine, but the first time you screw up, I'll have Serge work you over. I'm sure he's looking forward to that!"

Pressing a button under her desk, Sokoloff opened the door. "I'm allowing him back," Fat Zoya announced, "but one wrong move, and he's all yours, Serge!" A big grin appeared across the bully's face. He was escorted out to the lobby where a screen above his head displayed the picture of each available girl and how much each cost for the half hour. *It's like looking up at a board of food choices displayed at a hamburger joint.*

"Well, who will it be?" Sokoloff demanded impatiently.

Hank's eyes scanned the board, but he did not see Renata's photograph.

Have they killed her already? Again, he focused on the pictures until they settled on a statuesque blonde. Her name was Nonna and the price underneath her picture read 100 dollars.

"The price for Nonna is pretty steep."

"She is new," Serge exclaimed. "Straight off a Belarus farm. Is she the one you chose?"

"Yes."

"Pay at the register." A disheveled and bored-looking woman uttered, "Who do you want?"

"Nonna."

"One hundred dollars for a half hour." Hank pulled out a wad of cash bundled in a rubber band and peeled off the bills. He made sure that what he was doing was obvious. The girl and the bodyguard's eyes bulged.

"Room 12."

Hank left behind two stunned people. It's a good thing that Cass gave me this money.

Weldon knocked on the designated door. "Come in," a sweet voice replied. A 5'6" beauty with all the right curves stood before him in her nakedness. "Hello lover," she said. "Do you like what you see?"

My God, she looks like a model straight out of a photo from Town and Country magazine. Most men used their eyes to undress beautiful woman. Weldon imagined her in clothing.

"So, where are you from, Nonna?" he asked nervously.

"I am from Belarus, but enough about me. I'm here for you," she replied in a seductively purring voice.

Nonna strode toward him and pressed her naked body on him. Weldon immediately had a sexual response. Placing her lips on his, she kissed him as if she were trying to draw the breath out of his body. His head began to spin with sexual passion and desire.

The prostitute took him by the hand and led him to a bed, where the covers were already turned down. Nonna slipped between the satin sheets waiting for Weldon to join her. Taking off his clothing as quickly as he could, he got in and straddled her.

Perspiration and moans were emanated from the boudoir by both parties until they reached their climax. Hank collapsed by her side. After a few minutes, his breathing became regular.

He fought off the urge to ask Nonna about Renata's whereabouts, even though he now worried that she may be beyond his reach.

"What are you thinking about, lover?"

"I'm thinking about how beautiful you are, Nonna," he lied.

"I like you very much," she answered. "Maybe next time you come to see me again, no?"

"I'd love to see you again!" he said enthusiastically despite his alarm for Renata.

"That is good, but you must go now, lover." Checking his watch, he noticed that his half hour was almost over.

"Until next time, Nonna."

"Goodbye, lover," she purred as he left the room.

Outside in the hallway, Weldon came face to face with Max Greshnev who had just arrived at the bordello.

As the Russian boss passed him, Weldon called out, "Mr. Greshnev, may I speak to you for a minute?" Immediately one of the bodyguards stepped between them in a defensive stance.

Max turned and said, "Yuri, step away." The bodyguard, like a trained German Shepherd, heeled immediately.

"And who are you?" Greshnev inquired.

"My name is Henry Weldon. I've heard through the grapevine that there is an empty chair at your poker table."

"Henry Weldon…" Greshnev thought out loud. "It seems to me that your name is familiar to me."

"You may know me as Hank Weldon."

"Yes, that's it!"

"As I was asking, is there an empty chair at your poker game?"

"Hank Weldon…You're the ex-cop that is now a private detective, yes?"

"That's me."

"The private detective who goes around taking dirty pictures of couples making love, is that right?"

"I provide a service," the detective responded defensively. "I provide a service to husbands and wives whose spouses are cheating on them."

"My poker games are played for big stakes," Greshnev said his voice dripping with condescension. "I'm afraid it's too rich for a person like yourself with limited funds." It was at that point that Serge, who was listening to the conversation, came over to his boss and whispered in his ear. Max looked back at Weldon as Sokoloff continued to speak softly. Serge pulled away and Max declared, "It has come to my attention that you may have the funds needed. If that's the case, I host a game here every Tuesday night at eight. Should I expect to see you here?"

"You can expect me this Tuesday night."

"Very well." Greshnev and his entourage walked away.

Hank smiled. *I'm in!*

The moment Weldon told his co-conspirators he was in the upcoming Tuesday night poker game, the stress started. "We told you not to approach Greshnev until he got used to seeing you around the bordello," Parrish chided him.

"Do you think he's onto him as a plant?" inquired Cass with some reservation. Archie replied, "It makes no difference now. If Hank doesn't show up, Greshnev just might get suspicious and withdraw his consent for him to play."

For hours each day, they prepared him with counseling for all possible scenarios. For the next few days, Hank was drilled by all three men as to his approach of the crime boss.

"Fly under the radar the first few times you're at the game," advised Cass Baker. "Don't ask any questions for the next few weeks until he becomes comfortable with your presence."

"Yeah, lay low! Don't ask any questions about Kaz Titov or the two dead whores," Archie cautiously advised him.

"Whatever you do, don't push it or you'll wind up in a grave in Potter's Field along with Kurkov!" warned Parrish Wilson in a solemnly serious voice.

"Will I be wearing a wire?"

"Not this soon after Greshnev found the one on Kurkov," advised Cass.

"But what if something goes wrong?"

"If you follow our instructions, nothing will go wrong."

"Do you get it now or do we have to go over it again?"

"Alright! Alright! I've got it!" the decoy shouted back losing his temper on the final day before the poker game. "I've got it straight, already!"

"Okay," Detective Malone's voice was purposefully calm. "Take it easy.

Just play the game and let Greshnev do the winning. If he does, he'll invite you again and again, thinking that you're an easy mark, understand?"

"I've got it okay? Stop going over it! I'm ready!"

"Go home and relax," recommended Parrish.

Detective Malone interjected, "Try not to think about it anymore tonight."

Hank Weldon stood up and put his coat on to get ready to leave the hotel room. "I'll drive you home," Archie offered.

"Don't bother," was Hank's reply. "I want to walk home in the cold air and clear my head before I go to sleep."

Weldon took the elevator to the lobby which was pretty much deserted at this time of night. He pushed through the revolving door to be greeted by a cold blast of arctic air. Bracing himself for the journey home, he walked between mounds of shoveled snow on the sidewalk. As he walked mindlessly along the thoroughfares, his mind wandered.

Jesus, how did I ever get myself between a rock and a hard place. I must be crazy to think that Greshnev will just accept me in Kurkov's place! What if Max suspects something and this is just a trap? Am I already a dead man? These nagging questions, as well as the trio's voices of advice played repeatedly in his head.

Hank couldn't explain how it happened, but when he looked up he was standing at the neon sign that said, The Dive. Weldon knew he should just walk past it. After all, he had been abstemious for months and had felt the positive effects of his sobriety. Yet, there was a comfortable familiarity in the sign. *Besides, it's a cold night and what harm could one drink do to warm up?* He took the first step toward the entrance and found himself inside.

The atmosphere was that of greeting an old friend as he strode toward the bar. Bar flies in different states of inebriation were gathered at the watering hole. A couple of faces were new, but most of the people were instantly recognizable to him. Bellying up to the bar, Weldon got Ivan's attention.

"Well, it's been quite a while since you were here."

"Yeah, I know. I've been on the wagon."

"Did you come here for a drink or for the sparkling conversation?"

Hank took one more look at the customers who all were in their own worlds.

"I'll take a scotch just to warm me up from the cold."

Ivan smiled to himself. He had heard all the excuses used by alcoholics for a reason to drink. This one was not new. Pouring the liquor into a shot glass, Ivan delivered it to Weldon.

"Why don't you join me," Hank proclaimed. "It's on me." the bartender did not argue and poured himself one.

"To better days," added Ivan. They clicked their glasses together and downed the drink in one gulp. The warmth of the liquor traveling through his throat and down his esophagus felt so good and he realized how much he had missed that sensation.

"Pour us another," the private detective directed.

"You got it." There was no toasting this time as both men finished off their drinks.

The drinking went on for a while and as Hank's guard began to crumble he suddenly asked, "Have you been up to see Kaz lately? I wonder how is he doing?"

"What for?" Ivan shot back.

"Well, he is your cousin, isn't he?"

"Yeah, but he's a vegetable now. Kaz wouldn't know if I were there or not. You'd know that if you visited him in the rehabilitation home. After all, he was your friend and part-time colleague."

Weldon downed another drink before he replied. "I should go..." he answered, his words being slurred. "I should go, but I just haven't had the courage," he sheepishly replied

"You mean the balls!" Ivan challenged him

"What is that supposed to mean?" Hank barked in a surly manner.

"Well, if you had located Albina before she was murdered, Kaz wouldn't be in the condition he is today!"

"That's a damn lie!"

Henry Weldon didn't remember much after he voiced his objection to the bartender's accusation. What he recalled next was being shaken violently.

"What? What is it? Stop shaking me!" Raising his head off the bar, his blood shot eyes tried to focus.

"Get up!" he heard a harsh voice command him. With some help, he raised himself off the bar stool and looked at the face that was glaring at him. It was Archie Malone.

"Archie, my old pal," he garbled, inebriated as he patted him on the chest. "You're the best friend a guy could ever have."

Before they could leave, Ivan came running up. "He can't leave until he pays his bar tab!"

"How much?"

"Thirty-eight." Archie dug into his wallet and pulled out two Andrew Jackson's and slammed them on the bar.

"Keep the change."

"Gee, big tipper!" grumbled Ivan.

"Let's go!" Malone growled as he dragged Hank to his car.

"Stop!" Hank protested. "I'm going to be sick!" Leaning him against a lamp post, he vomited onto the street. Malone opened the passenger door of his car before he dropped him into the seat.

"I knew you were here when I couldn't get you on your phone!"

"I just stopped for a drink to warm me up."

"You could have burned up in spontaneous combustion with all the liquor you've downed!"

"Very funny," the private eye said before he nodded off. The next thing he remembered was the jolt of cold water. "God damn it!" he screamed as he attempted to get out of his shower.

"Oh, no!" yelled Archie. "Stay under there until you're fully awake. Pressing his hand against Hank's chest, he forced him back under the cold shower.

"You bastard!" he sputtered. Malone paid no attention to his protestations. After another few minutes, he pulled the drunkard from the shower and turned off the water. He roughly dried Hank's head, his hair going in all directions.

"What did you tell Ivan about our plan?" he demanded as he stripped him of his wet clothing.

"Nothing, I told him nothing."

"For your sake, you'd better be right!"

"I'm telling you, I didn't let the cat out of the bag."

Archie dragged him to bed and pushed him down on the mattress. He lifted Weldon's legs up and placed them in bed. Hank's head fell back on his pillow as his former best friend quickly covered him. "You're a pal!" Weldon said as Malone turned the lights off.

"Go sleep it off!" were Malone's parting words. You'd better be ready for tomorrow night! Detective Archibald Malone had his doubts as he closed the apartment door behind him.

CHAPTER

16

EIGHT FORTY-FIVE IN the evening and Henry Weldon was at the Russian Doll House ringing the doorbell. As always, Serge Sokoloff answered the door, his look even more menacing. His expression was that of the Grim Reaper!

The brute addressed him. "Take off your coat!"

Thinking the man was going to hang it up for him, Weldon tried to hand it to him.

"I don't want that!" he snarled. "Now unbutton your shirt!"

"Don't you only instruct that to the girls who work here?"

"Shut up and turn around!" Hank did as he was told. Serge frisked him up and down.

Thank God I'm not wearing a wire!

"Second door on the left," Sokoloff directed, pointing down the hallway.

The door was opened by another of Max's apes. The room was smoke filled by the men around the poker table puffing on Hoyo de Monterrey Cuban cigars. Max rose from his seat to greet Weldon. Hank was taken by surprise by this courteous gesture of the crime kingpin. Three other men sat at the table, all instantly recognizable: Walter Ronan, local Congressman, Michael Salazar, Fire Commissioner and Benjamin Kaiser, Police Chief.

After introductions, Hank was offered a drink. He was tempted but fought off the enticement. "No thanks."

The other men continued with their conversations.

"You can exchange your cash for chips," Greshnev announced pointing to a beautiful girl behind a counter.

"What is the minimum cash chip?"

"Five hundred," she declared pleasantly. *High Rollers!*

"Give me $10,000." She handed him the chips and took his cash. Weldon walked back and took the empty seat at the table.

"Gentlemen," proclaimed Greshnev, "the game is 5-Card Draw! Ante up!"

Weldon watched as the players each threw in a $500 chip. He followed suit. Greshnev shuffled the cards like a professional card shark, showing off his expertise. He went around the table dealing three cards down and four up. Hank tried to devise a winning hand by combining five cards from those that were down. Each man looked intently at his own hand.

"I'll open up with $500!" Kaiser said tossing a chip into the pot.

"I'm in!" Greshnev announced throwing his chip in. Salazar and Ronan considered their options. Hank reviewed his cards: Ace of Spades, two of Spades, Queen of Hearts, five of Diamonds, nine of Diamonds, Jack of Clubs, and ten of Clubs. I've got zilch!

"I'm out!" Weldon tossed in his cards with disgust. Ronan did the same, but Salazar stayed in and threw his chip in the middle of the table. Greshnev flung two chips into the pot.

"Too rich for me!" Salazar proclaimed, tossing his cards away.

"Well, I guess it's just you and me, Ben!"

"Looks that way! I'll raise you a $1,000."

"I call," Greshnev said throwing two chips in. "What are you hiding?"

Kaiser fanned his cards out for everyone to see. "Three of a kind and two ladies!"

"That's better than I've been holding," Max said displaying two pairs. Ben Kaiser gladly scooped up the pot and stacked his winning chips.

The hours wiled away with drinking, smoking, and laughing. Weldon's night was over, winning only one game.

"Better luck next time," Max wished his guest as the game broke up about 1:30 in the morning.

Walking to his car, his breath vaporized, and his feet crunched through frozen snow. He started the car and got out to scrape the windows. He drove home and climbed the stairs to his apartment to find the "Holy Trinity" waiting for him: Malone, Baker, and Wilson.

"Well, what happened?" Archie asked with curiosity.

"Give me a minute to unwind before you inundate me with your questions!"

"Come on, give!" demanded Parrish. "What went on?"

"I only won one hand."

"Cut the comedy!" Cass reproached him. "Spill it!"

"Well, they checked me for a wire before they let me into the game."

"I knew they would! It's a good thing we decided not to do it tonight." Cass and Parrish nodded their agreement.

Baker queried, "Who was there?"

"Michael Salazar, Walter Ronan, and Benjamin Kaiser."

"That's what kills me!" the police detective spat out.

"You mean, Kaiser?" asked Weldon.

"A police chief in Grehnev's pocket. It makes me want to toss my cookies!" Parrish asked, "How did Greshnev treat you?"

"Like a long-lost friend. Or maybe it was because I had enough lettuce to get into the game."

"Interesting," speculated Cass.

"What are you thinking?" requested Parrish.

"I just wonder if he's playing possum," said Baker.

"What do you mean?" deliberated Archie.

"Maybe he's trying to throw Hank from the scent of his crimes by being overly friendly to him."

"Are you saying that you think we can never trust Weldon with a wire because Greshnev's figured out our intentions?" theorized Parrish.

"I'm not sure, but I think he's playing it very cagy!"

"We'll have to wait and see. In the meantime, every Tuesday will be poker night and Hank will continue to attend," announced Malone.

As the two federal agents walked out, Hank tugged on Malone's sleeve.

"What is it?"

"Have you had any word about Renata?"

"Why don't you concentrate on the job you've been given."

"Don't put me off, you made me a promise!"

"There's nothing yet."

"Try harder!"

"Listen, I know that you wanted only me to know about this, but I think I have to get Cass and Parrish involved."

"Why do they need to know?"

"The FBI has many more resources available to them. There would be a better chance locating her if they were involved."

"I guess so," Weldon capitulated.

"Get some sleep and don't get on the sauce again, okay?"

"Yeah." Archie Malone left him to the silence of his apartment.

A quick shower and Weldon was off to bed, but sleep did not come right away. His anxiety for Renata had been increased when he didn't see her name or image on the selection board. *Is she already dead? Have they killed her, and her body is floating under the Atlantic Ocean? Will I ever see her again?* The thought of seeing her in the same condition that the prostitute Karina was found, made him gasp with fear.

It had been two months since Kazimir Titov had been rendered a shell of a body that harbored an incoherent mind. It had been two months since Henry Weldon had seen him. Hank was experiencing great trepidation in seeing a man, once with such vitality, turned into a bed-ridden invalid. He had thought about seeing him very often, but each time he had an excuse for not going. It was after his last drinking binge at The Dive when Ivan had accused him of lack of courage, that finally Weldon had discovered his spine and went to see his former colleague.

March was blustery even though there was the slightest tinge of spring in the air. Kaz had been transferred to the Maria Skobtsova Nursing Home once the rehabilitation center at the hospital found that there was nothing else they could do for him.

The nursing home was an imposing edifice that had been built on a huge plot of land donated by the Eastern Orthodox Church, and was named after a female saint. The lobby resembled a 5-star hotel rather than a home for hopeless medical cases. Going directly to the information desk, Hank inquired, "I'm looking for Kazimir Titov. Can you help me?"

"Of course," the older woman answered helpfully. "Yes, he's on the 5th floor, room 516. The elevator bank is right over there," she pointed out.

"Thank you." I wish that I could turn around right now and go back out the front door!

When the elevator door opened, he entered along with a young woman who held a bundle of flowers in the crook of one arm and had the hand of a young boy about 7 years old. "Six please," she asked as Weldon pushed her button as well as his own.

"Are we going to see Nana?" the child inquired of his mother. Sniffling his mother replied, "Yes, we are."

Reaching the 5th floor, and glancing at the directory on the wall, he turned left and walked down the corridor. He noticed several patients sitting outside their rooms. He drew near to an older man seated in a wheelchair. Instantly the elderly male reached out and grabbed his coat sleeve. "Mister, mister..."

"What is it?" Hank inquired.

"Help me!" he cried out.

"What can I do for you?"

"Just wheel me outside so that I can get out of this place!" he said with tears pouring down his cheeks. "They won't stop me if you do it!" He looked around to see the other patients rocking back and forth and mumbling to themselves. The pathos of the whole scene around him was charged with a sense of desperation. It made Weldon extremely uncomfortable.

"Now Joe," a nurse announced as she walked down the hall towards them. "You know better than to bother the visitors." Joe's arm dropped into his lap as heavy as his heart that had lost all hope.

Weldon continued until he reached the door marked 516. He looked through the narrow glass window, but the curtain had been pulled so he could not see the person in the bed. Inside, he heard a television. *Is Kaz out of his coma?* Around the curtain of the private room, he saw Kaz lying under the clean white sheets, his eyes closed. The TV program was The Jerry Springer Show, loud enough to have awoken the dead. Hank lowered the volume with the remote.

"Kaz," he called in a low voice. "Kaz, wake up. It's Hank." Titov didn't stir. Placing his hand on his arm, he called a little louder. Nothing. Before he could try again, a woman entered the room. "Mr. Greshnev?" she queried.

Why does she think that I am Max?

"I'm not Mr. Greshnev," he answered.

"Oh, pardon me," she apologized.

"My name is Henry Weldon."

"I see. Are you a family member?"

"No, I'm not. I'm a friend. What's with all the questions?"

"I apologize. I should have introduced myself. My name is Mrs. Uvarov. I'm the supervisor here."

"Has Kaz come out of his coma?"

"I'm sorry to tell you that after a short time of alertness, he has not regained consciousness." Weldon wasn't really surprised by this news.

"Do you always approach the visitors armed with all these questions?"

"Not really, but Mr. Titov's situation is somewhat different than the other patients."

"And why is that?"

"Well, first, you are the only visitor who has come to visit him."

"There's been no one? I'm the first?"

"That's true."

"And what's the second reason his case is unusual."

"A Mr. Greshnev has been paying all his bills." Hank was instantly shocked by this bit of news. "Are they related in some way?"

"He's paying for everything here?"

"Yes, even to the fresh flowers that are delivered every day."

"No, they are not related."

"Mr. Greshnev is certainly a generous friend to Mr. Titov."

"Yeah, generous."

"Well, I'm sorry for disturbing your visit. If you could encourage his family to visit him, I would greatly appreciate it. After all, he may respond to one of their voices."

"You mean he could wake up from this?"

"There is always hope. That's why we leave the television on. I'm going to leave you now. Please talk to him." Mrs. Uvarov turned and left the room.

Weldon turned toward the window and looked outside. Kaz's room faced the front entrance that was lined with trees that would soon be in bloom again. Will Kaz ever be awake to see it? From what he was seeing, the answer was "No".

He saw that Kaz's hair was trimmed and his face cleared of whiskers. *God, he's never looked better!*

Slipping his hand into Kaz's, he said. "Kaz, if you can hear me, squeeze my hand." The patient's hand remained limp. "If you hear my voice do something so that I know you're still in there." The big man remained motionless. "I'm sorry this happened to you, but you should have never been screwing around with Albina especially since she was Max's woman."

"Bean," Kaz suddenly blurted out. "Bean."

"My God, even in this pathetic circumstance, she's still on your mind!"

Kaz became silent and Weldon withdrew his hand. Hank looked once more at his placid face before he left the room.

When Hank returned to the "Holy Trinity", he related what had gone on in Titov's room.

"Has anything changed?" inquired Archie.

"He's still in a coma, but occasionally, he'll say "bean"."

Parrish interjected, "I guess it's hopeless."

"I had a visit from the nursing home supervisor. She was trying to be upbeat about his condition, but from what she was telling me, I think she assumed the same."

"Until he wakes, we can never find out who beat him into unconsciousness. There's no news about that."

"I do have one bit of news," Weldon trumpeted.

"And what's that?" Cass queried.

"Greshnev is paying for everything Titov needs."

"Get out of here!" Cass answered with incredulity.

"Doctors, medication, television, even fresh flowers in his room every day." Parrish inquired, "What's up with that? Has Greshnev suddenly developed a guilty conscious?"

"A guilty conscious?" Archie retorted. "The man has no conscious, guilty or otherwise!"

"Then what could be the reason for his sudden generosity?" contemplated Parrish.

Malone concluded, "He's probably keeping him as a constant reminder of what happens to somebody who dares to cross him."

After a few weeks at the poker table, Hank revealed to the two federal agents, "It's been the same every time I've been there."

"You're still the only one being frisked for a wire? Cassidy Baker questioned.

"Every time." Weldon replied.

"Are you sure the others are not being patted down?"

"I've gotten there before the other three. They're never given the same treatment."

"He still doesn't trust you," acknowledged Archie Malone. "This is not a positive sign."

"I'd say so. What am I supposed to do? Just go on being a part of these poker games for an eternity?"

"We need to shake things up if we are ever going to get the goods on Greshnev," Malone suggested.

"Have you got something in mind?" Cass inquired.

"I'm going to confront Police Chief Kaiser. He'll being wearing the wire now." Parrish was skeptical. "He'll just deny his involvement with Greshnev. It will be his word against yours. We have no proof!"

Archie turned toward Hank. "My proof will be right here!" he said holding up the device.

"But will he consent to wearing the wire?" Baker related.

"He will if he doesn't want to stain his reputation or lose his job!"

"So, you think this will work?" Weldon expressed with some reservation.

"Like a charm!"

"When do we approach him?"

"There's no time like the present."

A quick trip to the 60th precinct in Malone's unmarked car brought them to the front of the building. It was like old home day as Archie was greeted by many of the detectives. Weldon didn't recognize anyone. *Been gone too long, I guess.* Walking up to the sergeant on duty, the police detective was greeted with enthusiasm. "What's up Archie? Slumming today?"

"Not when it comes to you, Sean!"

"You're just full of blarney today, aren't you? Well, how can I help you?"

"I'd like to see Kaiser if he's not too busy." Sean dialed the Police Chief's office and said, "Archie Malone is here to see you."

After hearing the answer, he replied, "Go right in. It was good to see you again Archie."

"The same here."

Archie turned to Hank saying, "You wait outside until I call you in." Weldon nodded his understanding.

Malone entered as Hank stood outside the office close enough to hear their conversation, his back against the wall. "Well, look who's here," the Police Chief stated, shaking Malone's hand. "How the hell have you been?"

"I'm good."

"Sit down." Archie took a seat as Kaiser returned to the chair behind his desk. "How's the family?"

"They're well, and yours?"

"Still going strong. So, to what do I owe your visit to me today?"

"I'm here about Maxim Greshnev." Kaiser continued to smile giving no reaction to Greshnev's name.

"What about him?"

"You already know his reputation for murder as well as being involved in the prostitution racket."

Remaining stone-faced, he replied, "I know."

"For years, we've been trying to get the goods on him with no luck."

"He's a slippery bastard."

"That's been true in the past, but now I think I have a way to entrap him."

"How is that?"

"By catching his confession while someone wears a wire."

"And who would wear the wire?"

Archie paused before he replied. "Why you, of course."

"What are you talking about, Malone?"

"I'm talking about your getting the dirt on him while wearing a wire at his next Tuesday evening poker game."

"I don't understand?" his voice now seemed somewhat strained. "Are you accusing me of having some sort of relationship with that scumbag?"

"That's exactly what I'm saying."

His voice became enraged at this accusation. "You need to get out of here before I put my hands on you!"

"I'm not leaving, but someone else is joining me!"

"And who would that be?"

Getting up from his chair, Malone opened the door saying, "Come in." As Weldon walked in, Kaiser's jaw slackened.

"Who is this supposed to be?"

"You know me," Hank answered.

"I've never seen you before in my life."

"Stop playing games," Malone warned him.

"I've been sitting across from you during Greshnev's poker nights, and I'm prepared to say that in a court of law."

Benjamin Kaiser's resistance suddenly waned in front of the undeniable truth.

"What are you planning on doing about this information?"

"As I said before, you'll be wearing a wire at this Tuesday's game."

"If he knows I'm wearing a wire, he'll have me killed."

The detective shot back, "No chance of that happening since he never has you searched."

Crestfallen, the Police Chief announced, "I guess I don't have any other choice."

"No other choice at all," Hank retorted.

"Once you get the goods on him, then what?"

"You're going to resign from your job as Police Chief."

"What if I refuse to do any of this?"

"Then we go above your head. I might even give this tidbit to the newspapers. Can you just imagine the embarrassment your wife and children will be feeling with the press right outside your front door?"

Taking a deep sigh, he declared, "Fine, I'll cooperate. But what can I use to explain my retirement?"

Malone suggested, "Say you want to spend more time with your family, or that you're getting too old to do the job any longer. Write anything you want. Be creative! I just don't give a damn anymore!"

CHAPTER

17

S IRENS SCREAMED AS police cars drove to the scene of a murder
committed behind The Dive. Detective Malone and his entourage
made their way to the crime scene, the federal agents in one car and
Malone and Weldon in the police detective's vehicle. By the time the four
of them arrived, the bar was already cordoned off with yellow police tape.

A crowd of curiosity seekers were already in the street outside the
watering hole. Archie and the others got out of his car and walked to the
police officers who were outside for crowd control. Flipping open his gold
shield, Archie led the others into the building. Other detectives on the
scene were already taking statements from the patrons inside.

Malone went over to one of the uniformed cops and asked, "What's
going on?"

"Murder. The lead detective is outside in the back of the building."

As they approached the murder scene, they saw the body covered by
a sheet. Malone approached the other detective. "What have you got?"

"A guy named Titov has been iced."

Hank immediately surmised to himself, *It can't be Kaz? Did he just
come out of his coma only to be murdered in this dirty back alley?"*

Archie bent over to lift the sheet. Sprawled on the ground was Ivan,
Kaz's cousin. Ivan's eyes were wide open with an expression of terror on
his face. He looked as if he had been caught totally by surprise by someone
lurking in the shadows. The method of the killing was immediately
recognized. Sticking out of his chest was an ice pick, but it was what was
between chest and ice pick that really caught all their attention. A snapshot
of the bartender smiling was pierced through it.

Scrawled in what looked like a red marking pen was the phrase, *"Smile,
you're dead."*

Again, Hank realized it was a turn of phrase that he used when capturing a spouse's infidelity caught on camera, *"Smile, you're caught."*

The lead detective started to speak. "It seems that he was surprised by the murderer when he went out to throw trash into the garbage pails." Weldon was made aware of a dumpster in the back, as well as an overturned pail with garbage strewn all around the body.

"Any clues?" Cassidy queried.

"Right now, we're still dusting for fingerprints. I'm waiting for the forensic experts to dust the hilt of the ice pick, but as of now, we have nothing."

"Was this Greshnev's doing?" questioned Parrish.

"It might be," answered Malone. "but it could also be anything from a disagreement with a patron to a simple attempt at robbery."

All four men went back inside to question one of the detectives. "What can you tell me about the customers in here? Anybody see anything?"

Detective Malone solicited. "A lot of the people are in different stages of inebriation from what we can gather."

"Nobody saw or heard anything?"

"We asked them whether any of the customers tonight had a beef with him. There was no problem that anyone could surmise with any patron this evening; nothing that wasn't out of the ordinary."

"What is that supposed to mean?"

"There were a couple of people that he cut off when they got a bit boisterous."

"How did he handle it?"

"He tossed them out of the bar."

"You've got names?" The detective checked his notepad.

"Vladimir and Stanislav Romanowski."

"Brothers?"

"It seems that way."

"Find out where they are and question them. See if they have any connection to Maxim Greshnev."

"Somebody's on that already."

"Did anybody hear a commotion outside?"

"A few of them saw the victim leave with a trash pail but heard nothing after he left."

"Get back to me when you find anything out."

"Yes, sir."

The four men moved back to Malone's white Toyota Corolla where they stood talking. "Do you think this is Greshnev's doing?" Weldon questioned.

"I wouldn't be surprised by that. He has his fingers in almost everything in almost every dirty thing that goes on in Brighton Beach."

"This guy seems to get away with anything," commented Cass.

Archie took umbrage to this remark. "What is that supposed to mean?"

"Just a thought. Nothing more."

"Are you implying the police are too incompetent to pin crimes on Greshnev?"

"Well," Parrish began, "he does have the Police Chief in his back pocket. Who knows how many other cops he has seduced with money."

"I will not have you smear this department based on the sellout of one traitorous police official!"

"I didn't mean anything like that by the remark."

"Sorry guys," apologized Archie. "I guess this latest murder just set me off."

"Forget it," Cass dismissed the apology. "We all have that kind of day. We'll see you in the morning."

"See you then," remarked Cass as the two federal agents walked back to Baker's car.

"So, you think that Greshnev is responsible for Ivan's death?" remarked Hank.

"I'd bet my life on it."

"Do you suppose Kaiser went back to Max to reveal what we are planning to do?"

"I doubt it. I am having Kaiser shadowed and we've had all his phones bugged. If he had any contact with Greshnev since we met, I'd have knowledge of it."

"Can you drive me back to my apartment?"

"Get in."

As they drove away, Malone asked, "You saw what was written on the photograph stuck in to Titov's body?"

"Yeah, "Smile, you're dead!"

"We found a similar picture in Kaz's room. It was a photograph of Albina Lukashenko."

"I know, Kaz showed it to me before he was beaten." Hank did not mention the argument he had gotten into with the Russian mobster.

"Kaz worked for you?" Malone inquired from Hank.

"Sometimes, when I was working on more than one case."

"Isn't "Smile, you're caught" your catchphrase when you trap your adulterer?"

"I've been using it for years."

"It's a real coincidence, don't you think?"

"I'm detecting a certain vibe from you. Are you accusing me of having something to do with these murders?"

"Not at all. I'm just saying that it's a strange coincidence."

"It's strange alright." The rest of the way to Weldon's apartment, the two men remained silent.

The body was driven to the Coroner's Office where the cadaver was thoroughly examined, while forensics examined the ice pick for any trace evidence. Both reports came back with nothing that would help the case. Word on the street however, was that someone in Greshnev's employ was sent to shut the barkeep's mouth about his cousin. There was no proof, but everyone pointed in Maxim's direction.

Immediately, Police Chief Benjamin Kaiser contacted Malone. Archie put the call on loudspeaker, so the others could hear the conversation.

The Police Chief began his rant. "I'm having second thoughts about tonight!" the police official stammered into the phone. "If he finds out I'm wearing a wire, I'm the next body on the coroner's table!"

"Listen, Kaiser!" shot back Malone without the respect of talking to a higher official. "You're not going to back out of this!"

"I tell you Greshnev is going to suspect something if I start questioning him!"

"Not if you do what we've been telling you. You better show up there tonight or I'll personally hand you over to Greshnev."

"I didn't say I wouldn't do it," he answered in a placating manner.

"I expect to see you at Weldon's apartment at 7:30. Don't be late and be prepared for us to go over the tactics you use on Greshnev."

"Again?"

"We'll keep going over it until you can repeat them in your sleep."

"Alright."

"Don't forget, if you don't show up, I'm going straight to the papers with your crimes."

"I've been thinking…"

"What do you want?"

"I want my family and me to be put into the Federal Witness Protection Program." Cass replied, "Get the job done and the government will accommodate you."

"Now, I want this understood. I don't want to be placed in some backwoods area. I want…

"Listen, Kaiser!" fired back Parrish. "You're not in any position to make demands! You'll go where we send you!"

"Fine!" he replied like a petulant child.

Hanging up, Archie said to the others. "It looks like a go tonight."

Weldon wondered out loud, "Do you think he'll go through with it?"

"He better if he knows what's good for him!" Baker replied brusquely.

The darkness of evening fell, cooling the air and giving it a chilly bite. The men waited for the arrival of their patsy. Jerry was there checking the equipment, his surveillance van parked outside by the curb. Right on time, Chief Kaiser arrived, his skin color a little ashen despite the bitter coldness outside. "Well, I'm here!" he announced.

"Good! Now take off your coat and shirt." The white-haired, potbellied city official stripped himself to the waist. Jerry began to fit the wire on him.

"We want you to bring up Ivan Titov's name and watch for Greshnev's reaction."

"You don't think he's just going to come out and admit it, do you?" Kaiser replied,

"He's not stupid."

"That's why you're going to wait until the game breaks up and everyone else is gone for the evening before you broach the subject."

"Will Weldon be with me when I talk to him?" Malone replied,

"Weldon is not close enough for Maxim to reveal anything. We've learned that over the last few months." The news that he was going to have to fly solo, raised Kaiser's heartbeat.

Jerry interrupted saying, "This guy's sweating like a pig!" Cass placed his hand on the official's shoulder to calm him down.

"You can do this." Cass's soothing voice seemed to do the trick. Immediately, Kaiser's pulse began to slow down. Kaiser answered, "Okay."

"Don't get sloppy drunk tonight and screw up. I'll be only too glad to stand on the side and watch one of Greshnev's apes do away with you. I wonder what method he'll use after shooting, drowning, and ice picking the last three?"

"I'm not going to wind up as another one of his victims!" Once more, Jerry checked the equipment. He gave a hand signal that everything was a go.

"Just keep that in mind," Parrish added, "And you'll do just fine."

Archie Malone piped in after he was dressed, "You go now. Hank will follow in a little while."

"I've got it."

"Good, then get started."

After he had departed, Malone turned to Hank. "Watch Kaiser closely tonight. See to it that he doesn't deviate from the strategy."

"Alright."

Ten minutes after Kaiser left, Weldon was sent on his way.

Jerry drove the three men to a parking spot not too far from the Greshnev's cat house. Jerry joined the others at the back of the vehicle. Turning on a few switches, he put the earphones on and listened. "As clear as a bell," he announced to the relief of the others.

As usual, the dour-faced Serge greeted each invited guest. Like the other two city officials, Kaiser was let in without a frisking. That was reserved for Hank. Jerry turned on the intercom so they all could hear the conversation. After 15 minutes of prosaic discussion, Maxim entered the room and the poker game got started.

The dialogue ranged from women to money, punctuated from time to time with card play and the triumphant sound of voices as different men won the pot. The four men in the van sat back and waited. They anticipated that it was going to be a long night.

Three and a half hours later, the group agreed to call it quits. Hank joined the others in the van and listened in. Jerry alerted the others that the moment of truth was about to occur.

"I hope he doesn't lose his nerve," Cass Baker voiced to the others.

"He better play it cool!" replied Malone.

Kaiser's voice came in loud and clear. "Max, can I talk to you for a minute?"

"It's late. Can this wait for tomorrow?" Everyone in the van held their breaths.

Once more, the Police Chief's voice was heard. "I was just wondering if you knew anything about Ivan Titov's death."

"Well, I heard that the Romanowski brothers are being investigated for the murder."

"I know."

"The rumor is that Ivan threw them out of the bar and one or both decided that was an insult they weren't going to let him get away with it."

Are the Romanowski brothers on your payroll?"

"Those pea brains? Please, give me a break! I wouldn't trust them as far as I could throw them!"

"So, you didn't order a hit on Ivan?"

"Why would I do that?" the crime boss queried. "And by the way, why are you so curious about this?"

"If Ivan were talking about the situation with his cousin, I would think that it would perhaps be a reason to permanently shut his mouth."

"Ivan knew better then to cross me."

"Okay."

Kaiser was about to leave when Greshnev stopped him. "Why do you have all these questions about Titov?"

"I just wanted to have a head's up when this case comes across my desk. I just wanted you to know that I have your back."

"I pay you enough not to have to worry about that," snarled a peeved Max. "You would be foolish to forget that, you know what I mean?"

"I'm sorry."

Greshnev tersely replied, "Don't ever bring this up to me again! Goodnight!"

###

They all met back at Weldon's place, disappointment etched in each of their faces. As soon as Kaiser marched through the door, Jerry began to take the equipment from the Police Chief's body.

"Damn it!" Malone cursed. "We've got nothing!"

"You heard me," explained Ben. "You heard me ask him directly if he had Titov rubbed out!"

Parrish responded, "We heard!"

"I said everything I could to get him to admit that he was responsible for Ivan's death!"

"I know," Archie replied.

"You know," Kaiser said as an aside, "there may be something you haven't thought of until now."

"And that would be…" answered Baker with sarcasm.

"Maybe, just maybe, Greshnev is telling the truth. Perhaps he did not have anything to do with these murders."

"Yeah, right!" was Parrish's reaction to that declaration.

"Are you kidding me?" reacted Cassidy.

"Well, I mean, it could be a possibility."

"Are you naïve or just stupid!" Malone shouted with irritation. "All three murders lead directly back to him. There is no mistaking that! He needs to be brought down before another person winds up in Potter's Field!"

Kaiser speedily buttoned up his shirt adding, "Well, there's nothing more I can do."

"We're not done with you, Kaiser."

"I've tried every way I could!"

"Not yet!"

"What do you mean?"

"You're going back next Tuesday, wired up of course, and try and get him to divulge his involvement with the other murders."

"You're out of your mind! You must have heard him threaten me, and he was not kidding. If I ask him again, I'm as good as dead!"

"I wonder how your wife and children will react to the news that you've been on the take from Greshnev all these years?"

"You won't do that!" Ben Kaiser reacted, panic in his voice and on his face. "I did everything I could to get him to admit his guilt!"

Cass retorted, "We're not finished with you until we catch him in an admission."

"He'll never admit to it!" Kaiser cried trying to wriggle off the hook like a trout that was being reeled in. "It's apparent that he doesn't trust me enough!"

"Until we find someone he will admit it to, you're our man."

"Give me a break!"

"You want a break," queried Malone. "Your break should have been the time Greshnev approached with a bribe and you could have said "no", but you were too greedy, too dazzled by what Greshnev offered you. You took the wrong fork in the road. Now it's too late to turn back."

Kaiser seemed to deflate before the four of them. "Fine, I'll keep doing it."

"And don't go back to your friend telling him what we have been trying to do," added Hank. "That would be a huge mistake on your part."

Malone piped up. "Yeah, especially if he were to find out you had a wire on your body when you played poker!"

"I'll do what you want." The Police Chief was resigned to his fate.

"Now go home and act normal. Pretend that each day is just like the days before we approached you."

"I'll try."

"You better make it convincing or else you'll be a goner."

With reservations, Kaiser walked dejectedly from the apartment.

"Do you think he'll be able to keep it together?" Weldon wondered out loud.

"He kept the charade going tonight. There's no reason to think that he will fall apart now," Parrish added confidently.

"I wish we could be sure," Hank responded. "After all, when we put this much pressure on Kurkov, he put a gun to his head and blew out his brains."

Malone answered, "Kaiser is no Kurkov!

He's not walking around harboring a death wish," Parrish remarked.

"Perhaps we're pushing the screws in him too tight," Hank noted.

"He'll do as he's told. I have no doubt in that," observed Cass.

Inwardly, Hank asserted, I wish I could be just as sure.

###

For Henry Weldon, the fact that there was nothing new in the search for Renata left him desolate. He couldn't help going back to the Russian Doll House and look once more on the board of feminine delicacies the establishment had to offer. Each time he was sorely disappointed to find that her image was not up on the board with the other girls. Hank knew that if he mentioned Renata, he would no longer be welcomed at the whore house. At least there he felt closer to her then any other place of which he could think.

The "smiling" face of Serge Sokoloff greeted him each time. "So, you're back?"

"Yeah, you got a problem with that?"

"As long as you obey Zoya's rules, you are welcome." Hank's eyes scanned the board. *Renata's still not up there.*

"I won't do anything to upset Zoya."

"Smart boy! So, who do you want?"

"I guess I'll go with Nonna again."

"Pay the cashier." As Weldon gave up his cash, Serge pressed a button that told Nonna to be prepared for a visitor.

Hank walked back to Serge, and the door guard said, "Go right down. She's expecting you."

"Come in!" Nonna sat on the end of the bed in a pink sheer negligee, her legs crossed. "It's so lovely to see you again, lover!"

"It's good to see you too," he answered with little enthusiasm. Nonna rose from the bed. The sheerness of the garment showed off her young, nubile body. Despite himself, Weldon reacted sexually.

"I can see that you're glad to see me." Weldon looked down at how his engorged member was pressing against his pants. He couldn't help his response even though he longed to be with Renata.

"I. I don't know…"

"Sssh!" she replied putting her index finger against her full, red lips. "Let me wipe away all the doubt in your mind. For now, it's only you and me."

Weldon allowed himself to go with that feeling. It had been so long since he had shared his bed with someone he loved, and it didn't make any difference anymore. *I just want to forget about everything!*

CHAPTER

18

I T WAS TIME to get back to work. Hank Weldon had let his business slide for months, but now dwindling finances dictated that he get back to what he was good at - spying on other people. Some of his clients had taken their business elsewhere while the private detective was distracted by murder and trying to re-connect with Renata. It had all been a colossal waste of time and effort.

He threw open his door to let potential clients know that he was back in business. Like swallows making their way to Capistrano, they poured in. Whinny wives and outraged husbands came to Hank to ask for help in their supposed marital betrayals.

A Mrs. Irina Petrov arrived at his office as he was unlocking his door. She had a handkerchief in hand and was blubbering. "Mr. Weldon?"

"Yes."

"The private detective?"

"That's me."

"I want to hire you."

"Come right in."

Weldon gave her the once over. *Attractive, late 30's early 40's I would say, and well dressed.* "So, how can I help you, Mrs. ..."

"Irina Petrov."

"How can I help you, Mrs. Petrov?" At this the woman cried hysterically holding the white linen hanky to her face. Placing his hand on her shoulder to comfort her, Weldon said, "I know this must be difficult, but you'll have to talk to me."

"Yes, yes, of course," she sniffled to a stop. "I'm so sorry."

"Is this about your husband?"

"Yes, it is. I believe that he's been cheating on me."

"What's his name?"

"Vanya, we've been married 17 years."

"I have to tell you Mrs. Petrov that after several years, husbands sometimes lose the desire for a sexual relationship with their wives."

"I understand that, but I believe that he has been seeing his secretary Anfisa Losevsky."

"I see. What makes you believe that?"

"He comes home late from work and he's intoxicated. I've seen lipstick on his collar and the scent of a woman's perfume that is not mine on his jacket. Besides, a wife knows when her man is stepping out on her."

"Okay."

"I want you to follow him and catch him in the act so that I have the proof of his indiscretions that I need to divorce him."

Reaching to the upper draw of his desk, he pulled out a standard contract. After going over the details to which she agreed, Irina signed on the dotted line. "I will need a deposit," Hank informed her.

"How much? Money is no object." Weldon's brain quickly calculated.

"Let's say $250?" He waited for her reply, but it didn't take long to come. Opening her purse, she brought out a roll of bills that were held together with a rubber band. Peeling off a couple of bills as if she were stripping layers off an onion, she deposited it on Weldon's desk. He dropped it in the drawer and locked it shut. Hank continued with his questions.

"What business is your husband in?"

"He's an importer-exporter dealing in Russian antiquities. *No wonder she goes around with a roll of bills that could choke a horse in her handbag.*

"I see, and where is his place of business?"

Irina opened her purse, and withdrew a business card. Hank recognized the name of the street located uptown on the eastside of Manhattan in one of the posh neighborhoods.

"May I ask you for your phone number and address?" Quickly, he jotted down the pertinent information.

"I will get back to you within a few days to give you the status of my investigation." Mrs. Petrov stood, extending her hand to the detective. "Thank you so much for your assistance," and she walked out of his office.

This could prove to be quite a monetary jackpot!

He usually handled this kind of high-class customer himself, leaving local cases in Brooklyn to Kaz who was much more familiar with Russians. He could no longer depend on his partner to do that. Every case would fall exclusively onto his shoulders.

Checking his image in the mirror, he decided that he looked enough like a collector to go to Vanya's place of business, "Petrov's Fine China and Furnishings". Taking the subway into Manhattan, he waved over a taxi and gave the driver the address.

After fighting the noon traffic for a time, the taxi pulled up to the destination. The store was one of many in which antiques of the world were offered to the discerning collector of fine objects d'art. He took note of the variety of luxury items on display in the windows. Two employees, a man and a woman, stood behind display counters. Inside, a middle-aged man came over to him. "Good day, sir. Are you looking for something special?"

"I'm interested in purchasing a silver Rococo candelabra." The gentleman behind the counter looked at him with skepticism. "Don't let my appearance fool you. I'm a serious collector."

"Yes, sir. This way." The employee led him to a display case.

"As you can see we have a variety of them. Did you have something specific in mind?"

"That one," Hank indicated pointing to a 19th century two-light candelabra. Gently, the employee lifted it so Hank could have a better look.

"And the price?"

"Fourteen thousand dollars."

"Put it away," Hank said as if it was offending his eyes. "I'm interested in one made for the Romanoff family before the revolution."

"I'm not sure…"

"Where is the owner of this establishment?"

"I will get him, sir."

Weldon waited for the proprietor to show his face. In a few minutes, a balding man, a bit on the plump side but meticulously dressed, emerged. *He seems to have indulged in too much champagne and caviar.*

"May I help you, sir?"

"Yes, I'm interested in purchasing a pre-revolution silver candelabra."

Vanya Petrov snickered to himself. "I don't have what you're looking for, but if I did it would cost you a small fortune."

"I have a fortune to spend," Weldon answered nonchalantly.

Petrov stopped snickering. "Your name is…?"

"Harold Wilhelm the Third". He sometimes used this persona when dealing with moneyed clients. "I was assured by one of your other customers that you could get me what I've been looking for."

"And who would that be?"

"She wishes to remain anonymous."

"I understand. Let me talk to my secretary and tell her to ask around." He rang a buzzer under the cash register and a wispy brunette in her twenties emerged from the back. "Miss Losevsky", this is Mr. Wilhelm."

One look at her fetching face and curvy body and he thought to himself, it's no wonder he's banging her!

"How do you do?" she replied sweetly. *Just fine since I've met you!*

"My pleasure!"

"Will you check with my contacts and see about a silver Rococo, pre-revolutionary Romanoff candelabra."

"Right away, Mr. Petrov." *I'm sure she doesn't call him Mr. Petrov when he's got her in the missionary position, her milk white thighs draped over his shoulders.* Anifa Losevswky went off to make some phone calls.

"May I have your card so that I can reach you?" asked Vanya.

"There's no need. I will stop back tomorrow." Before Petrov could answer, Weldon was out the door.

###

The private detective had taken up surveillance of the antiques store at a coffee shop across the street. He ordered a black coffee while he sat and waited with both eyes fixated on Petrov's Fine China and Furnishings.

Hours ticked by with only customers or window shoppers coming and going into the antique store. At last, the light grew dim as the daylight faded. First, the female employee left for the day and was followed by the man who had originally waited on him in the store. It wasn't too long before employer and secretary emerged together.

Hank rose from his chair, put some cash on the table and left the building. While Vanya locked the store door, Anifa hailed a cab. Quickly, Weldon hailed his own cab, and instructed his driver, "Follow that cab that's across the street."

"You got it!" the cabbie enthusiastically answered. Making an illegal U-turn, Weldon's cab driver began to tail the couples taxi.

Zipping in and out of traffic like a speed demon, the cab driver never lost sight of the other vehicle. Entering Washington Square in Greenwich Village, the cab pulled up to a brownstone a block away. Petrov and Losavsky got out of the car and walked up the steps to the brown wooden door. Mr. Petrov had paid the driver, and Hank quickly paid for his taxi. "Any time you need someone followed," the cabbie said with a broad smile on his face, "just give me a call," he said handing him his business card.

Hank walked into the lobby. The two lovers had already gone up in the elevator. Weldon checked the mailboxes until he came to one that read, Losevsky - 2B. Taking the elevator, he got off on the second floor, went straight to the window at the end of the hall, and opened it to the fire escape.

With the agility of a monkey, Weldon climbed up the stairs, peering cautiously into every apartment window until he located the couple he had been tailing. They stood in the bedroom kissing passionately like long-separated lovers.

He squeezed himself into the corner of the fire escape landing, biding his time until the two were in the act of making love. Hank surmised by their feverish kissing that it would not take too long before the two were undressed and in her bed. He slipped the camera from the pocket of his coat. The detective waited, counting to himself. Guardedly, he crawled to the window and got an eyeful.

Anifa's voluptuous body was on top of the uncovered bed, while Vanya stood by her, wearing only his boxers. She raised her arms up to him as an invitation, which Petrov immediately accepted, dropping his underwear around his ankles. Weldon could see that he was fully engorged. They were both too distracted to notice the "peeper" at the window.

Climbing on top of her, Vanya kissed her along the neck, his left hand fondling her breasts. The moment of truth at last arrived. Petrov entered her as Anifa moaned. Lifting her shapely legs onto his shoulders, Petrov rocked back and forth, slowly at first then with ever increasing exhilaration.

Hank focused his camera and took a couple of shots. Anifa caught sight of him outside her window and screamed, "Vanya look!" Pulling out, Petrov rumbled, "What the hell!", as he fumbled to pull up his drawers. Weldon yelled, "Smile, I caught you!"

It was at that specific moment that a comprehension came to him. *My God, someone is trying to frame me for Kaz's injuries and the three murders!* Frozen in motion, Weldon didn't realize that Petro was throwing the window open. He grabbed Hank's coat lapels, and screeched, "Give me that camera, you pervert!" Ripping his jacket from the madman's grip, Weldon scurried down the fire escape.

"Your wife will be very interested in these candid shots of you and your girlfriend!"

"Come back here, you bastard!" By that time, the gumshoe had already hit the pavement and was running down the street.

He stopped at the corner and looked back. Taking a well-deserved breather, he reassured himself. *It doesn't seem that I'm being followed.* He continued to walk until he got to the subway station and disappeared below the teeming mass of humanity that now walked above him.

Hank waited with the other commuters along the walkway, the dim lighting irritating his eyes, and the vile odor affronting his nostrils. The brakes of the train were applied as soon as it materialized in the tunnel. The crowd of tired workers trying to get home, bunched closer together in front of the doors that slid open. The passengers trying to get off had to fight their way out, as the incoming commuters scrambled to get to empty seats. Jostling with his elbow, Hank realized he was too late to get a seat, and he hung on to the strap above his head.

In the cramped subway car, which jerked the passengers back and forth, Weldon found the time for some introspective. *I never took it seriously before, but the words scribbled on the photographs of the murder victims is suspiciously close to a phrase I use when I catch cheating spouses in the act of infidelity. Smile, I caught you, and Smile you're dead are too much alike for it to be a coincidence. Is someone setting me up for a fall?* Weldon could hardly believe it. *Who would hate me so much that they would try to pin these murders on me?*

Hank mentally went over a list of people to figure out potential enemies. Within his close circle of friends, he couldn't think of anyone who would detest him that much, but when he thought of the list of people caught in the act of their unfaithfulness, the list of names seemed to stretch into eternity. He felt that he should discuss this with Malone as soon as possible. *After all, a guilty man would never mention it to the police. I can trust Archie with this information, can't I?* He would soon find out if that were true.

###

Malone phoned Hank Weldon one morning saying, "I want to talk to you."

"Do you have a lead on the murderer?"

"We'll talk in my car."

It wasn't long before Archie pulled up to the curb in front of Weldon's apartment. Hank left the building and joined the detective in the car.

This is an unusual place for our meeting. Where are Baker and Wilson?"

"What I have to tell you is for your ears only."

"So, spill it," said Hank with growing curiosity.

"The first bit of news has come as quite a shock."

Hank was intrigued by this remark. "What news?"

'"Police Chief Kaiser is reported missing."

"Missing? I thought you had a tail on him."

"I did."

"Then what happened?"

"Kaiser went into the lobby of the Municipal Building and pushed the elevator button. For some reason, in the crunch of people getting on, the cop lost him."

"Maybe he went back home."

"Checked his house and his wife claims he left for work hours ago. The thing is, she didn't seem upset by the news."

"Then she must know where he is."

"If she does, she's not talking."

"What could have happened for him to decide to make a run for it?"

"I would think it was the pressure we were putting on him to bring up Kaz or Ivan's name again to Greshnev."

"That's a real possibility."

"Greshnev warned him to never bring up the topic to him again."

"So, what happens to the Tuesday night poker game?"

"There's no point in your going anymore. The fact that he's still having you frisked tells me that he will never trust you, so you have to find an excuse to bow out."

"I'm not sorry to tell you that I'm glad that my participation in the game is over."

"There's something else you need to know." I've gotten some information about Renata."

Weldon held his breath. "Is it bad news?"

"Well, it depends on how you look at it."

"What's going on?"

"She's not dead."

"Thank God! Where is she?"

"That's the bad news."

"Tell me already," he answered with increased apprehension."

"Greshnev had her shipped back to Moscow."

"She's gone for good?"

"At least she's still alive."

"I suppose Greshnev thought that another murder would be too hard for him to explain."

"I guess so."

"There's another thing I need to speak to you about. Kaiser may have been right."

"About what?"

"We may be barking up the wrong tree when it comes to Greshnev's involvement with the killings."

"What makes you say that?"

"We've come at that bastard at different angles and he always comes up clean."

"So, are you saying that you're not going to pursue these cases?"

"No, we're just going to look in a new direction."

"You've got another lead? What is it?"

"Did you have an argument with Kaz before his attempted murder?"

"I wouldn't say it was an argument. Kaz was in a rage because he wanted me to find Albina Lukashenko, but she was murdered before I could get to her. Say, what are you getting at?"

"Did you have a relationship with her?" he asked ignoring Weldon's inquiry.

"I paid for her service a couple of times. I wouldn't call it a relationship."

"Did Kaz find out about that?"

"I wouldn't know. What's this all about?"

"You're still using the phrase, "Smile, I caught you!" when you photograph cheating spouses, aren't you.?

"It could be that someone is trying to pin these murders on me."

"Is that what you've concluded."

"Why? Don't you think it's possible?"

"Anything's possible."

"Why are you being so noncommittal?"

"I've just been thinking."

"Thinking what?" Hank demanded with an edge in his voice.

"I just think this is all too pat to be a coincidence

"Are you accusing me?"

"Did Ivan have the knowledge of who beat Kaz to a pulp?"

"How the hell would I know," Weldon shouted in rage.

"It's just very interesting, don't you think?"

"Look," Weldon began. "We've known each other since we both entered the police academy."

"I know that."

"What I'm trying to say is that you know me. How could you think I could ever commit murder?"

"I thought I knew you. Now, I'm not really sure."

"Come on! You know me. I'm not capable of murder."

"I'm beginning to wonder if I ever knew you at all."

"What is that supposed to mean?"

"When you started drinking, your personality changed. Just look how far you have fallen. You let your wife and child's deaths lead you down a destructive path, and you're still on it."

"You can't know what I've been through!"

Archie raised his tone of voice. "How many more years are you going to allow yourself to wallow in your self-pity? Grow a pair and take it like a man!"

Hank opened the car door and exited. Before he slammed the door, he screamed, "You can go to hell!"

CHAPTER

19

I T WAS LIKE watching his world slowly collapse around him and he was unable to prevent it from happening. *I can't believe Archie would think that I was a suspect in these murders. I could use a drink right now!* The Dive was the last place he wanted to be found now. He didn't need to have his brain pickled in alcohol. What he needed were clear faculties if he was to discover who was out to get him convicted of murder. *God, I wish I had a scotch and soda right now. Stop it! That's what's gotten you in this mess. I have no one to turn to since Archie suspects me. I could have a conversation with Kaz, but in his condition, he wouldn't be of any help at all.*

But he did need some sort of distraction. Something that could take him far away from his situation, even if it were just for half an hour. *Nonna! I'm always in a better mood after I've seen her.*

The midafternoon had the scent of Spring, along with the aroma of a mixture of Pelmeni (meat stuffed dough) and Shashlyk (grilled marinated meat on a skewer) from the local restaurants in preparation of evening meals.

He drove to the Russian bordello and parked nearby. He strolled to the front door and rang the bell. *I might as well tell Greshnev that I won't be attending his poker games any more.*

The smiling face of Serge Sokoloff greeted him. "Oh, it's you?" he ridiculed.

"I'm glad to see you too." *What's new laughing boy?*

"Are you here to see Nonna again?"

"That's right, but before I do, I have to speak to your boss."

"He can't see you now. He's in a meeting and doesn't want to be disturbed."

"It will only take a minute."

"Are you deaf? I told you he's in a meeting. Tell me what you want, and I'll see that he gets the message."

"Tell him that I won't be attending his poker games anymore."

"I'm sure he'll be all broken up when he hears the news!" Sokoloff scoffed. "There'll be no way anyone could comfort him." Sokoloff broke into riotous laughter.

"I'm here to see Nonna." he reminded his disdainer.

"Go pay!" Serge barely got out of the way before he broke out in laughter again. He laid his cash on the counter, and passed the big man as he went down the hallway. The sound of Sokoloff's amusement followed him.

Knocking on the door, he heard Nonna's voice asking him to come in.

She was simply stunning, dressed in a Mandarin-style turquoise robe with an oriental print of flourishing cherry blossoms on branches. Her blonde hair was cascading over her shoulders. It was enough to have him catch his breath. Hank couldn't help himself when his body rose to the occasion.

"I'm happy to see you too," Nonna greeted him in English with a faint Russian accent. Weldon allowed himself to enjoy the moment without any guilt. *I mean, I tried to save Renata. Her deportation to Russia can't be laid at my doorstep.*

"I'm happy to see you too, Nonna!"

She let her robe slide down her smooth body until it lay crumpled at her feet. Weldon stood drinking her sensuous image into his eyes. It was as intoxicating as any drink of hard liquor.

"What are you waiting for, lover?" Hank couldn't think of a reasonable response, so he stripped down to his skivvies. "I want you right now!"

"Well, I'm right here. Come and get me." Without a second thought, Hank dropped his draws and walked over to her. They both fell to the bed as Hank took his place on top of her.

"Take me, *golubuska*," she purred like a kitty. "For now, I am all yours." The rhythm of their bodies started out slowly but rapidly picked up the tempo. It wasn't long before the two of them lay side by side breathing heavily.

"Tell me truthfully, Nonna. Do you think that I could ever commit a murder?"

"You, *lyubov moya*? Don't be crazy. You wouldn't hurt a fly, would you?"

"Not if I could help it. In my line of business however, a person can make a lot of enemies." Sitting up she said,

"I'm sure you do, but do you think that any of them would intentionally do you any harm?"

"I'm beginning to believe that one of them would."

"What are you worried about, Hank?" It was the first time she had used his name instead of "lover".

They conversed a little while longer until a knock was heard at the door. It was a signal that the client's time was up. "I'm sorry Hank, but it looks like our time together is over for now."

Giving Nonna a peck on the cheek, he stated, "Well, thanks for listening to me."

"Any time," he heard her reply before he finished dressing and closed the door.

Serge was still stationed, like a statue, by the front door. "Well lover" he began as Weldon came into earshot, "did you have a good time?"

"What's your problem with me?" Weldon shot back at him. Shrugging, the big man stated,

"I just don't like you."

"And why is that?"

"You earn your living as a Peeping Tom."

"It's an honest living."

"You stick your nose into other people's business, a place that you don't belong!"

"What's the matter," mocked Hank. "Are you afraid that one day I'll catch you with your pants down?" As soon as he said it, Hank knew he had miscalculated. Sokoloff went off like Mount Vesuvius.

"Listen, you little worm!" he yelled grabbing his neck in a vise-like grip. "I could crush your larynx without much effort and nobody would ever miss you!" Serge did not seem to want to let go. Weldon beat him with his fists, but the guard did not flinch. Weldon began to feel as if he were going to lose consciousness. Suddenly, the giant released him. Hank fell to the floor gasping for air.

After a minute, he began to return to breathing regularly. "What's wrong with you? Are you crazy?"

Serge laughed. "Yes, I'm crazy. So, you'd better not make me angry at you. I could have easily finished the job."

Weldon knew he was right.

All at once, an idea flashed in his head. "How would you like to be my bodyguard?"

Sokoloff stared at him with disbelief. "Maybe you're the crazy one."

"Listen, I figured out that someone is trying to pin a crime on me."

"On you? Don't make me laugh!"

"I mean it, and I'll make it worth your time."

Sokoloff stared at him silently. "How much, big spender?"

"Fifty dollars a day?"

"Don't waste my time!"

Hank realized that he had no shot at making the Russian his bodyguard. As he walked out of the bordello the thought, *I'm no better off than I was before. I'm really on my own!*

Hank was busier than he had ever been. The line of people looking for proof against a cheating spouse seemed never ending. He became so busy that he did something he had never done before. He soon started turning potential clients away.

In a way, being busy helped him forget his current problem, but he kept a wary eye open for likely enemies. He soon came to the realization that he needed help. He was forced to admit that he needed Archie Malone's expertise, but first he had to win him over. After their last talk, he did not know what kind of reception he would get from the detective. The next day, he made his way to the precinct, where a plump desk sergeant sat. "What's up?" he asked with cool indifference.

"I'd like to talk with Detective Malone."

"And who might you be?"

"I'm Hank Weldon."

Picking up the telephone, the sergeant rang a number. "Sorry to bother you, but there's a Hank Weldon out here to see you." Nodding his head, the cop said, "Interrogation room 3. Go to the right…"

"I know where it is."

He passed the first two interrogation rooms which were both occupied by a detective and a suspect. Arriving at the next room, Weldon saw the "Holy Trinity" in conference. All three looked up at his entrance. None of them said a word. Their stares felt like laser beams of death to his head.

"Archie," he began, "I need to speak to you."

"You can speak in front of Cass and Parrish." He wasn't going to give him a break. Archie was playing hardnose. He must have already informed them about our last conversation.

"About our last talk, I came to clear things up. I want to assure you that I'm no murderer."

"I know that."

"You do?"

"I know it because the photos and your catchphrase are just too hard to believe. It's a little too obvious."

"But, the things you said to me…"

"You have changed from when I first met you, but you're not a killer."

"You don't know how happy I am to hear you say that."

"Sit down. We're going to try a different tactic with Greshnev."

"We're thinking of charging Greshnev with tax evasion," revealed Parrish Wilson.

"You mean like Al Capone?"

"Exactly!" Malone emphatically agreed.

"But what about the murders. Is he going to get away with that?"

"We've shined a spotlight in every one of his dirty businesses, but we've come up with nothing," Cassidy Baker declared.

"What about the fact that three murders are pointing to me."

Parrish noted, "We've figured out that he may be trying to set you up for a fall."

"Once he's convicted and incarcerated, the threat against you will end," added Cass.

"I don't know…" Weldon interjected. "He has a long arm outside of prison walls."

"This is the only way we can get him off the street," Archie informed him. "The longer he's out, the more bodies will pile up."

"So, what's been done so far?"

"We've contacted the Treasury Department, which is going over their records." added Malone. "A new member will be joining the team. Special FBI Agent Emma Fedosov.

"A woman?" Weldon inquired with disbelief.

Archie answered, "Not just any woman. She's one of the Treasury Department's top agents with over 10 years of experience."

"Besides, her grandparents were Russian and she speaks the language fluently," spoke up Parrish.

"What will she be doing?"

Archie Malone informed him, "She's going undercover in the Russian Doll House."

"You mean as a prostitute?"

"She has the look that Greshnev is drawn to," Cass made it known.

"Tall, statuesque, and a redhead. She's the right bait to catch our big fish," laughed Parrish.

"When does she arrive?"

"Tomorrow morning," Malone replied. "After a preliminary meeting, she'll be introduced to Maxim by a federal undercover agent who is part of Greshnev's inner circle."

"Wow," exclaimed Weldon. "This is some operation. Who's on the inside?"

"That's something that can't be revealed," warned Cass. *They've kept this information from me from the very beginning! It's obvious that the "Holy Trinity" doesn't fully trust me.*

"Watch your back," Malone counseled him. "Greshnev is still probably out to frame you. A desperate man will take desperate measures!"

"You feel threatened?" inquired Parrish.

"Can you handle it?" Cass followed up.

"I've dealt with characters as tough as Greshnev before. He doesn't frighten me."

"Perhaps it would be better if you were shadowed by a police officer," suggested Baker.

"No way! You'd be putting a target on my back. Greshnev will conclude that I know something and that he needs to eliminate me as a threat."

"Maybe that's how we draw him out," suggested Archie.

"You're not going to make a scapegoat out of me! I won't stand for it!"

Agent Wilson remarked, "You'll be a lot safer if you were being tailed by a cop."

"You might as well take your gun and put a bullet through my head. I'd be as good as dead!"

"Well it's up to you," responded Baker.

"Damn right! It's my life that I would be risking!"

20

J ANUARY OF 1968 during the outlawed Russian Orthodox celebration
of the birth of Christ, the Fedosov's made a daring escape out of
Leningrad, into Western Europe. Saving as much money as he could, Dr.
Pyotr Fedosov, a pediatrician, and his pregnant wife Galina, with some
money from their parents, were going to meet a Russian black marketer
who had agreed to secret them to a Finnish ship docked in Leningrad for
the short trip to Finland.

The day before, they were to meet the man in a butcher shop and pay
him their money, Galina wanted to pull out of the deal. "I don't want to
go, Pyotr!"

"What are you talking about? The plans are already made!"

"I can't leave my family behind."

Sympathetically, her husband touched her womb with his hand. Do
you want our son or daughter brought up in the severe conditions we were
brought up in?"

"No…no, I don't."

"Then we must see this through. We have no other choice." Galina
nodded her head in agreement.

They had already said a tearful goodbye to their relatives, knowing
that there was no hope of ever seeing them again. The couple walked away
from their apartment, their possessions and the lives they had known, in
exchange for a chance at freedom.

Husband and wife waited nervously at the agreed-upon meeting place.
Finally, a thin man with a bushy moustache approached. "Dr. Fedosov?"

"Yes, that's me."

"Follow me at a distance. Don't lose sight of me." As they trailed a few yards behind, twilight slowly faded into a dark starlit evening. The Fedosov's kept their eyes glued on their target.

In the shadows of a dark alley, a truck was awaiting them. They slipped him an envelope full of cash, and he thumbed through the contents. "Get in!" the man commanded, "and lay down! Garbage will be piled over you so that it looks like a trip to the dump. Each laid down as the foul garbage was shoveled on top of them. "Don't make a sound or we will all be doomed!"

The driver got behind the wheel and drove away. The married couple was bounced uncomfortably in the back of the vehicle. At last they came to a stop. They could hear voices. They had their hearts in their mouths as they heard the truck door open. "*To, chto von! Vernites' v gruzovike vpered!*" the guard yelled at the city check point. The door was closed, and the truck was shifted into drive. The Fedosov's realized that they had successfully passed their first obstacle.

Their trip was fraught with danger at each stop point, but every time, the malodorous stench of the garbage got them through.

After being driven night and day and only occasionally coming to a stop, they arrived at the edge of the Gulf of Finland. The soldiers that guarded the coast were busy inside the check point building making merry in the holiday season by knocking back glasses of vodka. Getting them free of the garbage by the driver, the Fedosov's were surreptitiously spirited away to a row boat waiting in the dark. A low whistle brought the boatman to his passengers. Pyotr said, "Spasibo."

Quickly, they entered the motor boat as the sailor took them out to the waiting Finnish tramp steamer. The air was frigid and the sea somewhat choppy, but finally the lights of the boat could be seen in the distance. Once they reached their destination, they clamored on board. The captain held out his hand, palm up, so he could be paid, then yelled "Anchor up!"

The steamer started forward, its destination - the city of Boston.

Each morning on the open sea, Galina felt sick and would vomit into a pail which her husband brought on deck to empty over the side. After almost three weeks, the harbor of Boston could be seen in the morning mist. Waiting for them with papers granting them asylum was Pyotr's cousin, Vadim, who had escaped two years previously.

They embraced fervently, kissing on both cheeks, after which Vadim escorted them to his car. They had much to talk about as he drove to Lynn, Massachusetts, where a small enclave of Russians had settled. Relative's greetings were warm and welcoming as Vadim showed them to his home.

Galina gasped when she first saw the white-washed brick house with a space for a garden in the front yard. "All this is yours?"

"Yes, it is."

"In Leningrad, this would house at least two families, maybe even three!"

"In America, no one dictates where you will live. You buy what you can afford."

"Are you sure we will not be in the way if we stay with you?"

"You will stay until you can afford your own little home."

All three walked inside, and the couple was amazed at all the conveniences that the house contained. Vadim showed them to a small guest room. "This is to be yours," their cousin told them. Opening the closet, he revealed some clothing that had been donated by the Russian community. As they looked around, Pyotr exclaimed, "This is all too much!"

"Tomorrow," his cousin replied, "I will take you to the restaurant in the town of Lynn where I am working as a waiter. I have convinced the management to hire you as a dish washer, if that's alright with you."

"I now have a home and a job in America! What could be wrong with that. Our baby, who will come in about seven months, will be born an American citizen. We are truly grateful!"

On the 18th of August, in the middle of a heat wave, a baby girl was born to Galina and Pyotr Fedosov. They named her Emma after Galina's mother. Mrs. Fedorov cried, the tears watering her cheeks as she cuddled closely to the baby wrapped in a pink blanket.

"What are you crying about, Galina?"

"Some of my tears are happy ones, because I have given you a healthy child born in a free country."

"And the other tears?"

"Those I shed because my parents will never know their grandchild."

"Be thankful that our baby will grow up in a country where anything is possible and she can be anything she wants."

"Yes...yes, this is true!" she replied. "God has been good to us!"

Emma Fedosov grew up in a happy home. Her parents weren't wealthy, but for the child, that made no difference. The little red-headed girl attended the local elementary school where she was popular and made many friends. Later in her parent's marriage, Galina gave birth to a healthy son, whom they named Stepan after Pyotr's deceased father.

When Emma graduated to high school, she became a part of the chess club, president of the Latin Club and a member of the girls' softball team. She grew to be quite a beauty with her warm smile and red hair down to her shoulders. Emma attracted boys like bees to honeysuckle, but she never gave them any encouragement. Her studies were her priority.

Because of her excellent grades through her high school years, Emma was offered many scholarships to universities. With no second thought or regrets, she chose Harvard University. She enrolled in pre-law classes in which she excelled for the next four years. To ease the stress of her courses, she took up karate and was a very adept pupil, earning a black belt.

Upon completion of her undergraduate degree, Emma got her acceptance letter to enroll in Harvard Law School. It was there in her senior year that Emma Fedosov met a recruitment agent who would change her life forever.

CHAPTER

21

I N THE EARLIER years of Federal Agent Cassidy Baker's career, the tall, dimpled-chinned, sandy-haired man looked more like he belonged on a surf board off Laguna Beach, California than a government investigator. His good looks and charm helped recruit some of the brightest students to the Federal Bureau of Investigation. It was how he first recruited Emma Fedosov, a top student ranked 5th in her class at Harvard University.

For her part, Emma had never let a handsome face turn her head, but Cassidy was someone special. From the time she had locked eyes on him, a tingling sensation had coursed through her body. She had never experienced that kind of feeling with any other man. He's not the usual collegiate lothario you can find anywhere on this campus.

Once he had made his presentation to her, she was caught, hook, line, and sinker. Emma signed on the dotted line, pledging herself to the agency. The idea of joining the FBI gave her a thrill.

On graduation day, Emma was awarded a Summa Cum Laude degree for her achievements. Saying goodbye to her proud parents, who had traveled to Cambridge for the ceremony, she took the train to Washington D.C. to join other recruits on a bus headed for Quantico in Virginia, where classroom instruction was combined with stringent tactical training. She was to learn survivor skills, even going through a mock town named Hogan's Alley, and training in fire arms, as well as defensive tactics. Her trainer and supervisor during her stay there was Agent Cassidy Baker.

Her experiences in the FBI varied over the years. She had been a part of a takedown of two Somali terrorists who had entered America on student visas. They had planned a bombing in the Mall of America in Bloomington, Minnesota just before Christmas, but were thwarted before the bombing could occur. Emma was also a part of the FBI team that infiltrated a ring of gangsters that captured girls living on the street, to sell them to men whose bid was the highest. Posing as a homeless person, she was snatched, her photo taken after she had been cleaned up, and her image put on the website these men had created to sell females.

With these and numerous other cases solved, Emma Fedosov became acquainted with the case of murder, prostitution, and money laundering involving Russian-Americans located in Brighton Beach, Brooklyn.

It was on a chilly Spring day in late March that Emma arrived at FBI headquarters at 26 Federal Plaza in lower Manhattan, and was greeted by Baker, who escorted her into a waiting black car. "It's been quite some time since we've seen each other," she mentioned. Baker, who sat next to her replied, "Wasn't it at the arrest of those Somali terrorists that we saw each other last?"

"I believe so. Why don't you tell me why I'm here?"

"It involves the Russian mob. The whole story will be related to you by Agent Parrish Wilson. With him will be some local men, Captain Archibald Malone and a private detective by the name of Hank Weldon. We've tried everything to get the goods on the head boss, a guy named Maxim Greshnev. But no matter what we've done, the bastard keeps coming out clean. We need somebody to get into the inside of his operation. That's where you come in."

The car pulled up to the FBI building and after their credentials were checked, Wilson escorted the female agent to his office. There, as he promised, were three men waiting for them. After a round of introductions, they all sat down.

"Maxim Greshnev is a blackmailer, pimp, and worst of all, a murderer," Parrish began. "We've tried everything to bring him down, but he's thwarted us at every turn."

"I tried to have him confess to the killings by joining in his poker nights," explained Hank, "but he's a stone wall. He revealed nothing."

"I understand," Fedosov nodded her head. "And what would you have me do?"

"We want you to go undercover as a Russian girl, sneaked into this country as a prostitute," related Agent Wilson.

"I see. How do you plan to get me into the inside of his operation?"

"I have an operative working for him."

"And who would that be?"

"A woman named Svetlana Zoya, nicknamed "Fat". *My God, Fat Zoya has been working with the FBI?* Hank could have been knocked over with a feather.

Parrish gave her a picture of Svetlana. She scanned the woman's features before she returned it to Wilson.

"I never would have guessed!" Hank replied with disbelief.

"We promised Zoya immunity and relocation if she would help take Greshnev down," supplemented Parrish.

"After your experience with the white slavery ring, and since you speak fluent Russian, you are the logical choice to go undercover." Cass made it clear, "Our superiors thought that getting you involved would be the natural step."

Emma spoke up, "That sounds perfectly reasonable."

"You'll get a new identity for the job." Cassidy held out her new identification papers which were in Russian. Emma looked at her new name. The female agent said the name and her information out loud to memorize to it. "Katrinka Shchetinin. According to this I'm seventeen years old, and was born in Omsk, Russia."

"That's the role you're going to play once you get in," Archie informed her.

"What's to say he'll ever accept me into his harem?" quizzed Emma.

Weldon interrupted, saying, "You're just what the doctor ordered, His type is young, shapely, beautiful, and red-headed."

Agent Fedosov smiled. "I see. When do you plan on getting me on the inside?"

"The agency wants you to be there in two days. In the time before that, you'll be receiving intensified training and directions. Could you do it?" questioned Baker.

"It won't be a problem."

"We've reserved a room for you at the Waldorf-Astoria, far away from Greshnev's operation," Cass informed her, "and I'll be your handler while you're undercover."

"Do you have any questions?" questioned Parrish.

"Not at this time."

"Good." indicated Wilson. "Then we'll get you to the hotel."

"Relax when you get there, order a good meal, and get some sleep," Cass advised her. "Tomorrow we'll get to work."

Cass took her down to the lobby where the same black car waited for them. The car stopped numerous times because of evening rush hour. "Your first time in New York City?" inquired the male agent.

"My very first time. I wish I had the time to go shopping."

"Maybe after we take this scum down."

The car pulled over to the curb and Emma got out. She walked over to the front desk and said to the young woman behind the counter, "My name is Emma Fedosov. I have a reservation."

The girl behind the counter typed her name in the computer and smiling, replied,

"Yes, Miss Fedosov. You're in room 937." She made her way to the 9th floor. She opened the door, turned on each of her bedroom lamps and looked around. Don't get too used to the present accommodations. *I'm sure I'll have to get accustomed to something far less sumptuous at the bordello!*

For two days, Emma was inundated with instructions from her handler, Agent Cassidy Baker. She was even shown a blueprint of the Russian Doll House, and familiarized herself with where the exits were, and in what area Maxim Greshnev's office was located.

"You won't be outfitted with a wire," Cass explained. "And as far as your pistol is concerned, you'll have to leave it with me."

"So, I'm to be there with no protection?"

"Exactly, but if there's any trouble, rooms there are already bugged. We'll break in before anything can happen to you."

Toward the end of the last day, a knock was heard on her hotel door. Cautiously, Cass opened it. It was Fat Zoya. She entered quickly, taking a furtive look down both sides of the hallway to make sure she hadn't been tailed. "I told Greshnev that I had to visit a sick cousin to get over here tonight.

Zoya got to the point of the meeting. "First," she suggested, "stay away from Greshnev's bodyguards. They are dangerous, particularly one man named Serge Sokoloff. His job is to guard the front door. He's crazy!"

"I understand."

"And Greshnev is a cold-hearted bastard. He'll kill you at the drop of a hat."

"I've heard the rumors about him."

"I must tell you," began Zoya. "Once you're inside the house, there is no way I can protect you without blowing my own cover. You'll be on your own."

"I get it," responded Emma. "Don't worry, I know how to handle myself."

"I hope so," were Zoya's departing words.

"Get a good night's sleep," Cass advised her before he left. "You'll be thrown into the thick of it tomorrow."

Agent Fedosov lay her head on her pillow and tried sleeping. It did not come easily that night. She could not help but think about her assignment. At last, sleep came to her as she realized that she had gone undercover before and had always been successful in bringing her target down.

Arriving at the bordello's door the next morning, wearing the short dress and stiletto heels of a woman from the street, Katrinka rang the doorbell. The door swung open, revealing a burly man. *This is most likely, Serge Sokoloff.*

"What do you want?"

"I'm here to meet with Zoya," she answered brusquely.

"She knows you're coming?"

"Of course she knows!"

"What's your name?"

"Katrinka Shchetinin."

"Call Zoya," he demanded of one of the prostitutes, "and see if she's expecting a Katrinka!" The girl did as she was told. After asking, she hung up and told Serge,

"She is expected." With a nod of his head, Sokoloff allowed her to enter pointing out the door of Zoya's office. Emma, now known as Katrinka, sashayed herself to the designated door and knocked.

"Come in."

After a small conversation between them, Zoya led her into the hallway and in front of Greshnev's office door. Zoya rapped her knuckles against the wood.

"Who is it?" the brusque impatient voice of the boss could be heard. "I said that I didn't want to be disturbed!"

"It's Zoya. I've got a present for you."

Relentingly, he replied. "Well then, come in!" Zoya opened the door letting Katrinka enter first. As soon as she entered Greshnev's office, she caught his attention.

"Who do you have here?" he queried in a much more pleasant tone of voice.

Zoya closed the door behind her. "This is Katrinka Shchetinin." For a moment, Maxim appeared paralyzed by what he saw, but he made a quick recovery.

"I am charmed, my dear," he told her as he got to his feet.

"Happy to meet you."

"To what do I owe the pleasure of your visit?"

"I believe," began Zoya, "that she will make an excellent addition to this house."

"I can see that. Where are you from, my dear?"

"Originally from Omsk, Russia, but I emigrated with my parents to this country at the age of six."

"And your age now?"

"I'm seventeen."

Coming around to the other side of his desk, Maxim observed every side of her with a discerning eye.

"She will be an excellent addition, Zoya. Tell Serge I want to see him." Zoya went out into the hallway to wave him in.

"Yes, boss?"

"Put her into Room 20," Maxim instructed his henchman, "And see that her image is kept off the board."

"But Room 20 is your room boss."

"I know that. Take her there now!"

"My dear," he addressed her again. "I will see you in a little while."

After Serge left with the girl, Greshnev told Zoya, "See to it that no one spends time with her. She is to be kept for me."

"I understand," responded Zoya and left for her office.

Once he was left alone, the owner of the business checked his image in a mirror. I have a touch of gray hair on both temples, but that only makes me look quite distinguished. He checked his eyes. *There are a few rings under both, but I can do nothing about that now.* He touched his taut belly. *Thank goodness my belly isn't showing, because I'm wearing my man corset!* Splashing on a little Invictus Cologne by Paco Rabanne, he used his fingers to comb his thinning hair to the side. *I'm in my mid 50's, but I'm still a vital man.* In all ways, he was now satisfied by his appearance, and opened the door to the hallway.

Calling out, he told Serge, "Make sure this time I'm not disturbed by anybody, do you understand?"

"I got it, boss," his flunky called back.

Assertively, he strode down the hallway to room 20. Greshnev knocked on the door.

"Who is it?" the coquettish voice answered from the other side.

"It is me, Maxim Greshnev," he replied, his voice an octave higher than usual. He felt like a young boy on his first date. The sensation was thrilling as it coursed through his veins.

"Please, come in." He entered, his anticipation was soaring.

Emma sat demurely upon a bogus Louis the 14th chair, by a large decoratively- carved bed, whose mahogany headboard was adorned with chubby putti prancing across the wooden landscape. Looking up, the FBI agent lifted her lips into an alluring smile. "Mr. Greshnev, I did not expect you."

Maxim returned a grin to her statement, saying, "Please, call me Max."

"Alright, Max. I was expecting my first client."

"Not before I get to know you. I like to welcome the new girls personally," he said, feeling like a pimple-faced lothario in her presence.

"Please, sit by me on the bed," offered Emma seductively.

As he gazed into her green eyes, Maxim could feel his manhood starting to rise to the occasion. Quickly, he sat covering his lap with his hands, hoping that she had not noticed his arousal. Still, he wanted to learn about her before he bedded the girl.

"What shall we talk about?" the agent inquired in a sweet tone of voice.

"So, you come from Omsk?"

"That is correct."

"I have some relatives who live there," he lied.

"What a coincidence."

"Yes, my Aunt Nataliya and Uncle Yakov, who raised me after my parents had died," he lied.

"Are you still in contact with them?"

"I call them every so often," he answered continuing the fabrication.

"I'm sure they appreciate it."

"It has been a long time since I was there and I've forgotten the district they live in."

"That's too bad," cooed Emma.

"They live very close to the Saint Nicolas Cossack Church. Do you recall the district's name?" Emma knew at once that this was a test even though she knew it was a clumsy attempt to go about it.

"Oh, of course! It's the Leninsky District!"

"Yes, yes, that's it. I always have trouble recalling it for some reason. Where were, you brought up?"

"On Lenina Street not too far from the Vrubel Museum of Fine Arts."

"It is very beautiful there," Maxim stated.

"Yes, very beautiful." A sudden stillness fell over them as each did not know how to continue the conversation. At that moment, Max could no longer hold his desire at bay.

"I really like you Emma."

"You barely know me, Max."

"It makes no difference. I know what I like, and I like you."

"You flatter me."

"This is not flattery. It is the truth." He moved his hand to her shoulder and let it slip down to her right breast. He sighed with desire and was about to move his other hand to her body when she explained,

"I don't sleep with my employers. I make it a strict rule!" she declared seriously. It was as if she had thrown a cold pail of water on his genitals.

"And why is that?"

"Things have a way of becoming difficult if I were to allow that to happen."

"You know," he declared in a strong voice. "I am the boss of the Russian Doll House, and no girl has ever spurned my sexual advances!"

"I am not like your other girls, Max. I am special! I was hoping that you would realize that!"

Maxim's mouth went dry. He knew that if he forced himself on her, he could never win her love. Emotionally, he suppressed his craving for her.

"I can see that," he retorted like a school boy who had just been dressed down by his beautiful teacher.

"I'm glad that we understand each other." She stood up giving the indication that their conversation had come to an end.

Max stood, declaring, "Well, I'll go now."

"When can I expect my first customer?"

Panicking, Greshnev replied, "Take today off and familiarize yourself with my business. Take the time to introduce yourself to the other girls. Tomorrow is another day."

An engaging smile became evident across her face. "That is very nice of you, Max. Thank you."

Sheepishly, he grinned back as he exited the room. As he walked back down the hall, he thought, *What is wrong with you, Max? I could have any woman in my stable by just snapping my fingers, yet I allowed this one to make a fool of me.*

"How was the new one?" a curious Serge inquired further down the hallway.

"Mind your own business!" he barked storming into Zoya's office.

"Yes, Mr. Greshnev?" began Zoya.

"What do you know about this new girl Katrinka?"

"Well, I know she's from Omsk and was orphaned at the age of 12."

"Have you done a thorough background check on her?"

"I always do with every girl before I bring them here."

"I'm not asking about the other girls!" he yelled, his temper boiling over. "I want to know about her!"

Fat Zoya got right to the point. "She is literate and has spent six years in the Holy Assumption Orphanage in Omsk."

"Is that all?"

"There is nothing more to her, Mr. Greshnev. Nothing at all."

"Then she is not a plant by some American agency?"

Zoya swallowed hard at this statement hoping that she would not give herself away. "She is not a plant I can assure you. She has been cleared by my contacts."

"I don't want any clients scheduled to her, understand?"

"That's fine but can I ask why? It is plainly evident that she would be a huge money maker for you."

"That's for me to know!"

"Yes, sir!" With that, Max left for her office.

Day after day, it was always the same. "No clients for Katrinka!" Greshnev would inform Sokoloff. "Keep her picture off the board!" Agent Fedosov smiled to herself with self-satisfaction. She had gotten into his head, and she was going to make sure that she stayed there. When they would bump into each other in the hallway, Max would smile sheepishly like a little boy caught with his hand in the cookie jar. *Except his hand has probably somewhere more personal!* The thought of him pleasuring himself with her image in his brain, made her wince with disgust.

With the time afforded her, Emma made friends with the other girls, garnering as much information as she could about Greshnev's operation. Some of the girls were reluctant to talk about their boss, but one or two spoke to her in whispers. "He's into anything that is dirty," the prostitute Nonna educated her one day as they sat in the blonde's bedroom.

"What does that mean?"

"There is nothing in this town that he doesn't control."

"Well, I'd bet the police are independent and beyond his control." Nonna smirked in response. "Then you'd lose that bet!"

"Even the police?"

"I told you, he has his hand in every despicable activity. How do you think he can get away with all of this?"

"Unbelievable!"

"He pays off the most powerful people in the police department as well as City Hall. He's a real snake!"

"I see."

"As far as Sokoloff is concerned, I'm warning you, don't cross him. He's a brutish animal. He'd step over his own mother's body without a drop of sympathy. Serge is one of Greshnev's pitbulls. The animal will do whatever his boss wants of him." Nonna moved even closer to Emma and in a soft voice continued. "There's even talk that he took care of two of the girls who used to work here."

"Really?"

"For sure. Their names were Albina and Karina."

"What did they do?"

"The rumor is that they betrayed Greshnev."

"In what way?"

"The talk is that Albina wanted to leave him with another bodyguard named Kaz. She's dead and he's lying in a permanent coma."

"And Karina?"

"The other girls say that Karina saw Albina die and her body was dragged out of the Atlantic Ocean."

"It's all sounds so gruesome!"

"It is. I'm just warning you. Greshnev won't put up with anybody's shit! Be careful with him."

"I promise, I will."

Before Emma could leave the room, Nonna grabbed her forearm and told her, "You must also give me your word that you'll never reveal anything I just told you to anyone else. Swear it!" She was deadly serious.

"I won't tell another living soul."

Emma knew all about Greshnev's blood-stained hands, but hearing first hand from one of his prostitutes made it come to life. He's got to be taken down before another person dies! Maybe I can get close to Sokoloff and get the goods on his boss.

Serge had the personality of a piece of lumber, and the intelligence of one. Emma watched as each perspective "John" came through the door. He treated each with disdain and made sure they knew that. The most dominant man in the outside world buckled under his withering comments.

She strolled near him before she queried, "Are you the man they call Serge?" Sokoloff looked at her as if she was some dirt under his shoe.

"What does it matter to you?"

"Nothing, it's just that I've heard a lot about you."

"Heard what?"

"Only that your Maxim's right hand man." Serge smiled a crooked grin which probably mirrored his twisted personality.

"Maybe I am."

"Now you're just being modest." *As modest as a snake in the grass.*

Suddenly, he turned on a dime and barked, "What the hell do you want from me? Why don't you go about your own business!"

Emma shrugged nonchalantly. "I just wanted to meet a powerful man like you." Serge was about to be sarcastic when the next client entered the door. It was Hank Weldon. The private detective hoped he wouldn't give her away by word or deed. He did not.

"Well, look who's back to have his tree trunk rubbed," Serge remarked laughing with glee.

"I'm here to see Nonna, if she's free."

"For you there's nothing that is free here. Pay the cashier!"

"What about her?" Weldon pointed to Emma as if he were meeting her for the first time.

Sokoloff sneered bellicosely. "You couldn't afford her on the money you make as a gumshoe!"

"Still, I'd like to know."

"She's off-limits!"

"Why is that?"

"You ask too many questions! Are you going to see Nonna or not! If not, get lost!"

"I'll see Nonna."

"You'll do more than that," he laughed with ridicule. "Pay the cashier!" Weldon placed his money on the counter. Sokoloff pushed the button that corresponded to the room the prostitute occupied. Bodyguard and federal agent watched as Hank walked down the hall, knocked and went into Nonna's room. Turning toward Emma, Sokoloff remarked, "What are you still doing here?"

"I'm just trying to get to know you."

"Well, I'm not interested in you. You're Maxim's property. No one touches what Greshnev owns, not unless he has a death wish!"

"That's too bad," Emma gushed romantically. "I'd really like to get to know you." Sokoloff stared at her with a contemptuous expression. "You're just another whore who works here. That's all you mean to me! Now, go away!"

"It's too bad," she conversed in her sexiest voice. "I could really go for a guy like you."

"Don't bother me!" he warned her and shoved Emma aside.

"Maxim is not going to like the way you've been treating me!"

"Maxim's not going to like the way you're coming on to me!"

Shrugging indifferently, she retorted, "Don't you know when someone is kidding you?"

"I'm not laughing!"

Emma walked to her room. *I've gotten under his skin just as I wanted! I wonder if I can get a minute to talk to Hank.* She realized that it would be too risky a move.

Weldon exited Nonna's bedroom after his appointment and scanned the hallway. No one was about, and Sokoloff was turned away bantering with another client. Stepping quickly and as silently as possible, Hank made his way to Fat Zoya's office and opened the door. Zoya was occupied in a conversation on the phone. Shocked to see Weldon in her office, she spoke into the receiver, "I'll call you back later."

Weldon took a seat in a chair on the opposite side of the "Madam".

She looked up with fright in her eyes. "What the hell are you doing here?"

"I'm checking up on how Agent Fedosov is progressing."

"Keep your voice down," Zoya presaged, "or you'll get us both killed!"

"The sooner you answer my questions, the sooner I'll be out of here."

"Does Agent Baker know you're here bothering me?"

"He requested that I come to you. He knows that the people here are already familiar with my face. What do you have to report?"

"Did you think that after a few days we would get the evidence against Greshnev and that all the pieces would fit together?"

"No, I didn't think that," he mocked her. "Tell me what has transpired these last few days."

"Well, Greshnev has taken a keen liking to Katrinka. That much is obvious."

"How can you be sure what he's feeling for her?"

"It's openly apparent. He's gone as far as keeping her off the board.

"Interesting. Has there been any pillow talk between them?"

"She has put off sleeping with him."

"And Greshnev is putting up with this?"

"He's like a bird eating out of her hand."

"Incredible!"

"I have to be careful so that I'm not seen talking to her too much, but from what she has told me, she wants to break down his resistance."

"Caution her not to push him too far, too fast, or he'll react like a cornered tiger."

"She is smart, and knows what she's doing. Of that much, I am certain."

Hank wasn't sure what sentiment he was feeling for Emma, but he knew it was more than just simple concern.

"There is no more that I can tell you at this moment."

Just then, Greshnev bolted through the door. He was as surprised as Zoya had been to see Weldon there.

"What are you doing here?" he queried with easily detected disparagement.

"I asked him the same question," unflappably added Zoya without skipping a beat.

"Well, I asked you a question," Maxim pressed his point. "Why are you in here?"

"I'm here to ask about Nonna," Weldon contrived.

Zoya raised her voice. "What about her?"

"I want to reserve her for myself."

Greshnev let out a loud belly laugh. "You are one funny bastard!" he said between guffaws. "What a hilarious son-of-a-bitch!"

"What do you think?" barked Zoya "Did you think you could reserve her like a table at a restaurant, you idiot?"

"You make me laugh!" interjected the crime boss.

"Well then, what about the new girl?"

At the mention of Katrinka, Max's face turned dark and brooding. "How do you know about her?"

"I saw her walking around the hallway. So, what about it, is she available?"

Fat Zoya yelled, "Forget her! She is not for you!"

"Why not? She works here, doesn't she?"

"She is not for a pig like you!" interjected Greshnev.

"I'm a pig?" sneered Weldon. "I wasn't a pig when I sat down and played poker with you!" Maxim scornfully replied.

"Taking your money was a pleasure, but as far as I'm concerned, you are no better than that rapist Kurkov, who blew his brains out in front of me. The idea of you touching her makes me sick!"

"What's the problem? She's just another whore, isn't she?"

Maxim Greshnev rushed toward him like a bull tearing down the streets of Pamplona, Spain. He knocked him from his chair and Weldon was sprawled on the floor.

"What the hell was that for?"

"That was for calling her a whore! I don't want to hear another reference about her coming out of your mouth, understand?"

"Okay…okay," he objected as he got to his feet and brushed himself off. "I don't need a brick wall to fall on me!"

"Get out!" screamed Zoya. "Get out before I ban you from this building for good!"

"I'm going…I'm going!" Hank opened the door and left. *Emma's really got her hooks into him. Still, she needs to move cautiously.*

Turning to his manager, Maxim spit out, "Is that all he was here for?" he suspiciously demanded.

Gesticulating her indifference, she said, "What do I know? He's just so annoying!"

"Has he ever brought up Katrinka's name to you before?"

"This was the first time."

"If he ever mentions her to you again, call for Sokoloff and have him tossed out on his ear. Never let him back in here again!"

"I understand."

Greshnev left the office, to Zoya's relief. She had been caught off-guard when her boss barged in on her and Weldon.

Serge saw his boss's dark mood and inquired, "Is everything okay boss?"

"No, everything is not okay!" Stopping at the door where Sokoloff was stationed he added, "Did Weldon leave yet?"

"Yeah, he left a few minutes ago. Did something happen between the two of you?"

"Shut up and keep your nose out of it!"

"Okay boss" the bodyguard answered in a placating tone of voice.

"Keep your eye on Weldon the next time he comes in!"

"Is there something I should know?"

"That's all you need to know! Now, get back to your work!" Greshnev stormed his way to his office and slammed the door.

###

Every first Tuesday of the month, in the morning, the van was loaded with 5 girls, on a rotating basis, and were driven from the Russian Doll House to a local gynecologist so that they could be checked for venereal diseases. Maxim's driver, a man named Gorski, drove the girls to the office of Dr. Vladimir Orlov a few miles away. For the women, it was like an outing, leaving their gilded cages for the open air for a few hours. They were as giddy and sociable as school girls on a field trip. Among the women being driven that day was Nonna.

Gorski sat reading a Russian-American newspaper in the waiting room as each girl was called in. It was about an hour and a half before Nonna, the last girl to be looked at, was called into the examination room. After a few minutes, the chattering of the girls as they waited was suddenly shattered by an ear-piercing scream.

"Get in the van!" Gorski urged the girls as he walked through the door to the doctor's back office. The woman who had screamed was the nurse. A crowd of employees crowded outside one of the examining rooms. "What's going on?" he yelled as he pushed people aside until he could see inside the room. There, Nonna lay on the examination room, her legs up, her feet in the stirrups. Her white gown was soaked with blood from a severed jugular artery.

Dr. Orlov arrived on the scene and yelled to his nurse, "What happened?"

His nurse answered through her sobs. "I don't know. I told her to get ready and that you would be coming in shortly. I closed the door, and after a while I opened the door and this is what I found!"

"Call the police! Call them now!" he yelled at the woman in the white uniform who seemed paralyzed with fear. The sound of his voice brought her back and she ran to make the call.

Gorski stepped into the murder scene. "You shouldn't be entering the crime scene until the police are here," Orlov warned him.

"Shut up!" shot back Groski in an annoyed voice. *Greshnev is not going to be happy to learn that one of his girls was killed on my watch!*

Nonna's blonde hair was visibly in disarray. She must have resisted her murderer. Her blue eyes were wide open in terror and her mouth agape, but the killer must have slashed her throat before she could scream for help.

With all the surrounding commotion, no one had noticed something laying on the victim's stomach. It looked like a Polaroid photograph.

Gorski looked at the image. It was Nonna, already dead from the slash along her neck. Across it was written in a red magic marker, "Smile, you're dead!" Gorski knew that this wasn't the first of Greshnev's girls to be found killed. *The shit is going to hit the fan when the boss finds out.*

In ten minutes Detective Archie Malone, accompanied by Cass Baker and Parrish Wilson arrived at the murder scene. "How the hell did this happen?" Malone questioned the gynecologist.

"I can't explain it," the doctor responded. "She had been prepared for her examination by my nurse, but when she looked in on her, she was already dead."

"What's her name," asked Cass.

A voice from the crowd answered, "Nonna!"

The three men looked to see who had answered. Hank Weldon's face appeared out of the crowd.

"What are you doing here?" Malone inquired with frustration.

"I was at the precinct when the call came in. I had to see if the murderer had struck again, and I can see that he did."

The coroner arrived and took charge of the body. While another detective questioned those at the doctor's office, Malone spoke to Weldon, "Come back to the precinct."

"Why?"

"I have some questions to ask you."

"I'll follow you back in my car."

Fighting the noon traffic, all four men finally arrived at their destination. It wasn't long before the questions were flying.

"How did you know that girl's name," Parrish posed the question to Weldon.

"How do you think?" sarcastically answered the private eye.

"Watch your attitude!" warned Malone. "This doesn't look very good for you."

"Don't you get it?" Hank answered back. "Someone is trying to frame me. It's as clear as the nose on your face." Cass came back with,

"It's clear to us that you have now become our number one suspect for these murders!"

"You're out of your mind! Why would I be stupid enough to leave evidence that would point directly to me?"

"Then give us a reasonable alternative," Parrish countered impatiently.

"Have you thought about people who might have it in for you?" Archie interjected. "Do you have at least one name we can investigate for these murders?"

"I'm telling you that I've wracked my brain trying to come up with somebody, anybody! But I can't think of a single person who would hate me enough to frame me!"

"You're not helping yourself at all," Baker observed. "What do you know about Nonna?"

"Not much. I know she's from Russia but that's about it."

"You were her regular customer?" Malone queried.

"If you're asking me if I ever saw anyone else, the answer is no."

"And why is that?" Parrish Wilson inquired with curiosity.

"Why do you think?" he retorted derisively.

"That kind of approach will only dig yourself into a deeper hole!" contradicted Archie. "You're making this harder for us than it has to be."

"I don't take kindly to people who accuse me of multiple murders!"

Cass Baker retorted, "We don't take kindly to a suspect's purposeful evasion of the questions."

"If I had a name to give you, don't you think that I would have done it by now?" Malone slammed both his hands on his desk. "By every right, I should hold you at least as a material witness."

"A material witness to what?"

"A witness to these murders. I mean you did have relations with all of them, didn't you?"

"You wouldn't!"

"I could, and I would. The only reason that it hasn't happened yet is because we were once friends."

"Come on, Malone," Cass urged, "That attitude is totally unprofessional!"

"What are you thinking?" demanded Parrish. "All the evidence points to your friend here."

"The evidence is flimsy at best," countered Malone.

"Evidence is evidence, flimsy or not. He should be arraigned for these murders!"

"Nobody's taking me in and booking me!"

Cass moved toward Hank, but Malone held his hand out to stop his progress.

"Cass don't!" Archie warned.

"Why are you letting him stop you? If this was anyone else but Weldon, the suspect would already be behind bars!" charged Parrish.

"Thanks, Archie!" Hank imparted in a relieved tone of voice.

"Get out of here, Hank!" Malone yelled. "Get out of here before I change my mind!"

"I'm leaving."

"And don't leave town, do you hear me?"

"Yeah, I hear you."

"Because if you attempt to leave, your heels will be cooling off inside a prison cell!" Weldon left while he still had the opportunity.

CHAPTER

22

"SHE NEEDS OUR protection!" emphasized federal agent Cassidy Baker to his colleagues. "Agent Fedosov is in as much danger as any of the other girls in Greshnev's brothel, even more if he ever finds out who she really is!"

Detective Archibald Malone responded, "I agree, but the question is how do we get a pistol to her without an employee at the bordello discovering it being smuggled in."

"There's only one way," contended FBI Agent Parrish Wilson. "We have to send Weldon in with the gun."

Malone made a phone call to his former friend. "I want you to come over to the police precinct."

"Am I going to be arrested?"

"I can assure you that this is not a trap to have you thrown in the clink."

Henry Weldon took a moment to ponder this declaration. At last, he spoke up. "I'll drive right over."

Twenty-three minutes later, Weldon stood in front of the "Holy Trinity" in Malone's office. Hank could tell from the look in the men's eyes that he was not trusted by them. "So, why am I here?"

Cass spoke up. "We want you to go back into the Russian Doll House.

"For what reason?" Parrish lifted a small pistol from the desk and showed it to the private detective.

"We want you to deliver this to Agent Fedosov," he declared holding out the weapon.

"After all that has happened there, I think that it's a good idea. When do you want me to go?"

"Right away," instructed Archie. "As soon as possible!"

Weldon held out his hand to Parrish. "Give it to me."

Cass added, "Somehow you've got to sneak it past Sokoloff and get it to Emma."

"I can do it!" answered Weldon. "I'll have no trouble getting past that animal Sokoloff."

Parrish picked up the phone. "I'll call Zoya so she can give Emma a head's up about what you're bringing over."

Stuffing the pistol in the back of his waistband, Hank walked back to his car. *It's about time that Emma had a gun for her own protection!*

He parked his car at the house of prostitution and gave himself a look over in the rearview mirror. *I need to make sure that I don't look flustered when I'm standing in front of Sokoloff!* Hank took a deep breath and opened the door.

Serge was in his usual place. "Back already?" Sokoloff taunted him.

"Yeah, what's it to you?"

"You give yourself too much status!" Serge snapped back. "If you would suddenly drop dead before my eyes, I wouldn't even notice it!"

"Nice!" retorted Hank.

"Well, who do you want to see today. You know that Nonna is not working here anymore, don't you?"

"I heard." Weldon looked up at the board. Nonna's picture had already been taken off. Pretending that it was going to be a hard decision, he kept Sokoloff waiting.

"So, who the hell is it going to be? I can't wait all day!"

"I suppose I'll see Irina."

"Go pay your 50 dollars," Serge instructed.

As Hank was paying, another client entered the room. "Well, look what the cat dragged in," he heard Serge sarcastically snipe at the new visitor.

"Cut it out, Serge! Why do you have to ride me each time that I come here?" he heard the client answer. Weldon slipped away while the two were engaged in conversation and speedily moved down the hall to Emma's room. He looked down the hallway. *Sokoloff is not looking in my direction.* He tapped at the door and entered quickly. Emma was sitting by a desk, but rose as he closed the door. *God, she is so beautiful!* "I was expecting you." Walking toward her, Hank took out the pistol and handed it to her.

"Do you have a place to hide it?"

"No problem," she replied and took the gun, lifted the mattress and slipped it under. She smoothed out the comforter to make it look as if nothing had been disturbed.

"What's the atmosphere been like here after Nonna's murder?"

"The girls are hysterical. They all feel as if they have a target on their backs."

"Does Greshnev know about this?"

"He knows now!"

"So, it's business as usual?"

"Nothing has changed since Nonna's death except that now when the girls go to Dr. Orlov, Fat Zelda will accompany them and wait with each girl for the gynecologist to arrive."

Hank swallowed hard before he asked her, "And how are you doing?"

"I'm fine and ever vigilant."

"That's good to hear. Is Greshnev going to replace Nonna?"

"No one has the courage to ask him. He's been in a very foul mood since he was told about Nonna's death."

"Has he confided in you?"

"He blames Gorski's negligence for Nonna's murder. Greshnev accuses him of losing a great money maker. He has decided to take money from Gorski as reparation for the money he is losing."

"Has he taken his mood out on you? Has he been violent with you in any way?"

"Not at all. When he's with me, he's like a reticent little boy with a crush on a girl in his school."

"Has he made a move on you?"

"He occasionally suggests that we have sex, but so far, I have been able to hold him off," she stated to Hank.

"Good, keep up the good work!" *He's a real jackass!*

Suddenly, the door opened, and Serge Sokoloff entered. "The boss wants you to…" Serge suddenly grew silent when he realized Weldon was there. "What are you doing here?" he demanded as he moved aggressively to the private detective. "You were told that she was off-limits to you!"

"It's an innocent mistake," Hank began holding up his hands in a defensive stance. "I thought this was Irina's room!"

"This guy just barged in on me," Emma said, going with the story that Weldon was weaving. Serge did not hesitate, he landed a right fist to the side of Hank's head. Stunned for a moment, Hank socked the bully in the face. This hit infuriated the Russian brute, who grabbed him by the lapels and head-butted Weldon. Hank lost consciousness and dropped hard on the floor. Lifting him over his shoulder like a sack of potatoes, Serge made his way to the front door. He dropped the client on the side of the building.

"Have a nice rest, Sleeping Beauty!" he said sardonically. "When you wake, you'll have some headache!"

People who passed him as they walked down the street simply chalked him up as a hopeless alcoholic sleeping his binge drinking off. Over an hour later, Hank's eyes began to flicker awake. As he lifted himself on his elbows, a terrific pain emanated in his head. "Oh, God!" he moaned. For a minute, he didn't know where he was or what had happened to him.

Suddenly, it all came flooding back. With some difficulty, he got to his feet and made his way tentatively back to his car. Weldon let himself drop into the driver's seat. He took a look at himself in the rearview mirror. There was a black and blue area where Serge had connected to the side of his head. When he turned to look at his forehead, a large red swelling appeared on it. *Well at least, the mission was accomplished! Stay alert, Emma!*

Hank Weldon couldn't wait to put his feet up and put a cold compress on the wounds he had received. He parked as close to his apartment building as possible. He knew his appearance would draw the attention of people passing, and the strange looks he got only confirmed his belief. He breathed a sigh of relief as he closed the door of his apartment behind him. Glancing up at the staircase, it felt as if he were to climb to the summit of Mt. Everest. One step at a time…one step at a time. With this mantra, he climbed one stair after another until he reached the 3rd floor landing. He saw a woman waiting at his door, her back turned toward him. *God, the last thing I need now is to get involved with a new client.*

"Can I help you?" he inquired as he ascended the last few steps. She spun around quickly, caught by surprise. When she turned, the shock of who he saw almost gave him a heart attack.

"Are you Mr. Weldon?" she queried.

"Albina Is that you? You're back from the dead?"

"No, I'm Anya Lukashenko, Albina's twin sister." The answer calmed Hank down.

"Come in," he offered as he unlocked his apartment door.

Weldon couldn't help but make a comparison of the two sisters. Both were great beauties, but that was where they also differed. It was well known that Albina had been quite a money maker for Greshnev. Her looks however, were brash and gaudy which was reflected in the cosmetics she applied to her face, and was also reflected in the tawdry way she dressed. In contrast, Anya's facial exquisiteness was heightened by her classically understated enhancements. With very little use of makeup, augmented by her sophisticated feminine attire, she stood head and heels over her sister.

Once they had entered Hank's apartment, Anya repeated, "Are you Mr. Weldon?"

"I am. Forgive me for my reaction. I knew your sister."

"In her profession, I'm sure she knew many men!" her voice was harsh and critical.

"The only difference between the two of you is your hair color."

"Yes, I know. We were both brunettes until Albina dyed her hair blonde. She believed she could attract more men that way." "Are you alright?" she inquired after observing his facial pummeling.

"Yeah, I'm okay," he responded. "I tangled with a Russia bear and came out the worse for it."

"If you say so."

Hank swallowed hard as he asked, "Do you know that your sister is dead?" Anya's voice became saddened.

"Yes, I know she's dead, and I also know how she died."

"You have my sincere condolences."

"Thank you."

"Why have you come to see me?"

"I am looking for a man named…" at this, she pulled out a scrap of paper and read it out loud, "Kazimir Titov, do you know where I can find him?"

"Why are you looking for him?"

"The last letter I received from my sister said that she was engaged to him and that he was going to take her away from her life of prostitution. I'd like to question him to see how my sister wound up dead."

"I regret to tell you that you've come too late to question him."

"Is he dead too?"

"He might as well be dead. Kaz is comatose and he lives in a vegetative state at a local nursing home."

Anya dropped into a nearby chair. "I was hoping that he could tell me why Albina was killed."

"It's only a theory, but I believe a man named Maxim Greshnev found out about their plans and had Albina killed. There is strong evidence that he had Kaz beaten to the point that he would never recover."

"Have I reached a dead end?" she cried, her tears surging from her eyes.

"Were you in constant contact with your sister?" Hank hoped that the information might lead to a path directly to Greshnev.

"Albina and I had a limited relationship ever since she turned to selling her body."

"Please tell me what you can about your backgrounds. It may help in getting Greshnev arrested for her murder."

"Our parents immigrated to this country in the hopes of raising their children in a free society."

"So, what happened?"

"My mother was pregnant with us when they came over. She gave birth to us in Brooklyn, which made as citizens. It all seemed so happy until my father took to drinking as his full-time profession. My mother would harp at him about his drinking and getting a job until one day he left us without saying a word. At that point, things went from bad to worse."

"In what way?"

"For a time, my mother tried taking in laundry to keep our heads above water, but she soon realized that we couldn't survive on the money she was making." She stopped at that point of her narrative, hesitating to continue.

Weldon drew a conclusion as to her vacillation and inquired, "Was that when your mother turned to prostitution?"

Anya answered with a sense of sadness in her voice. "Yes, she entertained men."

"You and your sister grew up knowing this?"

"It was pretty hard to miss because these men came up to our apartment."

"Both of you saw what was happening?"

"If the weather was inclement, my mother would send us to our rooms to play, but if the weather was good, she told us to play outside. We were young, but that didn't mean that we didn't know what was going on."

"I understand."

"Once Albina and I grew up, I swore that I would never go down that same road, but for Albina, she saw that life as an easy way to make a living."

"What happened to you after that?"

"Because of my excellent grades in high school, I was awarded a scholarship to earn my Bachelor's Degree at Emory University in Atlanta, Georgia. After my four years there, I graduated and continued at Emory University's School of Law." I waited tables, and became a mother's helper. In other words, I did anything to supplement my college loan."

"Very impressive!"

"Later, I worked for my law professor until she recommended me to the firm of Wyatt and Blair in Atlanta where I am currently working."

"And Albina?"

"When my mother died of heart failure, my sister took on her clients. While I was in school, I tried to encourage her to give that life up. Whenever I could, I sent her a little money, and told her I could get her a job so that she would no longer have to debase herself."

"How did she respond to your offer?"

"She took my money but refused to change her life. In time, I realized that if I didn't turn my back on her, she would have dragged me down to her level."

"And that was the last time you heard from her?"

"Yes, until she mailed me the letter I told you about. In the letter, she explained that a man named Kazimir was going to take her from her old life and marry her. Then I read about a prostitute that was murdered and had her body dismembered. The shock came when I read the name of the woman. I asked for a leave of absence from my firm and they agreed."

"How did you find me?"

"The article said that she had been working at a brothel called the Russian Doll House, and that your name was mentioned. I asked around until someone told me where I could find you. I made it my business to locate you and learn what I could about Albina's death."

"Can I offer you some water?"

"Yes, thank you."

After handing her the glass, Weldon said, "Just sit tight. I am going to call the police detective in charge of this case." He dialed and waited as it rang.

"This is the 19th Precinct, Sergeant Arnold speaking."

"This is Hank Weldon. I need to reach Detective Malone. Is he there?"

"Just a minute." the call was transferred.

"Detective Malone, how can I help you?"

"Archie, it's Hank."

"What the hell are you bothering me about now!"

"Are Parrish and Cass with you right now?"

"Yeah, and…?"

"The three of you need to come to my apartment immediately. I've got someone in my apartment that you need to meet!"

"Who?"

"Just get over as soon as you can! Once you're here, you'll understand why I'm asking you to do this!"

"Why can't you tell me now?"

"It would take away the shock value. Believe me, I was nearly blown away."

"You're making this sound very mysterious."

"Well then, come over and the mystery will be solved."

"Look we're very busy over here. If you want to see us, then come over with your mystery guest.

"We'll be right over!"

The drive to the precinct was quiet, until Anya realized that they were parking at a police precinct. "Are the police involved in trying to discover my sister's murderer?"

"Not only the police, but the FBI"

"Really?"

"Yes, in fact, that's who we're going to see now."

Hank made his way to Malone's office, followed by Anya. As they approached, Weldon instructed, "Wait here until I call you in."

"Whatever you say." Knocking on the wood door, Hank entered without being asked.

"Finally," Archie exclaimed. "So where is this mystery person?"

"Right here," declared Weldon as he waved Anya forward.

"What the hell?" Archie cried out as his jaw slackened with shock. Parrish and Cass looked at her with puzzlement in their eyes.

"What's going on?" demanded Cass.

"I want to introduce you to Anya Lukashenko, Albina's twin sister."

"My God," the detective intoned with some confusion. "I thought I was seeing an apparition, except for the color of your hair!"

"I know. She bowled me over too!"

"I'm sorry Miss Lukashenko, please have a seat," Parrish offered. Cass queried,

"Can I get you a cup of coffee?"

"I'm fine, thank you."

"I don't mean to be insulting," Malone began, "but are you in the same line of work as your sister?"

"I am an attorney in Atlanta, where I've now made my home."

"Again, I apologize for the question."

"After finding out that my sister had been murdered, I decided that I needed to travel here and find out what actually happened."

"All that we've been able to find out so far," Agent Baker commenced, "is that she may have been engaged to a Russian mobster named Kazimir Titov. After that, the story came to an end. Can you fill any of the blanks for us?"

"What do you want to know?" The questions came rapid fire as the "Holy Trinity" got down to business, but there was very little she knew about her sister since they had separated years before.

Parrish passed a photograph across the table to her and inquired, "Do you recognize this man?"

Anya studied the face for a while before she responded. "It's Kazimir Titov, I believe. My sister's fiancée."

"He was your sister's supposed fiancée."

"Why do you say "supposed"?

"We have only your sister's version of their relationship. We have no corroborating evidence that what she said was accurate."

"Her last letter to me said the same thing. Albina wrote that they were going to be married and that he would take her away from her sordid life."

"I see." Archie took the photograph and replaced it with another.

"What about this one?" asked Parrish. "Do you recognize his face?"

Once again, Anya took the photo and deliberated over the image. After a time, she answered back, "I think I know who he is. There's something about his evil looking eyes that brings me back in time." Once more, she stared at the picture.

"Well, what do you think? Do you recognize him?" asked Parrish.

"Can I have a pencil?" asked Anya.

Passing the writing utensil to her, Archie queried. "What are you going to do with the pencil?"

"You'll see in a minute." She began to fill in the white hair until only the temples remained white. She passed it back to Archie.

Staring at it, he inquired with inquisitiveness, "Why did you do that?"

"I thought I knew him, but I needed to darken the hair to make sure I did. He was my mother's pimp and he came quite regularly. In fact, we called him "Uncle Max".

"My God, are you saying your mother worked for him?"

"That's right. He's Maxim Greshnev."

"Incredible!" voiced Weldon. "Who would have thought."

"I haven't seen him in decades." Cass spoke up.

"Your sister worked for him at the Russian Doll House."

Archie inquired, "Do you think he realized who she was?"

"I doubt it. As I said, it has been a long time."

"Did your sister remember him?"

"If she had, I'm sure she would have told me in her letter."

"I have an idea," Cass suddenly interjected. "That is if Miss Lukasenko approves of it."

"Tell me."

"What if we have your hair bleached? There would be no telling you apart from your sister, is that right Archie?"

"They would be mirror images!"

"What would be the point of that?" inquired Parrish.

Weldon answered, "I know where you're heading with this idea."

"Pardon me for saying this," Agent Baker said, "but Russians are generally superstitious. What if Greshnev would begin to see Albina alive and well from a distance. It might jolt him enough to throw him off his game, maybe enough to begin to have a mental breakdown. He may give himself away and take responsibility for your sister's death."

"Brilliant!" Malone exclaimed.

"It might just work," Parrish added.

"What do you say, Miss Lukashenko?" Agent Wilson asked.

"If it means that my sister's murderer is arrested and punished, then I will be glad to participate in this charade."

"Good!" Detective Malone exclaimed with enthusiasm. "Then we need to start preparing this scheme as soon as possible."

"That means an appointment with a local hairdresser," interjected Anya.

"Not too local," cried out Weldon. "We'll have to go outside of Brighton Beach to make sure it doesn't get back to Greshnev." Anya asked,

"When do you think we can start?

"We'll have an appointment set up for you tomorrow."

CHAPTER

23

W ELDON RECEIVED WORD the next morning that Kazimir Titov had expired without regaining consciousness. *I'm so sorry Kaz that I was unable to bring you and Albina together. Rest in peace, my friend.*

Hank could not afford to wallow in his grief for Renata for very long. He had to pick up Anya for a 10 o'clock appointment for a makeover in Park Slope, Brooklyn at a beauty shop called, "La Petite Curl". Exactly at ten, armed with a photograph of Albina, they arrived for their appointment with Monseigneur Rene.

Weldon handed him the photo. "I want her to look like this."

"Are you sure?" the hairdresser with a French name and New York accent inquired with an incongruous expression on his face. "She is beautiful just the way she is. Perhaps a trim and some highlights in her hair, but that is all."

"Look!" pointed out Anya, "I'm the one paying to have this done and not you, so get started!" Rene looked at Weldon for support of his opinion.

"Give the lady what she wants!" With a shrug of his shoulders, Rene covered her with a smock and took out his scissors.

In four hours, a cut, dye job, blow out and styling of her coiffure cost $250. Looking at her image and holding the photograph up, the twin exclaimed, "I don't see any difference at all. What do you think?" she asked Hank.

"You're the spitting image!" Taking her wallet from her purse, she tipped the hairdresser before she went on to get her makeup done.

"Please," Rene begged. "Do not tell anyone you got your hair done by me. It would simply ruin my reputation. *D'accord?*"

"Don't worry, our lips are sealed," Hank reassured him.

After another hour of brassy and tacky application of cosmetics, there was no telling Anya from her sister. Weldon drove Anya back to his apartment where the "Holy Trinity" was impatiently waiting. When they got a look at Anya's transformation, all of them agreed it was a perfect re-creation.

On the private detective's bed were clothing that reflected her new image - trashy and cheap. "Where did you get your hands on these?" queried Anya.

"I sent my secretary out to purchase them," Cass Baker offered. "I think it will compliment your new look."

"It really does!" As she changed, the four men waited in the living room.

"I'm going to get in touch with Zoya and explain what we're up to so she doesn't think she's seeing a ghost.

When her phone began to ring, the Madam picked up. 'Russian Doll House. What can I do for you?"

"Zoya, this is Malone."

"Why are you getting in touch with me here?" she inquired nervously. "This is dangerous!"

"Don't worry, Emma has swept your office. There are no listening devices."

"Then tell me why you called and be quick about it."

"We have had contact with Albina's twin sister."

"She had a twin?"

"Yes. We've made her over to look like her sister to rattle Maxim's nerves, so don't think that you're having paranormal experience. Let Emma know what we are planning."

"Okay, but now I have something to tell you. Greshnev has offered to re-locate Emma to his home in Roslyn Harbor. Emma has accepted. He's driving her there at the end of the work day."

"Thanks for the head's up. We'll make sure that we tail him home."

###

Emma sat in her bedroom, thumbing through magazines, bored out of her mind. *Something better happen soon with Greshnev before they carry me out of here in a straightjacket!* It was exactly at that moment that Greshnev knocked and came into the room. "Are you busy?" the crime boss inquired as he stood at the threshold. *Is he joking?*

"No, Maxim. Come in and talk to me for a while." He made his way to a chair by the bed on which Emma was sitting.

"I have a proposal to offer you."

"Really," she asked coquettishly.

"How would you like to go to my home in Roslyn Harbor on Long Island?"

"It sounds like a very fancy place."

"My home is an estate on the Gold Coast of Long Island. It overlooks Long Island Sound."

"It must be very beautiful!"

"You're right, it is."

"Will you take me there for a visit?"

Greshnev smiled at her innocence. "I'm asking you to live with me there."

"But what would your wife and children say to that?"

"I'm no longer married. I have two grown children, but they don't live with me anymore. So, what do you say about my suggestion? I would be very upset if your answer was "No".

"Oh, Max! I'd love to live there with you." Emma got up and threw her arms around his neck. "Thank you, thank you so much!"

Greshnev couldn't help himself as he felt his penis press against the material of his pants.

"Splendid," Greshnev reacted as he tried to get his physical erection under control. "You'll love it there, I hope. We'll have plenty of privacy. You can count on that!"

"I know I will! I can't wait!"

"Make sure you pack up all your things," he suggested before he turned to leave. "We'll leave at about five this evening."

"I'll be waiting for you to take me there." As he left, she blew him a kiss. Greshnev closed the door.

"Ugh!" she said as she remembered how it felt with her face against his scruffy cheek. *This move better give me the results I'm looking for.*

She entered Zoya's office and related her story. "Make sure you tell the three of them what's happening. Tell them to have Greshnev's car followed this evening."

"I'll do that."

Emma returned to her room to pack. She placed the pistol at the bottom of her suitcase. She piled her clothing on top, making sure it was thoroughly hidden. *If he thinks he's going to party and take me to bed with him, he's got another thing coming.*

She heard a knock on her door. Zoya was waiting outside in the hallway. She declared, "I have something important to tell you."

"What's up?"

"I've just hung up with Malone."

"Is there any trouble?"

"On the contrary. Malone has been in touch with Albina's twin sister, Anya."

"Are you serious?"

"That's what he told me."

"So, what's going to happen?"

"They've already given Anya a makeover to resemble Albina. They're going to try and make Greshnev's guilty conscience reveal that he is the one who had ordered her murder."

"My God, I hope this will work!"

Winter's stranglehold on the weather had finally been broken by the warming temperatures of Spring. Like the hope of the more welcoming climate, the "Holy Trinity" and Henry Weldon wanted the case against Maxim Greshnev to warm up enough to get an arrest warrant issued. The four men waited in Malone's car at a safe distance, but where they were, they were still able to detect the comings and goings of people at the cat house.

At 4:55 p.m, a black limousine pulled up to the front door. "Okay guys," Archie alerted the others. "It's going down." After a few minutes, a chauffeur came out of the driver's seat and opened the passenger door. Max came outside followed by Emma. The driver took Emma's luggage as he held the door open. Once his passengers had been settled, the chauffer opened the trunk and dropped the bag inside. He walked to the driver's seat and turned on the ignition. The limousine pulled away. "We're on their tail," announced Malone as he started his car and pulled away from the curb.

"Stay on them," Cass Baker advised to the driver.

"Don't worry," shot back Malone. "This isn't my first rodeo."

###

Inside the limousine, Greshnev and his companion sat back on the comfortable, contoured leather seats. Emma Fedosov absorbed her surroundings. *He does not spare himself any luxuries. That's for sure!* "May I offer you a drink?" asked Max as the limousine turned onto the Belt Parkway. With a push of a button, a panel in the car dropped, revealing an interior bar. "As you see," he declared with braggadocio, "I have anything that you could want."

Emma stared at the cut-glass carafes that were lined up, each bottle with a silver label defining the bottles contents. "I don't drink hard liquor," explained Emma.

"Then what about some water?" Using his index finger, he pushed against another panel that opened a small refrigerator

"No thank you." *Who knows if these bottled waters have something in them to make me more pliant to his desires.*

Greshnev became talkative. *Sounds as if he's nervous.*

Emma remembered the last thing Zoya had said to her as the madam pretended to kiss her on both cheeks.

"Be careful with him."

"I think you will like my home," he began as his voice burst back into her sub-consciousness "It is very big and even has tennis courts and an inground pool."

"Oh, you play tennis?"

Greshnev paused and in a sad voice replied, "Not anymore." Perking up, he added, "My mansion abuts the beach on the Long Island Sound."

"Yes, you mentioned that."

As Greshnev continued to talk, the limo slowed down on the entrance ramp because of traffic on the Northern State Parkway. Allowing Greshnev to talk, Emma gazed out the window. The homes along the Parkway were expansive. Emma watched children frolic in the warming rays of an afternoon sun.

Stop-and-go traffic gave the federal agent enough time to look at the scenery. Weeping cherry trees were adorned with aromatic pink flowerets. Scattered among them, pops of white could be seen from the flowering Royal Star Magnolia trees. Below them, multicolored tulips began to peek up from the ground.

"I have two children," she heard Greshnev continue to babble.

"Oh really?" *Two that he knows of for sure!* "How old are they?"

"Liliya is 21 and studying at Stanford University and Nikolai has just turned 19 and attends Dartmouth. My daughter is studying…"

Maxim's voice began to fade in the background once more. *How do I put him off if he tries to get me to sleep with him tonight? I've got to play this smart.*

Glancing over to the dashboard, Emma took a quick look at the time. It was 6:17 p.m. *I wonder how long this will take?* Within 10 minutes, the limo drove off the ramp leading to the service road. They traveled until they made a left turn onto a road with a sign that read, Willow Way Road. After a few minutes, the driver turned right onto Shelter Island Trail.

Emma observed that along these streets, mansions were gated, and the houses buffered from the road with emerald green lawns that acted as safeguards from the real world. Every home faced the sandy beach that lined the shore.

"Here it is," she heard the crime boss announce as they pulled up before a white brick wall with two iron gates.

"It's beautiful!" said Emma thoroughly taken aback by the expanse of land before her.

The chauffer blew the horn, and she saw the guard, led by a leashed tan and black Doberman Pinscher, whose pointed ears stood straight up, and whose bark could raise the dead. He unlocked the gate, holding the dog, who aggressively continued to bark and lunge.

The limo drove up a curved driveway and stopped. The chauffer got out and opened the passenger door. "Don't worry about your bag," Greshnev alerted his guest. A butler opened the front door as Max ordered, "Take the bag to the guest room that has been prepared.

"Yes, sir," the servant responded.

Emma stepped into an opulent foyer bedecked with cherry-wood paneling and antique furniture. "Do you like?" he asked in a pleasure-seeking manner.

"It's just lovely!" she lied. More like an ancient mausoleum.

"I had an expensive interior decorator redo it according to my specifications." *If for nothing else, this interior designer should get the electric chair for inferior decoration.*

"It's just so much exquisiteness to take in at one time."

"I've spent a lot of money on this whole place!" Greshnev emphasized his thought by spreading his arms out.

"I can see that!" *I'd get a good lawyer and sue!*

"But, you haven't seen anything yet. Come and I will show you around." Acting as if he were a museum tour guide and not the scum who had his fingers in every dirty thing Brooklyn could offer, Max took her from room to room explaining things as they went.

After the tour of the ground floor rooms, they climbed the grand staircase to the second floor. Max went from bedroom to bedroom explaining every single detail. "And this is the master bedroom," he declared opening the door.

Emma walked into a room that would have put an Ottoman Sultan to shame. A crystal chandelier lit up an overly decorative boudoir that was painted in a dusty rose. She tried to absorb everything about the room. Suddenly, a picture on an enormous dresser caught her eye. It was a photo of Greshnev's wedding day. Emma picked it up to observe the photo better. The bride, holding a bouquet, had red hair and a figure much like Emma's. That's it! Here's the reason I have not been treated like the other girls in the bordello. I have a strong resemblance to his late wife!

"That's my wife Vera. She's dead now."

"I'm so sorry," sympathized Emma as she replaced it on the dresser.

"The last room I have to show you is the guest room, the bedroom you'll be staying in." Greshnev opened the bedroom door directly opposite his. This room caught the last light of day that streamed through its windows. Everything in this room was just as sumptuous as the other, except this was painted and decorated in a light lilac and yellow combination. *Now, this is more pleasing to the eyes.*

"Where is my bag?" she asked panicking that her pistol might be discovered. Just at that moment, a maid entered the room saying, "It's on the other side of the bed."

"She will unpack it for you," Max announced snapping his fingers at the young woman.

"That's alright," countered Emma. "I'd like to rest for a while, if you don't mind. It's been a long day."

"Of course, Katrinka. Take a rest and freshen up for now. The butler will come to the door to announce dinner.

"Thank you for everything." Greshnev winked at her as he closed the door. *At last, I'm alone and don't need to see his eyes on me constantly. I'll have to unpack and carry the gun on my person if it is to remain undiscovered.*

"Keep your eye on the car," Baker told Malone as they entered the Northern State Parkway.

"In this heavy traffic, he won't get away from me. Besides it's the only limousine around," Cass responded, sitting in the passenger's seat next to Archie.

Parrish noted to the others, "Emma is playing it cool."

"I hope she continues that way," added Hank.

"Don't worry," Cass advised. "She is the consummate professional. She knows how to handle herself in these situations. Emma has been through this before many times."

The conversation inside the car ended abruptly as Archie focused on following the limousine without being detected. Hank looked out the window hoping to lower his stress level, but it didn't seem to help him at all. *I wish I were seated next to Emma in the limousine. I'd feel much better if I were there protecting her from Greshnev.*

The car passed private homes with expansive lawns. The sounds of horns by impatient drivers punctuated the air with their frustration. Traffic moved along at a snail's pace so that Detective Malone had no problem keeping the long, black vehicle in his sight.

After 90 minutes, Archie observed the limo turn onto an off ramp. "Hold back a distance," advised Cass.

"I know," answered Archie with some annoyance.

In a while, the limo driver made a turn and the car that was following slowed its speed. The area they had entered was filled with enormous estates surrounded by high walls. Trees were everywhere.

"This certainly is a very secluded area," commented Weldon to his companions. Cass Baker explained, "It's just such a place that Greshnev would choose if he wanted to have some privacy, and isolate himself."

Detective Malone observed the limo making another turn. Archie sped up until the turn came close. They saw the vehicle turn into a driveway where an iron gate opened as the vehicle approached.

"We're finally here!" Parrish Wilson stated with a sense of relief. "Once the limo is inside, we'll check out the perimeter on foot." They did not have to wait long as the iron gate was unlocked, and the vehicle was allowed entrance. When the gate was once again locked, the trailing car parked under a tree to not be so noticeable and they exited the car.

Cass spoke in a whisper. "Parrish and I will walk to the left of the gate and Malone and Weldon will walk to the right. Test the perimeter to detect if there are any weaknesses in the wall that we might take advantage of later. When we're done, we'll meet back here at the car." All three men nodded their understanding of the directions. They quietly walked around the surrounding walls.

Dead leaves underfoot crunched as Malone and Weldon walked around, but the noise was not detected by anyone on the other side of the wall. Suddenly, a dog began to bark. The two men didn't dare breathe as they listened to the dog's repeated snarl and yap. A voice from the other side said, "Shut up, dummy! It's just a squirrel!" Immediately, the dog calmed down. The two listened as footsteps from the other side faded away.

"It's a Pinscher," Archie observed to his cohort in a whisper. "My family had one when I was growing up. I know it when I hear it."

They moved along the wall, observing every brick to determine if it had any weaknesses that they could broach. As time went on, the idea of finding a chink in the brick buffer seemed to become more and more hopeless. Soon, the enormous residence came into view.

"My God," Weldon uttered. "Look at the size of this place!"

"It's tremendous, but it has been purchased with blood money. If we convict Greshnev, he'll have to start getting used to living in a much smaller space, called a prison cell."

"From your mouth to God's ears!"

"This has nothing to do with God. We are the ones who have to find and collect the evidence, make a case against him, and then slam the prison door shut on him for good."

"You're right," Hank had to admit.

The investigation of the mansion walls continued as they rounded a corner in the woods. From there, they could hear the waves of the Long Island Sound lapping along the pebbly shore. Shortly, they came upon a part of the fortification that had crumbled a bit, the bricks and cement scattered on the ground. It had certainly fallen enough for an intruder to climb over and get inside the barrier. "It's probably too far back for anyone to have noticed it," opined Hank. "This looks like it's been here for a while."

"I'm sure you're right."

Being careful not to make any noise, they clamored over to the ground filled with roots. "This is probably how the wall was weakened and fell apart," Detective Malone observed.

"Let's see how close to the building we can get."

"Don't' forget," Archie reminded. "When we next attempt this, we will have Anya by our side."

"Well, I'm glad to see that there are enough trees back here to give us hiding places."

Cautiously, the two men made their way forward, getting closer and closer to the residence. Every time they heard a noise, they quickly took shelter behind a tree. As they drew near, they noticed a light shining in what looked like the dining room. They both observed Emma and Maxim there. The crime boss was doing all the talking. "This would be perfect for Anya to make an appearance," said Archie.

"Yeah, we'll have him choking on his dinner before you know it!"

Suddenly, the lights on the chandelier went out and the two left the dining room. "He's probably going on and on about what he has and how much he has spent," Weldon interjected.

"Come on, let's go before we're caught here." Both men carefully made their way back to the broken wall, turning their heads as they went and hoping that no one had spotted them. Dodging between trees, they finally reached the wall and made their way back to the car.

They were the first ones back. Cass and Parrish were nowhere in sight. "I hope they're alright," said Hank.

"If they weren't, we'd be hearing some kind of commotion."

As the sun began to sink into the horizon, the two agents could be seen making their way back. "Did you find anything?

We saw no way to get in where we checked," informed Parrish to the other two.

"We found a break at the back of the wall," responded Hank.

"Let's get the hell out of here!" Malone advised. "We can discuss everything on the way back to Manhattan." After the car pulled away and was once more on the Northern State Parkway, Cass Baker spoke up. "So, the break in the wall was big enough for the two of you to get in?"

"Very easily," Weldon answered back.

"When do you think we should give Greshnev the scare of his life," asked Malone. Wilson counseled,

"We can't wait too long. The more we put it off, the more we're putting Agent Fedosov in danger."

"Tomorrow!" Cass announced. "Tomorrow night we'll go for it!" None of the men in the car objected.

As Malone drove along the lighted highway in the dark, he reiterated, "Tomorrow is the day."

CHAPTER

24

WORD HAD TO be given to Emma about the plan that was going to take place that evening. Maxim had left for the day to go to the Russian Doll House, which left Federal Agent Fedosov in the house to explore every inch of the elaborate abode. Starting with the master bedroom and bathroom, Emma couldn't find anything illegal or out of the ordinary.

She had more time however, to stare at the photograph of the crime boss's dead wife. The more she focused her attention on the picture, the more she saw the likeness of herself and his deceased spouse, Vera. The red hair was just the beginning of their similarities. Emma estimated that she was a little taller than Vera, but not by much. Their body types were almost exact and the cleft in Vera's chin was a match for Emma's. *Amazing, we could have been cousins.*

Out into the hallway, Emma was walking to the next bedroom when she was intercepted by the butler. "You have a call, Miss."

"A call for me?" she answered with a puzzling surprise.

"Yes, you can take it in your bedroom. Just press #2 on the phone."

"Thank you."

Hurrying off to her bedroom, Emma lifted the receiver.

"It's me, Zoya," a voice came back at her. "Are you alone?"

"Yes, Maxim has left already."

"I know. He's just arrived here."

"What is so important that you called me here?"

"I just received a phone call from Weldon who asked me to pass along a message to you."

"What's going on?"

From this point, Zoya lowered her voice so that she could not be overheard. "Tonight, while you're eating dinner with Greshnev, Anya

Lukashenko is going to make an appearance outside the dining room window. They're hoping that he'll think it's Albina making a paranormal appearance and that he'll break down and admit to you that he had her killed."

"This will be quite a performance!"

"Just make sure that he is seated at the table so that he's facing the window."

"I will."

"When he does see her, make sure you pretend not to."

"I've got it."

"I've got to go," stated Zoya before she suddenly hung up.

Emma thought about how the plan might go down that evening. *I hope the bastard freaks out when he catches sight of her. With any luck, he'll reveal his involvement in the girl's death. Then he'll be slapped with handcuffs and be charged for the murder.*

But Emma knew that nothing always runs that smoothly.

A soft knocking was heard at her door. "Come in," answered Fedosov. The door opened to reveal a slight built maid. "Excuse me, Miss. I'm the maid. May I make up your bed and clean the room for you?"

"Yes, I'm done in here now." The girl brought in fresh sheets and towels before Emma left for the hallway. She noticed other maids cleaning the other rooms upstairs. *I can't examine any other rooms until the maids are through.*

Winding down the stairs to the street level, Emma wandered into the kitchen. Two women were busily cooking. "Hello," she said trying to make her voice as pleasing as possible. A heavy-set woman in a white apron looked up. "Hello," the woman answered in a thick Russian accent. The younger of the two women just looked at her silently.

"You're the cook?"

"Yes, Miss." Wandering over, Emma stood over the boiling pot.

"It smells delicious. What is it?"

"It is borscht made with beets and chopped sirloin steak. It is one of Mr. Greshnev's favorite meals because Mrs. Greshnev used to ask me many times to make it for dinner," she announced proudly.

"And what is this girl doing?" Emma asked about the girl who was cutting onions, potatoes and cabbage. "Is she preparing for this meal too?"

"Her?" the cook sniffed in disdain. "She is just my assistant. Tanya couldn't prepare a decent meal if her life depended on it!" The expression on Tanya's face was priceless. *She shouldn't mock her while she has a knife in her hand. If looks could kill…this cook would already be dead.*

Emma stood for a while watching the two women buzz around the kitchen like bees at a hive. Losing interest, she went out the back door where the patio and the swimming pool were located. The weather was a bit blustery as the wind picked up velocity. The elm and oak tree leaves fluttered violently in the wind as the branches and twigs bent in the current of air blowing across the landscape.

Gathering her sweater around her body, she tried to stay warm in the brisk Spring weather. Emma saw the shoreline of Long Island Sound. Sail boats that had been out, had already turned into a safe harbor as the wind picked up speed. She caught sight of threatening clouds as they moved across the sky and obliterated the rays of the sun. *Seems like a storm is heading this way. I wonder if this will cause a change in my plans tonight? Time will tell.*

Back at the house, Emma noticed that a few of the maids were already cleaning downstairs. The butler approached her and said, "I've started a fire in the library. I think you'll find it comfortable and quiet in there."

"Thank you," she answered as the butler pointed the way.

She strode into the room and closed the door. Two ceiling-to-floor windows looked out onto the front lawn strewn with fallen leaves. The room had a serene atmosphere, accomplished by the tranquil color tones of the room. The walls were painted in a light mauve. The crown and base moldings were painted in a cream color. The couch and chairs were tufted with light gray material, with navy blue throw pillows and a carpet of the same color. *This actually is in good taste.*

She strolled along the book shelves, surprised by the large number of volumes that were lined there. Emma started reading the authors names: Tolstoy, Dostoyevsky, Pushkin, Lemontov, and Tsvetaeva. The names went on and on as she realized that the room housed only Russian authors. *Quite impressive for a crime boss and murderer.* Emma removed a volume entitled, "Dead Souls", by Nikolai Gogol. Seems to be a very suitable subject for the slaughterer who owns this house!

The fireplace crackled in the hearth as the flames danced across the logs. Taking the book to the sofa, she lifted her feet and settled down, facing one of the windows. Emma began to read.

"To the door of the inn in the provincial town of N. there drew up a smart looking Britchka - a light spring carriage of the sort affected by bachelors, retired lieutenant-colonels, staff captains, land owners possessed of about a hundred souls, and, in short, all persons who rank as gentlemen of the intermediate category. In the britcka was seated such a gentleman..."

Emma continued to read, getting caught up in the story of the main character named Chichikov, a man who comes to town appearing to be warm and honest to the townspeople, but in reality, is a superficial man, a person who hides his true colors. Emma couldn't help thinking how there was a parallel between this character and Greshnev. Like Chihikov, Maxim was a man of greed and dishonor, simply interested in showing off his wealth, property, and possessions. And like the main character of the book, did whatever he had to do to keep and extract more and more. It was a major character flaw she found in the Russian temperament.

The sound of the rain hitting the windows drew Emma's attention to the outdoors. The wind was still blowing, while only a light rain fell, washing away the muck and mire. Agent Fedosov wondered if the rain would accomplish the same ending for Maxim, cleaning away the false façade Greshnev had carefully constructed as a cultured gentleman, so that the beast of a man he was would be finally revealed for all to see.

By mid-afternoon, the rain started to pummel down. Cass stared out his FBI office window and observed, "The weather report stated that this rain would start slowly but would become a heavy, continuous storm into the evening."

"Maybe, we should cancel this evening's plan," suggested Parrish.

A frazzled Anya spoke up. "I don't think I could spend another 24 hours thinking about doing this. I would like to get this done this evening!"

Hank Weldon watched Miss Lukashenko as she spoke. It confused and threw him off to see her there looking exactly like her sister. "I think we should follow through no matter what the weather is like," the private eye answered.

"I agree," Malone piped in. "Tonight's the night, rain or no rain!"

"We'll need to leave early," Weldon stated. "You know how the Northern State Parkway gets at rush hour when it's raining."

"Perhaps, the Southern State Parkway would be a better way to go."

"It makes no difference," Hank stated sarcastically. "Whatever road we take, traffic will be crawling like a snail."

Archie glanced at his wristwatch. "We should leave right now. If we get there earlier than Greshnev, we'll just wait in the car until he gets home."

They made their way outside the building and waited on the sidewalk, umbrellas opened to shield them from the downpour. They stood there until Malone retrieved his car from the parking lot and pulled up to the front entrance. The three men and one woman piled in. Malone drove to the Queens Midtown Tunnel which took them over 40 minutes. The stop-and-go movement of the cars continued through the tunnel and out on the Expressway.

"My God!" Anya stated. "Is this road always like this?"

"It's just one of the privileges of living in New York City," Malone answered sardonically.

"Welcome to the L.I.E." Cass Baker added. "New York's longest parking lot!"

The persistent drumming of the wipers on the windshield beat out a rhythmic tempo as the occasional blasts of the horn by frustrated commuters punctuated the dank air. The conversation in the car grew silent as Malone focused on crowded car lanes that surrounded them. Urban settings of buildings set one on top of each other eventually gave way to the more open suburban environs. "I need a cigarette," a growingly anxious Anya finally said to break the stillness.

"If you need to smoke to calm down," Parrish suggested. "then, light up!"

Weldon recommended, "I'll crack open the window so we can get a little fresh air."

Nervously puffing her cigarette, she glanced at the time on the dashboard. "God, it's over an hour and a half since we first got into the car!"

"We still have a way to go," declared Malone.

"One good thing," Cass offered. "If we're having trouble getting to our destination, so is Greshnev."

"You're right!" replied Anya. "How much longer do we have to travel on this road?"

"We have to pass five more exits," a knowledgeable Weldon answered back. Anya sighed with annoyance. "This is taking forever!"

"Sit back and relax," suggested Archie. "Focus on what you have to do once we get to Greshnev's house."

"I know what I have to do!" Miss Lukashenko shot back. "It's the only thing I've been thinking about since you all concocted this scheme!"

Cass rejoined, "Calm down! You're working yourself up for nothing!"

"We have worked everything out," commented Parrish. "Nothing can go wrong!"

"Yeah, I've heard that song and dance before!" Malone spoke up.

"You're getting yourself overwrought for nothing. You'll do it and you'll be out of there before you know it. I guarantee that the plan will run smoothly with no glitches."

"Says you!"

"Look!" Archie retorted losing his temper. "If you've had a change of heart about avenging your sister's murder, just say the word and I'll turn this car around and go back to Manhattan!"

Anya stared out through the wet windshield. "I never said that I had changed my mind." she replied calmly. "It's just that this trip is taking forever, that's all."

"It's been long for all of us," Hank mollified in a soothing voice. "You won't be alone," he reassured her. "We'll all be there to see that no harm comes to you."

"I knew that, but it's comforting to hear it."

The five of them fell back into quietness as the vehicle inched forward. Almost 30 minutes later, they pulled out of traffic and drove up the off ramp.

The wind had managed to leave the roadway with wet leaves and torn away branches strewn along their way. At last they reached the outer wall of Maxim Greshnev's mansion. "He hasn't arrived yet," Malone observed.

"How do you know that?" Anya queried out loud.

"He doesn't leave the Russian Doll House before five in the afternoon. That gave us an hour's head start."

Anya replied. "I guess you're right."

As Malone pulled the car off the side of the road, he suggested, "Everybody needs to loosen up and settle down. We've got some time before his limousine shows up."

They waited without a word passing between them. Almost an hour later, a pair of headlights approached.

"This must be Greshnev now," observed Parrish. They watched as the vehicle moved past them. They saw the guard and watch dog approach to open the gate. The limo slipped through and drove to a protective portico where the driver let the passenger out. Maxim hurried out of the damp weather and entered the front door.

"It's show time!" Weldon calmly declared.

They calmly waited in the car, giving Greshnev time to come to his dinner table. As they passed the time, the rainstorm grew more intense.

"You can still change your mind," Weldon suddenly announced to Anya. The "Holy Trinity" did not look pleased by Hank's suggestion.

"It's now or never!" she steadfastly answered. "I couldn't deal with the stress for another day!"

Checking his watch, Agent Baker said, "It's time. Parrish, stay with the car and wait for our return." Wilson's expression remained stoic even though he was disappointed about being left behind. "Alright."

Immediately, the three left the confines of the car for the dismal weather outside. Cass called out, "Let's go!" Hank held an umbrella over Anya as they set out for the house.

Making their way slowly through the woods to the back of the estate, they trudged through the muck and mire. The weather did not give them a break. The wind started to pick up velocity as the distant rumbling of thunder commenced.

The broken wall at last came into view as the three men helped Anya through the rubble. The first flash of lightning crackled across the sky lighting up the mansion. The lights inside fluttered for a minute but remained on. Sloshing through the rain soaked- lawn, they drew near the picture window of the dining room.

Taking Anya by the arm, Cass Baker said, "It's time. Make your way to the window and stand there until he sees you. Once he has, get back here. Understand?"

"I get it," her eyes seemed wild with fear.

"Just be careful," warned Hank.

She gave him a slight smile before she trudged forward. Once more the crack of lightning lit up the exterior as thunder boomed.

Anya did not hesitate. She steadily made her way to the glass panes of the dining room window. Though her hair hung wet along her face and her clothing was saturated to her skin, Anya watched as Greshnev and Emma entered the dining room.

"You were late tonight. Was the traffic particularly awful?" Katrinka said in the sweetest most concerned voice she could muster.

"The Devil take it!" he spewed in Russian. "The roads are always worse in this kind of weather!"

They took their seats at either end of the table, Emma with her back to the window and Maxim facing it. Cook came in, carefully carrying a white soup terrine which she laid gingerly on the table. "Does my nose deceive me, or have you made borscht?"

"You have a very keen sense of smell, sir," the cook answered gleefully. She took off the cover and began to ladle out two portions. A minute later, the butler entered with a dish of sour cream.

"You are a dream," Maxim expressed to the cook in a happy frame of mind after tasting it.

"Do enjoy it," she replied as she left the room. Greshnev scooped up a generous portion of sour cream and placed it on the soup in the bowl. He slurped the spoonful with the palate of an epicurean.

"My God," he exclaimed loudly. "The woman is a magician! It tastes just like my mother's borscht! Go ahead, taste it," Greshnev encouraged Katrinka.

Taking a spoonful, the federal agent sipped it. "It is so delicious!"

"I told you!" The two of them continued to concentrate on their dinner.

Anya cautiously made her way to the window and stopped just before it. *All I need to do now is stand here until he catches sight of me. I probably look a fright with all this rain soaking me.* She waited patiently outside as the host and guest continued to dine without catching sight of her. Damn it! When is, he going to…?

A crash of lightning exploded, and the night was lit up for a few seconds like it was day. Maxim's attention left his meal as he looked out the window.

Greshnev's mouth dropped open, his eyes as wide as saucers. Katrinka had not paid attention to him until he dropped his spoon into the dish with a clatter and the soup spilled onto the tablecloth. Suddenly looking up, she stared at the startled crime boss. "Why Maxim dear, what's wrong. You look like you've seen a ghost!" For a moment, Greshnev seemed frozen in his pose.

"God damn it!" he screamed pressing a hidden button under the table to call for the guards.

From the appearance of shock, then anger on his face, Anya realized that he had caught sight of her and quickly backed away. She ran back to where Weldon and Baker were waiting. When she reached them, Hank inquired, "Did he see you?"

"Oh yeah, he saw me!"

"Let's get out of here," Cass advised them. They took off back to the vehicle where Wilson was stationed.

"What's wrong?" Katrinka asked feigning ignorance.

"There...there!" Greshnev stuttered pointing to the window. By the time the federal agent turned around the pretend apparition had already disappeared.

"What is it that you've seen?" she asked with concern in her voice.

"Didn't you see her?"

"See whom?"

"That woman!"

"What woman?"

"The woman who looks like Albina!"

"But Albina is dead, isn't she?"

At that moment, the guard entered the dining room. "You buzzed for me, sir?"

"What the hell is going on out there?" he screamed at the top of his lungs.

"I don't understand."

"There was a woman standing outside my window," he pointed in the general direction. "Go out and bring her to me now!"

Emma thought, *He doesn't believe he has seen the ghost of Albina. So much for a full confession from him.*

"But sir, the dogs hate going out in this kind of weather. And besides, all this rain will interfere with them picking up the scent."

"I don't give a good God damn! You get them out now and find her or you're fired!"

"Yes, sir!" The guard left the premises to return outside to the foul weather.

"What has got you so upset, Maxim?" his guest queried.

"Someone is prowling on my estate pretending to be a dead woman!" *He didn't take the bait at all!*

"I'm sure the guards will get whoever it was," she declared trying to comfort him with soft words.

"They'd better if they know what's good for them!"

"What do you mean you couldn't find anyone?" Greshnev yelled at the top of his lungs. "Incompetent, totally incompetent!"

"But sir, I told you that the dogs would never pick up the scent of the intruder in this kind of weather," the guard reminded him.

"Get out of my way," Maxim shouted, roughly pushing him out the front door. "I'll look for myself!"

The rain still poured down heavily as Maxim made his way to the back of the house. The lawn was already saturated to the point of being muddy. Not thinking about a coat or hat for protection, Greshnev was soon soaked to the skin. The lights in the dining room still glared from inside with Katrinka peering out to see what was going on. Although he searched every inch of the vicinity, the area was so wet that it didn't reveal any footprints. *There must have been somebody out here. I know what I saw, and it couldn't be Albina. She is dead!*

A rapping sound on glass drew his attention. It was Katrina at the window waving for him to come back inside. Taking one more look around, Greshnev decided to give up the search. Sloshing back to the front door, he found his house guest waiting for him with a bath towel. "Draw a warm bath for Mr. Greshnev," she instructed the butler as she helped dry off Maxim's head. She queried, "Did you find anything?"

"Nothing at all," he spat out in exasperation.

"Go and get out of these wet clothes and take a warm bath. I'll have the fireplace in the den lit when you come back down." Like a little child being given orders by a worried mother, Greshnev quietly made his way up.

When the butler returned, she told him to start a fire. Emma watched as he entered the den and using a bit of kindling and a match, he got a fire going. She closed the doors after he left.

Federal Agent Fedosov went to the wet bar and pushed a button on the wall that he had shown her previously. A reproduction of Vincent van Gogh's delicate painting entitled, "Almond Blossom" rose from the wall, revealing a fully stocked mirrored bar with crystal glasses. The lights over the bar went on automatically.

Taking a cut-glass tumbler, she poured a drink of vodka that would be waiting for him when he returned. Looking around to see if she was still alone, Emma took a pocket of "angel dust" from her bra, ripped it open and poured it into the drink using a swizzle stick to make sure it was thoroughly dissolved. She placed the glass on a small wooden table next to Maxim's favorite leather chair. She then sat in an overstuffed chair and waited for his return.

After fifteen minutes, he returned, in a silk pair of paisley blue pajamas, a red silk robe, and slippers that had "G" embroidered top, indicating that they were designed by "Gucci". His hair was combed back, and his flesh still had the red glow of a warm bath. "How are you feeling now, Max?"

"Much better, thank you," he responded as he took his seat in the leather chair. Katrinka commented,

"You look much better than you did before."

Maxim stared at the flames in the fireplace as they danced around.

"Have your drink. It will also warm you up. After all, we don't want you getting a cold."

He downed the vodka with one gulp. "That is good. Give me another."

Katrinka rose from the chair, took his glass and poured another shot. I shouldn't have to wait long before he begins to feel the effects of the drug. Another drink will make him react to it sooner.

Once again, he swallowed the whole drink down. She watched as he began to unwind.

"Who do you think you saw at the window tonight?"

Greshnev turned his head to her. From his glassy eyes, she could tell that the drug was having the desired effect.

"Someone wants me to believe that it was Albina Lukashenko."

"You mean it wasn't this woman called Albina?" Maxim was breathing heavily, and his answers began to take longer to get out.

"It looked like her, though."

"If it looked like her maybe it was this woman."

"No…no…no. It couldn't be her."

"Why not?" He looked at her like he was having a spiritual experience.

"She's dead. That's why."

"Dead? Are you sure?"

"Yes, you must have seen her also."

"I didn't see anybody. Are you sure there was someone standing there?" Greshnev squeezed his eyes shut as he thought about his answer.

"I could have sworn that I did."

Good, the angel dust is making him second guess what he saw.

"Maybe it was just a branch or some object that the wind carried past the window."

"Maybe, but I'm sure it was a woman that I saw."

"But, I thought you told me that she was dead."

"She is, I think."

"Did you find any footprints outside the window?"

"No, there was nothing there."

"Perhaps…" began Katrinka

"Perhaps what?"

"Perhaps she was there, but not in the flesh."

"What is that supposed to mean?"

"Did she die in a violent manner? Was she murdered?"

"Albina was strangled. She was hacked into pieces, put in plastic garbage bags, dumped and abandoned in a nearby sanitation heap."

"That may be the reason."

"The reason for what?"

"Maybe her spirit is restless because of her murder and coming back because her soul cannot rest."

Greshnev's eyes grew wide.

"You mean she's Albina's ghost?"

"I don't see any other way to explain what happened here tonight."

Emma could sense the rationality in Maxim's mind start to evaporate and be replaced with fear.

"You really think that's what I saw?"

"It is a proven fact that murdered people's souls cannot rest until the person who has killed them dies for what they did."

"Why is she haunting me?"

"You're the only one who can answer that question."

"I didn't kill her!" he said with a strained voice. "I never laid a hand on her!"

"Maybe you didn't kill her but instead ordered her death by one of your men."

"I don't know. I can't remember," Greshnev mumbled.

"Then how can you be sure that you didn't kill her yourself?"

"Perhaps..." Maxim didn't finish the sentence as his head dropped to his chest.

I'm finally getting somewhere with this investigation.

She rang for the butler. "Help Mr. Greshnev to his bedroom. He's very tired."

"Yes, Madam." The butler draped his bosses arm over his shoulder and slowly made it up the staircase.

Before too long, I'll have the truth and enough evidence to toss this guy in prison, and throw away the key.

As they approached the car, they noticed that Parrish was waiting outside in the rain for their return. Catching sight of the four runners, Agent Wilson jumped into the driver's seat and started the car. The fugitives jumped into the car and slammed the doors.

Weldon screamed, "Burn rubber!"

The car pulled out from its hiding place and entered the flooded road. It plowed ahead, spraying water on either side of the road.

"What happened?" Parrish demanded.

"He saw me," replied Anya.

"I wish I could have been there to see his face!" added Hank.

"I don't think he thought I was Albina's ghost," related Anya.

"You can't be sure of that!" countered Cass.

"What do you mean?" questioned Parrish.

"At first Greshnev's look was one of shock," the woman explained.

"And after that…?" Cass inquired.

"His face was enraged. An expression that seemed to say, "Who's playing with my mind!" They sat silently as the vehicle reached the main road.

"We'll know for sure what he is thinking once we contact Agent Fedosov," Cass concluded out loud.

As the car had pulled out, a single person lurked in the shadows of the woods. This person had been standing behind a tree a few yards away, dressed in black and camouflaged. The person watched through binoculars with great interest. Nothing had escaped this person who watched their plan unravel.

CHAPTER

25

THE MORNING PHONE call from Fat Zoya had been quite disturbing. "Anya told me that Maxim doesn't believe he saw Albina's ghost last night!"

"What does he think?" Malone questioned his informer.

"Greshnev believes that someone is trying to intimidate him with an Albina look-alike. He's as angry as hell and says he won't stop searching for the person who tried to trick him."

"That's not what I wanted to hear."

"Nevertheless, that's what Emma told me. Do you have a message for her?"

"Tell her to sit tight and keep vigilant." Archie hung up the receiver.

Parrish spoke up first. "Your conversation with Zoya did not sound very promising."

"It wasn't. Instead of provoking a guilty conscious in Greshnev, he is convinced that someone was trying to trick him, and now he's out for blood."

Cass interrupted by saying, "We're like dogs chasing our tails. We're getting nowhere in this case."

"I suppose you're right. What do you suggest?"

"Perhaps we've been barking up the wrong tree," related Parrish.

Cass explained, "Even though we realize that Greshnev's hands aren't clean, it may be that he had nothing to do with these murders."

"Where do we go from here?" Malone queried.

Cass and Parrish looked at each other momentarily.

"Weldon has to be questioned," volunteered Baker.

Parrish added, "He's the next logical choice."

"No," Malone emphasized emphatically. "You don't know him the way I do. I can't believe that he would have anything to do with these killings!"

"You can't just eliminate him because he's your friend," scolded Cass. "Do it whether you like it or not!"

"If I do, it will have to be just between us, is that understood?" Before they could answer, the door opened, and Hank came in.

"What have I walked into?" Weldon asked as he gazed at the facial expressions of the "Holy Trinity". Cass and Parrish got up never addressing Hank's inquiry.

"Do it," Cass warned. "Or we'll do it ourselves!" The two men quickly exited the office.

"What's wrong with them?" questioned Hank.

"Sit down," Malone instructed him. Weldon sank into the chair next to him. "I got a call from Zoya this morning."

Peaked with curiosity, Weldon asked, "What did she have to say?"

"Greshnev wasn't fooled. He's as angry as hell at the person who tried to hoodwink him. It appears that he may have had nothing to do with Albina's death." Disconsolate, the private detective asked, "Then where do we go from here?"

"Cass and Parrish have a theory."

"And what's that?"

"They believe that you have a strong motive to have committed all these murders."

Hank sat back in his chair and laughed heartily. "My God, those two are way off the mark!" Archie did not join in on the laughter.

Hank took note of Archie's facial expression. "You are not seriously considering that I was involved, are you?" Archie stared silently at him. Weldon jumped out of his chair. "This is insane! You know I had nothing to do with these killings!"

"We need to have a serious talk."

"I can't believe this!"

"It would go a long way to prove your innocence if you could account for your whereabouts at the time of the murders."

"This floors me!"

"It shouldn't. I've mentioned this theory to you before."

"I never thought you were really serious!"

"Well, I'm taking it seriously now. Let's talk about Albina Lukashenko, shall we?"

211

"I'm your friend," Weldon underscored effectively dodging the question.

"We really haven't been friends for years. Did you know Albina?"

"You know I did," Weldon defended himself.

"You're a frequent customer of Greshnev's brothel, aren't you?"

"Yeah, so what?" he answered belligerently.

"In fact, you paid for Albina's favors many times. Is that true?"

"That doesn't mean I killed her!"

"Were you sleeping with her at the time of her death?"

"And what if I was?"

"Did you know she was leaving her profession?"

"Yeah!"

"How did you find out?"

"Her boyfriend Kazimir Titov told me."

"And how did you react to this bit of news?"

"I didn't give a shit!"

"Did you fall in love with her and take this news bitterly?"

"Are you kidding me? She was a whore!"

"And yet you were looking for this woman."

"That's because Kaz hired me to find her."

"You mean she was missing?"

"Yeah, that's right!"

"But she wound up dead, didn't she?"

"That's not on me!"

"She was found with a photograph of her dead image and a message laying on top of her body. Words were scribbled across it in red marker. Do you know what it said?"

"It said, "Smile, your dead!"

"As a private detective, you've taken pictures of unfaithful spouses, haven't you?"

"Many times."

"And you have a special catch phrase that you use as you take their pictures while they are proving themselves to be cheating spouses. Remind me what that is again."

Weldon took a gulp and felt his mouth suddenly become desiccate. "Smile, you're caught."

"Yes, that's it," answered Malone pretending he couldn't recall it.

Weldon churlishly replied. "That doesn't mean anything!"

"There could be a connection."

"Only in the minds of the "Holy Trinity", he barked back.

"I suppose you're referring to Cass, Parrish, and myself."

"That's right! You're all "holier than thou!"

"Okay," Archie responded never addressing Hank's accusation. "Let's talk about a prostitute named Karina."

"I don't know anything about her."

"Did she die because she witnessed you murdering Albina?"

Jumping out of his chair, Hank screamed, "You're fucking nuts!"

"Sit down!" Malone warned Hank in a harsh tone of voice. "Sit down or I'll cuff you to the radiator!"

Weldon relented and did as he was told.

Almost five hours after he had entered the police station, Detective Malone finally finished questioning Hank Weldon about every murder related to the Russian Doll House. During that grilling, Weldon had been tempted to articulate that he wanted an attorney, but he had refrained from saying that for two reasons; he thought it would make him look like he had something to hide, and he had done nothing wrong so why would he need one.

"Listen to me carefully," Archie had warned him. "As of this moment, you've just jumped up from a list of possible suspects to become our number one."

"You know me," Weldon responded angrily. "You've known me for a long time and you still believe I would do such things?"

"I used to know you, but over the last six years, you've become someone I barely recognize."

"Really, Archie?"

"Really! You can go now, but don't even think about leaving Brighton Beach. I'll be calling you back for more questioning."

"Screw you!" Hank walked out, his back aching from the lengthy time he had been sitting on a wooden chair.

Mindlessly, his brain had shut down as his feet retraced the familiar path back to his apartment, but he never made it home. Instead, his feet stopped at a one-time familiar haunt. He realized that he had found his way to The Dive.

For months, he had been able to refrain from drinking, but now he felt no restraint. What's the point!

The familiarity of the place gave him an instantaneous sense of security. It was the same smoky, ramshackle bar that he remembered during his days of heavy drinking, but one important thing had changed. With Ivan now laying in his grave, a new bartender had been hired. This time it was a beautiful, young woman.

Strolling to the bar, he slammed his hand on the counter to call for some service. The beautiful brunette behind the bar approached him with a warm smile. "What is your name gorgeous?" he flirted.

"Martina. What will you have?"

"Chivas, neat." She took the bottle and a clean glass and put them down in front of the customer and poured him a drink. Hank reached for it and poured it down his throat in one gulp. "Another." The process was repeated.

"More?" she asked. Taking a $20 bill from his wallet, he responded,

"Just leave the bottle." Martina did what she was told, and walked away to another customer.

The haze of cigarette and cigar smoke hung low in the stifling air, making it difficult to see anyone more than 15 feet away. But that was just fine with Hank. He was there to get drunk and not to make idle conversation.

Weldon stared at the bottom of his glass as he downed another drink. *This is how I got into trouble the first time, but I don't give a rat's ass anymore.* The fog in his mind began to clear as he relived that terrible moment six years ago.

From the other side of the bar, a pair of interested eyes watched as the private eye increasingly became more inebriated. A tiny smile appeared on this person's face, reflecting self-satisfaction. Having seen enough, the person made their way out of the premises.

CHAPTER

26

WELDON DID NOT know how he had managed it, but he woke up the next morning to find himself in bed in his own apartment. His head ached, and he thought that without much effort, it would crack like an egg shell. His thoughts were muddled, and he felt nauseated and dizzy as he tried to raise his head.

Hank gave up on the idea of rising from his bed. His mouth felt as if he had traveled across a desert - it was dry and parched. His stomach turned over loudly as he realized that he had had nothing to eat since breakfast at the Tick Tock Diner, 24 hours ago. The idea of food made him want to heave, but he fought back the queasiness in his gut.

He could not tell how long he had slept, but the long rays of the Summer sun gleaming through his window gave him the impression that it was probably late afternoon. Gingerly, he lifted himself up into a sitting position. He breathed deeply trying to fight off the feeling of vertigo.

Slowly, he got to his feet and made his way to the bathroom to take a piss. He went to the sink to throw some water on his face, and glanced up to see a man with a haggard expression looking back at him. *How many more times do I need to look at myself like this?*

Wandering over to the refrigerator, he opened it and examined its contents - container of milk, which had turned sour, a quarter loaf of white bread that was somewhat stale, a half a bottle of pimento-stuffed olives, and a cardboard container of Chinese Pork Lo Mein from The Bamboo Garden restaurant. He took the box from the shelf, grabbed a fork and sat down to eat at the kitchen table.

As he ate, he reminisced when he was hiding Renata, and all the delicious meals she had prepared for him. *She's gone now too! I destroy anyone I love or loves me! I can't hold on to any woman. They either wind up dead or deported to Russia. What kind of a man am I anyway? What kind of man kills himself slowly with liquor?* He answered his own question. *Not much of a man at all!*

"Stop feeling so sorry for yourself! He screamed as he threw away the empty container. I cannot stay on this road of self-destruction anymore. *If Archie won't help me clear my name, I must do it myself!*

Taking a pad of paper and a pencil from the kitchen drawer, he sat down to draw up a list of possible people who would want to see him indicted for murder. As time went by, he soon realized that the list was growing longer.

The name of every man that he had caught in infidelity to his wife began to build the list. He couldn't remember how many times he had heard the phrases, "I'll get even with you!" and "I could kill you" shouted out to him, but he never took them seriously until this very moment. He wrote down as many names as he could think of. The next time Malone calls me in for questioning I will be ready and armed with this list. He'll have to investigate these guys.

Determined to take hold of his own destiny, he resolved to bring the list to Malone's immediate attention by delivering it to him that day.

He turned on the hot water in the shower as he stripped away his rumpled clothing. Weldon allowed the hot water to hit and cascade down his back. He stood there for some time luxuriating in the feeling of comfort and relaxation. At last, he picked up the bar of soap and lathered himself up. It felt great to wash away the dirt and sweat that had clung to his body. He watched as the suds and dirty water got sucked down the drain. He shampooed his hair and rinsed it out. Reaching for his safety razor, he sprayed some shaving cream on his stubble and glancing at the mirror attached to the shower wall, he scraped away hair until his face was clean. Hank turned off the faucet and grabbed for a towel to dry off.

He combed his hair and entered his bedroom. He once more caught sight of his image in the mirror. For a moment, he was reminded of the man who had been Clare's husband.

As the sun dropped closer to the horizon, Weldon got in his car with the folded list of names in his pocket and drove to the precinct. The streets were crowded with people trying to get home from work, and it took him a little more time than usual to reach his destination. Marching past the receptionist, he walked directly to Malone's office. He opened the door to find the "Holy Trinity" in conference.

"What do you want, Weldon?" Cass inquired with mistrust.

"Go away," Malone added. "We're in conference."

Ignoring the advice, he made his way to Archie's desk.

"Beat it," ordered Parrish, "or we'll place you under arrest!"

"I'm here to deliver something into your hands."

"Unless it's your confession to the murders," Archie announced, "I'm not interested!"

He slammed the list on the wooden desk.

"What's that?" Agent Baker queried with mild curiosity.

"It's a list of names that I've put together."

Archie took the list and glanced at it. "Who are they supposed to be?"

"These are the names of men I have caught in the arms of women who were not their wives."

"Why did you think that this would be of any interest to us?" Parrish demanded tossing the paper back at Weldon with condescension.

Pointing to the list, Hank explained, "These are the names of men who threatened to either kill me or get even with me."

Cass snorted with ridicule. "This list is useless to us. Are you trying to have the spotlight turned on them to shift our suspicions off you? This is a pretty pathetic attempt of you to get yourself off the hook."

"Look, I've been a member of your investigating team up to this point. I can go down the list myself to find out if one of these men has set me up to look like a murderer."

"My God," Cass shouted back. *Look at him giving himself airs because you allowed him into your confidence, Archie!*

"That was a mistake that I take complete responsibility for. I knew him when he was a good cop. I was stupid enough to let him back in my life. I will not make that mistake again!"

"You're not even going to look at this list?" inquired Hank as he picked up the paper.

"Go back to The Dive, Malone advised him. "You can investigate all of them through the bottom of an empty whisky bottle."

The rebuke was harsh, and Hank bristled at the insult.

"Fine! If you're not going to do anything about this, I'll take care of it myself!"

"I'm warning you," threatened Agent Baker. "Do not interfere in our investigation!" If you do, we'll slap handcuffs on you and put you behind bars. The only reason that that hasn't happened yet is because Detective Malone has vouched for your character, but that is not going to keep you out of jail forever. Before long, you'll wind up at a state penitentiary where murderers like you belong! Now get the hell out of here!"

Weldon turned his head to look at Archie. The detective diverted his eyes away from his former friend. He believes I'm innocent. By God, I'm going to find out who is setting me up for murder if it kills me!

He walked out the door, list in hand, there's no time like the present to get started.

The first name on his list was Jerry Selden. As he recalled, he had found this company president shacked up with his secretary in an expensive apartment Selden provided for her. Not that he blamed him. Anything she lacked in secretarial skills, she made for with a curvaceous body and full pouty lips.

He had followed a paper trail after his wife had hired him to investigate the loss of her husband's affections. He recalled how she cried in her living room as he asked her some pertinent questions. Hank had followed him from his office in Midtown Manhattan to a swanky condominium on the Upper West Side, in an area named Riverside Park. He watched as Selden entered the building. Weldon followed him just in time to see him get into the elevator. He watched the lights as it came to each floor. It had stopped on the 18th floor. "Can I help you?" the doorman asked with suspicion.

"Yeah, I'm looking for Mr. Selden. I've got a message for him from his office."

"Give the message to me and I'll deliver it to him."

"Sorry, I was told to deliver to him in person."

"Well, I'm not letting you up!" he defiantly answered.

"If you could just give me his condo number I could mail it directly to him." The doorman didn't see any harm in that.

"Okay. He's on the 18th floor, condo 18 B."

"Thanks a lot," he said leaving the lobby for the street, but Hank wasn't done yet. He walked around the corner to the freight elevator and pushed the button to the 17th floor. He walked down the hallway to a window that overlooked the fire escape. He climbed outside and quietly made his way up to the next floor.

Once he reached the landing, he looked inside the window. It was a bedroom done in lush furnishings. He thought about how this building had been a pre-war jewel that needed a good facelift. When it had been completed, only people with money to burn could afford to buy into the multimillion-dollar complex that looked over the Hudson River to the glittering lights of Palisade Avenue of North Bergen New Jersey.

As he contemplated the fact that he could never afford to live in such a building, the bedroom door opened. Selden and his office playmate entered. Selden was a man in his mid-fifties who already looked like an old man. His girth was large, and Hank estimated he probably weighed about 250 pounds. Being careful not to move, he took out his camera and waited patiently.

She toyed playfully with him for a few minutes, taking off his tie and suit jacket and unbuckling his belt. His mistress would not allow him to touch her, teasing him even more as she stripped down to her bra and panties. It was at that point that Selden dropped his pants to reveal his erection held back by a pair of striped drawers. As he grabbed her to plant a kiss on her lips, Hank took out his camera and focused the lens on the image inside. The flashing light of his camera was caught by the woman who started screaming.

"Smile, your caught!" Hank yelled through the window as he climbed down the fire escape to the floor below as Selden fumbled, lifting his pants yelling back, "I'll kill you!"

From the 17th floor, he pushed the elevator button. It arrived, with a grand dame of society carrying her long-hair white Maltese dog with a pink bow above its eyes. "Good evening," Hank said tipping his hat as he got onto the elevator.

"And who might you be?" she questioned with snobbery. "I haven't seen you here before!"

"Just passing through, madam."

Hank returned to the penthouse apartment of Mrs. Selden. When he showed her the photo, she did not breakdown into tears as he expected. Instead she screamed, "I'll take him for every cent that he has!" She hired an expensive lawyer and she did. After giving Weldon a check for the agreed amount, the private detective left, never thinking that he would see her again.

####

Now, at the former Mrs. Selden's apartment, he rang the doorbell. "Yes", said a voice from inside. "Who is it?"

"Mrs. Selden, I'm Hank Weldon, the guy you hired to find out if your husband was cheating on you." The door opened to Mrs. Selden's familiar face.

"Hello, Mr. Weldon. How can I help you?"

"I was wondering if you have any contact with your ex-husband. I need to talk to him."

"That rat-bastard died over a year ago. Heart disease I was told, although the only contact I had with him was his alimony check each month. I'm sorry that I can't help you with anything more than that."

"But you have, Mrs. Selden. You've cleared up a problem for me. Good evening."

"Goodbye," she answered as she closed her door. Well, I can cross that name off the list!

CHAPTER

27

T HE TASK OF getting in touch with people he had caught in the act of adultery soon became too overwhelming. Even though there was some distrust of Hank by the others, the "Holy Trinity" decided that he was a major person of interest whom they needed to keep their eye on, and what better way to do it then by asking him to come back on the team.

The four men entered the apartment of Hank Weldon like drowned rats, hair stringy and clothing soaked to the skin. "Well that was a total disaster," Agent Parrish Wilson opined as he dried his head with a towel. The others tried to dry themselves as best as they could.

"There's no point in staying here anymore," Albina's sister declared. "If Maxim Greshnev hasn't cracked now, he never will!" Agent Cassidy Baker retorted,

"There's no need to cry defeat just yet."

"What do you mean by that?" Weldon wondered out loud.

"Just because Greshnev may not be our murderer doesn't mean that he was our only suspect."

"What do you have in mind?" inquired Parrish.

"We will use Miss Lukashenko as bait as we trawl the streets of Brighton Beach."

"Wait a minute," Anya protested. "This sounds very dangerous!"

"Cass," Hank added, "This is too much of a risk!"

"I'm not saying that this isn't perilous, but the risk factor will be diminished because we all will be trailing her. The killer is still out there somewhere, and he must be caught!"

Parrish Wilson now took up the cause. "This may be the only chance for all of us to learn who has murdered your sister, don't you see?"

"I'm not sure."

"Listen, Anya," Weldon began. "Don't forget the reason that you came to Brooklyn. You can't lose focus now. If you do, you may never discover the killer!"

"He's right," Cass added. "This is your best hope."

Anya looked at all of them, who seemed in total agreement.

"You're right of course. Let's go ahead with the plan." The five of them sat down in Weldon's living room to strategize.

"What are you thinking?" Weldon inquired of the FBI agents.

"We'll let Miss Lukashenko stroll down Brighton Beach Avenue."

"And?" Anya asked warily.

"And you'll walk nonchalantly down the street to have the maximum number of people on the boulevard recognize you."

"What do you think will happen?" the somewhat distressed woman queried.

"I want to draw him out into the open, to reveal his identity whoever he is."

"But what about my safety?" the frantic woman inquired.

"We'll have you covered."

"How can I be involved?" Weldon wanted to know.

"Well, Hank you'll tail her from across the street."

"I've got it."

"Agent Wilson you'll follow her from behind."

"And where will you be?" Lukashenko demanded of Agent Baker.

"I'll be following from my car so that if he approaches you in his vehicle, I'll be able to put the brakes on his plan."

Wilson answered, "We have all options covered. There's no need for you to be apprehensive." Anya gave them a weak smile of understanding.

Hank spoke out. "What if that doesn't work?"

"People will see and recognize her as Albina and tongues will begin to wag," Parrish indicated. "The rumor will start spreading around the city until it reaches the right ears."

"Whoever the murderer is, he will soon get wind that Albina has been walking through Brighton Beach. He will feel the need to check on the allegation. We will force his hand!" proclaimed Cass Baker.

Wilson adjoined. "It's the perfect trap!"

"Do you plan on putting this in motion tomorrow?" Anya asked skeptically.

"There's no use in wasting any time," the senior member of the FBI retorted.

"And what if we aren't able to make him show his hand?" the private detective wanted to know.

"Then she'll walk down a different street the next day, and the next day after that, and so on and so on until he makes a mistake. You better wear a comfortable pair of shoes," he advised her.

"I understand."

"You better go back to your hotel room and get a good night's sleep. You'll need it for tomorrow."

"I'm afraid to stay by myself in my room tonight!"

"Don't worry. I'll assign an agent to stand outside your door the entire night. Will that make you feel better?"

"It will certainly help me to get a better night's sleep."

"Great, Agent Wilson, would you please escort Miss Lukashenko back to her hotel room. I'll have another agent assigned to your post." Without saying word, the two left.

The men who were left sat down. "Tell me the truth," Hank queried. "Do you really think your plan will work?"

Baker took his hand and ran it through his hair before he replied. "It's all I've got for the moment."

"How much danger do you think we're putting Anya in?"

"I tried to downplay the danger, but realistically we can't prepare for all the possible contingencies."

Weldon sat back in his chair. "I can't have this young woman's blood on my hands, I just can't!"

"Pull yourself together!" barked Malone. "The only reason I'm trusting you with this assignment is because of your knowledge about this case. Don't make me sorry that I banked on you. If you're having any second thoughts, back out now! I won't have Miss Lukashenko's safety jeopardized by someone who has doubts about the outcome, understand?"

"Yeah, I get it."

"So, are you in or out?"

"I'm in!" he said with determination.

"Good," announced Baker. "Get a good night's sleep. We'll meet at Miss Lukashenko's hotel room at nine in the morning." Malone and Baker left the premises. *He has more confidence in his scheme than I do. Baker is probably hoping that Greshnev will finally show his guilty conscience, but I wonder if he has a conscience at all.* Weldon trudged off to bed.

Federal Agent Emma Fedosov sat in the kitchen sipping her morning coffee while Maxim Greshnev remained upstairs sleeping. She could see that last evening's downpour had stopped, and the morning sun was drying up the puddles of water and mud on the ground. As she drank her morning latte and ate a buttered croissant, her mind worked overtime. *I've noticed the resemblance of his wife's photograph to me. If I didn't know any better, I would say that he has been treating me like his late wife. I believe I may be in control of this situation after all, because I've been here for days and he hasn't tried to touch me.*

Her serene sunrise contemplation was suddenly shattered by the noise of someone running heavily down the stairs. Katrinka walked through the marble hallway and into the foyer to see an enraged Maxim waiting impatiently at the opened front door. He wasn't alone for long, as Katrinka saw his head of security arrive with a guard dog. "Well," began the raging Russian. "What have you found?"

"Whatever footprints may have been left behind have been washed away," the muscular, broad-shouldered employee responded.

"What about the dog's picking up a scent?" he yelled querulously.

"The dogs would need dry conditions to be able to follow a scent."

"Did you at least discover how the hell they were able to get close to my home?"

"I believe they entered over the crumbling wall at the back of your property." In an instant, Greshnev raised his hand and struck the man hard across the cheek.

"I told you weeks ago to hire a mason to repair that wall! You're fired!" he screamed stridently, his fists balled up in anger. "Pack your things and get out of my sight!" He ended the verbal bombardment by slamming the door in his former employee's face.

Maxim was startled to see his guest looking at him.

"Are you alright?" she asked with as much worry as she could dredge up.

"I apologize," he answered with genuine regret. "I did not mean for you to see that."

"What's wrong?"

"That jackass allowed an intruder to enter these grounds last night! It's inexcusable!"

Katrinka chose her words carefully. "Are you sure you saw someone outside the window last night?"

"You mean you didn't?"

"When I turned toward the window, I didn't see anyone."

"There was someone there," he answered never saying who it looked like. "I know that I'm not losing my mind!"

She walked over and put her hand on his arm comfortingly. "No one is saying that. Come into the kitchen and have some breakfast. You'll feel better afterwards."

As compliantly as a lamb, she led him into the kitchen where the cook was already preparing Greshnev's usual breakfast, plain yogurt with nuts and honey, and black coffee. Katrinka sat down next to him and ate the rest of her meal.

"What are you going to do about hiring another head of security?"

He put down the spoon and walked to the wall phone. He pressed a red button. It wasn't long until someone on the other side of the line answered. "Vladimir, you are now the head of security. The first thing to be done is having a mason come and fix the back wall of my estate. Can you handle the job?" He paused to hear the man's reply. "Fine, then get it done!" He returned to the breakfast table.

"Do you think he'll do a better job for you?"

"He better or he too will find himself on the unemployment line." When he had finished his meal, he rang for his chauffer.

"Are you off to work now?" Checking his wristwatch, he answered, "Yes, and I'm already late."

"Take me with you today. I'm so bored here," she pleaded.

"The Russian Doll House is no place for you, anymore" he gently scolded her.

Is he kidding? Has he already forgotten that he hired me there?

"Please, Maxim," she tried to sound pitiful. "At least let me visit Zoya."

It would be a good time for me to check in about my progress, and to get word to Agent Baker.

Greshnev grudgingly gave in. "Alright you can come with me, but you can't stay long." Suddenly he softened and smiled. "But then I want you to go into Manhattan on a shopping spree. Is it a deal?"

"Maxim, I don't need anything."

"That's the deal, take it or leave it."

"Alright, you win."

"Hurry and get ready. I should have been on the expressway by now. The limousine will be waiting at the front door."

Emma made sure she had her pistol in her purse when she came downstairs. Once they were comfortably inside the limo, the chauffer announced, "I've gotten a report about a 3-car pileup at the Jericho exit, sir."

"Then try the Southern State," directed Greshnev. Although traffic was moving a little better on the parkway, it was still stop-and-go traffic all the way into Brooklyn.

When they at last pulled up to the bordello, the driver got out and opened the door. The two passengers got out and went inside. "Good morning, boss," the familiar face of Serge greeted them. Greshnev did not acknowledge his salutation. Instead, he turned to Katrinka and stated, "Before you leave, drop by my office."

"Of course, Maxim." She was greeted by the working girls whom she stopped to talk with. She then knocked on Zoya's office door. "Come in." Katrinka walked in and closed the door. Zoya looked up from her paperwork. "It's been a couple of days since I've heard from you," the fat woman exclaimed. "What's been going on?"

"I've been afraid to call you from the mansion in case anyone should overhear my conversation."

"Have you anything to report?"

"He hasn't touched me."

"Not even once?" inquired a shocked Zoya.

"Not once. I'm getting the feeling that I am reminding him of his dead wife. That may be the reason."

"Have you found any evidence of murder or fraud in the mansion?"

"Nothing so far, but that doesn't mean that there's nothing there. The little escapade that went on last night didn't go off as planned."

"Yeah, I heard about that. The best laid plans they say."

"Tell Agent Baker what I've told you. I've got to go before Greshnev starts looking for me."

Entering Maxim's office, she interrupted his phone call. He handed Katrinka his platinum American Express Card. "Have a good time," he declared and bent over, and kissed her on the cheek. He had never been so forward with her before and she was shocked by his presumptuousness.

"Thank you, Max."

"Just be sure you get back here in time for us to go home." She was driven into Manhattan. She looked through different boutiques for clothing, but had no intention of buying. When she got hungry, she had the chauffer stop at a burger shop and paid for the meal herself. *I'm not taking a penny from him!*

CHAPTER

28

THE MORNING DAWNED overcast, gray, and gloomy. The two agents and the private detective arrived together in front of Anya Lukashenko's hotel door. "Any disturbances?" Cass asked the officer in the hallway.

"It was quiet the entire night."

Parrish knocked, and they entered. Anya stood waiting in a robin's egg blue cashmere sweater and a pair of tapered black pants.

They all stared at her before Hank said, "What you're wearing will never do." Looking down at herself, she responded, "What's wrong with what I'm wearing?"

"Too subtle," Parrish answered. "You don't look the part of a prostitute." Suddenly another knock was heard at the door. Parrish opened it and received a hanger of clothing from the cop outside.

"This just arrived," he commented to the federal agent. Parrish brought them in and draped them over the living room chair. Curiously, Anya went over to examine them. She took the snake skin skirt and floral blouse off the hanger and held them aloft. Turning toward the men, she exclaimed, "Are you kidding me? This outfit will scarcely cover my body!"

"If you're going to masquerade as your sister Albina, you're going to have to dress the part," Cass Baker announced.

"I can't go out in public looking like this," Anya stated in distress. "I don't think that I can do it!"

"Do you want to find your sister's killer or don't you!" Weldon harshly proclaimed. "Just don't waste our time!"

Without saying another word, Miss Lukashenko marched the clothing into her bedroom and closed the door.

While they waited, another knock was heard. Parrish opened the door to find an angry Detective Archie Malone. He pushed his way past the federal agent and entered the room. "What the hell is going on here?"

"Detective Malone, what are you doing here?" inquired Cass.

"Did you think something like this would be going down without my getting wind of it?" he fired back. "Nothing goes on in this precinct without my knowing about it!"

"Listen, Archie..." began Parrish.

"No, all of you listen! I'm going to post police officers around to protect this woman you're using as bait!"

"Out of the question!" barked Baker. "Police presence on the avenue will simply scare away the man we're looking to trap."

"Then, I'm going out with you. The more eyes following Albina's sister, the better." There was no arguing with that.

Anya came out of her bedroom. She looked mortified by the outfit she was wearing. The snakeskin skirt was hiked up to mid-thigh and the blouse barely covered her ample bosom. The spiked red heels culminated the entire lady of the evening look.

"I've been added to your detail to further your protection on the street," Archie declared.

"The more of you there are, the better. Well, I'm as ready as I'll ever be."

"Detective Malone," Baker announced, "You can help by joining me in my car as we tail her." With a simple nod, the five of them left the hotel room and piled into the elevator. As it dropped nine floors, Cass gave Anya her last instructions. "Walk down the street slowly allowing as many people outside to see you as possible."

"Okay."

"Walk with confidence not like a woman who is embarrassed about the way she looks."

"I understand."

"And for God's sake, ditch that nervous look if you're ever going to emulate your sister!"

"I'm doing the best I can!" she blurted out with impatience.

"If anyone on the street approaches you, don't worry. We'll all have you covered."

As the elevator doors opened into the lobby, the passengers disembarked. At the reception desk, the employees gawked and wondered how a prostitute had managed to get by security. "Go outside," instructed Parrish. "And don't worry. We'll be following you." Taking a deep breath, Anya Lukashenko passed through the revolving door which deposited her on the concrete sidewalk.

"Get going," Cass commanded Wilson and Baker. "My car is parked just up the street,"

At first, Anya drew no attention from the people on the street. For most of them, passing a whore on the avenue was an everyday occurrence. Mothers with children drew their little ones away as she neared them as if they were trying to avoid leprosy. The bait walked a few blocks east along Brighton Beach Avenue before a thin balding man with a patch over his right eye stopped and stared as she passed by him. His jaw dropped as he suddenly recognized her. *But, she's dead and buried, isn't she?*

He was about to approach her with caution when something told him not to do it.

As she crossed Coney Island Avenue, another man, stocky and short, stopped dead in his tracks as he realized who she was. No, it can't be Albina! She's been dead over six months. Curiosity overwhelmed his anxiety and he drew up next to her. "Albina, is that you?"

"Get away from me you pervert!" He immediately halted and had a thought. She remembers me!

Parrish instantaneously moved in on him and after a few questions ascertained that he wasn't the man he was seeking. He continued to tail the female bait.

More and more people began to recognize the supposed dead woman as she made her way down the crowded thoroughfare. Recognition turned to whispering as she continued on her way.

That's when the clouds turned threatening and began to drizzle. People hurried off the street before the drenching downpour began. And it came all at once. Ducking into a store doorway, Anya tried to stay as dry as possible, remembering the soaking she had received the night before. Cass pulled up in his car and waved her in. She was soon joined by Hank and Parrish, and the car pulled into the street.

"I guess that's all for today," Archie opined.

"I suppose it is, but our mission was accomplished despite the timing of the lousy weather," Cass proclaimed.

"How do you figure that?" a confused Malone queried.

"Didn't you see how many people thought they recognized her?"

"One of them even called me by my sister's name," Anya informed them.

"Yeah," added Parrish, "but looking at his rotund size, I realized we'd be looking for a younger, spryer individual."

"Exactly," commented Cass. "Word is now going around that Albina has been spotted on the street. It will get around like wildfire!"

Malone declared, "And then what?"

"And then the murderer will begin to second guess himself. He'll have to come out of hiding to see her for himself."

"We'll get him so rattled that he will begin to make mistakes, revealing his identity."

"That's a long shot," Hank lectured. "We have no guarantee that will happen."

"You've got a better idea about how to capture this criminal?" Parrish sneered.

"No, not really."

"Then keep your negativism to yourself and stop making a bad situation any worse!" Cass castigated. "Tomorrow we'll continue trawling the streets!"

###

It wasn't long before the news reached Greshnev's ears. The first to come forward was Oleg Galinski called "Patch" because of the loss of his right eye. He came barging into the Russian Doll House, drenched from the downpour. Serge immediately held him up. "I've got to talk with Mr. Greshnev!" the slender man pleaded.

"You're creating a puddle on the floor," the guard answered with infuriation.

"Is Mr. Greshnev here?"

"If you're here to spend some time with one of the girls, it's cash on the barrelhead. Your credit here ran out a long time ago!"

"I'm not here for the girls," he retorted somewhat irritated by the statement. "It's Mr. Greshnev that I've come to see!"

"Well, Mr. Greshnev has no time to see you. Get lost!" he shouted shoving the man to the door. It was at that moment that Maxim exited from his office. He looked up to see the commotion going on in the corridor.

"What's going on?" he snapped at the two men.

Serge answered, "He's here to visit with one of the girls, but I told him…"

"I'm not here for that!" protested Oleg. "I've come to talk to you."

"I'm too busy," Maxim fired back.

"You're going to want to hear this," advised Patch. Maxim wasn't sure why, but he sensed that the bald man might be right.

"I'll give you a minute,"

"I need to tell you this in private."

"Come on," commanded Greshnev as the visitor followed him into his private office. Galinski closed the door behind them.

"Do you think I could have a little whisky? The rain has left me with a chill." Maxim glowered at the rain-soaked man before he took out a glass tumbler and poured about two finger's worth of liquor into it.

"This better be good," he warned, as Patch gulped it down.

"That was good," he exclaimed putting the glass down on Greshnev's desk.

"Alright, you've had your drink. So, what is it that you've come to tell me?"

"I think this information is worth some monetary compensation," he reported cockily.

"I think that if you don't tell me what's on your mind, I'll hand you over to Serge to have a little fun with you."

"Okay," Oleg relented. "I saw Albina."

Maxim didn't say a word.

"Did you hear me? I said I saw Albina Lukashenko."

"You're drunk!"

"All I've had today is the drink you just gave me! I'm telling you that I've seen her, and she's alive!"

"Albina is dead. What you saw was probably a figment of your soused imagination," he answered dismissively. "Now, get out!" For Maxim, however, the siting by another person validated what he had seen the night before.

"I'm telling you that I just saw her walking down Brighton Beach Avenue as alive as you and me!" The flashback of the image of a soaking Albina instantly entered his brain. *This can't be true. I saw her dead body.*

"Now do you think this information is worth some money?"

"All it's worth is you getting out of here without a hammering from Serge. Beat it!"

"Is that the thanks I get…"

"I said get out!" Maxim screamed as he came around his desk in a threatening manner. Oleg didn't hesitate. He made a hasty retreat.

Maxim was not usually prone to headaches, but he had a raging one at that very moment. He turned off the light, lay back on the couch and closed his eyes. The likeness of the dead prostitute came to him as he had seen her last night, outside his house. *This is madness!* he told himself. *None of this can be true!* Maxim tried to let his mind drift, by concentrating on Katrinka, the girl for whom he was falling hard, but even that didn't seem to ease his head pain.

Greshnev couldn't remember how long he lay there before he fell asleep. The sound of voices nearby woke him up. The headache had almost completely gone away when his eyes finally opened. Annoyed by the racket outside, Greshnev got up from the couch and opened his office door. "What the hell is going on here today?" he demanded.

Serge turned toward his employer apologetically saying, "I'm sorry, but now, Demetri Potemkin wants to talk to you." Greshnev focused on the fat man down the hallway. He had received numerous complaints from his girls that the fat man was just too disgusting to have sex with them. Maxim had agreed and banned him from the premises.

"What are you doing back here, Potemkin? The last time you were here, I threw you out and told you never to come back!"

"I know, I know, but you're going to want to hear what I've come to tell you!" Maxim got a sick feeling in the pit of his stomach, but waved the man down anyway. Demetri waddled his way to the office door, his fat thighs rubbing together as he made his way down.

"Get inside!" he ordered the rotund man. "Let me guess," the mob boss told Potemkin as he closed the door. "You've seen Albina too. Am I right?"

Demetri's eyes opened in amazement. "Yes, just a little while ago."

"And just where did you see the dead whore?"

"She's not dead I tell you. I saw her on the corner of Coney Island and Brighton Beach Avenues."

"Has the whole world gone crazy?" Greshnev asked rhetorically.

"I don't know about the whole world, but I thought I must be imagining it."

"So, is that it? Is that all you've come to tell me?"

"No."

"Well, what else?"

"I couldn't believe what I was seeing, so I approached her."

"And…?"

"And I called her by her name."

"So, I'm assuming she said something to you?"

"Yeah, she said, "Get away from me you pervert!""

"You're saying that Albina Lukashenko is walking and talking her way through Brighton Beach? Maybe they're filming a zombie movie here in Brooklyn," Greshnev said sardonically.

"Look," the corpulent man responded. "I'm just conveying to you what I saw, what others saw. This is no bullshit!"

"This is absurd. Maybe this woman looks something like Albina?" he replied beginning to second-guess himself.

"There was no mistaking her. It was Albina in the flesh!"

"Well now that you've told me what you wanted to say, why are you still here?"

"I think this bit of news I've brought you deserves some kind of reward."

"And what were you thinking of as payment?"

"I want to sleep with one of the girls."

"That's out of the question. None of them would consent," he proclaimed with revulsion. "And I don't blame them!" A sour expression flashed across Demetri's face.

"Then I'll take money."

"And how much were you thinking would be enough?"

"A nice round figure like $1,000 dollars will do just fine." Opening the top draw of his desk, he watched expecting Maxim to pull out cash. Instead a Glock was flashed in his face. Potemkin stepped back in alarm, his hands up in a defensive gesture.

"What if I let you walk out with your life? Would that be enough?"

"Look, I'm just here trying to do you a favor. I even debated with myself whether I should come to you with this information."

"I guess your common sense didn't win! You can go now!" Potemkin gratefully left the office, his life intact, leaving Maxim in sullen silence. *I'm going out to see this for myself!*

###

The rain continued to pummel man and beast on the streets of Brooklyn, but that did not prohibit Maxim from trying to leave the bordello. "Boss", Boris his bodyguard declared in a concerned tone of voice. "It's still raining cats and dogs out there!"

"Get out of my way," his employer snarled pushing the bewildered guard away. "And don't come with me!"

"At least take an umbrella with you," he pleaded like a concerned wife. Maxim didn't bother to answer as he stepped out into the downpour. It wasn't too long before he was completely soaked. Walking swiftly on the street, he stopped and stared at every blonde woman still on the avenue.

"Albina Lukashenko!" he called out randomly as he roamed in the streets. The people still out either stared at the man in the wet suit or ignored him completely. Maxim wandered about aimless seemingly oblivious to the rain that battered down on his shoulders and head. Almost 15 minutes of this unrelenting behavior continued as he searched frantically. As he continued down the street in a distraught frame of mind, the limousine with Katrinka in it drove down the street.

"Oh my God," she gasped as she caught sight of him on the pavement. "Pull over!" she ordered the chauffer. He immediately came to a stop. Taking her umbrella with her, she got out onto the sidewalk and ran after him. She grabbed him by the wet sleeve of his suit.

Maxim turned to see who had accosted him. "Albina?"

"What are you doing out here?" asked the agent as she pulled him underneath the protection of her umbrella.

"Have you seen her out here?" he queried his eyes in wild excitement.

"Seen who?"

"Albina, Albina Lukashenko, of course."

"Come into the limousine," she encouraged him, "or you'll catch your death of pneumonia!" Like a child being led by his mother, Greshnev allowed her to get him into the limousine.

"Take Mr. Greshnev home!" she ordered the driver.

"No!" Maxim protested. "I have to get back to the office."

"Your workday is done. Drive him home." Without uttering a word, Maxim sat back and let Katrinka make the decision for him. Katrinka reached out and turned the dial to make the heat higher so that Maxim did not catch a chill.

It was a few minutes after 3 in the afternoon and traffic out to Long Island hadn't quite started to build up. However, the rain, which had not slackened, created traffic that crept along the Expressway. It wasn't long before Maxim's head dropped to his chest as he slipped into a deep sleep. Emma watched as the "Mad Russian" as he was sometimes referred to, slept as peacefully as an innocent child. No innocent child is he. *I can recite at least 20 names of victims he has had rubbed out, and yet he appears to be putty in my hands. Let's hope the situation remains this way long enough that I can get evidence that will make the charges stick.*

She gazed out the window and watched the raindrops hesitate and then fall together as they made their way down the glass. *What if he eventually wants to get too close to me? How am I going to discourage him without him losing his temper with me? I'll cross that bridge when I get to it!* Emma watched the mob boss continue to sleep peacefully. She touched his forehead with her hand, and felt the flush of a fever beginning.

When the limousine pulled up to the estate gate, Vladimir, the new head of security, accompanied by a snarling Doberman Pinscher was there to greet them. He watched as the limousine pulled through and drove up to the portico in front of the house. Katrinka hurried to the door and rang the bell. When the butler appeared, she announced, "Help me get Mr. Greshnev up to his bedroom!"

"What's happened, Miss?" he asked following her.

"He has a fever!" As they pulled him out, he never awakened. The chauffer and butler dragged him through the doorway and up the staircase. "Get him out of his wet clothing, dry him off, get his pajamas on and put him to bed.

"Yes, Miss," they said in unison. Leaving the men to do their work, she waited outside in the carpeted hallway. She instructed the maid, "Get me the thermometer, and ask cook to prepare a hot cup of tea.

"Yes, Miss!" The maid slipped into the master bathroom and removed the thermometer from the medicine cabinet. Handing it to Katrinka, she went downstairs to the kitchen to retrieve the cup of tea.

Once he was under the covers, the two men were dismissed, as Katrinka shook the thermometer and then placed it between his lips. Counting off the minutes, she removed and read it. "One hundred and three," she gulped and walked out to the hallway. "Call Mr. Greshnev's doctor. He's very sick!" she exclaimed to the butler at the bottom of the staircase. As he dialed, the maid brought up the cup and saucer. "Thank you."

"You're welcome, Miss." The agent lay the cup and saucer on the end table.

"Maxim!" He didn't stir. She suddenly began to worry that he would pass away under her watch and escape being punished for his crimes. Again, she called his name and shook him until he was groggily awake. "Drink this tea. It will make you feel better." *You're not going to die on me, buddy! No, I won't see you die peacefully in your bed when all your victims died such horrible deaths! I'm going to pull you through this so that hopefully you can be strapped into the electric chair and have the deadly current course through and burn your body!*

Determined to see this through, she waited anxiously for the call from the crime boss's personal physician.

CHAPTER

29

WELDON HAD FALLEN asleep to the sound of the rain beating against his bedroom window. It was a soothing sound, a sound that had lulled him into a deep slumber. The only other sound in the room was the ticking of his bedroom clock, its minute hand quietly turning.

Images came to the private detective appearing and evaporating into the mists of his dream world. Kaz was the central figure appearing over and over again. The beefy man with the quick grin seemed to be trying to tell him something, but Weldon was unable to hear him. "Speak louder!" he begged the dead mobster, but all he did was to fade away.

He was instantly replaced by his cousin Ivan, the former bartender at The Dive. He was followed by the specters of Albina, Karina and Renata. All three women smiling and waving at him. Slowly they began to dissolve. "Don't leave!" he shouted out. "I thought Greshnev said he'd sent you to Moscow, Renata. He lied to me. Now I know you're dead. I want to know who killed all of you?"

Before he could hear them, a jolting ringing woke him from his reverie. "What the hell?" he yelled as he got up. Realizing it was his phone, Hank answered and asked, "Who is this?"

"Weldon? It's Zoya." Hank reached for his clock. It was only ten in the evening. His voice calmed down. "What's going on?"

"I got a call from Emma a little while ago."

"What did she say?"

"Greshnev is seriously ill. He has a high fever because he was outside in the rain this afternoon."

"Why was he outside?"

"Two of his former clients came in to tell him that they had seen Albina on the street."

"Then the plan worked!"

"It may have worked too well. If he dies, we may never be sure who the killer is."

"Now what?"

"Get in touch with Baker and Wilson and find out what they want to do."

"Will do," he answered hanging up. He dialed Cass Baker's hotel.

"Hotel Petersburg," a woman's voice greeted him.

"Mr. Baker's room please."

"One moment." The phone began to ring.

"Hello?" Baker's voice answered.

"Cass, it's Hank. I just got a call from Zoya who was in touch with Emma."

"What's happening?" Weldon related the facts as he had heard them.

"We need to go over there quickly!"

"I agree. You get a hold of Parrish and I'll phone Archie. We'll meet you at Greshnev's estate."

Two cars sped their way across Long Island on the Expressway despite the rain- slicked roads. Baker and Wilson arrived first and parked a little distance from the main gate. Weldon and Malone pulled their car next to the FBI agents and rolled down their window. "What's the plan," Detective Malone inquired.

"We're going to flash our badges and barge through the gate if we have to."

"We'll be right behind you," Weldon yelled to the two men.

The cars took off until they reached the front gate. Parrish got out to ring the buzzer. Vladimir and another man came out with their dogs. "What do you want?" growled the security head.

Parrish Wilson responded, "We're here to see Mr. Greshnev!"

"Are you expected?"

"Just open the gate!" he shouted flashing his government identification.

"Get lost copper! Mr. Greshnev would never allow you entry into his home!"

"Open it or we'll ram it down with our car!"

"I wouldn't try that if I were you!" threatened Vladimir.

Parrish merely got back into the car as Cass moved the vehicle back and revved the engine. Baker yelled, "This is your last notice before I put my foot on the gas pedal! Then see if you can tell your boss how the gates were damaged!" Both men behind the gate looked at each other as they spoke Russian. "Well, what's it going to be?" Vladimir pushed a button and the gates opened wide. The two cars drove through and went on to the main house.

Emma was there to open the door for them. "Thank God you've come." she expressed with a sense of relief. The men entered the lobby.

"Where is he?" Archie wanted to know.

"He's in the bathroom tub. The doctor ordered ice cubes be filled around him to bring down his temperature.

"Is he lucid?" Cass wanted to know as they all made their way up the staircase.

"At times."

They all entered the master bathroom to find Maxim's body covered with ice. He was blue in the face and shivering. Malone said with a concerned voice, "Is he going to make it?"

"The doctor says that if he survives the night and breaks the fever, he'll have a better chance at recovery." Cass sat down on the edge of the tub. Maxim's eyes remained closed.

"Maxim," Baker called out. The sick man never stirred. "Maxim!" he said in a stronger tone. "Maxim, open your eyes!" The mob boss's eye lids suddenly fluttered open.

"Albina?" he answered back. Cass decided to go with the false identity.

"Yes, Max. It's me, Albina." Cass looked into his eyes and saw that they were glazed over.

"Albina?"

"Yes, Max. I'm here with you. Do you have something to say to me?"

"Where are you?"

"I told you that I'm right here. What do you want to tell me?"

"Where have you been all this time? I've missed you! You were one of my best money makers."

"I was murdered, Max. Don't you remember?" Maxim nodded lethargically to the statement, his teeth chattering from the cold.

"I remember."

"Tell me, Max. Who murdered me?" No answer was forthcoming. "Do you know who killed me?"

"The bastard!" the mob boss grumbled.

"Which bastard?"

"If I get my hands on him, I'll kill him!" The five of them began to think that they were on the brink of making a breakthrough.

"You'll kill who?"

"That rat bastard!"

They could see that Cass was about to lose his patience. "What's the bastard's name?"

"I don't know, but when I get a hold of him, he's as good as dead!"

"That's it!" Malone reacted in disgust. "All we've discovered is that Greshnev is probably not the killer. We're back to square one!" Agent Baker stood up from the tub.

"You're most likely right, but at least we've eliminated one of the suspects."

"What now?" remarked Weldon. "Where do we go from here?"

"Anya goes back on the street tomorrow. We'll keep trying to lure our suspects until one of them takes the bait!"

The next morning was Saturday and the sun rose on the first warm day of May. Like bears awakening from a long winter hibernation, the residents of Brighton Beach came out to soak up the warm rays. People walked the avenues, stopping to shop or to peer into store windows. Older people sat on the benches around the band shell at Asser Levy Park while children played around them.

At Maxim Greshnev's estate, a phone call was made to his doctor. Emma told him that Max's temperature had spiked again after it had initially gone down. "Rush him by ambulance to Mt. Sinai Hospital in Nesconset! I'll meet you there!"

The ambulance arrived with the sound of a screeching siren. The attendants were shown upstairs where he was lying feverishly in bed. Federal Agent Emma Fedosov watched as they got him on a stretcher, carried the seriously ill man down the steps and into the back of the emergency vehicle. "Are you coming with him?" one of the attendants inquired. Emma shook her head.

"The doctor will be there. He knows what's been going on." Once more the ambulance raced through the open gates and disappeared down the rustic road.

"Do you think he will recover?" the butler asked her. Emma simply shrugged and retorted, "It's in God's hands now."

Emma walked upstairs to her bedroom and closed the door. She dialed a local cab company to be picked up. "Ten minutes," she heard the dispatcher tell her. Quickly, she dialed Cass's hotel room and informed him that she would be returning.

She moved around the room gathering her things. From inside the closet, she removed her piece of luggage. She neatly packed her things and carried it to the front door. "Are you going to the hospital?" the butler queried.

"No, I'm leaving." A look of shock registered on his face, but he said nothing and walked away. A yellow cab approached the gate. Vladimir rang the house and Emma picked up. "There's a cab here," he announced.

"Let him through," she answered. She walked down the brick stairs and handed the bag to the cabbie. Emma looked back at the house. *Well this has been quite the experience!*

She gave the driver the address of Cass and Parrish's hotel. The car drove over the gravel drive to the front gate. Vladimir gave her a strange look as the taxi drove out. *He'll never say anything to Greshnev about what happened last night. Greshnev would kill him if he found out that he had been talking to the FBI and had let them pass inside the grounds!* She sat back and relaxed as the cab drove to Brooklyn.

The verdant open suburbs soon gave way to the brown and swarming boroughs of New York City. Traffic slowed as they approached the Jackie Robinson Parkway, and crawled after they entered the Belt Parkway. It took over two hours before the cab finally pulled up in front of the hotel. She took her luggage and made her way straight to the elevator. She pressed the 11th floor button on the elevator. She walked to the room and knocked on the door.

"That took a while," commented Cass.

"Traffic was a mess. I think the Mets are playing a home game at Shea this afternoon."

"That'll do it!" Weldon scoffed.

"That was quite a scene last night," opined Agent Baker as Emma dropped her luggage and sat down.

"It certainly was strange," Emma remarked.

Parrish now weighed in. "Who would have thought we would grill Greshnev in his home inside a tub filled with ice? It was almost laughable!"

"Still, we learned one thing," private investigator Hank Weldon added. "We can eliminate Greshnev as a suspect."

"I don't agree," Archie spoke up. "He couldn't have been in his right mind when we questioned him. Anything he said last night can't be taken seriously."

Emma asked, "So you still think we should keep Greshnev at the top of the list of suspects?"

"In my mind, he should not be ruled out."

"I think we should keep him on our suspect list, but perhaps no longer on the top," remarked Agent Baker to the others.

"You believed that raving he did yesterday?" the New York City Detective inquired incredulously.

"I don't think he had the ability to hide the truth from us given his condition."

"I'm in agreement with Archie," Weldon articulated. "He's one of the biggest scumbags in "Little Odessa". I wouldn't believe a word that came out of his mouth, sick or well!"

Agent Parrish Wilson interrupted. "One thing's for sure. Anya will have to go back on the street."

Anya who had sat quietly listening, now spoke up. "I'm uncomfortable doing that again," she answered meekly. "I just don't think I can do this anymore."

Emma spoke to her woman to woman. "I can understand how you feel." No woman wants to be degraded like that."

"Finally, somebody understands the way I feel."

"I get it, but there's the question of who killed Albina. Without your help, we may never know what happened to her. You wouldn't have come to New York if you didn't care about your sister. Am I right about that?"

"Albina and I were very close until she left to become an "actress" in New York. It was soon after that she stopped communicating with me. I didn't know what kind of life she had turned to. I guess she just didn't want me to know how far down she had fallen." Anya burst out into tears.

Putting her arm around the weeping woman, Emma queried in a soothing voice, "Do you really want to go back home never uncovering the truth about your sister's death?"

"No, not really."

"I have an idea." Everyone in the room listened intently.

"You probably feel all alone and vulnerable out there, don't you?" Anya nodded her head.

"We're out there with you," Hank volunteered.

Emma eyeballed him, and Weldon stood down.

"I'm going to walk the streets with you as another prostitute, side by side. Would that make you more comfortable with the situation?"

"It would help."

"Then that's settled." Looking toward Cass, Emma asked, "Is that alright with you?"

"If Anya will feel better, then I'm good with it."

"Alright then, it's a go!"

Boris and Zoya stood at the foot of Greshnev's hospital bed in his private room. Around him, bouquets of multicolored flowers were positioned, and greeting cards from well-wishers were taped on the wall in front of him. They had both been summoned into his presence. An intravenous antibiotic drip was still attached to his arm, even though his temperature had finally returned to normal.

His two employees had arrived just as a private barber had finished shaving the mob boss's face. "Get out of here!" Boris barked, paying the man, and the barber beat a hasty retreat into the hospital corridor.

"How are you doing, boss?" inquired Boris.

"How do you think I'm doing?" he snarled. "I'm stuck in this place until the doctor's sees fit to release me!"

"Don't get yourself upset," counseled Zoya. "You don't want to get yourself sick again, do you?"

"I know...I know. How's the business going in my absence?" he directed the question to his guard.

"No trouble, boss. Everything's running as usual, just as if you were still there."

"If I'm not there, nothing's the same!" he fired back.

"Sure, boss. You're right," his employee placated.

"What about the girls?" Max directed his inquiry to Zoya.

"It's business as usual, Maxim."

"I don't want either of you discussing the fact that I've been ill. If anyone asks why I'm not around, just tell them that I'm on vacation."

"Okay, boss," his male flunky responded.

"I haven't seen Katrinka in days. I tried calling her at my home, but my butler says she has left the house. Do either of you know where she is?" The two of them looked at each other.

"Well, she hasn't been back to the Doll House, Zoya mentioned.

"Do you know if she's contacted any of the girls?"

"Not that I know."

"I want you to question them," said Max to Boris. "Press them hard for answers and let me know the results of your inquiries."

"I will, boss."

"I'll be back in a day or two at the most," he told them.

"Is that what the doctor told you?" Boris wanted to know.

"I tell him and not the other way around, get it?"

"Sure, boss. Anything you say."

"Now the two of you get out! I'm getting tired."

"Okay, boss."

"Feel better soon," Zoya said as they both left the room.

Max pushed the button that lowered the head of his bed. He lay his head down and closed his eyes. *Where's Katrinka? Why has she disappeared?* The idea that his house guest was missing disturbed him very much.

Greshnev thought back to the night he had been put into a tub of ice. He remembered how painfully cold it was and how his entire body ached. Vaguely, he recalled a group of people in his bathroom questioning him, but he was damned if he could remember what they were asking him. *They must have been doctors asking me about my fever.* But for the life of him, he just could not recollect the incident very well.

"Well, Mr. Greshnev," his thoughts were interrupted. "How are you feeling today?" Maxim opened his eyelids to see his doctor reading his chart at the foot of his bed.

"Actually, I'm feeling just fine."

"Well your temperature is finally normal. That's good."

"When can I leave?" the Russian demanded of him.

"I can't discharge you until your temperature remains normal for two days."

"I want to leave tomorrow!"

"That's out of the question," advised his doctor. "It would be far too soon for that."

"That was not a question. Either with or without your permission, I'm signing myself out of here tomorrow!"

"I will not be held responsible if you were to have a relapse!"

"Don't worry, Doc," he replied nonchalantly. "You'll be in the clear!"

"Then I guess this will be my last hospital checkup with you."

"I guess so."

"Well good luck to you, Mr. Greshnev."

"I make my own good luck," he answered back sarcastically.

As soon as the doctor left his room, Max buzzed for the nurse. A shapely brunette came to his room. "What can I do for you, Mr. Greshnev?"

"I want you to prepare my release papers for tomorrow."

"The doctor usually orders them for his patient."

"I'm releasing myself tomorrow morning."

"I don't think your doctor would agree to your actions."

"Screw him!" The young woman was shocked by his reaction.

"Excuse me?"

"He has nothing to do with it! Just make sure I get my release form early tomorrow. Is that clear enough for you to understand?"

"Very clear," she responded coldly.

"Well then, get out of here! I want to be alone!"

CHAPTER

30

A RM IN ARM, Emma and Anya walked along Coney Island Avenue in clothing that loudly broadcasted their trade, the sun warming and brightening things. Discreetly behind them, keeping pace, walked Agent Parrish Wilson, and across the way, Private Investigator, Hank Weldon. Following all of them in a car was Federal Agent Cassidy Baker and Police Detective Archibald Malone.

The followers of the Jewish faith known as "The Hasidim", with women outfitted in long dresses and wigs and pushing baby strollers, quickly drew away from the pair on the street, shaking their heads in repugnance and mumbling to themselves.

"I hate the way they are looking at us, as if we were diseased!" commented Miss Lukashenko to her companion.

"Ignore them," advised the agent. "Sticks and stones…"

A few men approached them on the street to ask them for the price of their services, but Emma could see that they did not recognize Anya as Albina. "Beat it!" Agent Fedosov would say with disdain in her voice and waving her hand. "You couldn't afford us!" The men usually walked away with their tails between their legs, but occasionally, they would find one that would become boisterous. "You dirty whores" one of them began and gave the appearance of becoming violent. That's when Parrish would come up and flashed his badge.

"I'm with the FBI and if you don't move off right now, I'll arrest you for soliciting a prostitute, get it?"

"Okay, buddy. I'm leaving!" He speedily moved off, leaving the duo to continue their walk. Parrish quickly dropped back behind them to continue his surveillance.

It was like this all afternoon as the sun hurriedly made its descent. Cass made the decision to end the day and picked up all the members in his car. He made his way back to the hotel. The man behind the registration desk eyeballed them suspiciously as they made their way through the lobby. He quickly rang for the manager and pointed them out as they waited for the elevator. Moving hastily, the manager confronted them at the elevator door. "Excuse me," he began, "I'm the manager here. Are all of you registered at the hotel?"

Cass and Archie turned toward him. "We're involved in a police matter." Both men showed him their badges. "Please do not interfere with our work." The door to the elevator suddenly opened and the others walked in.

"But how long is this to continue?"

"Until further notice!" Cass abruptly ended the conversation, and with Archie, joined the others on the elevator. The door finally closed on the manager, whose mouth was agape. "That should take care of him for a while," Agent Baker stated as the elevator rose. The others remained silent until they got to the hotel room.

"That was another wasted day," harangued a disappointed Anya. "How long do we go on with this?"

"As long as it takes until we get a bite."

"That's not an answer, besides I still have Greshnev topping my list of suspects! It's a total waste of time to continue this. Greshnev needs to be arrested," noted Malone.

"And where's the evidence that he has committed these crimes?" shot back Parrish. "We could never hold him."

"Okay boys, take it easy. Stop making this a pissing match," Emma said stepping into the verbal fray.

"Parrish is right," Cass spoke up. "We have nothing on him."

"Let me have him alone for a little while and I'll have him singing like a canary!" Archie boasted.

"Those old police tactics don't fly anymore," mentioned Hank. "He'll be screaming about police brutality!"

"Let him scream. My methods are very effective!"

"I'm sure they are, Archie," Emma replied in a mollifying voice, "but that's never going to happen. Let's be realistic. What information do we have to support Greshnev's arrest? Even the worst attorney would be able to get the charges dismissed if we don't have anything concrete."

"Well," Hank began, "we know that Albina worked for him and it's rumored that he even was having a relationship with her."

"And what about Kaz," offered Parrish. "He worked for him and wound up dead."

"That's true," noted Weldon.

"He also worked for you, Hank," Malone pointed out.

"What's that supposed to mean?" the private detective answered angrily.

"It means that just because you're helping in this plan, it doesn't mean I've forgotten about your involvement with some of the people who are dead."

"You know me better than that," countered Hank.

"I used to know you. I knew you when you were married to Clare, and when we graduated the police academy together when we were best friends. But now…"

"Don't mention my wife's name," Weldon answered caustically. "You don't know anything about us."

"I know that she kept you grounded, kept you from doing things that you would harm yourself because you're self-destructive."

"Stop now while you still have your teeth in your mouth!"

"Now you're just a hopeless alcoholic, a drunk who is subject to occasional blackouts. How do any of the rest of us know what you do during those memory lapses. Murder isn't too farfetched."

"I haven't had a drink in a while besides, I'm no murderer. I can say that right here and now."

"As far as you know, but that doesn't prove anything, does it?"

"I don't have to defend myself to you!"

"I'm the cop. You are no longer on the force. What if you're just playing along with us, going through the motions to throw us off your scent. What better way to throw suspicion off yourself than to be seemingly cooperative with the FBI and the police."

Hank suddenly made a bull's rush toward his former partner, a look of hatred and loathing on his face. Parrish tackled him to the floor before he could reach Malone.

"I'll kill him," he screamed in a voice that would have raised the dead.

"Why don't you just leave and go back to The Dive. You know that you're dying to get a drink," remarked Malone.

"Get off me!" Hank screamed at Parrish who kept him pinned down.

"Not until you promise not to get into a fistfight."

"Let him loose," Malone taunted. "I'll dispatch this rummy in no time flat!"

"Enough," Cass yelled above the mayhem. "Nobody is going to get into a physical altercation, is that understood? Archie?"

"Yeah, alright."

"Hank?"

"Fine, just get Parrish off me!" Agent Wilson got up.

"This has gotten way out of hand," scolded Baker. "We can't have this infighting. Focus on why we've come together, and that's to help Miss Lukashenko discover who killed her twin sister."

"Do you consider me a suspect?" demanded Weldon of him.

"No, not right now." The flare that had almost sparked into a fight slowly went out.

"Tomorrow we start again," Cass instructed. "Eventually we will draw the murderer out from whatever rock he's been hiding under. Until then, everybody get a good night's sleep. We're back here tomorrow at nine."

Everyone left Anya's room, and moved into the hallway. Soundlessly, they all entered the elevator. Once they reached the lobby, everyone went their separate ways. Cass grabbed Hank by the shoulder to speak to him alone. "Are you alright?"

"Yeah," Weldon answered resentfully. "I'm just pissed at what Malone started with me upstairs."

"Can I trust you to go home tonight and not get drunk?"

"I'm not going to risk my sobriety for anyone," he fired back.

"Good. I'll see you tomorrow morning bright and early." Baker turned away. Hank Weldon had black thoughts enter his brain as he walked out. *Malone is a bastard!* He seethed with antagonism. *I could have killed him upstairs just now. It was lucky that Parrish stopped me from stomping in his head! God, I need a drink right now!*

###

A crescent moon rose into a starry sky as Hank Weldon walked down the street to his home. The evening was still mild, and many residents of the community seemed to be outside. Conversations between neighbors sitting on the stoop went on while children played tag on the street, but Hank didn't notice any of it as he walked on.

A few yards away, a pair of dark eyes followed behind casting a shadow on the sidewalk towards the detective. This unrelenting stalker kept eyesight trained on the man that he was monitoring while brushing passed other people.

This continued for a few blocks until the trailer noticed that Weldon had just passed The Dive. The detective walked on, never looking back when he suddenly stopped a few steps away. Not wanting to be caught in the act of following him, this person took out a ring of keys and stepped into the street as if they were looking for the ignition key to start his car. The person watched carefully as Hank made his way back to the front door of the establishment. Weldon just stood there between heaven and purgatory not knowing what he was going to do. The pursuer thought, *Go in and order yourself a drink! One drink couldn't hurt you!*

Hank grabbed the doorknob, opened the portal and entered. Cigarette smoke hung all around the room at first stinging his eyes, but he soon got used to it. Walking to the bar, he expected to see the beefy Ivan pouring out shot glasses of whisky and filling steins of beer. *Wait a minute! Ivan's dead, killed by a knife wound in the back alley of this joint!* Strolling up to the bar, he remembered that the new bartender was the shapely dark-haired beauty Martina. He took a seat at the bar and waited for service.

As he lingered, waiting patiently, he turned the bar stool around to stare at the patrons. Some of the faces were the same as when he used to go on benders. These were mixed with other faces he did not recognize. While he visually polled the patrons, the pair of eyes stared at the detective from outside the bar window, watching and hoping that the alcoholic would order a drink.

At last, Martina came up to him while his back was still turned to her. "What will you have? She inquired of him. He turned the bar stool around at looked at her. "Listen, buddy" she began when he didn't have an answer for her. "I can't waste my time waiting for you to make up your mind! Either give me your order or hit the bricks!"

"I'll have a vodka and tonic with Grey Goose, he blurted out before he could even stop himself.

"Finally!" she replied with exasperation and relief. Before he knew it, the glass appeared before him. He lay his money on the counter and Martina rang it up and pushed the change toward him. Hank's hands remained on the counter without moving, never reaching for the libation because he felt that if he did, he would be shaking hands with Lucifer himself. At last, his arm reached out and his hand grasped the drink. The glass was cold as he drew it towards him. Once again, he hesitated before he moved. He tilted the glass towards his mouth. He sat there as if he were frozen in time debating with himself as to what his next move would be. He eyed the liquid carefully as he detected the scent of a freshly cut lime section balanced on the edge of the rim of his glass. *It smells so good.*

What the hell are you waiting for, the person on the outside told himself. *Go ahead and do it already you lily-livered son-of-a-bitch!*

Anybody else paying attention to Weldon would have thought the man was a statue, as if he were waking up from a deep sleep. He put down the glass without taking a sip. Snapping his fingers together to get Martina's attention, the bartender walked over. "What's the matter? Something's wrong with the drink?"

"Not at all. I've just changed my mind," he replied pushing the glass toward her.

"Well, do you want something else?"

"I'll have a carbonated water with ice, please." She stared at him for a second before she took the glass and drained its contents into the sink.

"Fine, although it's a waste of good liquor." Weldon simply shrugged at this statement. A glass of carbonated water and ice was set before him. Once again, Hank laid his money on the bar. A voice outside grumbled, "God damn you!" and then the person walked away.

After some time and a few sips, Hank Weldon got off the bar stool and made his way to the door. *I did it!* He smiled to himself. *I really did it!* He opened the door and walked onto the cement pavement outside. There was a sudden spring in his step as he continued his way home, and the grin stayed on his face as if had been plastered on.

He climbed the three flights of stairs to his apartment and his footsteps resounded in the empty hallway. Weldon entered the apartment and turned on the light switch. The lamp by the couch lit up the dreary surroundings.

Hank threw his jacket on the chair. As if replaying a movie in his head, Weldon went over the scenario that had occurred when they all went back to Anya's hotel room. *Malone had no right accusing me the way he did! I'm not a killer. An alcoholic, but not a killer! Where does he get off saying those things to me! Because he's a detective doesn't give him liberty to smear my name with hollow denunciations!*

Undressing himself until he was in his underwear, he slipped under the sheets of his unmade bed, lay his head on the pillow, and reached over to turn off the lamp.

The wheels in his mind began to turn. *It looks like Malone has Greshnev and myself at the top of his list of defendants! I won't rest until I prove to him that I'm not the man he is looking for!*

It was decided that instead of posting a cop outside of Anya's hotel room, Emma would become the young woman's roommate. It was after the men of the group had departed that both women sat down to look at the hotel menu. Anya ordered a chicken salad sandwich from room service while Emma went with a cob salad. The two also requested coffee.

They enjoyed their repast and talked for hours, Anya providing more details of a troubled childhood.

Emma glanced at the alarm clock on the table between their beds. "My goodness, it's after 11. We need to get to bed." Turning off the lamp between them, they both said goodnight. Before she dropped off to sleep, Emma thought, *Poor kid, she's really had a hard time of it, but it won't be over until her sister's killer is found and brought to justice!*

CHAPTER

31

A S GRESHNEV WAS being driven into Brooklyn, he sat back and reviewed the last few days in his mind. Two women were haunting him now, an ostensibly dead Albina, and a living but missing Katrinka. Women will drive a man mad!

The limousine finally left the mechanical mayhem of traffic at Exit 8 and entered Coney Island Avenue. The sidewalks teemed with people, men on their way to the subway and their jobs in Manhattan, and women holding the hands of their children, or pushing a stroller on their way to the supermarket. *The proletariat who are like robots going through the motions each day, their minds anesthetized, void of any emotions. At least that is what Karl Marx wrote in The Communist Manifesto. Those fools in the Soviet Union don't know how much money a person can make illegally under Capitalism. You'll never find me in their bland world!*

From Coney Island Avenue, the vehicle pulled up in front of the Russian Doll House. The chauffer came out to open the passenger door and Maxim exited. *The good weather is continuing,* he told himself as he looked up into the azure sky.

He strode to the front door. As usual, Serge was already at his post. Turning, his guard was taken aback. "Boss, should you be back at work so soon?"

"Just do your job and mind your own business." He hesitated a moment before he inquired, "Has Katrinka been here? He hoped beyond hope that she had turned up at the bordello.

"No, boss. Is she missing?" Maxim ignored the inquiry.

"Is Zoya in yet?"

"She's in her office."

"Tell her I want to see her with the books."

"Right away, boss," he answered and went off like an obedient dog. None of the girls were in the hallway since it was too early for any of them to be up.

Just as Maxim sat behind his desk, a knock was heard at the door. "Come in," he barked. Zoya entered the office carrying the books that listed assets and debits for the last month. "It's good to see you back," the house madam greeted him.

"It's good to be back," answered Maxim. "How has business been?"

"We've done very well," she told him laying out in front of him the open books. Using his index finger, Greshnev followed the columns down to the sums.

"Good," he related to her as he closed the books. "Is there anything that I should know about?"

"We've got two new girls arriving from Vitebsk, Belarus at the end of the week from our agents there."

"Remind me what they look like?" Zoya took out two photographs from one of the books and handed them over to her employer. One was a brunette with an hourglass shape and deep soulful brown eyes. The other was a blonde statuesque with a charming smile. "Yeah," he answered tossing the pictures on his desk in Zoya's direction. "I remember them now."

"Are you sure you should even be here?" she inquired, trying to sound as genuine as possible.

"I'm fine," he retorted. "Besides, if I stayed home, I'd be as bored as I was in the hospital."

"I'm sure."

"Has Katrinka been around?"

"No, boss. Is she missing?" Maxim ignored her query, saying, "Zoya, tell Anton and Ilia to come to my office."

"Right away."

The two henchmen were at their posts at the back of the building where shipments of liquor and other commodities arrived for the bordello. "The boss wants to see the two of you!" The two brutish men did what they were told and walked down the hallway. Ilia knocked on the door. "Come in." The henchman walked in and closed the door behind them. "You want to see us, boss?" asked Anton.

"Yeah!" The pair of goons had never been in their employer's office since they had been interviewed for the job.

"What can we do for you, boss?" queried Ilia.

"I want you to go out and walk around." The two men looked at each other with puzzlement.

"You want us to just walk around?"

"No, you idiot! You're not going out for your health. I have a job for you!"

Anton replied, "Sure boss, anything you want."

"I want you to be on the lookout for Albina Lukashenko!" Once again, the two men stared at each other.

"But she's dead, boss. Don't you remember?" Ilia reminded him.

"I know that!" the mob boss retorted impatiently. "But a few people have said that they've seen her on the streets." *He's either losing his mind or sending us on a wild goose chase!* thought Anton.

"What do we do if we see her?" Ilia inquired, figuring that this would be a total waste of time.

"You grab her and bring her to me."

"And that's it, boss?" queried Anton with some incredulity.

"Yeah, that's it! You two mental midgets can handle that, can't you?" The two bristled at the insult but kept their thoughts to themselves.

"Yeah, we can handle it," responded Ilia.

"Good, then go out there and start looking!" Taking their leave, they left by the front door, and stopped just outside. Anton said, "Is this guy for real?"

"Maybe his recent illness has put him over the edge," responded Ilia, his voice filled with bewilderment.

"Yeah, that's probably it, but we get paid to do what he wants no matter how stupid it sounds."

"Listen," Anton began. "We'll start on Brighton Beach Avenue, each of us on a different side of the street. This way if she's out there, we're sure to come upon her."

"You don't really think Albina's still alive, do you?"

"Hell no, but we've got our instructions."

From inside his office, Maxim watched with fascination as the two men stood there talking. *What are they telling each other?* He asked himself as he watched them conversing. It was almost laughable what he had told them to do, but he had to find out if she had really come back from the dead. Maxim had a difficult time believing that she was resurrected and on the streets of Brighton Beach, but he felt that he needed to find out whether what he had been told was true or just pure unadulterated hogwash. Maxim watched as the two walked to Ilia's car and drove away. They won't find her, but I need to take a chance.

The mob boss picked up the receiver and made a call to Josif Andropov, the man to go to whenever someone was looking for a missing person. He was a man of independent wealth, whose father had been a powerful man back in the Soviet Union. Although he didn't belong to the mob, he had connections to powerful city officials. A woman's voice answered that Maxim believed was his wife Svetlana, a hard-faced woman with a raspy voice. "Andropov residence," she answered.

"Mrs. Andropov?"

"Yes."

"Is your husband at home? Tell him it's Maxim Greshnev."

"Hold on for a minute." It wasn't long until the receiver was picked up.

"Well, I'll be a monkey's uncle. Maxi, you old dog. Where have you been hiding yourself?"

"I can always be found at the Russian Doll House.

"How have you been?"

"I've been well," he lied. "And how have you been?"

"As good as ever. So, what do I owe this phone call out of the blue?"

"I want you to find somebody for me." Josif became business-like in his demeanor.

"Who do you want located?"

"Her name's Katrinka Shchetinin."

"Have you got a recent photograph of her?"

"Unfortunately, I don't have one."

"You're really hamstringing me without her picture. How would you describe her?"

"You remember my wife, don't you?"

"Of course, a beautiful woman. She died way before it was her time."

"Yes," Maxim added sadly. "Katrinka looks a lot like her."

"Really? How did you ever meet her?"

"She worked for me for a little while."

"Do you have anything else I can use?"

"She's originally from Omsk."

"It's not much, but I'll do the best I can."

"Thanks, Josif." Greshnev hung up wondering if he'd ever see her again.

###

"My feet are killing me," Anya complained as she took her right foot out of a red pump with a stiletto heel. "Don't you find them uncomfortable?"

"I'm sure your business attire is a lot easier on the feet, but this is not the first time I've been undercover. I'm used to it by now." Slipping the shoe back on, Albina's twin sister asked, "Can't we at least stop at the deli across the street and get a cup of coffee? I could rest my feet." Emma looked around, making eye contact with Parrish and Hank, indicating that they were about to take a break.

They walked across Brighton Beach Avenue, darting traffic as cars screeched to a halt. "What's the matter honey, business is slow so you're looking to kill yourself?" a heavy-set cabbie demanded.

"Listen, baby!" Emma shouted out in her best Brooklynese accent. "I see more action in a day than you've seen in your lifetime!" She raised the middle finger to punctuate her insult.

"Go to hell!" the cabbie shouted before he drove away. They entered the busy deli.

"The coffee is on me," Emma told her partner. "How do you take it?"

"Black, no milk or sugar." Emma walked to the counter as the owner turned to her. Realizing what she was, he said,

"Get out of my place of business! I serve decent people with families here!"

"My money is as good as anybody's!" Emma argued back. People in the store began to turn toward the commotion. Now the owner's wife piped up.

"You heard my husband! We don't serve whores here!"

Emma turned, "Come on," she said to her companion. "We'll go someplace else." Anya stood up in the direct line of vision of the owner.

"Albina?" he asked, his face turning in a grotesque expression. "I heard the rumors that you'd been seen, but I just can't believe it." Before he could say another word, his wife slapped him hard on the back of his head.

"You know this kind of woman?" She did not wait for his answer before she slapped him hard across the check. It appeared to awake him from his torpor.

"Yes…I mean no!" he stumbled verbally. The two women didn't stick around to hear what else would go on.

"He's in deep shit now," Emma concluded as they left the store.

"Word of my sightings have really gotten around," analyzed Anya.

"I believe the odds of the killer approaching you are now tipping in our favor."

"I hope so. I don't know how much more my feet are going to take."

It was around noon, when the streets and sidewalks were filled with local workers that two men approached them. Startled by their sudden appearance, one grabbed Anya by her neck, his hand over her mouth. Emma withdrew her pistol from her blouse, but the other man clocked her in the nose and she dropped to the pavement like a sack of potatoes. Pedestrians either stopped to watch or continued down the street. No one said a word as the two men dragged the women into their vehicle.

Parrish was the first to notice that he could no longer see them and radioed Hank. "Do you have them in your sight?"

"No, do you?" They ran to the spot where they had last been seen. As Parrish ran, he radioed the car Cass and Archie were in.

"They're gone," Agent Wilson screamed into the radio.

"What do you mean their gone," Cass barked back. "Are you telling me that you lost them?"

"Did anybody see two prostitutes who were just here?" Weldon questioned the people who were around. No one who lived in Brighton Beach was stupid enough to say what had happened. Greshnev's hand of violence and retribution had a long reach.

"Somebody must have seen something?" yelled Parrish as the car with Cass and Archie double parked on the street. They began canvasing the group in the area, but everyone claimed not to see anything.

"It's Greshnev," Cass told the others. "They're afraid to open their mouths because of the repercussions that will follow if Maxim gets even a hint that someone has spoken about him.

"What are we going to do?" asked Parrish. Cass said,

"We're going down to the Russian Doll House and gain entry even if I have to kick the door down

Business was up and running in the Greshnev's illegal place of business by ten in the morning. All the girls had eaten, applied their make-up, and got into the briefest costumes possible. Once the door was opened by Serge for the day, the regular morning clientele entered, chose a woman, paid for her time, and were off for their rendezvous. And things continued as they did six out of seven days of the week. No business was conducted on Sunday.

The back door opened, and Anton hurriedly entered the building. Running into Boris, the henchman requested, "Is the boss still here?"

"He's in his office with Zoya. Is there a problem?"

"Not anymore," expressed Anton over his shoulder as he kept walking. A couple of raps on the door, and Maxim's voice could be heard bidding him to enter.

"Boss can I talk to you privately?" Greshnev nodded to Zoya, who didn't hesitate to leave. Anton waited until the door was closed.

"Did you see her?" Greshnev inquired with curiosity.

"You've got to come outside in the back. I have something to show you."

"You found her?"

"Come see for yourself." He led the mob boss down the hallway and out the back door. Ilia sat in the driver's seat as two women sat bound and gagged in the backseat. Opening the back door, he could clearly see who was sitting there. The view made him suck in his breath in astonishment. "Albina, Katrinka?"

"Two for the price of one, boss!" Anton intoned triumphantly.

"Why did you bring them here?"

"I thought you'd want to see them for yourself."

"I told you to find Albina, not bring her back here! Where did you find them?"

"Walking right down Brighton Beach Avenue as bold as brass," answered Ilia.

"People saw you taking them off the street?"

"They know better than to cross you, boss."

"Untie Katrinka now," he ordered. "Why does she have a bloody lip?"

"Boss, I hate to tell you this, but she was packing a gun and a badge."

"A badge?"

"Yeah, she's an FBI Agent."

"What?" he fulminated, the blood rushing to his face."

"It caught me by surprise too."

"Well get them out of here in a hurry."

"Where do you want us to take them?" questioned Ilia.

"Take them to my warehouse on the Brooklyn docks and keep them there! Now get going!" The two men didn't ask any questions, but drove off immediately.

Maxim entered the building, slamming the door hard behind him. Zoya had overheard the conversation at the back door and approached her employer, pretending not to know what was going on. "Are you feeling okay?" she asked fairly dripping with apprehension.

"I need to speak to you in my office." His voice was grave and serious. They both walked in and shut the door for privacy. "They found her."

"You mean Albina is alive?"

"That wasn't the only shock," he added.

"What else?"

"They had Katrinka in the back seat."

"Well, thank goodness they found her."

Greshnev fumed angrily, "She's an FBI agent!"

"There must be some mistake!" *My God, they've found her out!*

"There's no mistake! She was carrying a weapon and a badge! The government must have faked Albina's death and are trying to drive me out of my mind! They think that if they drive me into a nervous breakdown, I'll confess all my sins, but they have another think coming!"

"Where are they now?"

"Don't worry. I have them safely put away until I can decide what to do with them. Right now, I need you to hold the fort down. I don't know how long I'll be gone."

"Sure," she answered. *Where is he hiding them?* Leaving Zoya in the dust, her boss rushed out of the building.

Zoya began to sweat. *If they break Emma, she could reveal that I was an accomplice in trying to bring Greshnev down. I'm in deep shit!*

She tried to calm herself down and convince herself that there was nothing to get excited about. *Emma is a government agent and I'm sure that they've trained her for a scenario like this!* Although she told herself the right things, she was not confident that her fate was not in danger.

A commotion in the hallway brought her outside her office. Serge was confronting her conspirators. All four of them were taking issue with the guard's attempt to stop them from entering. "You can't come in here!" Serge yelled at the top of his voice. "I don't care who you are!" Because his voice was raised, a few other of Greshnev's men joined the fray at the front door.

"Get out of my way or you'll all be put under arrest!" Cass yelled back, flashing his badge.

"Move out of the way," Parrish commanded them.

The henchman closest to Agent Wilson pushed him away yelling, "Just try to make us move!"

Before the situation could get any worse, Fat Zoya approached, saying "Everybody relax!" For a minute, the arguing died away.

"Where's Greshnev?" Malone demanded.

"He's not here."

"Where is he?" questioned Hank.

"I don't know and that's the truth!" Cass caught her by the wrist and dragged her outside. The other three men remained to make sure their conversation couldn't be heard. When they were far enough away, Cass asked her, "Are you sure you don't know where he is?"

"I swear I don't, but he knows Emma is a government agent. He has both women stashed somewhere."

"Jesus!" he swore, combing his fingers through his hair. "Don't you have any idea where they might have been taken?"

"I'm not sure, but I thought I heard him tell them to take them to the docks."

"Damn, there are hundreds of empty and deserted warehouses around there. I've got to call for reinforcements." As he was about to go, she grabbed him by the arm.

"What if Emma tells him that I've been in collusion with you. He'll kill me before I draw another breath."

"You'll be protected, I promise!" Loosening her grip, he went to join the others back inside.

CHAPTER

32

I T WASN'T LONG before Greshnev arrived at the Brooklyn Navy Yard. Although it was once a place that saw thousands of sailors and Navy vessels, it was now a place of dereliction and neglect.

He drove his own car to the warehouse so that his chauffer didn't know where he was going. Greshnev had exited the back of the bordello, entering a shed where he threw off the green tarp revealing a special-order cobalt blue Ferrari GTS Turbo, in which he drove away. Making sure he didn't run stop signs and traffic lights, he eventually found himself in the rundown and seedy remnants of what was once one of the busiest ports in New York City.

Driving down the cracked cement road where weeds sprouted as high as a small child, he turned the corner and pulled up behind a rusting hulk of a warehouse. Ilia was waiting outside the building. "They're inside?"

"Yeah, boss."

"Keep yourself hidden, but keep your eyes open for anyone who gets too close. Understand?"

"I got you, boss."

Maxim entered the interior where broken windows let the sun's rays light up the interior. It was cavernous and empty except for litter that had accumulated over the years. Pigeons had made nests in the rafters and could be heard cooing and flapping their wings.

In the back of the building, Anton sat on a rickety chair, watching the two gagged prisoners who had been chained to shackles in the rafters. Anton stood up as his employer approached.

"Well, I'm so glad we could have this little gathering," he expressed acerbically. He ripped the gag from Anya's mouth.

"So, Albina," he said. "That was a neat trick! How did you manage to come back from the dead?"

"I'm not Albina," she sputtered.

"What are you talking about?" he yelled irascibly. "If you're not Albina, who the hell are you?"

"I'm her twin sister, Anya."

"It was you who appeared at my dining room window during the rainstorm?"

"Yes, that was me." Taking his hand, he slapped her hard across her face. Anya screamed in shock and pain.

"You, bitch! You come to my home to try to make me think that I'm crazy?" He turned to face Katrinka. "Take off her gag!" he ordered Anton. He untied the gag and she coughed. "So, what's your real name?"

"My name is Emma Fedosov."

"Oh," he fired back. "Don't be so modest! You're a federal agent too, isn't that so?"

"You're right."

"You're damn straight I'm right!"

"You're in big trouble. Not only have you kidnapped Anya, but also a federal agent!"

"I'm quaking in my shoes!" he retorted dismissively.

"Set us free now if you know what's good for you." Once more he raised his hand and struck Emma across her face. She did not say a word.

"What's really remarkable is all the research you've done on my personal life. I mean for you to dress and look so much like my late wife. You really knew how to get to me. I bet your hair color isn't even red, is it?"

"You'd lose that bet."

"Brilliant maneuver!"

"You give me too much credit. It didn't take that much effort to fool you."

"I would have given you everything. I invited you to live in my home and treated you like a lady the entire time you were there."

"Do you think I could ever be with a man who uses women and is a killer. I mean look at what you did to Albina!"

"You had no right to kill my sister," Anya cried out. "She never harmed anyone!"

"Although I don't owe you any explanation, I'm going to be honest with you. I did not kill your sister."

"Then you ordered one of your men to do the job," Emma accused him.

"I swear on the soul of my dead wife; I did not kill or order someone else to murder her." Something inside Emma told her that she was hearing the truth.

"If that's the case," the federal agent began. "it's important that you should set us free now!"

"Unfortunately, it's a little too late for that, especially after the kidnapping charges you mentioned."

"Emma, get us out of this," whined a distraught Anya. "I don't want to die!" she sobbed breaking down into tears.

"Don't worry," confidently answered Emma. "Maxim wouldn't be that foolish. I'm sure Cass and the others are already heading to our rescue."

"You seem so certain about that! How would you like to bet your life on it?" Maxim laughed heartily, his voice resounding off the walls and ceiling.

"I tell you now that you would lose."

"Before Agent Baker and his cohorts get here, the two of you will be gone," he said waving his arms around. "There will be no evidence that you were ever here!"

Turning to Anton, he commanded, "Gag them and get them out of here."

"No...no...no," Anya screamed at the top of her lungs while Emma remained cool and silent."

"Right away, boss!"

"Gag that one first," he pointed to Anya. "Her screaming is getting on my nerves." Anton quickly gagged the emotionally distraught Anya and then he gagged Emma.

Maxim called him to his side. "Once we have them in the trunk, where do you want us to take them?"

In a soft voice, his boss said, "Drive them over to the landfill just south of Starrett City along the Belt Parkway. Kill them and then bury them deep so that no one will ever find them."

Just then, Ilia burst inside. "What is it?" impatiently asked Maxim.

"A car has just entered the complex and is going back and forth as if they are looking for something or someone."

"It has to be Agent Baker and his group! Get these two out of here as quickly as possible and do what I told you," he told Anton.

Picking up a couple of shovels, he replied, "Right away, boss."

You're going to be just too late to be able to save these women, Baker! A faint smile appeared on Maxim's face as the women were dragged away.

The women lay in the darkened and cramped trunk of the car. While Anya cried incessantly, Emma's mind was working overtime. Instantly, the federal agent came up with a solution.

Slowly, she began to loosen the gag that had been wedged in her mouth. She'd used her tongue to block some of the gag in her mouth. Finally, it fell off. "Anya," she called out in a hushed voice. The woman continued to cry. "Anya" she whispered a little louder. This time, her companion heard her. "See if you can loosen the bindings on my hand.

Since Anya was already positioned behind Emma, she raised her rope-bound wrists and began to undo Emma's binds. After working at it for over 15 minutes, the rope fell off. Emma pulled the gag out of the other prisoner's jaw. Anya gagged for a moment until she could catch her breath. Agent Fedosov undid the rope around Anya's wrists.

"You have a plan to set us free?" Miss Lukashenko asked with the dim glimmer of hope in her eyes.

"Keep your voice down," Emma answered with admonishment.

Feeling around, she located the tire iron. "When they stop to open the trunk, we have to move quickly. I'll knock one of them over the head with this thing and you jump out and kick the other as hard as you can in his scrotum. We'll disarm them and lock them in the trunk. Do you understand?"

"I'll do it! You can count on me!"

The car weaved back and forth in traffic until it came to the entrance of the landfill. Pulling into a deserted part of the garbage dump, Ilia brought the car to a halt and turned off the ignition.

"Okay, let's get started," Anton told his partner in crime.

"It's too bad."

"What's too bad?"

"That two beautiful broads like that should be wasted."

"You've got another idea,"

"Yeah, why don't we have sex with them before we kill them."

Anton smiled at the suggestion. "What the hell, why not!"

"We'll give them a little pleasure before the pain." They exited the car, Ilia with the car keys in his hand. He unlocked the trunk and let it fly open. They were shocked by the ferocity they experienced when the trunk opened. Emma swung hard and connected the tire iron across Ilia's face. He immediately sank to the ground with a moan. Anton stood frozen for a moment. It was just enough timed for Anya to thrust her foot into his groin. Screaming out in pain, he dropped to his knees and fell over on his side. Taking the tire iron, Emma gave him a shot to the head. Anton lay there in silence.

The women stared down at their kidnappers with hard-earned satisfaction. Disarming each of them of their pistols, and grabbing the car keys, Emma said, "Help me get them into the trunk." Although they struggled, they managed to load them inside.

"Nighty night, boys" Anya said with scorn before Emma slammed the trunk shut. "That was quick thinking on your part," she related to Emma.

"We've been highly trained for all kinds of scenarios in Quantico. It didn't take much to outsmart those numb skulls."

"What should we do with them?"

"We're going to bring them to Agent Baker and the others and charge them with kidnapping and attempted murder."

"But what about Greshnev?"

"After we testify, his days will be numbered."

"Do you think he's the one who had my sister murdered?"

"Maybe it's my female intuition, or maybe my FBI training, but I got the sense that he was telling the truth for once in his life. I don't believe he was the killer."

"Then we're back to where we started and no closer to finding out!"

"Regrettably, I'd have to admit that you're right."

"It's hopeless," Anya declared in frustration. "We'll never find the right person."

"I do believe that although Greshnev wasn't involved, somebody in his nest of rats is the man we are looking for."

"I hope so."

One of the men began to groan as he regained consciousness.

"Let me out!" he screamed.

Emma banged her fist on the trunk and answered, "Shut up in there! Now it's our turn to take you on a little ride!"

The women got into the vehicle with Emma in the driver's seat.

Following the narrow road back between mountains of refuse, they drove through the front gate. Traffic was heavy on the Belt Parkway because it was the time in the afternoon when most people were driving home after work. "It must be getting hot in that trunk," reflected Anya.

"It was just as hot for us, except now it's their turn to fry a little!"

After almost an hour of stop-and-go traffic, Agent Fedosov was able to get off onto the exit ramp. She drove to the police precinct where Detective Malone worked. They walked directly to the desk sergeant. "What can I do for you ladies," the bespectacled, thin-haired officer queried.

"Is Detective Malone here? Emma inquired.

"Not now, but how can I assist you?"

Agent Fedosov took out her FBI identification and passed it to the sergeant.

"I'm turning in two criminals to face charges," she answered.

The sergeant looked around the room. "And where are they?"

Emma held up the car keys. "You'll find them in the trunk of the light blue '89 Chevrolet Malibu parked outside."

"What are you charging them with, may I ask?"

"Let's start with kidnapping and top that with attempted murder."

The sergeant was taken back by what she said.

"Don't worry, we've disarmed them," added Anya, laying the weapons on the sergeant's desk.

He stared at the pistols and called out, "Officer Reilly, accompany these ladies outside and arrest the men who are in the trunk of their car." Reilly looked back and forth as if it were April Fool's Day, but when nobody reacted with laughter, he walked outside with them.

A car screeched up to block a blue Ferrari that was just pulling around one of the dilapidated warehouses on the abandoned wharfs. The four men charged out of the car. "Turn off the motor and get out of the car Greshnev!" Cass yelled, drawing his pistol. The others followed suit revealing their weapons.

Letting the driver side window down, the mob boss said with a grin, "Well this is a surprise. What are you all doing here?"

"Where are Agent Fedosov and Anya Lukashenko?" charged Parrish.

"How would I know," he answered innocently.

"You were told to turn off the ignition and get out of the car," Detective Malone reiterated in a strong voice.

Greshnev did what he was told in a nonchalant manner. "Never let it be said that I did not do what you fine police officers told me to do."

"Weldon, Wilson, go inside and check out the warehouse!" Baker ordered. The two men went through the door.

Baker stated, "I'll ask you one more time. What are you doing down here?"

"I like to come down here when I need some time to be alone and think."

Detective Malone followed up asking, "And what were you here to think about?"

"Oh, this and that."

Wilson and Weldon returned. "It's empty," Hank declared, "but there's evidence that people were recently there."

"Probably hobos," Greshnev responded casually.

"Turn around," barked Cass loudly. "You're under arrest!"

"Arrested for what?"

"Loitering for now, but kidnapping for sure!" It was at that moment that the phone rang in Cass's car. "Parrish get that for me," he called as he slapped on the cuffs. Agent Baker read Greshnev his rights as Malone called for a patrol car to take their prisoner to the precinct.

Agent Wilson hung up the phone saying, "We just got a call from the precinct. Agent Fedosov and Miss Lukashenko are safe. Their two kidnappers have been apprehended."

"That's a relief," expressed Hank as the patrol car pulled up. Taking the crime boss by the arm, Archie escorted him to the vehicle.

"I had nothing to do with this!" Maxim stormed vehemently. "I want to call my lawyer!"

"All in good time," Cass retorted as Greshnev was placed in the car.

"Let's get back to the precinct and see if the two women are okay," suggested Hank.

"Forensics is on their way out to go through the warehouse for any evidence left behind," Parrish informed them as they piled into the car.

Forty-seven minutes later, Cass's beige Chevrolet Caprice pulled into a reserved spot at the police station. They were directed to a room where the two women were being debriefed. While Detective Malone went off to see about booking Greshnev, the other men walked into the room. The smiles on Emma and Anya's faces said it all.

"Well, I'm glad to see that the two of you are still alive," called out Agent Wilson.

"It's good to be still breathing," Fedosov answered.

Emma related the story of how they were pulled off the street by the men who brought them to the Russian Doll House, and then to the abandoned warehouse, and how they were tied up and slapped around. "Greshnev ordered us killed," Anya informed them. "I heard the words come straight from his mouth."

"The bastard almost had us become a part of the landfill."

"But it was Emma's quick thinking that turned the tables on them."

"Once we untied each other, I grabbed a tire iron and waited for them to open the trunk."

"Boy, they both got a big surprised when you got the drop on them!" Anya praised.

"Well, at least we got Albina's murderer off the street," crowed Hank jubilantly. Emma spoke up in a soft voice.

"I don't believe he did it."

"What?" intoned Cass. "What makes you say that?"

"It just doesn't add up."

"Why?" Weldon wanted to know.

"She was his biggest draw to the Russian Doll House, his meal ticket. He would never have her killed, maybe slapped around a little, but not killed."

Archie came in and listened to the conversation. "I agree with Emma. Greshnev is first and foremost a businessman. He was making too much money with Albina to kill her."

"But he must have discovered that Kaz was going to take her away from that life and marry her."

"That would be an excellent reason to kill off Kaz, not Albina!" Archie's voice became hard and cold as he answered Hank.

"At this point," related Emma, "I believe that Anya's sister's killer is still out there on the loose."

"It's a viable alternative," related Cass. "But let's grill Maxim first and see if he'll crack."

All four law enforcement agents went into the interrogation room where the prisoner was held, and Anya and Hank walked into the room next door where they could watch from a one-way mirror.

"I demand to see my lawyer!" yelled Maxim as soon as the agents and detective came into the room.

"Unfortunately, all the police phones are tied up, but let's talk a while until one of them is free."

"I don't have to answer any of your stinking questions! I know my rights!"

"That's true," Emma Fedosov told him. "But, you forget there are two witnesses who are alive after you ordered our deaths.

"It was a gag!" Maxim said peevishly. "Nothing was going to happen. We were just going to teach the two of you a lesson."

"So," Agent Baker said. "Did you want to teach Albina a lesson for trying to go off with Kaz?"

"Kaz"? he answered spitting on the floor. "He was nothing but a traitor!"

"Is that why you nearly killed him?" yelled Parrish.

"I'm a forgiving person, ask anyone. I live by the adage of, "Let bygones be bygones".

"So, you deny killing Albina?"

"I've told you that she was a big moneymaker for me. I'd be stupid to have her knocked off!"

"Do you believe what he's saying?" Anya asked Hank in the other room as they looked through the one-way mirror.

"It certainly sounds plausible."

###

They grilled the suspected murderer, but he kept his mouth shut, not uttering a word until his mouthpiece finally arrived. "Where the hell have you been?" he angrily inquired.

"I came as soon as I got word you were being held here," the attorney answered defensively.

Facing the law enforcers, the lawyer added, "If you don't mind, I'd like to speak to my client alone." The four interrogators left the room and entered the next, where Anya and Hank had been listening.

Parrish inquired. "Where are Anton and Ilia?"

"They're being questioned separately," Malone informed them.

"Do you think they'll crack under the pressure about the killings?" Fedosov quizzed.

"We can try," Baker answered.

"I agree with you," Malone referred to Emma. "Greshnev had nothing to gain by knocking Albina off!"

The room fell suddenly silent as if everyone was waiting for the next shoe to drop. It finally fell. "You're under arrest, Weldon," Malone announced as he approached the private detective.

"What the hell are you talking about?" Weldon yelled resisting the detective's advance toward him.

"I'm arresting you for the murder of Albina Lukashenko and the others!"

"You know," Hank began. "You've had a real hard-on for me from the beginning of this murder spree! I'm telling all of you that I had no reason to kill any of them!"

"Are you referring to the photographs that have been found with the bodies that say, "Smile, you're dead?" Agent Baker asked directing his question to Archie.

"You bet your sweet ass!"

"You've known this before, but never arrested me," stated Weldon. "What makes this time different?"

"You're right, but something new has been added."

"What's that?" Parrish inquired.

"It seems that under questioning, both Ilia and Anton swore that you were having a relationship with Albina outside the bordello."

"That's not true," Weldon defended himself. "Yes, I paid for her time, but we never saw each other outside of Greshnev's bordello!"

"Maybe that's why you kept putting off Kaz about finding her for him. You knew that she was already dead!"

"You're talking out of your head, Malone. Don't the rest of you see that? Are you just going to stand there and let him take me away?"

The others remained silent until Cass answered, "Malone makes a good case for your possible guilt."

"Mr. Weldon, you killed my sister?"

"It's a lie. Don't believe anything he says!" Roughly, Archie turned his former friend around and cuffed him. "Why would I be trying to help you to find the slayer if I had done the killings?"

"To make sure that if anything did turn up as condemning evidence, you'd be around to throw us off the scent!" Malone's voice insisted. He read him his rights as he dragged Weldon out, and Hank screamed, "How can you let him arrest me like this?" Although Emma looked on sympathetically, no one said a word in his defense.

CHAPTER

33

I N ALL HIS years, it was the only time Henry Weldon had been brought to the precinct as a suspect. Archie uncuffed the wrist shackles, and ordered, "Sit down!" It all seemed so unreal in Weldon's mind, a sense almost as if he were walking in a dream world, a nightmare.

"Are you telling me that I am now on the short list of suspects?"

"Yes, you've graduated onto the primary suspect list in my opinion."

"You're embarrassing yourself," Weldon announced to Malone.

"How do you figure that?" the detective inquired intriguingly.

"When you have no evidence that I've committed these crimes, you'll be busted down to patrolman."

"And who says I have no evidence?"

"If you have something, why don't you try to prove it!"

"Let's start with the notes that were found on all of the corpses." Going to his desk, Archie brought out a cardboard box. He spilled the contents onto the table. "Recognize them?" Weldon went through them.

"I didn't write these!" Hank remarked emphatically. "Besides, the words were printed. I always write with cursive lettering."

"It's not the writing that turned me on to you, it's the message." Taking one of the notes in his hands, Archie quoted, "Smile, you're dead!"

"So, what does that prove?"

"It's what you say when people hire you as a Peeking Tom."

"Not true! I say, "Smile you're caught!" It's very different."

"Not different enough to count you out as the killer."

"You've told me this before, but never arrested me. What do you claim you have now, because if that's it, I'm walking out of here!"

"Don't jump the gun! I've discovered something new."

"You're bluffing. There's nothing new to discover!"

"What about your relationship with Albina?"

"I had no relationship with her."

"That's funny, because her diary was discovered in a false bottom in her dresser draw." He tossed it in front of Hank. "Go ahead!" he commanded the reluctant prisoner. "Open it!" Unenthusiastically Weldon took it into his hand. "I've left a book mark on the page that I want you to examine. The suspect opened it to the book mark. "Read it, out loud!"

"Dear Diary",

"I'm in love, for the first time, I'm truly in love! I never thought it would happen to me! I love Hank Weldon and I sense that he loves me too. The problems are Greshnev and Titov. Maxim will never let me leave him and Kaz believes that I love him too. Although I've had a flirtation with Kaz in the past, it wasn't love on my part. Now I need to break the news to him. I know he will not take this news well, but I want to be with Hank so much that it's worth the trouble."

Hank sat for a moment stunned at what he had just read. "This condemns Greshnev and Titov more than it does me!"

"True, but Greshnev is already arrested and Titov's dead. That leaves only you!"

"This is bullshit! I never told Albina I had undying love for her. I don't know where she got this idea!"

"Kaz did hire you to find her once she disappeared, isn't that right?"

"Yes, but Kaz told me not to tell the police. How did you find out?"

"I'm asking the questions here! Tell me, did you even try to find her for Kaz?"

"Of course, I did!"

"But you never found her?"

"No, I never did!"

"That's because she was already dead, isn't it?"

"I didn't know."

"You knew from the beginning, didn't you?"

"I never killed her, I didn't even know where she was. I told Kaz this many times!"

"She confronted you with the idea that the two of you were in love!"

"I never heard those words come out of her mouth. I tell you that I had nothing to do with her death!"

"The two of you argued when you denied it to her face!"

"That never happened!" Weldon screamed jumping up from his seat.

"Sit down!" ordered Malone at the top of his voice. Hank unenthusiastically sat back down.

"This is just conjecture on your part. None of it is true."

"Tell me," the detective's voice grew softer. "You do blackout when you're drunk, don't you?"

"I haven't had a drink for a month."

"That's not what I asked you. You have lapses of memory when you get drunk. It's what you told me once after your wife Clare had died and you'd been hitting the bottle heavily for a while."

"Don't bring up Clare!"

"That's when your drinking problem started as I recall."

"I told you, I'm sober now!"

"I bet you could use a drink just about now. Would you like a little bracer?"

"I'm not drinking anymore."

"That's what all alcoholics say, but it couldn't be further from the truth, could it?"

"What are you trying to do to me?" accused Hank.

"Did you go to see Albina outside the bordello while you were already drunk?"

"I was sober!"

"So, then you're admitting that you did see her outside the brothel!"

"You're confusing me!"

"You went over there drunk and confronted her. That's what happened!"

"Listen, I'll admit that she was one of the girls that I used to have sex with at the Russian Doll House, but that's as far as it went. I saw her for sex, not for love!"

"Oh, I see. That's what you told her when she said she loved you."

"We never had that conversation!"

"Albina was furious when you spurned her love, wasn't she?"

"You're hallucinating! Nothing like that ever happened."

"Did she get mad and turn on you?"

"I'm telling you that none of this ever transpired."

"Did she strike you once or many times?"

"I wasn't with her!"

"After she struck you, did you want to get even and finally get this slut out of your life?"

"No," an exhausted Hank responded.

"In a fit of rage, your hands reached out and then you choked her to death, is that how it occurred?"

"I never laid a hand on her!"

"Perhaps you waited until her back was turned so you wouldn't have to look in her eyes while she was dying. Was that more like it?"

"You're wrong! That couldn't be further from the truth!"

"Or maybe you were blacked out from your drinking when this took place and just can't remember that you killed her? Is that more like it?"

"You're trying to drive me insane!" a visibly upset suspect uttered almost incoherently. "My God, for the sake of our friendship, don't do this!"

"Friendship? What friendship? Our friendship died the day you turned to the bottle instead of me after Clare died!"

Archie reached for the phone. "Come in now," he uttered before hanging up. A young police officer arrived in the interrogation room. "Book him and then lock him up in the holding cage!" he instructed the officer.

"Book him with what, sir?"

"For now, second degree murder."

Weldon was marched through the patrol room where officers who knew Hank looked up with morbid curiosity, but none of them approached him. The young officer unlocked the door to the holding cell, and Hank walked in. Removing his cuffs, the patrolman locked the door.

"Well, look who graced us with his presence!" Hank didn't have to look up to hear who it was. It was Greshnev, his two thug guards by his side.

"Is this your first time inside the cage?" Anton smirked, "or does the drunk tank count?" All three of them laughed.

Maxim approached the dejected man. "What happened? Did your old friend toss you in here with us career criminals?"

"Shut up, Greshnev, and go back to your side of the cage!"

"Or what?" Maxim baited him. "Are you going to kill me like you killed Albina?" Before the crime boss realized it, Hank had landed a punch directly on Greshnev's nose. The blood began to pour out. Ilia and Anton charged their boss's attacker, dropping him to the floor and kicked him viciously about the head and back.

"Break it up in there!" a patrolman screamed as he was joined with others of his police brothers to break-up the beating. "Lock these three in another cage!" the senior officer instructed the other patrolmen. Maxim and his henchmen were incarcerated a few cages down. None of the patrolmen came to Hank's assistance. They just relocked the door and walked away.

Hank lay there for a while, his ego more bruised than his body. Standing back on his feet, he walked to a bench and sat down. *I'd give my soul to the devil in exchange for a stiff drink!*

His mind blotted out all the noise and movement of the precinct, the same building where he had once been a young officer himself. *It seems as if it were a million years ago.*

After a while, he was escorted to be finger printed and have his picture taken. He walked through the process as if in a daze. It all seemed so surreal. Before he knew it, he was back in the cage just watching time torturously move on. The world passed by while Weldon felt that he was stuck in a time warp.

He didn't know how much time elapsed before his cage door was opened. "Get up so that I can cuff you!" the patrolman brusquely ordered him. Like a robot, Hank did as he was told. He was escorted back to the interrogation room and cuffed to the table. The patrolman left, leaving him in deafening solitude.

Weldon's eyes wandered around the room aimlessly. It had a spartan appearance, with only a table bolted to the floor and a couple of chairs. On the wall was the obligatory one-way window that acted like a mirror. He stared into it, wondering if there was anybody studying him as he sat there waiting. At last the door opened, revealing Federal Agent Emma Fedosov. She walked in and sat down next to him.

"Does Malone think that if he sent a pretty face in that I'd break down and confess to these crimes? I'll tell you what I told him. I'm innocent!"

"What happened to your face?" were the first words out of her mouth.

She put her hand on his chin and turned his head one way and then another. This maneuver reminded him of all the times Clare had held her fingers to his chin. Inside, his heart ached with great sorrow and longing. *Don't lose it! Hold on to your composure!*

"It's no big deal," Hank dismissed her worry. "Greshnev's boys wanted to play."

"How are you doing?"

"How do you think I'm doing? I'm doing great."

"I came in to tell you that I'm not convinced that you had anything to do with these murders."

Weldon stared at her in shock. "Come again."

"I don't think you're guilty of these murders."

"And what makes you say that when Malone is so convinced that I'm a cold-blooded killer?"

"I can't say for sure, but I'm not convinced Greshnev has done this, and I get the same feeling about you."

"Too bad you don't have any evidence that might exonerate me." Hank looked up hopefully.

"Unfortunately, I have nothing but what my instincts are saying to me."

"It's regrettable that your instincts are not enough to release me from this place."

"It is, but that won't stop me from pursuing the truth on your behalf."

"I know where Malone stands on this, but what about Cass and Parrish? Have you talked to them?"

"I think there was some resistance on their part when Archie had presented his theory to them, but now they appear to be on board with your incarceration."

"I'm cooked! I'm as good as dead! Don't waste your time on me, Emma. I'm on the brink of being convicted for these crimes."

"Stop it!" she raised her voice to him.

"Stop what?"

"Stop trying to convince me that helping you would be a waste of my time."

"Cut your losses now. Don't get caught up in a losing battle."

"Enough of this self-pity! Help me fight back to prove that you're innocent. What does Malone have on you to prove his theory?"

Swallowing his pride, Hank replied. "First there's the fact that the notes left at each murder have a connection to what I have the reputation for saying."

"You mean, "Smile you're dead"?

"Yeah, I usually say, "Smile you're caught."

"So, it has to be someone you have worked with or someone who was caught breaking their marriage vows. Does any of this bring some names to mind?"

"There is a long list of deceitful husbands or wives I've caught over the years. It could be anyone of them."

"What about people you may have worked with?"

"The only one that pops into my brain is Kazimir Titov, one of Greshnev's men who would sometimes help me with my job for financial considerations, but he's dead and buried now." Other than him, I have no other ideas."

"It's a place to start," Emma said trying to raise his spirits. "Don't let yourself fall into a depression."

"It's hard not to," answered Hank. "Someone has gone to a lot of trouble to frame me. I feel as if I'm at the end of my wits."

Emma got up from her chair. "This is a frame up!" she answered him decisively. "This whole case seems to be tied up with a big red bow like a present for the District Attorney. It's too neatly done to be true!"

"So, you do believe I'm innocent?"

"For the time being, I do, until I'm proven wrong, and I don't see that happening. Do not speak about our conversation with the others. I want the freedom of investigation to be unhindered. I'll get back to you as soon as I can, but don't lose hope. I'm going to need you at the top of your game. Do you understand?"

"I've got it."

Emma walked out, leaving Weldon a little more optimistic. He had no further time to ponder this, because a cop walked in, handcuffed him, and brought him back to the cage. He sat for the rest of the day trying to dredge up more names that Fedosov could investigate.

The next morning, Hank had gotten very little sleep and refused the meals that he was given. He met the defense lawyer who had been assigned to his case. He was less a lawyer than a kid who had just graduated from law school. He introduced himself as Gerard Poole. Attorney Poole, from the Public Defender's office, took out a yellow legal pad and a sharpened pencil. "So, tell me, Mr. Weldon, why have you been incarcerated?"

"You mean you took my case without knowing my story?"

"I'm familiar with your case, but I want to hear it in your own words."

Taking a deep breath, Hank began his story with Kaz coming to him to find Albina and the deaths that followed in quick succession. Poole listened intensely, only stopping to ask some pertinent questions. "The word is that you had a relationship with this Albina, is that true?"

"My relationship with her consisted of money given for sex. That's all there was to it!"

"I see," Poole responded in a tone that seemed to imply that he wasn't getting the truth from his client. "Do you know about a certain diary that Miss Lukashenko wrote, stating that the two of you were in love and that you intended to take her out of her present circumstances?"

"I know about it, but she was delusional. I never promised her anything like that because I was never in love with her."

"It's pretty damning evidence though." Hank looked at him in disbelief.

"Are you here to defend me or judge me on evidence that was concocted in the feverish mind of a dead whore?"

Poole bristled at the question. "I'm here for you, of course!"

"By the way," Weldon wondered. "Who is paying to defend me, because I certainly don't have the means to pay you."

"I'm a Public Defender. I was assigned to your case by the court judge. Can we get back to your statement now?"

"That means that you don't necessarily believe what I'm telling you?"

Putting down the legal pad, Gerard adjusted his glasses on the bridge of his nose and emitted a heavy sigh before he responded. "I don't know if you're guilty or innocent, and really don't care much either way. I'm here to take your statement. Let's get back to it."

Hank had the driving urge to fire him, but came to his senses when he remembered his dire financial difficulties.

"As I've stated before, Miss Lukashenko and I were not romantically involved."

"I see," he replied.

I'd love to haul off and deck this pompous ass!

Questions, questions, questions; the string of questions asked by Poole seemed never-ending and his attorney's voice began to grind on his nerves. After nearly an hour, the Public Defender put his legal pad and pencil in his briefcase and stood up.

"Do I have any chance of being acquitted?"

"Perhaps," he retorted non-committedly. "There's always a chance."

"But not a very good one, is that what you're implying?"

"It doesn't look good with the evidence already gathered by the authorities, but that won't stop me from providing the best defense I can give you."

"Yeah, right," answered Weldon sounding crushed by the circumstances.

"Guard!" Poole called out, and a cop walked up and unlocked the cell. Gerard Poole turned to say, "Try and keep your hopes up, Mr. Weldon." He stepped out into the corridor and walked away. Weldon sat on the cot with his head in his hands and bemoaned his dilemma.

Dreary and alone, he spent the next day in his cell wishing to see another human face, a smile, or tender voice telling him everything would eventually turn out right. More and more he hoped to hear the voice of Emma Fedosov. When she didn't come, he even caught himself wishing that he could see Archie Malone, once his friend, now his nemesis.

On the third day, his wish was fulfilled. He was dragged out of his cell and into an interrogation room where the "Holy Trinity" was waiting for him. Agent Parrish Wilson sat at the very end of the table, his left leg crossed over his right, and his arms folded over his chest. His appearance was cool, calm, and collected. Agent Cassidy Baker leaned against the barred window, a cigarette perched between his lips, with the smoke wafting upward in lazy swirls as he checked his watch. Detective Archibald Malone paced the floor, his hands folded together at the base of his spine, his shirt sleeves folded up above his elbows.

"At last," Hank moaned. "Some human contact," he thought out loud.

"Sit down, Weldon!" Malone barked pointing to the chair placed nearest to him. "This is going to be a long session!" Hank shuffled to the chair like a defeated player who had just lost match, set, and game of the tennis tournament at Wimbledon.

"We gave you this time so you could think," exclaimed Parrish. "Sometimes being alone can help clarify the facts for a person."

"Yeah, I've been thinking." Hank stopped there not saying another word.

"Well, enlighten us," demanded Cass.

"I've been thinking what a load of shit the three of you are peddling! Maybe you should go into screenwriting because you sure do stink at investigating."

"A wise guy," Malone commented with a grimace on his face. "Maybe you'll get the warden to laugh when he says to pull the switch on you in the electric chair."

"Why are you being so hard on me, Archie? You know that I could never be a murderer."

"Under the right set of circumstances, anyone could commit murder!"

"Tough guy!" Weldon opined. "Would you be that tough if you were questioning your mother in this chair?"

"If I believed she was the killer, I'd drag her from the grave right now!" Weldon had no doubt that he would do what he said.

"Why did you kill, Albina?"

"I've told you, I was not the one who killed her!"

"Yeah, and we don't believe you," Baker snapped like a rabid dog. "You're not going to wriggle out of this, you know. You're going to crack as easily as a raw egg and it will be just as messy!"

"Should I take it that you're going to implement violence to get a confession out of me? You know that's against the law, don't you!"

"A few well-placed punches to the solar plexus will do the trick, and there will never be any telltale marks that anything ever happened," advised Parrish, "and I'm just the man to do it!"

"You may not know this about Agent Wilson, but when he was in the Navy, he was welterweight champion two years in a row," mentioned Cass smugly.

"Well, I'm very impressed," beamed Weldon as he clapped his hands slowly. Malone charged toward the private detective like an enraged bull, grabbing him by the collar and screaming, "You're going to give us what we want, asshole!"

"I want my lawyer present!" The three interrogators looked at each other and roared with laughter. "What's so hilarious?" They stopped sniggering long enough for Agent Baker to remark,

"I guess you haven't heard."

"Heard what?"

"Poole made a petition to the court to be officially withdrawn from your case."

"What the hell for?"

"It seems that he doesn't want his first case to be a losing one," mocked Parrish.

"The bastard!" Weldon spit out. "One of the last things he told me was to not give up hope!"

"I guess after reviewing the evidence stacked against you, he decided to bail out. It's a smart guy who can figure out when he's wasting his time," Cass observed nonchalantly.

"Well then, I want a new mouthpiece!"

"That's going to be a problem," taunted Malone. "I hear every law firm in the city sees you as a pariah whose case can't be won in a court of law. Besides, they'll reject you as a client because you can't pay their fee. It's such a shame, isn't guys?"

"Too bad!" Cass commented.

"I'll say," added Parrish.

"Now, let's all get down to the reason we're here - your confession!" Agent Baker announced as he landed a punch to the prisoner's chest.

Sitting on a park bench that overlooked the police precinct, a person bought the Morning Gazette from the newsstand and sat down to read. The paper was held at eye level to give the impression of someone who was perusing the articles, but instead, eyes watched as Hank Weldon, cuffed and dejected, was marched inside to the station. A smile appeared. *This is just the beginning, Weldon, just the beginning!*

34

"TELL ME AGAIN what the hell we're doing here?" challenged Cass as he and Emma made their way up to the third-floor apartment of Hank Weldon.

"I told you already, Cass. We're looking for a possible suspect who is trying to frame Hank for Albina's death."

"Hank? You're calling him Hank now?" the trace of astonishment was in his voice.

"Well, that's his name!" When they reached the floor, Agent Fedosov opened the apartment door. The living space was disheveled.

"He probably keeps a list of his clients." Cass started trolling through the scattered papers on every piece of worn-out furniture as Emma tackled the file case.

"His file case is as disheveled as this room," Fedosov observed. After about ten minutes, Cass spoke out. "Find anything we can use?"

"Nothing yet, but I still have plenty of file folders to go over."

"When are you going to admit that we already have our man?" he inquired angrily.

"I'm telling you," she stopped to face Agent Baker. "I have a feeling which I intend to explore."

"This is not one of those women's intuition things, is it?"

"Don't dismiss it so easily. I've been right in other cases."

Cass dropped the papers he had been looking through and made his way to Emma, whose back was turned toward him. Putting his hands on her shoulders, he gently turned her until they were face to face. He drew her body toward him and kissed her passionately on her lips. The passion was not returned. "Not now," Emma dismissed him.

"Then when?" demanded Cass. "We're finally on a case together and you haven't touched me once!"

"It was a fling, Cass. A couple of night hookups which I never should have given in to."

"You're wrong," he fired back. "You fell in love just as strongly as I did."

"Cass," she responded, her voice an almost quiet whisper. "A relationship with you will go nowhere. You have your wife and children to consider."

"I'd give them all up for you! I love you!"

"I don't want you to do that. I don't feel the same way about you."

"But you feel that way for Weldon, don't you?" he contested trying to hold down his temper.

"Don't be silly, Cass. This is just another case. Hank means nothing to me." Cass took his frustrations out on the furniture around him, kicking an ottoman and a sofa leg with infuriation.

"Don't act like a spoiled child," she reprimanded him. "We have a job to do."

"We're never going to find anything in here," Agent Baker announced as he looked around the room. "Besides, we have Weldon dead to right for these murders!"

"It's circumstantial evidence," Emma told him. "You couldn't convict him on what you have."

"I beg to differ! If you weren't so in love with him, you'd accept the truth that Parrish, Archie, and I agree with. Weldon is as guilty as sin!"

"If that's the way you feel, you should leave!"

"My pleasure," announced Cass as he kicked crap out of his way to the apartment entrance. "If you think our relationship will go nowhere, what kind of relationship will you have with a convicted killer. Think about that for a while!" With that parting shot, Cassidy Baker slammed the door.

My God, I should never have slept with him!

It took hours to make any headway with the paperwork all around the room, until she came to a manila file entitled "Outstanding Bills". Mixed with final notices from the electric and gas companies, Emma found a worn list of names at the end of which was Kazimir Titov. Next to each name was an address, phone number, and a check which indicated that the private detective had been paid in full.

By some names however, written in ink, was the word "Delinquent" which meant that Weldon was still owed money. The word was seen far too often on the list. It's no wonder that he lives in a dump like this!

Skimming the rest of the list she thought, this must be his list of clients! Titov was his last client before all this began to happen. She carefully folded the list and put it into her pocket. Climbing down the stairs, she got a taxi by the curb that drove to Coney Island Hospital on Ocean Parkway.

Emma had tried to visit him days ago when she found out he had been rushed to the hospital with a concussion, but she had been told that he couldn't have any visitors. *I hope he's recovered by now. I need to speak to him.*

Emma made her way to the reception desk in the lobby. A pretty young candy-striper sat at the desk. She was gazing into a compact mirror as she moved some wisps of blonde hair from her face.

"What room is Henry Weldon in?"

A glance of annoyance sprang up on the girl's face as she put the compact back in her purse. "What was that name again," she inquired as she snapped the bubblegum in her mouth.

"Weldon, Henry," the agent repeated. "Do you need me to spell it for you?" she queried sardonically.

"No," the annoyed answer came back. "I've graduated high school!"

Good for you!

She went through the directory and answered, "He's in I.C.U. on the 10th floor."

"Can he have visitors?"

A cold and icy stare appeared before she turned back to the card. "Yeah, he can have visitors! Anything else?"

"No, you can go back to your personal grooming!"

Emma made her way to the elevator bank where she waited impatiently for the cage to descend. At last a chime rang indicating one of the elevators was approaching the marbled lobby. After people poured out, she and several visitors got on. The cage rose, releasing people each time it came to the lower floors.

Finally reaching her destination, Emma got out and found the arrow on the wall that read, I.C.U. She came to a nurse sitting behind a desk. "I'm looking for Henry Weldon," she told her.

"He's in room 5, but the doctor has ordered that he shouldn't have any excitement."

"I'll keep that in mind." The agent passed four rooms until she saw Hank. A cop sat outside in the hall. Weldon appeared to be gray, his head wound in bandages with his eyes closed.

Emma moved to the side of his bed and touched his arm.

"Hank," she mouthed quietly as she gently shook his arm. His eyes fluttered open and it was then that she noticed that his left eye was blackened. "What the hell happened to you?"

Grimacing as he moved his body, his right wrist cuffed to the bed railing, Weldon answered, "I owe my condition to your friends, the "Holy Trinity!"

"They did this to you?"

"Yeah, they tried to beat a confession out of me, but I'm not going to cop to a crime I didn't commit!"

"Who gave you the back eye?"

"That was Agent Baker's gift to me, and Parrish bruised my chest by pounding on my solar plexus!"

"Who gave you the concussion?"

"That I got from my old friend Archie. When I stood up from the chair, he pushed me back down, but I lost my balance and hit my head on the floor."

"My God, how could they?"

"Everything after that is a blank until I woke up earlier today in this hospital room."

"Are you feeling any better?"

"Except for a slight ringing in my ear and a headache, I'll live."

"Are you up to having a look at this for me?" She took out the folded list she had found in his apartment.

Weldon scanned the names. When he had finished, he asked. "What about them?"

"Are these all names of your former clients?"

"Yeah, why?"

"If you're up for it, I'd like to go over the list with you."

"I looked up everyone I could find and got nowhere, but why not," he shrugged. "I've got nothing better to do with my time."

Starting from the top of the list, Emma asked Hank his impressions of each client. "Self-absorbed…Cheap bitch…Dim wit…Playboy…Tax Evader. The comments and labels went on and on until they reached the end of the list.

"Do any of these names stand out for you as a client who might have threatened you?"

"I didn't deal with the brightest people, but I don't think any of them would have actually threatened my life."

"I'm going to start looking them up."

"That will take a while."

"That's alright! I have nothing better to do."

The next day the weather was cool and blustery for Agent Fedosov to hunt down each name on Weldon's client list. In some cases, the client either moved or was no longer using the phone number, and Emma had to search the phone directories to locate them. In a few cases, the former client could not be found. Of those that were still at their listed addresses, she could not get any vibe that they were framing him for murder. "I haven't thought of him in years," a housewife declared when Emma approached her for a conversation.

"The bastard tried to sue me for his money, but he never completed the job and the court denied his law suit!" an elderly man exclaimed. "I could care less about him!"

It took almost three days to go down the list, and the answers were by and large the same.

Returning to her hotel room, Anya asked, "Any luck today?"

"I've been pounding the pavement with nothing to show for it!" an exasperated agent declared as she threw the list on the desk, and plopped down in a wingchair next to it.

"I don't believe Weldon killed my sister either. He just doesn't seem like the type. Is there anything else you can do to prove his innocence?" Taking the list from the desk, Anya silently poured over it. "What about the names that haven't been crossed out," she inquired.

"Either they've left the place they were living or they're dead."

Anya stared at the list mutely. A few minutes went by before she spoke again. "I think I have an idea, but it may mean nothing."

"Well, I'm ready to hear any idea to solve this case. What's on your mind?"

Anya looked up saying, "What if this whole killing spree was started by a person who is now dead?"

Emma mulled over the idea.

"It's stupid, isn't it?"

"Not at all!" Fedosov declared. "In fact, it's really a brilliant one!"

"Are you going to tell the others?"

"Let's just leave it between us girls," suggested Emma with a wink. "I don't think the boys would appreciate our going out by ourselves on this."

"I'm going with you?"

"Of course. After all, it was your idea, but before we do, I want to petition the court to grant an exhumation of the body of Kazimir Titov. You can identify his body, can't you?"

"Albina had sent me many photographs in which they were together. You think he could be the one who started all of this?"

"I don't know but we're going to find out."

It took over a week before Fedosov received the decree to exhume Titov's body. In that time, Emma visited Weldon, who had been sent back to jail.

"Where have you been hiding?" Archie inquired acerbically when he saw her in the hall.

"Here and there," she answered evasively.

"I hear you've come to visit Hank. Maybe you can get him to confess. He stubbornly resists doing it."

"You mean after the three of you sent him to the hospital, he still hasn't admitted his supposed guilt to you?"

Archie smiled, replying, "That was his own fault!"

"Are you saying that he beat himself up and gave himself a concussion?"

"You're funny," he answered dead serious.

"I've been told that by a few people."

"You know; it would really help the team if we were all back on the same page."

"That's going to be a bit of a problem, Archie. You see, I don't believe he is guilty."

"Are you blind?" he queried in a loud voice. The evidence is stacked up against him. There is no question about his guilt!"

"As I've tried to explain before, it is all circumstantial. He'll never be found guilty."

"That's not what the District Attorney thinks. He wants to push ahead with this case and get Weldon formally charged."

"Well good luck with that. I'd hate to see the D.A. with egg on his face, but if he goes ahead with this, it's bound to happen."

"Go ahead and visit Weldon," he announced dismissively. "Whatever you're cooking up to save Weldon from the chair, it won't work."

Taking her cue, Emma went to talk to Hank in one of the interrogation rooms where he had been escorted by one of the cops. The man in blue stood outside the door waiting to take the prisoner back.

"Hey Emma," the prisoner greeted her. He still sported a black eye.

"Hi Hank, how are you feeling?"

"Much better than the last time I saw you."

"I've come to bring you some news."

"What's going on?"

"I'm waiting for an order of exhumation to be issued by the court."

"Exhumation? Who do you intend to dig up?"

"Kaz Titov."

"Kaz, whatever for?"

"I've got a suspicion that I might not find him there."

"Are you kidding? Before he died, he was incoherent for months. He couldn't possibly have pulled all this off!"

"I suppose, but this feeling persists."

"But you've never seen him. How will you be able to identify him?"

"That's where Anya comes in. She's seen photos of her sister with him. It won't be a problem."

"Keep me abreast of what happens will you, Emma."

"You'll be one of the first to know. Please don't give up hope. This will all work out, Hank."

"I heard what you're up to," announced Cass in the police precinct.

"Oh yeah, and what is that?" Emma simpered.

"We heard you're becoming a gravedigger," added Parrish.

"And where did you hear that?" Agent Baker replied,

"I have friends in the city court. They let me know what you've planned."

Wilson asked curiously, "What do you think that's going to prove?"

"That Hank is not the murderer?" Cass demanded,

"When are you going to admit that you've been wrong all this time?" questioned Parrish.

"The day you admit that you have the wrong man in jail."

"You're like a hamster on a treadmill," chortled Parrish. "Running like crazy and getting nowhere!"

"I've got an idea," mentioned Emma. "Why don't the two of you and Detective Malone join me in Potter's Field and we all can see who's buried in that plot."

"It's a waste of time," opined Parrish. "The guilty person is already incarcerated."

They were interrupted by a court officer who appeared in the doorway.

"Agent Fedosov?" he asked

"Yes, that's me," answered Emma. He walked over and placed the court order into her hand. Unsealing the envelope, she took the document out and perused it. "Well guys," she said, "it's a go. All I need to do is contact the undertakers and then we can get started. The offer still stands, gentleman. Are any of you going to take me up on it?"

Cass responded, "Okay, I'll go with you. I used to love field trips when I was a kid. Besides I want to be there when you have to admit that you've been wrong all this time."

With a sly smile, Emma replied, "We'll see about that."

The next day, an entourage including Emma, Anya, Cass, Parrish, and Archie approached the place where people who had died penniless were buried. In a small shack waited the undertaker and his assistants waited.

Agent Fedosov flashed her badge. I called yesterday and told you that I had a court order to exhume the body of Kazimir Titov." She pulled out the order and showed it to the disheveled man in front of her. He took the paper and looked at carefully.

"Well," she responded impatiently, "Let's get going!"

"We're going to have to walk a little way down."

"There's no time like the present."

With a nod of his head, his two assistants followed him out the door and the others followed. Emma walked with the manager. "Where was he buried," she inquired.

"He's buried under the marker 529. It's just ahead of us."

They walked a few yards more before they turned to the left. Each of the small headstones had a number on it rather than a name. They walked for a while until they got to the marker for which they were looking. A mechanical excavator waited nearby. With a wave of the undertaker's hand, the machine began to break into the dirt and lift buckets of dark brown soil. The noise droned on deafeningly until it exposed the wooden casket.

"Bring it up!" the manager told the man on the control panel, and slowly the coffin was lifted and laid gently on the ground. "Open it." he told his assistants, and the men with crowbars began to pry the cover loose. The visitors stepped closer to the cadaver. There was an immediate stench of rotting flesh that assaulted their nostrils and hands were held up to their faces.

"Well, Anya," Emma addressed Miss Lukashenko. "Do you think that's Titov?" The body was already in partial decay as Anya explored it with her eyes. She turned to Emma saying, "Unless his body has shrunk, this is not Titov!"

Archie spoke up, "These idiots must have dug up the wrong grave!"

"I resent that," the manager fired back. "My records are a source of pride for me. Inspections occur a few times a year and I have never screwed these burials up. This is the grave of Kazimir Titov!"

"That can mean only one thing," Fedosov declared. "Titov is still alive!"

"This can't be," Cass spoke out.

"You've heard what Anya said. This is not the man who's supposed to be buried here."

"But the evidence against Weldon..." recalled Archie.

"The evidence is fabricated. All charges against Hank should be dropped. We need to locate Titov. He's the one who should be jailed."

"I don't know..." Cass started to say.

"I know one thing," answered Fedosov. "You've never been a person who would put an innocent man in prison. You're not going to start now, are you?"

"Well, no."

"Do you still have any doubts?" Emma asked Detective Malone.

"I suppose not," he answered contritely.

"Somewhere in this city, Titov has been hiding and having a good laugh for himself at our expense, but today we're going to turn the tables on him."

"What are you waiting for?" snapped Archie to the undertaker. "Get this body reburied!"

CHAPTER

35

B Y THE NEXT day, Kazimir Titov had joined an exclusive club, the Federal Bureau of Investigation's Ten Most Wanted List. New York City's finest were put on alert. Flyers were distributed with the Russian henchman's mug on it, supplied by Anya Lukashenko.

It was with no fanfare that Henry Weldon was released from jail and was out on the street looking for the man who had so cunningly framed him for murder. It was a mystery to him as to the reason he had gone after him. "The only reason I can think of, is that he blames me for not finding Albina before she was murdered by Greshnev." Hank made a conscious effort not to rehash the unfortunate incidents of his imprisonment and beating.

"There is no proof that Greshnev was involved in that," Emma cautioned him.

"So, what's the plan?" he inquired of them.

"We hit the pavement hard and start rousting the members of the Russian mob and take them in for questioning," explained Detective Malone.

"One of them must know something of the whereabouts of Titov," adjoined Agent Parrish Wilson.

"Too many have already died to keep this mobster's secret," Cass proclaimed. "We can't allow anyone else to be sacrificed."

As they left the room, Archie stopped Weldon to speak to him alone. "Listen Hank," Malone started, "I'm really sorry about what happened here." Hank stared mutely into his former friend's face. Awkward with the silence between them, Archie added, "You know there was nothing personal in it. I mean all the evidence seemed to point directly to you. I had no other choice but to arrest you. You were a cop at one time, and know what the job entails."

Without warning, Weldon balled his hand into a fist that flew toward

Archie's face. The sickening crunch of cartilage could be heard as Malone was stretched out on the floor. Touching his fingers to his nose, Malone complained, "Jesus, was that really necessary?"

"That's just a small payback for the beating I took from you and the others."

Rising to his feet, he took out a handkerchief and dabbed his bleeding nose. "Can we at least shake hands and put an end to this?"

"This was a wall you built brick by brick between us. It's going to take me a long time to trust you again, if I ever do. And no, I'm not shaking your hand."

"Fair enough."

Around noon that same day, the precinct was filled with men and women involved in the "Little Odessa" Russian mob. In one of the interrogation rooms, Emma and Hank worked on Boris Vasiliev, one of Greshnev's multiple bodyguards.

"So," Emma began as the disgruntled mobster sat in the chair. "What do you hear from your old pal Kaz?"

"Listen lady," he began gruffly. "Haven't you heard the news. Kaz Titov is dead and buried."

"Are you sure about that?" Weldon quizzed.

"As sure as I'm sitting here right now! Say, is this why you hauled me in, to see if I'd seen a dead man. I haven't had nightmares since I was a child."

"Funny thing about that," continued Emma. "We dug up Titov's body, and guess what? There was another body buried in the coffin!"

Weldon spoke up. "You don't look surprised, Vasiliev."

"Why should I be. This has nothing to do with me! Maybe there was a mix up at the cemetery."

"There's no mix up," the private detective answered. "Because Titov is not dead."

Laughing, Boris answered, "You're crazy! It's been months since he died. I visited him in the hospital when he was comatose. I knew that if he had lived, he was never coming out of a coma."

"Which school issued you a medical degree, Dr. Visiliev?" Fedosov said.

"Actually, you don't have to have a medical degree to figure out that Kaz was never going to come out of it."

"You figured that out all by yourself, did you?" shouted Hank. "Where is he hiding

"Where is who hiding?" Boris answered with a grin.

"Stop playing games with us," Emma yelled, getting into his face.

"Did anyone ever tell how blue your eyes become when your angry?"

"Listen," Emma remarked. "That kind of line might work on the hookers you work with, but I'm not diverted by your charming words."

"You know where Kaz is. I can see it in your demeanor. Not once were you surprised by the news we told you," Weldon retorted.

"Prove it!"

"We're going to keep you here under intense questioning until you crack!" bellowed Hank.

"Better people than you have tried to crack me, and have gotten nowhere!"

Emma indicated with a nod that she wanted to speak to Hank outside in the corridor.

"Can I go now?" Boris sneered.

With a curled lip, Emma replied. "Are you hard-of-hearing? I just told you that we weren't done with you yet! Just cool your heels until we get back."

Outside the interrogation room, Fedosov turned to Hank. "It doesn't matter how long we interrogate him, I don't think he's going to give us anything."

"Do you think he knows where he's hiding?"

"I'd bet the farm on it."

"Even if we threw him behind bars, that wouldn't break him. He's already done hard time for trafficking drugs. Have you got any ideas?"

"We'll keep questioning him for a few hours just as we planned, but then we'll release him to the street."

"You're thinking he'll try to contact Titov to tell him that his cover has been blown?"

"Exactly!"

"But Vasiliev is too street smart for that trick to work. He'll know immediately that he's being tailed."

"We'll assign two patrolmen to follow him discreetly, and when he shakes them, he'll think he's free to get to Titov. What he won't realize is that we'll still be following him. It takes one rat to catch another rat."

Hours passed, and just as Agent Fedosov predicted, Boris Vasiliev never broke down. "Get out!" Emma finally screamed at him. "But I'm keeping my eye on you.

"Go ahead," he smirked getting up from the chair. "You'll finally see that I don't have the information you want." Boris strode out of the interrogation room as if he were taking a stroll through the park.

Quickly, Emma picked up the phone. "Get Patrolmen Norris and Pendleton to follow Vasiliev. Tell them to shadow him discreetly, but to show themselves so that he knows he's being tailed. Understand sergeant?"

Hearing the answer, Fedosov hung up. "Vasiliev won't try to contact Titov today, but he might try by phone."

"Then we need to set up taps on the phones in the Russian Doll House."

"I've already taken that under consideration. Zoya has given access to the building to federal agents posing as electricians. Instead they've wired every phone in that bordello. I have someone covering the phone calls. It will only take a few days before we have the man we're looking for."

"Do you think all these preparations really will pay off?"

"It's in the bag. Even if he doesn't contact Titov in the next few days, he won't be able to keep what is going on to himself. Now all we need to do is tell Malone, Wilson, and Baker so that we are all on board with this plan.

"I can't wait to have that rat bastard in my hands. I'll kill him!"

"Not before we find out the reason he started this conspiracy in the first place. I'm sure it will be a charming story," she discoursed with acerbity.

"After that, I'll kill him with my bare hands!"

If Vasiliev knew where Titov was hiding, or how to reach him, the next two days of intense questioning brought no results. His routine remained the same - from his apartment to the bordello, and at the end of the day, back to his apartment. His only deviations were his stops at The Dive a couple of nights a week for shots of vodka. Boris never got drunk enough to show his hand, and those tailing him soon grew restless with frustration.

"This is a waste of time," Hank complained to his companion as they sat in the interrogation room of the police station. "Are you sure he knows where Kaz is hiding?"

"He's playing it cagey, not wanting us to think he knows how to contact him. It's all a ruse!"

"But how can we turn the tables on him and put us in the driver's seat?"

"We'll arrest him on drunk and disorderly conduct when he comes out of The Dive.

"You think he'll give up Titov when he's drunk?"

"Not just drunk, but highly intoxicated."

"Boris never leaves the bar in that condition."

"We're going to help him along."

"How's that?"

"I'm going to turn off the electric fan in the interrogation room and pound him with accusations until he becomes overheated and asks for water."

Hank's face lit up. "You're going to give him glasses of water mixed with vodka instead?"

"Exactly! That will loosen up his tongue. It's the only drink we will offer him. He'll take it when he gets hot enough."

"Brilliant! I think I'm falling in love with the way you think. It's more like a man than a woman."

Emma didn't know if this was meant as a compliment or a dig. "Excuse me?"

"Oh no, don't get me wrong," declared Weldon. "Your mind may think like a man, but your body is all woman!" As soon as he said it, he could have kicked himself in the behind.

Am I developing feelings for her? He knew the answer to that question. Of course you are, you idiot. I think I felt something for her from the first day we met. After all, she was the only one who thought I was innocent, and went about proving her theory. But what if my feelings are not returned? I'm going to look like such an imbecile if she doesn't feel the same way about me!

Emma laughed, and he turned beet red from embarrassment. "Are you saying what I think you're saying?"

"Well, kinda, yeah." Now what am I going to do?

He didn't have to do anything. Emma turned toward him and kissed his lips tenderly.

Weldon was stunned by her sudden passion toward him. "You feel the same?"

"I have for a while, but before we act on these feelings, we need to put this case in the "Crime Solved" file."

"Yes, you're right, of course."

"Let's call in the others and explain our strategy to them." Emma called the three men into consultation. They came in deflated, irritated by the lack of progress in shadowing Vasiliev.

"This is becoming tiresome," Archie nagged to Agent Fedosov as soon as they all assembled.

A disgruntled Parrish added, "We're getting nowhere fast!"

"I'm beginning to doubt that Vasiliev has any knowledge about the whereabouts of Titov," Cass announced. "Your theory is unraveling before our eyes."

"Before you start any condemnation about my idea, Hank and I have decided to take the bull by the horns. In this case, Boris is the bull."

Parrish looked at them oddly. "What are you driving at?"

"I think we have a way of getting Vasiliev to give us the information."

Cass's face immediately showed his distaste for any more of Emma's ideas.

"This whole plan is going off track. We should start a new strategy!"

"I agree," confirmed Archie. "If Titov is in fact out there, we've been wasting a lot of time!"

"It hasn't been a waste of time!" Hank indignantly countered. "We've learned that Boris likes to have a few drinks at The Dive a couple of nights a week."

"And how is this information going to help us in our search," Parrish demanded. Emma Fedosov replied, "We're going to arrest him after he leaves the bar and bring him in for questioning."

"We've had him in for questioning, and that did absolutely nothing in our search for Titov," accused Agent Baker. "In fact, the last few days haven't offered any of the results we wanted. I don't believe any new idea the two of you have cooked up will change the outcome!"

"Give her a minute to explain," Hank answered reproachfully.

"When we get him here, we're going to ply him with more vodka."

Detective Malone peevishly challenged. "And how will we do that?"

"We're going to make sure there is no fan in the interrogation room, and after a while, we hope he'll ask for water."

"How will that help?" queried Agent Wilson.

Emma responded. "We'll mix water with vodka!"

"Oh, that's a great idea," smirked Cass. "Why don't we all just become his drinking buddies?"

"You're not seeing the entire picture," retorted Fedosov. "He's going to know we've switched it, but it will be too late. Perhaps, he will drop his defenses and open up to us."

"This is dumb!" Archie chortled with utter contempt. "And this is your big new plan?"

"Maybe," Hank fired back, "You've come up with a better idea, because I don't hear any genius strategies coming out of your mouth!"

"Oh, this is so cute," Baker pronounced sarcastically. "Are the two of you starting to finish each other's sentences now?"

"Listen," Weldon stood up to confront the FBI agent. "If you weren't so jealous, you'd be able to see the intelligence of this idea! Don't let your emotions interfere with the logic of this proposal."

"What is that supposed to mean?"

Emma jumped in before Hank could answer. "Listen, if all of you have doubts about my plan, step aside and let us put it into motion as soon as possible."

"I didn't say it wouldn't work," Parrish remonstrated. "It may just do the trick."

"And what about you two," pressed Weldon. "Where do you stand on this?"

"I'll go along with it," grudgingly responded Archie.

Cass waited for a moment before he annoyingly added, "Fine! I will too!"

###

"Get him out!" Emma instructed the cop who unlocked the door to the drunk tank. The cop opened the door to half a dozen men in different stages of intoxication. Agent Fedosov walked up to an unkempt man who had buried his head into his hands. With a nod of her head, the cop lifted the drunkard to his feet and walked him unsteadily out of the cage and into one of the interrogation rooms.

When the door opened, Boris Vasiliev was met by four men who had been waiting for him. "What's this!" he demanded.

"Sit down!" Agent Baker commanded the hood, "before you fall down!" Vasiliev fell into the nearest chair.

"What am I doing here again?" he interrogated, his eyes red and watery.

"You were arrested for being drunk and disorderly," Hank advised him.

"What kind of bullshit is this?" he slurred. "This is beginning to feel like police harassment!"

"All we want is to have a few questions answered," Parrish spoke up. "Answer them and we'll drop the drunk and disorderly charges."

Instead of answering, Boris loosened his shirt collar and looked around the room.

"It's as hot as hell in here," he announced. "Someone turn on the fan!"

"Sorry," apologized Cass, "but the fan is out being repaired."

Emma began the interrogation. "When's the last time you saw Kaz?"

"Kaz, Kaz, Kaz, what's this obsession with all of you over a dead man?"

"But he's not dead, is he, Boris old boy?" You've been helping him hide somewhere, haven't you?" Parrish sneered at him.

"All of you need some psychiatric help!" he replied as he tugged on his collar and unbuttoned it. "Someone open the window in here. It's getting stifling!"

"Shut up about the heat!" Malone snapped back. "It's hot for all of us in here! When's the last time you saw Titov?"

"He's dead and done for Christ's sake," he yelled trying to rise from a chair.

"Sit down!" warned Parrish as he shoved him back down. "We're not even close to finishing with you!"

"Well, I'm finished with you! I want my lawyer!"

Emma turned to Cass. "Did you hear him say something?"

"He's so drunk that I couldn't make it out."

"I said I want my lawyer," he screamed out louder.

Hank suggested, "Let's get back to the last time you saw Titov."

"Can I at least get a drink of water?"

"Of course," Cass replied. "Agent Wilson, will you get the man a drink of water?"

"Right away." As he left to fill a glass of water with vodka, the cross-examination continued.

"So, when are you going to answer the question?" Weldon asked belligerently.

"I've told you over and over. The last time I visited Kaz was in his hospital room. He'd been unresponsive for weeks. It was soon after that he passed away."

Parrish returned with the glass and gave it to Boris who immediately downed the liquid. "This can't be water," he said looking up at the group.

"It's water alright," confirmed Emma. "Where are you hiding him? We know that you are somehow involved in his disappearance!"

"You cops are barking up the wrong tree! If he's not in his grave, I don't know where he is!"

"You look thirsty, Boris. Get him another drink of water, Agent Wilson," exclaimed Archie.

"I'm telling you the truth! I don't know where he is!"

"Here," said Parrish thrusting the glass toward him.

"This isn't just water," Boris said. "It's got vodka. Are you trying to get me drunk?"

"We can hardly do something you've already done to yourself," Archie commented. "Drink it or I'll pour it down your throat myself with a little help from my friends!"

"The joke's on you," snickered Vasiliev. "I can't get drunk." To prove his point, he downed the drink in one gulp. "Keep them coming," he ordered thrusting the empty glass with his hand.

"Do you know about Kaz framing me for murder?" Weldon demanded. "Did you help him with that?"

"You've been framed for murder? It couldn't happen to a nicer guy!" Without warning, Hank brought his open hand hard across the suspect's cheek."

Leaping from his seat, he screamed, "No one slaps me and gets away with it!"

Cass and Parrish stepped between them and forced the Russian hood back into his seat."

"Get Mr. Vasiliev another drink." Parrish returned this time with a newly opened bottle of Belvedere Vodka.

"Give me the drink," Boris bellowed loudly. "This time only filled with vodka."

Parrish handed the full glass to him. Boris quickly drank it down. Laughing, and wiping his mouth with the sleeve of his shirt, he commented,

"This is very good! Better than the shit they serve at The Dive. As he spoke, the interrogators watched as Boris slipped into a real bender.

"So, tell me, Boris," with a soft voice, Archie got into his face. "Where is he hiding?" God, his breath smells like sweaty old socks and rotting fish. "You can tell me. I won't tell anybody else." Boris cackled with glee and put his index finger perpendicularly across his lips.

"Sssh! It's a secret!" he remarked getting more drunk with each gulp of liquor.

"I can keep a secret," replied Archie. "It will be safe with me."

"What about them?" he queried pointing his unsteady finger at the others scattered around the room.

"They can be trusted too."

"I want another drink," he blurted out suddenly.

"No more drinks until you tell me what I want to know."

"The others have to leave," he slurred. "I don't trust any of them. Only you, Malone. After all we both work for Greshnev."

"Yes, we do," Archie confirmed. "Everybody out," the detective said to the others winking his eye at them. The others left until only the two men were left in the room.

"So, tell me, where is Kaz?" Vasiliev moved his mouth to Malone's ear and said,

"Give me another drink and I'll tell you."

"No more drinks until you give me what I want!"

"Okay, you win." Once again, Vasiliev leaned into the detective's ear and told him.

"Here," he said to Boris. "You've earned yourself another drink."

CHAPTER

36

T HE CAR WENT screaming down the street with five passengers. They drove out of Brighton Beach to a tenement in the next town named Brownsville. The car pulled up to the Van Dyke housing building at 372 Blake Avenue. In the car that pulled up after them, were plainclothes policemen.

"We're going upstairs. I want the rest of you to scatter yourselves around until I call for your help, understand?" ordered Malone. The cops nodded their heads and went about blending themselves into the street population.

While Cass, Emma, and Archie rang for the elevator to take them up to the 8th floor, Parrish and Hank climbed the stairs to make sure Titov was not in the stairwell. When they reached apartment 8K, they all withdrew their firearms. Archie looked at his companions before he knocked on the door saying, "Here we go!"

Knocking three times, a female voice answered, "Who is it?"

They stared at each other expecting to hear a male voice.

"It's the police! Open the door!"

No answer was given.

"Open it or I'll kick the door down!" the police detective screamed at the top of his lungs. Silence continued from the other side of the door.

"Kick it down!" Cass encouraged him.

"You've been warned!" Archie declared as he got ready to raise his leg. Suddenly, the door opened. A woman stood before them. It was at that time that Hank and Parrish arrived at the doorway. Hank stopped dead in his tracks when he caught sight of her.

Her hair was colored brunette, but Hank recognized her right way.

"Albina?" They stood staring without saying a word. "You're not dead?"

"Move inside," Emma instructed the woman who complied with her order. "Have a seat," she told her. The others moved around the apartment, guns drawn to search for Kazimir Titov. He wasn't there.

"Where is he?" Archie demanded of her.

"Where is who?"

"Don't be cute!" Agent Fedosov declared. "Where's your boyfriend, Kaz?"

"He went out for some smokes."

Archie commanded, "How long ago?"

"You've just missed him."

"Looks like the two of you are going somewhere from the luggage on your bed," Parrish commented.

Albina remained sullenly silent as Cass got on the phone. It rang a few times before it was picked up. A plainclothes detective who was on the street answered.

"The suspect is not here," he advised. "Keep a watch out for him. When someone catches sight of him, ring me up. No one is to approach him," he ordered. "Stand down until I call for all of you to come upstairs." Cass hung up.

"Where were the two of you off to?" Archie examined their prisoner.

"Barbados," she unwillingly answered.

"That would have made a quite enjoyable vacation if you had made it!" declared Hank.

"It wasn't a vacation. It was for our honeymoon."

Hank was shocked by her response. "My God, the two of you almost pulled your plan off, didn't you?"

"Almost."

"Why did you create this elaborate plan in the first place?"

Albina laughed. "You'll never find out from me. I'll never betray my husband!"

"I suppose," Emma continued, "that we'll find another woman's body in your grave just as we found when we unearthed Titov's."

"That's true."

"Who's buried in your place?" Hank challenged.

"Some nameless streetwalker," she answered, shrugging unsympathetically as if she were referring to an insect. "Nobody missed her."

"How did Titov manage to get that arranged?"

"Only Kaz has the answer to that. You'll have to ask him."

"We intend to!"

"We're all going to sit around and wait for your husband to return," expressed Parrish.

Archie added, "Don't even think about warning him when he gets to the door because you'll be gagged and handcuffed to the chair."

"You can't do this to me!" she yelled challenging their authority.

Cass replied, "We'll just see about that!"

Albina tried to get out of the chair, but Emma pushed her back down.

"You're not going anywhere, Sweetie!" Speedily, Hank took a napkin from the kitchen table and stuffed it into her mouth.

"No!" was her muffled scream as Emma took her handcuffs and locked her into the chair. She continued to scream.

"If you don't stop screaming," Emma warned her in a threatening voice. "I'll slap you!" Albina did not cease her protestations. With one quick, hard slap across her cheek, the prostitute suddenly grew quiet. Tears rolled down her reddened cheek.

The arresting officer and agents took seats around the living room.

"It shouldn't be too much longer," commented Parrish as he checked the time on his wristwatch.

Cass informed all of them, "As soon as he is detected, I'll be getting a call." Weldon started pacing back and forth in the suspect's living quarters.

"Sit down will you Hank. You're making me nervous!" expressed Detective Malone.

"Shut your mouth!" Weldon fired back. "If it were up to you, we wouldn't even be here because you would still have me behind bars!"

"I've already apologized to you for that. It was Titov and this woman who created the false evidence that led right to your door."

"And that's something I'm going to have the pleasure beating out of Kaz!"

"Quiet down," Agent Baker warned. "We don't want to tip Titov off that we are in here."

"I can't wait until I have him in my sights," Weldon expressed.

"Archie was right," said Agent Baker.

"Right about what?"

"You need to sit back down and relax before you blow this "surprise party" for Titov. We may not get another chance to track him down." Hank had no argument for that and returned to his seat.

###

Time ticked by slowly. They looked at each other, trying to contain their enthusiasm for finally catching this evasive murderer. Suddenly the phone rang. Archie walked over and picked up the receiver. "Yes…okay," he answered before he hung up. The others looked at him with intensifying anticipation.

"Well?" Private Detective Weldon wondered out loud. "Is this it?"

"He's been seen walking to the building and going through the door."

"Good," Parrish commented.

"Agent Fedosov," began Cass. "Get her into the bedroom, close the door and for God's sake keep her quiet!" Emma unlocked the handcuffs and took their female prisoner in the next room before she closed the door behind them.

The apartment assumed a deathly hush as time went by, second by second. After an inordinate amount of time had passed, no one was heard on the other side of the door.

The ring of the telephone shattered the silence. "God damn it," Detective Malone hissed as he ran to pick up the receiver as the others watched him tensely.

"What?" he susurrated into the receiver and hung up after the answer was given.

"What's going on?" Agent Baker demanded.

"We've got a runner!" Cass informed them. They ran out of the apartment.

###

"What the hell spooked him?" Cass demanded of the senior officer outside the building.

"I can't say," he tried explaining. "He walked into the lobby and a few minutes later, he was fleeing the scene."

"I want him captured, do you understand me? And I want him alive!"

Archie, Hank, Parrish, and the plainclothes policemen who had been waiting outside, were in hot pursuit of their suspect.

Kaz looked back in desperation to see how far away his pursuers were as he pushed and shoved his way through the crowded boulevard. "Move!" he screamed. "Get out of my way!" People shrieked in terror as they noticed the man in the khaki overcoat was holding a pistol in his hand.

Titov's eyes darted back and forth looking for a place to somehow lose his chasers. He couldn't tell how long he had been fleeing as his feet nearly flew across the concrete pavement until he reached the IND subway system on Nostrand Avenue. Kaz took the steps down, hoping to get lost in the crowd. "What the hell do you think you're doing?" one commuter yelled as he was knocked to his knees. A woman next to him screeched, "Oh God, he's got a gun!" People on the stairs started screaming trying to get out of his way. Titov reached the station, springing over the turnstile to get to the platform. As he turned on the speed, he tried to reach the train that had stopped at the station.

"Hold the door!" he yelled, but the doors closed and the train started to pull out, it's steel wheels screeching on the rails as it moved forward. "Shit!" he yelled looking behind, seeing the first of his followers coming down the stairs. His eyes focused on Private Detective Hank Weldon in hot pursuit with a few other men. I need to move fast!

Without thinking twice, he jumped from the platform onto the tracks and ran into the tunnel. As he ran, he was careful to avoid the highly electrified third rail.

"Excuse me…Pardon me," his followers called out as the made their way through the stunned mob of travelers. Detective Malone stopped in his tracks and got to a phone booth. Dialing up the Transit Authority number, he identified himself and told them, "Shut down the electricity between the Nostrand and Kingston Avenue Stations! A suspect is running through the tunnel!" He then called the local precinct and ordered a contingent of cops to occupy the next stop, so that Titov could not give them the slip there.

Weldon jumped on the tracks followed by Parrish, who had borrowed a transit worker's flashlight. The first thing that Hank detected was the noxious and offensive odor that came from inside the tunnel and assaulted his nostrils. He screwed up his face in a distasteful expression.

"Kazimir Titov," Agent Parrish Wilson yelled as he ran, his voice resounding off the tile and brick walls, "Give yourself up! You'll never escape!" As his voice died down, another sound took over. It was the sound of fleeing feet as Titov made his way deeper into the tunnel.

As they took off, Archie Malone joined them on his trail. The three of them made their way into the darkness, their only reference points were illuminated by the small arc of brightness provided by the flashlight, Hank had an overwhelming feeling of panic shroud over him. *I can't let him get away! He has too much to answer for me.* Suddenly, the sound of a gunshot echoed throughout the dark tunnel. The men crouched down wondering if any of them might be hit.

A familiar voice followed the sound. "Stop following me! I'll shoot to kill!"

"Kaz," Weldon answered, his voice carried like an underground wave that kept bouncing along the walls. "It's Hank! You can't escape! The Kingston Avenue Station is flooded with cops. You'll never get past them!"

"I'm warning all of you, keep away from me! I'm desperate and will do anything to get out of this alive!"

"This is Detective Malone!" Archie out. "Drop your gun, and raise your hands over your head! Then follow my voice in this direction!"

"You want me to give up so I can be captured alive?" I'll never go back to prison!

"This is FBI Agent Baker speaking now. Titov, we want you to testify against Maxim Greshnev!"

"So, if I don't die in the electric chair, one of Greshnev's buddies will put a bullet through my brain? No thanks…no deal!"

"We can put you into the Witness Protection Program and send you somewhere far away from Brooklyn and the Russian mob!"

"You could never send me far enough away! The Russian mob has long tentacles that can reach anywhere you hide me. If I agree to do what you want, I'm slitting my own throat!"

"Kaz, what happened? Why did you try to frame me for murder?"

"I'm truly sorry about that, but I was left with no other choice!"

"Explain it to me!"

"It would take me a long time to tell you, and I feel as if I'm running out of time!"

"Titov, we have to come after you!" yelled Parrish.

"Do it and I can guarantee you that one or two of you will die along with me!"

The three men moved cautiously forward as Parrish continued to scan the area with his flashlight. The only movement and sound they heard were the squeaks and scurrying of the vermin as they scampered back and forth along the tracks.

Kaz could hear the footsteps get closer as he moved further into the tunnel, with his hand on the wall to keep his balance. Once more Cass called out, "Don't throw away your life for Greshnev, he would never do the same for you!"

"I want to get back to Albina! Everything I did was to protect my wife!"

"She doesn't want to see you dead!" verbalized Parrish in an understanding tone of voice. "Albina doesn't want to be a widow so soon after the two of you were married, does she?"

"It's no use!" he cried out. "I realize now that our relationship was doomed from the start! It's hopeless!"

"It doesn't have to be. Give up so your wife won't lose you!" Hank cried back.

"It's too late!" Kaz preached. "It's all too late!" Another shot went off as his pursuers hit the ground.

After a few seconds, Agent Baker called out, "Titov, are you there?" Not a sound was made. "Titov can you hear me?" his call was met with silence.

"My God," Weldon declared. "He must have shot himself!

They rushed forward until they came to a body strewn across the tracks. They kept their guns drawn as they came close to the suspect. Parrish noticed the bullet-hole in the respondent's head, the blood pouring out.

Weldon got closer and kneeled down. Kaz moaned in pain. "He's still alive," Hank exclaimed. "Call 911 for an ambulance."

"Hank," Kaz whispered as his eyes fluttered. "Tell Albina that I love her, that I'll always love her."

"Hang on, Kaz!" Weldon yelled. "You'll be able to tell her yourself!"

Suddenly, Titov's head slumped to the side and his eyelids remained still. Hank bent down to Titov's nose to detect any sign of breathing. There was none. "Forget the ambulance," Weldon told the other two. "Just call for the coroner."

Albina Lukashenko had been driven to the police precinct and now sat in one of the interrogation rooms. A policeman was stationed outside in the corridor as the woman inside wrung her hands waiting for some word of her husband. She stood up and wandered around the room, only occasionally stopping at the barred window.

The door opened and Agent Fedosov entered with an emotionless expression. "Have they found Kaz?" she asked with desperation. "Is he alright?"

"You need to sit down," Emma advised her.

Albina stopped in her tracks. "Why? What has happened?"

"Have a seat." Albina meekly did as she was told.

"Is there word about my Kaz?"

"Yes, and it's not good."

"He's hurt? I must go and see him!"

"Kaz is not hurt."

For a second, a sense of relief flashed across Kaz's wife's face. Thank God!"

"You don't understand…" began Emma and then paused. "Kaz has died."

"No", she muttered. "It's not true. He is hurt, but not dead."

Albina broke out into sobs as she rocked herself back and forth.

"You have to be brave now," Emma added. "I'm here to escort you down to the police mortuary so that you can identify his body.

"No…no," Albina cried lamentingly. "It can't be true! It has to be some mistake." Emma walked over to the distraught woman and took her by the elbow. With a little gentle pressure, she got her to stand up and walk out of the room. The cop outside escorted them.

They moved her toward the elevator where Emma pushed the "Down" button. Albina continued to cry as the elevator door opened. For Emma, it felt like an eternity before the cage reached the basement. They moved along the chilly hallway until they came to the door with the word "Mortuary" painted in black letters on the wooden door.

It was a cold and sterile room. Along with the forensic pathologist, stood Malone, Baker, Wilson, and Weldon. The three that had just entered moved to a wall of metal draws. The pathologist pulled one draw out. A body lay with a white sheet covering it. "Mrs. Titov," the pathologist said. "I need you to look at the body and tell me if it is your husband."

Albina cried even harder as both cop and federal agent kept her standing. With one sweep of the arm, the mortician exposed the body. Albina dissolved into a waterfall of flowing tears.

"Kaz. Kaz…she kept screaming his name as if her voice could raise the dead.

"This is your husband, Kazimir Titov?" the thin pathologist queried.

Albina broke the grip of the two people who had held her and threw herself onto her husband's cold body, and closed her reddened eyes.

"My husband, my darling Kaz, why have you left me all alone?" She found herself staring at a bullet-hole in his head. "Dirty bastards!" she yelled, raising herself up into a standing position. A countenance of pure defiance and hatred was immediately reflected in her face. "You murdered him?"

"You're wrong," Archie Malone declared. "That was a self-inflicted wound."

"He didn't commit suicide," yelled Albina. "He would never do anything to himself that would take him away from me! One of you did this to my poor Kaz!"

"I'm telling you," reiterated Hank. "I know it's hard to accept, but he put the gun to his head and pulled the trigger himself as we closed in on him. He decided to take the coward's way out, and leave you here holding the bag."

"Liar…liar!" she screamed repeatedly. "And he was your friend!"

"Take her back to the interrogation room," Cass Baker instructed Emma and Albina's guard.

Parrish advised, "Give her a glass of water and get her to calm down. There are a lot of questions that only she can answer now."

Emma and the cop took her back and sat her in a chair. Agent Fedosov walked out into the hallway and dropped some coins in a vending machine and pushed the button for a plastic bottle of water.

At the precinct front door, Anya Lukashenko walked in and ran into Detective Malone. "I'm here as you requested," she told him.

"Come with me," he declared and led her into an adjoining interrogation room.

"What did you want to see me about?" she asked laying her handbag on the tabletop.

"I have some shocking news for you."

"Well, don't keep me in suspense! What is it?"

"Your sister Albina is alive."

Anya just looked at him with a stunned appearance. Finally, she spoke. "No, you must be mistaken. I saw the photograph of her dead body. There is no way she can still be alive!"

"I'm telling you the truth. She is sitting in the next room."

"I won't believe it until I see her with my own eyes."

"Then come with me." Anya followed Archie out to the door of the other interrogation room. As soon as she was inside, Anya immediately recognized her sister even though she was a now brunette.

"Albina!" she screamed as she rushed over to throw her arms around her sister, who did not respond to her A rush of anger coursed through Anya's body and she broke away from her twin. "All this time I believed you were dead! Why did you put me through all of this?"

"I'm sorry Anya, but it couldn't be helped."

"What kind of an answer is that?" she asked. "You've put me through hell over the last months worrying about someone who was just playing around!"

"I was not playing around," Albina defended herself.

"I saw your dead body in a photograph! Why did you do such a thing?"

"It was staged. It was meant to get Greshnev off our tails."

"Let's start at the top," Cass instructed her. "How did this whole charade begin?"

"It started when Kaz and I fell in love. We decided to marry."

"And after that?" inquired Parrish.

"We knew Maxim would never let me go. He always told me that I was the biggest money maker of all the girls. I knew he would never release me to Kaz."

"How did Greshnev finally find out that the two of you had wed?" Archie piped in.

"That bitch Karina. She was supposed to be my friend and I told her our secret. Karina stabbed me in the back by going to Greshnev and telling him. Kaz had to kill her to avenge what she had done to us.

Maxim went wild with rage and had my husband beaten within an inch of his life. You found him in time Hank, before Maxim's henchmen could finish the job."

"What happened after that?" Agent Wilson asked.

"Kaz was sent to the hospital in a coma and I thought I had lost him."

"But you didn't, did you?" questioned Malone.

"No, thank God. My prayers were answered, and he returned to me."

Emma spoke up, "What did the two of you do after that?"

"We realized that Greshnev would never relent, so we staged Kaz's death."

"That part confuses me," replied Hank. "How did he stage his own demise?"

"Kaz knew someone in the hospital morgue that owed him a favor. He just slipped the toe tag on another body that was also ready to be buried. In the meantime, I pretended I had been slain but we needed a body. That's when we decided to kill Renata."

"You killed her?" Weldon screamed.

"Well, she seemed like the best choice at the time. Kaz strangled her, I dyed her hair blonde and Kaz chopped her up so that she could be mistaken for me."

Hank felt physically sick as his stomach churned, remembering how he had looked inside the bag at the garbage dump, and didn't recognize Renata.

"Greshnev was grief stricken and swore he wouldn't stop until he found my killer."

"I see," commented Detective Malone.

"That's when Kaz came up with a brilliant idea. If he could pin the murder on someone else, the two of us could escape and start a new life."

"And what was this brilliant idea?" charged Weldon knowing full well what she was going to say. "What the hell!" he screamed at her.

A contrite looking woman lifted her head until their eyes met. "It was the one thing in his plan that he was sorry to have to do."

"But he did it anyway, didn't he?"

"Yes. He was very reluctant to make it seem you were her killer, but he felt he had no other choice."

"Unbelievable!" shouted Weldon. "It boggles the imagination!"

"He had worked so long with you, Hank, and knew your catchphrase when you caught an adulterer. He slightly changed it to appear you had killed me. We had planned to escape right after that, but Nonna got in our way."

"What do you mean?" Parrish challenged her.

"She caught wind of our leaving. We could have just left, but Kaz didn't want to leave any loose ends behind."

"So, he killed her too?" Agent Wilson queried.

"He was hiding in the office with the help Dr. Orlov's assistance. He told me that he came up from behind while she was undressing and strangled her."

"Go pick Orlov up and arrest him," Malone ordered two cops who immediately left the precinct.

"And, what about his cousin, Ivan? Why did he have to die?" Cass asked.

"Ivan found out what we were doing and threatened to go to Greshnev. Instead, he extorted us for money. Even after Kaz had paid him the hush money, he did not trust him. That's when my husband decided that he could no longer remain alive."

"And so, he made it look like I had done the job!"

"I'm afraid so, but Kaz always told me it was nothing personal against you.

"Well, that makes a world of difference! I feel so much better!"

"What about the diary pages?" Hank inquired as he fought the urge to grab her by the neck and choke her.

Albina shrugged. "That was my idea. I thought that if I wrote about my undying love for you, it would solidify the case against you and I was right."

Detective Malone approached Albina and began to read her her rights.

"You're going to arrest me?" the brunette asked in shock. "Kaz committed those murders, but now he's dead!"

"You knew about the murders and did nothing to stop him. You were an accessory to those crimes," declared Cass Baker. A cop led her away to a holding cell.

"Congratulations everyone for all your hard work in solving this crime," Federal Agent Cass Baker went around shaking everyone's hand. All the law enforcement officers left the room except for Hank and Emma.

"Well, thank goodness that's all finished," stated Emma.

"It may be done, but I can't get over how they tried to frame me for murder! It's driving me out of my mind!"

"I bet I know how to get those thoughts out of your head," said Emma as she walked up to him and planted a passionate kiss on his lips.

Weldon reciprocated.

"You're right," he answered after their lips disengaged. "I can't remember a thing."

Printed in the United States
By Bookmasters